Moh & Maya

Mortality was the only reality

Sun:Jeev

ISBN 13: 978-93-90976-06-5
ISBN 10: 93-90976-06-5

Printed in India and published by BUUKS.

ABOUT THE AUTHOR

Sanjeev grew up in Bombay, today's bustling metropolis of Mumbai.

He has spent a majority part of his life in the city and travelled extensively in India. His first ever travels outside Mumbai were due to his job in sales and marketing, and his later travels were due to business and leisure.

Sanjeev has experience in diverse sectors like IT, Insurance, and Investments in a career spanning twenty-six years post his education. He was educated in Mumbai, with a BE. Electronics and MBA degree in International Marketing, both in 1st class Honors.

Sanjeev knows he was fortunate to receive an English medium convent education from St. Andrews School and St. Theresa's school in Bandra, Mumbai and pays a tribute to all his teachers of both these schools who helped to groom him.

Any measure of gratitude felt towards our teachers is less.

"A man is able to live, because he has with him the love of his life and friends. Yet, he lives for what he defines as his family. Who he lives with, is determined by circumstances, choices and destiny!"

Sanjeev started writing unpublished poetry in 2011 and this book is the first piece of fiction inspired by some common people he met during his travels.

FOREWORD

I am what I am, courtesy:

My grandmothers
My mother
My father
My sibling
My friends – my real family.
My spouse
My son
My daughter.

Some parts of this book, I owe **to each** of them.

In my travels across India, I have come across a beautiful country that fights deprivation with solidity, yet its people and the landscape they travel and live within provide the most memorable, diverse and enjoyable experience to the senses. I discovered love, and every illusive human emotion in India. Some of the images on the cover are from photographs clicked by me in my India travels after 2011. I experienced much joy and freedom in this country:

> "*It is here, where life, is alive.*
> *You get what you seek.*
> *Yet, what you see,*
> *may not last forever.*"

I thank my family, who helped encourage my first attempts at writing. A big thank you to my daughter *Yanya*, who was my editor, and my son, *Shritanjay*, who was my first reader and cover designer. To my wife, on our 25th anniversary. It is my gift to you Deepali. To my in-laws *Saroj & Suresh*, I received your biggest gift in my life. To my parents, *Asha & Munish*, I thank you for my 'education' by way of your life, on how to be and not to be. That's the best gift I received from you with love.

To my grandmothers, *Late Mrs. Janki Bhatia and Late. Smt. Kaushalya Bhatia*, the gift of unconditional love that I received from them remains with me to pass on to the next generations.

~SUN:JEEV_07May2021

Front cover: Carter Road, at the opposite end of Bandstand, Bandra Mumbai.
Back cover: Mt. Mary Church, Mumbai

Sanjeev has been inspired by various Indians in his life, to whom he dedicates this work, in no particular order

"I offer my salutations to the great people I learnt about and read over a period of time. I have revisited their works again and again and message during the very tough pandemic year of 2020-21. Many were always with me since childhood and made me feel like a proud Indian. I have looked up to these people mentioned below and often followed their lives and the message their life and work reflects:

Sadhguruji J Vasudev, Shri Kapil Dev, Shri Amitabh Bachchan, Shri Azim Premji, Resp. Lhamo Thondup

(14th Dalai Lama), Late Raj Kapoor, Late Dev Anand, Late Kishore Kumar, Late Rahul Dev Burman, Late Vinod Khanna, Late Swami Vivekananda, Late Satyajit Ray, Late M.K. Gandhi and most imminently the Late Rabindranath Tagore."

I was fortunate to have lived in their India, a free India, and experience their works. The work and output they have given to India, has helped me to live a peaceful and content life.

MUSICAL REFERENCES

Song#	By	Song
1.	Ed Sheeran	Shape of you
2.	Geeta Dutt in Kagaz Ke Phool	Waqt ne kiya…
3.	Lata Mangeshkar in Aawara	Ghar aaya…pardesi
4.	Manna Dey Shailendra Singh in Bobby	Na Mangoo Sona Chandi.
5.	Kishore Kumar in Julie	Dil kya kare, jab kisiko…
6.	Kishore Kumar & Mukesh in Dharam Karam	Ek din bik jaaye ga…
7.	Mukesh in Mera Naam Joker	Jeena Yahan, marna yahan…
8.	Mukesh in Anari	Jeena Isika naam hai
9.	Kishore Kumar in Yaarana	Chu Kar Mere mann ko…
10.	Kishore Kumar/Md. Rafi/ Asha.Usha / Naseeb	Rang Jama ke…

11.	Amitabh Bachchan/ Kalyani Anandji	Jiski Biwi…,Mere Agne main
12.	Md. Rafi in Hum Kise se Kum Nahin	Chand Mera dil…
13.	Kishore Kumar in Sharaabi	Inteha ho gayi…
14.	Manna Dey in Abdullah	Lalla Allah Tera Nighebaan
15.	R D Burman in Zamane Ko Dikhana Hai	Dil lena khel hai…
16.	S.P. Balasubrahmanyam & Asha Bhosle/Saagar	oh Maria…
17.	Pankaj Udhas & Anuradha P in Dayavan	Aaj phir tum pe pyaar…
18.	Mohd. Aziz & Sapna Mukherjee in Hatya	Main pyaar ki pujaran…
19.	Kishore Kumar in Namkeen / RD Burman	Raah pe rehte hain…
20.	Louis Armstrong by G. Weiss and Bob Thiele	What a wonderful world…
21.	Mohd. Aziz & S Janki in Aakhree Raasta/L.P.	Lo Jee Shuru hogayi Lovestory
22.	Manhar Udhas in Jaanbaaz/ KalyanjiAnandji	Har kisiko nahin milta yahan...
23.	Pankaj Udhaas/ L.P. in Naam	Chitti aayi hai, watan se...
24.	Kishore Kumar / SD Burman in Prem Pujari	Phoolon ke rang se…
25.	Kishore Kumar/ LP in Machali	O Manchali, kahan chali…

26.	Kishore Kumar/in Kasme Vaade/RD	Aati Rehengi Baaharein...
27.	Kishore/Rafi/Mukesh/ LataAmarAkbarAnthony	Humko tumse ho gaya hai...
28.	Kishore Kumar & Lata / RD in Devata	Chaand Chura ke Laya Hoon
29.	R D Burman/RD in Sholay	Mehbooba, Mehbooba...
30.	Udit Narayan/Alka Yagnik Raja Hindustani	Pardesi, Pardesi...
31.	Bhappi Lahiri/Disco Dancer	Krishna Dharti Pe aaja tu...
32.	S.D. Burman/S.D. Burman / Guide	Wahan kaun hai tera...

All Musical* references to any song and lyrics are to help build the narrative background in which the characters operate. It is NOT an attempt in plagiarism or to infringe any rights of the master owner of those works. The music, song or melodies referred to are merely to give a background context or situation in which the characters in the novel, are operating or thinking. All rights to those songs, lyricsand music remain reserved and are entirely owned by the creators and copyright owners of that work. The characters of this fictional novel enjoy the same like any music lover.

This book can be best enjoyed by the reader listening to the real songs that the charactersseem to enjoy, along with their place in the story.

LIST OF CHARACTERS

Maya Singh
Khazan Chand Singh
Nanna (Maternal Grand parent of Khazan)

Sulakshna and Sudarshan (*Son of Khazan's Father's employer Karorimal Rathod*)
Jyoti and Raj (Children *of Sulakshna and Sudarshan*)

Mony & Nirmala Malhotra (*Employers of Sanjeevni*)
Sonny Malhotra (*Mony and Nirmala's son*)
Thappa and Rupa (Workers at Malhotra's)
Khemu (*Sanjeevni's driver*)

Shop Owners
Khan (Sialkot), Gurupreet Singh (Papaji - Solan)
Pran (Delhi)

Maya and Khazan's family

Children

Sanjeevni (BootiBhai), Ashwini (Ashu) and Hari

Grand-children

Ekjot, Mohini (Moh) and Lakshmi/Durga

Cattle & pet

Nandu, Hariya and Tiger

Mumbai Characters

Megha & Kiran (School teachers)

Father D'Costa (School principal and priest)

CONTENTS

1

MOHINI AT BANDSTAND

(Bandra Bombay)
20 APRIL 2020.

"Mohini, come here, come here right now I say. Won't you listen to me? Come here!"

"Ashu relax, why are you getting hysterical?", screams his wife.

"Mama, please tell Pops, I am not getting in there, I'm leaving", replies Mohini to her mother, rather than replying to her father.

She walks out of her bedroom, avoiding to look into her grand-mother Maya's bedroom. She crosses her mother who stands at the door frame of the kitchen, glares at her father in the living room and walks out of the two doors of the house. Her eyebrows raised she winks at her dad, as she shuts the wooden door silently and *bangs* the ivory wrought iron door against the outside wall leaving it ajar. Some loose cement falls off the wall. Mohini's sneakers take two steps at a time to jog down the eight floors in her apartment block. She has a mask in one hand, her iPhone 11 in the other, as she puts on her ear-pods. The Ed Shereen song, '*Shape of you*' blanks out her memories of her concerned father and emotional grand-mother. Each of them is fighting their self-imposed challenges in the pandemic of 2020, that has knocked the lights off the world.

Due to the corona virus epidemic families are locked-down inside their homes. Her father Ashwini is not too keen that Mohini goes for her morning run, but she is keen to go look out for her friend. Ashwini is not aware about a possible emerging love interest of Mohini, and assumes it's the run that beckons her.

Mohini wants to take in the sun at Bandstand, stare at the sea and have her walk from the Mount Mary chapel steps, down to the mega star's house at the ocean front. She passes the famous Mt. Mary Steps also known as the Bomonjee Jeejeebhoy steps – that were presented by H Bomonjee to the 'Bandora Muncipality' in 1879.

She walks, then hopscotches the steps, running past the Mehboob Studios that have had to down its shutters due to the pandemic. The virus has shut the Indian film industry, the city as well as the entire country down. She ambles around the cemetery and the St. Andrew's church, till she crosses the closed Milk booth and the shut and very anchored Yacht Bar, to buy herself a sandwich at the *American Express Bakery*. She finds it open, as bakeries are classified as essential services.

Prior to the pandemic, she used to alternate between fruit buns, sandwiches or apple pies at *Amex bakery* and the chicken rolls at the *J. Hearsh Bakery*. Both are iconic simple bakeries of Bandra since over three decades, more popular than the *Andora's opposite St Andrews School*. Mohini is sixteen, optimistic, and despite a face mask, smiling within and happy. She has a sprightly step in her stride, keen to count her walking steps on her iPhone to stay fit. She believes that the pandemic will blow away in a few months. The virus is known to be selective about age and it is her granny who needs to worry, not her.

At home, Mohini's mother looks up at her hubby Ashwini, "Darling, she has done her fair bit, we have to handle '*Maya Memsaab*' ourselves.

"Don't call my mother a *Memsaab*, she is the most down to earth person in our family. She is a simple lady, rustic at heart, divine in spirit. It's just that she has a mind of her own. That's all!" shoots Ashu straight from the hip, albeit taking care to end a bit defensively.

His wife, with her hands on her hips is simply staring down at him.

"Ya, ya, I know, you are the most down to earth lady in entire Mumbai my *Jaan. Thank you* for being there with me through all this. Our life till now and not just this lock-down. It's a good change to be at home, especially since I am surrounded by three loves of my life."

"That's true Ashu, thank God she's not a Diva like you! But our *Moh* is going to turn out like Maya when she is older. Let's treat this as our training experience. If we can handle your mother, I am sure we will be able to live with our daughter when we are ourselves '*Memsaab's age' so let us not become difficult.*" Ashu's wife has again referred to his mother being difficult.

Ashwini and his wife have been contemplating the situation since Maya moved in last year, and realize that '*their time*' due to age, shall come too. The pandemic all over the world has brought mortality in focus into the living rooms of all urban couples. Some have tried to enhance their immunity while others have commenced fitness walks. Many parents have been forced to live near or with their children due to restrictions imposed by the state and the country on elders. There is no vaccination in sight and the population at large, considers itself to be immune to masks, since they have a fair share of turmeric, ginger and cardamom in their daily diets. Maya had taken that decision in the previous year, choosing to stay with Ashwini over her younger son,

Hari. It had been generally thought that she would get all her check-ups done at the nearby Holy Family hospital and return to her farm house in Nawalgarh, after '*her Ashu*' shows her around Mumbai.

Ashwini's wife places the incense sticks she has lit in the kitchen before the dining table altar cabinets. There is the Sikh emblem, of swords crossing, alike the stand on which the *Granth* is kept. There's *Guru Gobind Singh's* picture and that of *Lord Krsna* in one wooden frame. On the side is another frame inside the upper glass cabinet which has Ashu's father's youthful photo and three sets of cards, an Ace and queen of hearts, two fives and a joker, from a deck of playing cards. They are kept open like a Chinese fan. Ashu's wife has never understood the reason for collecting the child like memorabilia but persists with it as Ashu's touchy about the cards, and she is about the God and Guru in the same frame. She touches them with the tips of her fingers and crosses the same on her forehead and chest, crossing her heart like a catholic. This is done before Maya enters the room. Mumbai's compact homes allow all individuals carrying out their individuality and faith in silence, yet giving the elders their mark of respect that is possible in the confines of the small rooms. Privacy, arguments and love notwithstanding.

Ashu tilts his forehead upwards, plants his tea mug onto the center table merging the tea drops that jump out of the mug, with the distress polish on the table. The color of the tea drops merge with the old bohemian color of the table. He realizes he has to get his mother out of her bedroom. She is awake, perhaps in her sulking mood since last night and is afraid his mood will merge with hers like the tea on the table. He flicks the tea drops away, with his fingertips as he gets up, wipes them off on the back pocket of his jeans. He tucks his white t-shirt into his jeans to look a bit proper for his mother, despite his two-day stubble. He wears his hair short at the back and the tuft of hair on his forehead still makes him look young and cute, as he knocks his head sideways, left to right, to move his static hair on the forehead back in a head tilting motion. His wife pulls at his cheeks on the way, he caresses her shoulder and arms slowly. She winks at him, pleadingly to get *'Memsaab'* out and ready for break-fast ignoring his overtures.

"Ma, come on, let's sit out near the window, breakfast will be ready soon and you don't like soggy toasts. I owe you the history behind Mt. Mary's Chapel, which I told you about last night. It was the local Koli fishermen who discovered the mother Mary's statue in the sea, and ...".

Maya, rubs her eyes off the drops and looks up at her son, dewy eyed. "I don't like oats and milk either, save me for a day from your wife's insipid drink, get me a brandy with *ThumbsUp* instead! And I will bless you for a long life. Otherwise very soon, you will have to shift me into the old St. Andrews

Church cemetery nearby." One of the oldest churches, set up by the Jesuits in 1575. These are the only two shrines Maya has visited and seen, since arriving in Mumbai. While the St. Andrew's church had stood the test of time, the Mt. Mary shrine had been broken down due to attacks by the Arabs and the Marathas, and rebuilt around 115 years earlier.

"Oh, Ma..." goes Ashu, very concerned, all his steadfastness melting away.

"These are just eye-drops, - they call it Just tears! I know I got carried away last night, but do you not think the government could have done something for the migrants? Sanjeevni has walked half-way out of Delhi on foot to reach back home. No planning this, this, unbelievable way to shut transport of all kinds. We all have to die someday, here, death is not upon me and there my son has to walk in the sun-light for days all together to reach back home."

The pandemic and the sudden lockdown, had thrown urban workers in disarray and many yester year rural folk felt, that they had been ignored or forgotten about. Maya was always critical of the government of the day and believed that citizens should always keep politicians on their toes. As a widow she did not have her husband, so it was the government that attracted her ire.

Ashwini, the younger sibling of Sanjeevni, does not want a repeat of last night's argument, he picks his mother by one arm, gets her off the bed in one swooping action, making his mother stand on her own feet. He knows, she reveres her eldest child, as much as he does, and he does not want to exaggerate her feeling, neither negate it.

"Your balance is perfect now, walk after thirty seconds. Remember the doctor has said you have a health problem of Postural Blood-pressure. Don't move too fast when you get up." He catches her walking stick himself and walks out of the room as she waits the extra few minutes before following him out.

Breakfast is laid at the dining table by the window. They can see the sun shrink wrapping the sky, light blue with orange marmalade all over it. The strawberry jam on the light brown toast for Maya is looking like a luscious contrast brick-red. There is white *Amul* butter on Ashu's parathas for variety and competition. There's a feast of green apples and pears, a red water melon diced into cubes and milk with malt powder on the side.

"Be here in the moment, this is where we are at Mumbai now. Things are not in our control. I cannot take you to the bank branch yet, as it's not safe with the pandemic, we have enough cash at home, so please be patient, Ma..." Ashu cuts off.

He can see that Maya is lost in thought as she hums the tune of, "*Waqt ne kiya, kya haseen sittam....*" and revels in *Guru Dutt's* expressions of sadness, piety and yet a stoic calm on her face, not ashen, but not bright either. Neither entirely awake, nor asleep on her '*chorpoi*' bed either like in her past.

Ashu feels for his mother. He feels, that he feels the most for her. Maya has so many other connections with her other relations, that whatever Ashu exudes is lost like dust in the sands of a big dessert. He attempts to make his wife and Mohini feel the same way. He feels for them too. Does he feel too much for all the three women he quizzes himself?

He looks at the photo frame of Lord Krsna at the other end of the room, almost for some inspiration and wonders how he could manage so many gopis and wives.

In contrast, Ashu struggles with all the three goddesses of his life. Yet he feels an equal fondness, love and affection for all of them. His daughter is named on love and affection- the Indian word '*Moh*' like Mon Amour in French. Name keeping in their family had had its moments...theirs was a simple choice. The love of their hearts.

Maya, feels for the whole world. The night duty watchman in Ashu's building has contracted a cold, is someone she is as concerned about as much as Moh. Maya looks out of the window and tries to look for the day security guard in the opposite building premises, whom she usually waves to from the breakfast window.

She does not believe like Mohini, that there is any reason to mistrust these workers, as she feels they do not have the evil eye, that the young see in them. Besides her eldest son Sanjeevni has had to work in a similar role and aspect in Delhi.

Maya is like the universal mother and she understands her middle-son Ashu. She feels he is the most comfortable about sharing her, gives her full freedom and yet loves her equally without any sense of competition. He has inherited her genes and her love for love, love for loved ones, and love for life. Due to his open heart and an open mind, debates were fun in the family but never combative.

She gazes out at the cloudy horizon of the sea, in between buildings standing before her at the Bimal Roy lane. She has a vantage position at Bandstand, as if that of a lighthouse lookout, scanning the misty sea. She worries. Her eldest son is walking without transport into Rajasthan during one of the hottest months, due to the pandemic. She has seen countless disturbing images of jobless laborers and workers on television. She remembers the time when she insisted to her husband, to quit life in Calcutta and move to Rajasthan on a lark, after their vacation. '*Oh how freely possible it was, to move about in trains in the India of the 1970's!*'

She feels guilty in the comforts of Ashu's home and the conveniences she enjoys, that in fact they all enjoy. She is unable to find the food palatable, and due to that, ends up giving wrong signals to her doting daughter-in-law. She is used to her own style of cooking in Nawalgarh.

Maya thinks to herself and talks to herself often through the day. *The son you live with, nearby, is the favorite son, but really, once you have three children, can you have any favorite? Each one is like an eye.* Yes, Ashu is her third eye. Shiva's eye. He has the foresight, the sixth sense. He has called her over in 2019 to Mumbai under the pretext of showing her the city, the nearby forts built in Bassein and the port of Alibaug. The churches and the temples attracted her, and so did the Portuguese-built villas on the *Salsette* lands of Bandra. It had kept her glued to Mumbai. She has overheard her Konkani and East Indian neighbors talk of the British cranes breaking while attempting to lift the Elephant of *Elephanta Caves. It* now rests at the Bhau Dajji Museum.

Ashu has told her that the British had landed in Bombay and were fascinated by the caves, they had simply got 'Bombay' undeservedly as a gift in dowry to the King Charles II. Maya has landed at her own son's home and discovered her higher blood pressure merely upon standing on her two feet.

"My postural B.P.!" she sighs aloud. Ashu looks up, and gives her a weak smile.

Maya's thoughts are coming to her at the speed of light from the rays of the summery sun.

'These daughter in-laws do not understand, especially as they have only one child these days. The times of Maya, multiple children, juggling so many domestic duties, running a large kitchen, governing the house, cleaning the

compound, breeding bulls with cows...would these urban daughter-in laws survive? Without a micro-wave oven and cooking gas?'

She broods...she tries to tell herself, not to grudge the young, they always have it better than the old, but do not realize, that it only goes downhill with age for them too.

Off late, her third and youngest son, no longer speaks with her. This eats her up from inside. He is overseas in Singapore trying to expand his Delhi Malhotra *Seth's* optician business, with some talk of import Korean lenses to New Delhi. It makes Maya wonder how old Delhi would look through new eyes. Eyes of the young. She has not been able to see or talk with her youngest son since moving in with *'her'* Ashu. This youngest son Hari, has all of a sudden developed an acute sense of jealousy and possessiveness despite himself living a life in the good land of Singapore.

In side conversations, when she overhears her son and his wife talk, Maya also feels concerned for her grand-daughter Mohini. She believes that *Moh* is safer here, in this *Salsette and sea* bordered Bandra. She tells Ashu not to send her to Goa or elsewhere for studies. The news and papers are filled with filth and negative events even in good times.

She starts talking with herself again, as she wipes off the strawberry jam and few crumbs of her toast fall into her morning tea. Her daughter in law comes and picks up the cup, and replaces it with black tea. Piping hot the vapor from the mug, fogs up her glasses. Maya pulls them off and lets them hang from her chain. Ashu looks at her smilingly while devouring his parathas.

"Ma, no more milk tea. This is the second and last cup of the day. The next cup will be oats"

Before Maya can respond, her daughter in law walks away back into the kitchen. She admires the efficiency of her urban daughter in-law, already dressed in slacks and a tight pink t-shirt. A bit too tight for Maya to handle. Her dark pink sneakers ready to whisk her away into the back lane of Bandstand after Moh comes back in.

Occasionally Maya rues the fact that she finds herself in Mumbai. It's the dichotomy of life. Yet she cannot but express satisfaction for the speed of Mumbai and Ashu's life. She finds him somewhere to be the average in between Sanjeevni and Hari, and yet the more emotive and understanding of her sons. Ashu is someone whose life she can relate to, he's not extravagant, despite his modern outlook.

She does not want to be stuck in nostalgia and the past herself. Neither can she join her youngest son Hari, and live outside her country. It was not always like this. She wonders why and how her life changed so much, with the progress of Hari and Ashu.

The life she had thought she would have at Nawalgarh, got so quickly obliterated and feels like many moons and years ago. She nods her head, smiles, and greets the fragrance of her memories of Nawalgarh and the pickles she would enjoy making with her elder daughter-in-law.

She looks around her neighborhood from the window she is seated at…taller buildings next door, one by *Raheja's*. She *watches* the next door *'watchman'*. The security guard, aptly called 'watchman' lives his Mumbai life out of a small cabin between the iron gate and the street outside. He lives more than three fourth of his day in the cramped space giving up his farm life in UP or Bihar. Her heart melts and goes all out for Sanjeevni again.

Mumbai houses, small, compact, expensive, cramped, yet, cosy and so tightly knit, are apt for close family life. The neighbors not knowing their own, on the same floor. She wonders why her son's apartment is in a building, which is called a villa, and that too of a Captain. There is no merchant, or retired navy personnel living in *'Captain's Villa.'*

Perhaps numerous residents came and went, using the apartment like a port, to dock their part time ships of life events, and effectively sailed the higher seas, carrying off their families like containers, far away, like her youngest son Hari.

"Oh, I should not grudge him. Ashu when will you show me around this Portuguese Bombay, or Maharashtra's Mumba Devi city?" she sighs looking at Ashu.

Ashu had delayed the oft repeated request to show her the *Elephanta Caves and embark upon the vacation at Alibaug*, fearing to step into ferries from the Gateway of India. He had taken her often to the lobby of the next-door Taj Hotel at Bandstand, but avoided the visit to show the façade of the south Bombay Taj, the first iconic hotel of the country.

Ashu pre-occupied, looks at the television screen, the Sensex diving down further south, hitting new lows. He stares at the ticker on the television screen, and at his two mobile phones on the dining table on both sides of his plates, and murmurs to himself some names and numbers.

Maya realizes he is already lost into his working day. She has to hold her tongue - the magic potion - for living together. She waits for Moh to come back, as her next light moment in the day is before lunch with the grand-daughter.

After an hour has elapsed, Moh has showered and enters her grand-mother's room freshly shampooed a little after noon. Moh's mother is now walking the slope up and down from Mount Mary hill getting her cardio exercise at 12 noon after her oats milk drink. She is her optimal self, disciplined like the British band at bandstand, maybe over a hundred years ago. Ashu is still lost in the living room behind his laptop, his one mobile phone on his ear, the second before him as he is tapping feverishly into it.

So 'Maya Memsaab', says Mohini cheekily, to her grand-mother. "What shall we discuss today?"

"You tell me", retorts Maya.

"Can we speak about family, or our past history or even my ancestors?" Mohini, quizzes optimistically wanting to know about her paternal side of the family. Oblivious to its roots, its history. Her maternal grand-parents not being around, her curiosity unfolds unabashedly before Maya.

"Do ask what you wish to know?" says Maya, as she drapes her wine-red saree over her head.

"No fairy tales, I'm too old for that now, treat me like your friend." responds Mohini.

"Yes, yes, Moh *betta*, you are my best friend. I am as young at heart as you are, just that I do not enjoy your Ed Green music" assures Maya.

Maya is anyways story challenged, never having been told any in her own childhood by her gypsy parents. She buys time to collect her thoughts, never happy to alter true narratives. She was happier to tell her the ways of the past, observe the current and future trends and ask all her children and grand-children to change with the times. She has never really thought about her own family characters much.

"It's Ed Sheeran Mayaji!" laughs out Mohini. "Maataji I know, your sensibilities are Indian."

Maya looks at her grand-daughter with soft eyes, full of love, almost as if piercingly looking through a time sand clock. She can see the dust of sandstorms flying in the air.

The cycle used by Sanjeevni parked behind the well, Tiger wagging his stout tail, the *Gulmohar* tree's image flashes past her eyes standing as she is inside the compound of her old house; even as she looks at Moh in the foreground, she can see all that's in the background. The past. Gone.

"Moh, when I was your age, where we had access to this electronic music and wires and devices like you children? Let me tell you, your arms, fingers, bones, ears, all have to last you a lifetime. You neither let me put coconut almond oil in your hair, nor you let me put eye-drops in your eyes. They have to last you a lifetime" she says lovingly, as she places her coarse hands on Moh's eyes, almost feeling her youth, and her youthful energy.

Maya pats Moh's cheeks, feels her skin, and tucks her hair away, behind her ears.

Mohini looks at Maya. Maya just looks back, quiet, serene, silent.

"I wish they grew less here, and more up here" as Mohini points to her arms with one finger and raises her thin eyebrows. "Anyways. Chill." Mohini breaks the thoughts that Maya was trying to collect from her spent past.

"What is more important in life? *Moh, or Maya*?" comes the query from Mohini.

"That's the name of our village home at Nawalgarh, my '*Moh & Maya.*' Your father gave you the name from there perhaps... and from the bottom of his own heart." Maya, adds hastily taken a bit off guard. She is forced to propel her thinking backwards. Her mind's recorder starts throwing up images in reverse order, like what a rewind button would do on the old video images of a camcorder.

Maya senses a purpose in being a grand-mother and has to come out of her own time wrap, into the moment she is facing with her inquisitive and intelligent grand-daughter. She is Ashwini's love child. The child of her most romantic son. The son, who has always come back to her, seeking her, looking for her wellbeing. The son who loved her the most, and loves to love. Someone who learnt to love at a very young age and sought love from life.

At the same time, Maya is anxious, that Mohini stay in Mumbai, and not travel to Goa for her studies as she intends. If she has to share her story, she desires to showcase the rich tapestry of their family history, to give Mohini a personal hook to be with her father in the years ahead.

Moh cuts in, "Yes, that I know, but which is more important? And what really is Maya? Just an unending illusive desire, that can turn evil or a dream that is merely an illusion of the mind?"

"Mohini, I can only answer from my heart. You should speak to your father; he has great knowledge about matters of the heart. Matters of love. Matters of the mind."

"So do you! You tell me, do you think from the heart, and he from his mind?' asks Mohini, "...and are love, affection more, or as important as desire?"

"Darling, they are like pearls, put together in a necklace. If one pearl falls or slips out from the break in the thread, they all fall out. Love, affection, desire, these can be illusive to some, illusion to many, and real pleasures to seek and keep in memory for many. But all these are transient, like phases of life. Only love with commitment and loyalty can go the distance, like that of your father. In matters of the heart, always think with the heart. One must find a person, with their heart in the right place to make him a life-partner. Brains every human has, whether used or not it is okay. They will just live senselessly themselves. But it is when people do not use their heart, they become rough and rigid people in relationships, causing harm to others, which then never works. Yet, we have to eventually leave things here, behind, in this '*Sansara*' and go to the next part of our universe."

"What should I seek then grandma? Love, or affection. Aren't they two sides of the same coin? Like mind power and intelligence?" muses Mohini. "Well dear, so is 'Moh & Maya'." says Maya flatly. She realizes that their conversation could now taper toward the birds and the bees, and it sounds like one old owl of a bird is talking to a fledgling nightingale.

Maya buys some time, thinks, looking up at the ceiling, staring at the antique Chinese made rotating fan with its thread hanging in suspension to stop or make it faster. As she stands un-steadily, she increases the rotation speed of the fan, and collapses back unsteadily on her bed… "Yes, yes, I know, my Postural B.P." she grimaces at the walking stick and looks at Moh, giving her the look to discard it for her.

"We wanted love, affection and desire to remain in our home, and that is why the name was chosen to our village house. Just like your father came to Bombay, we had gone to Nawalgarh to set up home and seek a life ahead of ourselves."

"So fancy and romantic to have your own place, your own land, naming your own house, growing your own vegetables, making your own pickles, here we are, cooped up in Captain's Villa at Flat 802!" gushes a visibly impressed Moh.

"If you do not seek it, if you do not look for the illusive in the big wide world, how will you find it? Only if you seek, imagine, look for the love of life, can life be lovely. This life, this city is your parent's dream. You must find yours."

"I find it difficult to walk in this city of no pavements. Tell me about your city grandma!"

"Ha, ha." laughs on Maya, "It will take days... I rather study the history of Bombay city its forts, or the 19th century history of the Mt. Mary, and walk up the steps to see Virgin Mary, or pray in the September

Bandra fair…offer her some candles, that history will be more interesting. My own history is not like that of the British and the Portuguese in this city."

"You already know so much I promise to tell you all about Big Mumbai city," cuts in Mohini, "... if you tell me your story. Please grandma, please, tell me your story." Moh pulls out her small pen, pencil, and dairy out of her school bag, and dives into Maya's bed. She throws away her shawl and the Rajasthani sheets on to one side.

Maya glances at the Rajasthani print on the sheets, the pear shaped and flower shaped patterns in blue and pink. The goat skinned water bag '*Mashq*" is hanging from the door stand from which she still has her cool water. Images of her own parents, her husband in Calcutta her husband's first visit to Solan to see her in-laws come back to her.

Her first view of *Khazanchand*, in the little sweet mart in Solan. All the mixed-up memories come back to her, in a mixture of colors out of the Rajasthani bed-sheets and hits her like the pillows that Mohini pounds her with softly.

"Tell her Ma!" says Ashu, standing at the door of the bed-room; "She has all the time in the world with school shut now and Grade XI gives her the time to reflect and chronicle our family history. Next year, she will go away to some university in India. She might as well know about our story, our family story and what brought us all here. Why bother about the

British and the Portuguese? They are long gone. It's just *our little ol' Bandra* now. In a way we live in Bandra and not Bombay. This is where I belong. Tell her where do you belong?"

Mohini stares on, eagerly pen in hand, pencil in mouth, dairy open to its first page with hundreds of pages to fill. She draws a balloon bubble, to write down the words – '*Moh & Maya*' – perhaps a working title to her dairy, a novel some day?

"Dear son, I belong, where you are…but okay, I get the message." Maya thinks hard, and breathes deeply.

Moh gapes on, while Maya spins her web of illusion and how she had made it their family reality.

It was all illusive, till she made it her own.

2

HARI, NANDU AND HARIYA

Nawalgarh, Rajasthan(1990's)

Hariya attempts to move, but Nandu's ox like obstinate paralysis and the twitch of his tail, signals a warning to him to wait.

Maya's youngest and third son Hari, is farm boy and farmer in the Singh family's private estate. Hari is chiding the stubborn black bullock Nandu, to pull the plow for the last few steps before wanting to break for lunch himself.

Hari is impatient as he is hungry, having forgone his morning breakfast over a squabble with Maya. Beads of sweat break out from his tanned brow, slip over his long fine nose and are about to enter his mouth from his sun burnt torn upper lip. The white and second big horned bullock Hariya, his favorite, is more obliging and understands him like his son.

Nandu has stalled and is about to let go off some steam, by generating yesterday's chaff and passing it out in the form of today's pile of green. Circular, lacey and warm, it settles just behind Nandu, about two feet away from where Hari is trying to hasten Nandu. Hariya, with his red painted horns filled with balanced proteins surrounding its inner core bone, is attempting to nay-say what Nandu is up to.

But Nandu does not give a shit. He's done.

Having obtained natural fertilizer without expecting it at that time, Hari has to abort his attempt to plow his field. The farm land is more than muddy and slimy wet due to the early morning drizzle. He has to rush back through the slush, his *dhoti* pulled up, to his external shed behind his mother's main house. The family house that is called '*Moh & Maya*'

Hari wants to be able to pick up the excreta provided by Nandu into his collection box, a makeshift storage tin. The tin box will keep the produce lacey and useful with Nawalgarh's weather, he knows he has to collect Nandu's output, to cool the inner walls of his out-house. The afternoon sun can ratchet up temperatures of 48 degrees Celsius. It's his only experience of an air-conditioner in real life for his nap in the afternoon and he sure knows he has a hot head.

Nawalgarh is a small town in the *Shekhawati Region* of the state of '*Rajo-ka-sthan*', thirty-nine kilometers from Jhunjhunu and thirty odd kilometers from Sikar.

Hari imagines himself to be the prince of his own family as the only resident male family member in his household. His sister-in-law Jyoti and mother being the other residents.

Hari makes it back to the stalled jam of the bullock duo who are rearing their heads. One nods vertically in pleasure and relief, and the other in contempt and disgust horizontally and vigorously. The plow is shaking both up and down at the same time and Hari fears a split at the center. He angrily shouts, at Nandu while calming Hariya down by patting him on the buttocks.

"Now you have given me your gold for the day, let me at least pick it up before it settles into the soil." He bends and with his spade, - *a make-shift shovel using a brown card-board paper,* heaves up the 'gold' pickings quickly and cleanly loads it into his tin box.

The work comes to a stop as Hari feels like taking a natural lunch break. His 2 acres farm is a simple piece of land owned by the family since only two generations. He is the cultivator and the care-taker of the land, but he jointly owns and manages it with his other two brothers Sanjeevni and Ashwini, who both work in cities.

Their Mother, Maya, a widow, keeps the family together by providing the vision of *Mother India* for the family and reminds Hari repeatedly that he is only the care-taker.

"Sanjeevni and Ashwini are the co-owners, don't forget that. Your *BhabhiMa* is awaiting the return of Sanjeevni, it's been eight months. At least don't make her wait for dishing out your lunch."

Hari gives a sheepish look to Jyoti from the outside of the house, via the four and half feet courtyard, and the step-up verandah. He washes his hands and pulls at the checkered cotton '*gamcha*' off the clothesline. As he wipes off his hands, he makes the towel into a ball and softly throws it at his mother.

"It's ok Mai" says Jyoti. "I'm used to it. He's just like his brothers, at least he manages the fields and is there with us." She gives Hari a reassuring look as he steps in and hands over to him the stainless-steel plates, with 2 mini-bowls. There is a large chili in the circular plate, with five large wheat *rotis* and some dry vegetable in one bowl.

She gets the next *roti* off the pan with her bare hands, she fills the second bowl with blackish yellow lentils using the ladle in her right. Hari gets his plate and moves to sit, when his mother also enters. She passes him a brown earthen glass with white curdled milk, filled to the brim with a lace of butter and cream at the top.

"Mai, what about the butter for my *rotis*? See your bahu has not given me any butter with my food!"

Jyoti looks at Maya and suggests to her to give her share of the butter from the curdled milk to Hari, when Maya disagrees. "Hari, you should not be greedy. I know you are the *Bheem* of our home, but Jyoti is due next month. Let her also get some butter for my grand-son on the way."

As Jyoti is about to offer the butter, Hari interjects, "*BhabhiMa*, I know you love me more than your child on the way, I was just pulling a fast one. If I get any fatter, I will become slow like Nandu. Come you also sit and lets all eat together. I wanted to suggest names for your son to be born, the fourth generation '*Waaris- the inheritor*' in our family"

He licks his fingers and gesticulates to her to also sit down. Maya sets their two plates and they both sit with Hari to eat, chat and enjoy their afternoon meal, before he knocks off for his siesta.

"Vishnu!" says Maya, very persistently. She is a fan of the blue God, who has so many avatars. There are sticker posters all over the house, many turning edges off the grey raw earthen walls of their brick main house.

"Hey, Mai, he is blue, like the sky and oceans. In our arid state, with less water and pitter-patter drizzle, where can you have oceans to dream of? And what if I give birth to a baby girl? Then can I call her Laxmi?" reasons Jyoti, looking pleadingly towards Hari.

She has a mother son relationship with her brother-in-law and dotes on him. She knows the disappointment her family will face if she can't deliver a son. She expects him to kick in and build awareness to keep options open for the unborn girl child.

"BhabhiMa, you will have a son, as like our fathers, we are known to only father sons. It's our contribution to our wife. Ask Mai, it's been like that for three generations. And the Resort friend of Sanjeevni was telling us it's the man's contribution to your womb, only then can you have a son."

He gives a gap, so that the male female chromosome theory sinks into Maya's mind.

'So, if you have a girl, it will be by the blessing from Mai's Vishnu only! We will then have Laxmi in our arms and more and more wealth in our house with a bumper bajra crop. I will be the millet prince of Rajputana and maybe brother wins the lottery in Delhi."

"I'm just hoping he makes it in time next month for the delivery. That will be my lottery." Jyoti rubs her hand on her swollen belly, as she rests her head back against the wall.

"Moo!", say Nandu from the courtyard outside while filling himself up with water from the pail below his thick lips.

Hariya denies his declaration negatively, with his horizontal denial of a low probability, with his red horned head.

3

SANJEEVNI IN LAJPAT NAGAR

New Delhi.

The day starts at dawn in Lajpat Nagar 1 of Delhi, a cow mooing, as if answering back to Nandu and Hariya in Nawalgarh. She is crossing the 15th road as if to embrace Sanjeevni, the security guard of 17 Lajpat Nagar.

Nandi the cow is being led by this strapping, tall, handsome young man in his thirties, lovingly remembering early morning images of caressing his wife's brown hair from her fair face, looking at her in the eye.

Nandi moos again. Sanjeevni fondles and picks at the zip of the athleisure second hand t-shirt hoodie, a hand-down from his boss's teenage son, Sonny Malhotra. The son and Sanjeevni are like friends, but social class keeps them on two different sides of the lawn of 17 Lajpat Nagar 1.

About to be a first-time father, Sanjeevni knows he has thirty days, before he can take his annual holiday during the monsoons to go back to Nawalgarh in time for Jyoti's delivery. The last time he had overstayed enjoying the harvest time till late after Diwali, he had got Jyoti pregnant.

He is excited and has an extra step in his stride, as if imagining to take those hurried steps the same way, to see his wife before the mid-wife delivers him his baby. For the last three years he daily starts his morning, guiding a grey city cow – 'Nandi' to the nearest Krishna temple for her morning '*aatta ladoos*', before he runs the hundred-meter dash back to Malhotra Niwas in 13 seconds.

Nandi was orphaned as a calf and the entire suburb of Lajpat Nagar adopted her three years back. That was when Sanjeevni took the pledge to walk her in the morning to the temple, and the temple priest had agreed to the elaborate arrangement to ensure she got her daily water, hay and grains – or the tempting 'wheat *ladoos*' that the house-wives of three lanes of Lajpat Nagar donated.

Often Sanjeevni would get to whisk away few for his own peers at the Malhotra Niwas, if Nandi or the housewives and young dames and maids of the suburbs, did not gobble them fresh in the morning hours itself.

Sanjeevni has to move quickly.

He has a pressing schedule to finish before his boss Mony Malhotra gets ready and steps out at 10am sharp. A stickler for time, money and paying debt on time, Mony Malhotra does not like the absence of Sanjeevni at the gate before he leaves. He has transferred the tensions of the little brain that sits on his fat neck, all to Sanjeevni, so that he can leave the rich Lajpat Nagar area and go to squat at his shop's cashier's desk at G Block South Extension.

Since his shop is smack near the center of the old popular commercial street of Delhi, Mony Malhotra has to walk forty steps a day to fetch his favorite meal during lunch. He does this without fail, three days a week from Bengali Sweets. His home tiffin is eaten sumptuously by his two staff - the ophthalmologist and the sales girl on those three days.

Two other days of the week he takes out his visiting customers for a spontaneous lunch to retain their loyalty and his connect with them. Times are bad and he has learnt to keep things tight from Papa Malhotra, though he failed to keep his pants that way. His belt does not fit the first and closest hole in the leather as he is compelled to use his colorful suspenders as a back-up. This requires him to open the hook atop his trousers, the moment he sits at his cash counter daily, waiting for his repeat buyers. He appears like a frozen frog, about to pounce upon unsuspecting new customers or old loyal ones who buy their goggles.

The loyal clientele is built up on the back of treats from '*Bengali Sweets &Chaats*', while the buccal cavity of Mony Malhotra swells like the vocal sacs of a fat toad. The same frog-like demeanor is there in the squat pose, as is in the length and use of his tongue. Most new customers lose out to the sales pitch, negotiation and verbosity of Mony Malhotra and want to eventually get away with a pair of shades that they simply look good in. Mony in the meanwhile has imposed a diabetic attack on the sugar senses of his customer and added many hundreds of calories to himself.

Sanjeevni picks the water pail, a make-shift *Asian Paints* white distemper box, with its rusted handle covered in a square dusting cloth. With water sashaying over the dry green grass in the garden of Mrs. Nirmala Malhotra, Sanjeevni in his three fourth knee covering Adidas shorts, strips off his single piece night suit zipper t-shirt to expose his white vest inside.

A thin overnight dried towel is picked up from the cooler at the back-bedroom of Mr. & Mrs. Malhotra. Sanjeevni's vest looks sullen like a musk melon, light brown with stains of tea and light yellow from stains of dust and dirt over a period of time. His strong arms and tall height, allows him to wash the SUV roof of his boss's '*TATA Sierra*'. He stands on the support ladder of the back-side door to reach out to the left side roof of the vehicle. In a swift motion he moves to the right side of the car, opens the front driver cabin and cleans the steering wheel, hanging the wet muslin cleaning cloth on it to dry in the Delhi heat. He daily lets driver Ramlal take it from there before he drives his common boss to the market.

It's mid-June and rain clouds are not above the dry capital city. The ex-Mughal capital and current seat of central government has a pale blue sky. Rulers have changed over *Hindustan* but India's unpredictable rains are still difficult to fathom in New Delhi's weather forecast. It had rained heavily in March, for a week and the city was flooded and now with the rainy season approaching there was always a cool breeze by early evening, but no real rain to speak of. Umbrellas were ready in the boots of all cars, but people knew, rain was still a few weeks away.

Sanjeevni could beat the rain today, but he pondered every morning, if he would beat the monsoon to reach Nawalgarh back before mid-July? Will they have that much elusive daughter that the Singh family has always expected from Maya's time, but never had? The musings flood his head, like the rains had filled up the lawns in March. Every time he has called back home, it is a matter of debate over phone calls between him, Maya and Jyoti. They still had to think of a name.

The Delhi sun wastes no time however, as it is about to explode like a heat ball. Sanjeevni runs to the back of the house he guards for Mony Malhotra.

He knows his boss to be a surly optician, yet a burly retail owner who does not himself use glasses. He wonders how Mony can maintain this lifestyle selling just glass and glasses. There are tons of glass and earthenware and color clayware makers in Rajasthan who do not display their riches the way Mony does.

The double role Sanjeevni executes is of security guard at night, and car cleaner in the morning. He gets to bathe behind his owner's house in the servant quarters toilet-cum bathroom – both of which are distinctly different back home in Nawalgarh. For this he has to enter the quarters, occupied by the Nepali cook Thappa, and side-step his devious Bengali wife Rupa. He crosses over their feet and hurdles across to the toilet.

He has fifteen minutes to pass his morning ablutions before he can wear his uniform on the dry servant quarter house floor, without bumping into Rupa. By then, she is busy boiling the milk for the entire household in the make-shift kitchen. Having curds set at home is a tradition that the Malhotra household maintains, but it is Rupa who boils and sets the curd for all. She manages the same for Thappa and Sanjeevni, in small bowls as the Delhi heat allows them to partake in these small joys after their lunch. She systematically fills up all the stainless-steel bowls of all sizes, with milk, and penny drops a stainless-steel spoon of curd into each one of them.

Rupa had married Thappa, more to enter the Malhotra household, than to establish kinship with Thappa. She has a mischievous eye on Sanjeevni and though she knows he is married she makes a teasing offer of embrace with him in the morning as a fun start to her own day. The time it takes to boil the milk, is the time she has to needle Sanjeevni, tease him over his name, or his unshaven fuzz. Yet she playfully moves away before Thappa wakes up.

In full fairness to Sanjeevni he avoids her like the plague always. He is afraid more of breaking Jyoti's heart than Thappa's but cannot totally avoid Rupa.

Sanjeevni must wear his dark green trouser in a dry area after the bath. The small toilets in servant quarters of the big sahibs, do not permit his pants to remain dry, if worn by their staff after the toilet floor is wet.

This is well understood by the sari clad, fun seeking Rupa.

The servant quarters kitchen is really an extension in the open compound and yet partly visible from the sleeping quarters of Thappa and only roughly covered with a see-through thatched bamboo separation from the garden. The terrace balcony of Mrs. Malhotra's master bedroom also has a partial view of the kitchen through the bamboo screen and is a convenience set up specially to holler for Rupa, as the need be during parties or emergencies. At times, Rupa sends up fried fish from her own kitchen on a string pulley basket apparition, that Nirmala Malhotra dishes out to Mony with his whiskey on a quiet Friday night.

It works quite well if the sahib does not wish to step out for the early start to a lazy weekend.

Sanjeevni looks at Rupa. Rupa looks teasingly at him, pouting her lips, inviting him, with milk held in a glass for him.

Sanjeevni buttons up his shirt, with lapels on it hanging from both sides as they do for a guard uniform. Slowly afterward, he stretches out his left hand, for the glass, delicately balancing the trouser wearing act with the right, without tipping over the knot of the cotton towel to expose his under-pants.

He hastily over looks to see if Thappa is off the bed, and in the bathroom. He knows that Rupa makes the biggest moves when her husband is in the toilet, knowing that he takes the longest there first thing in the morning.

Sanjeevni understands she is harmless and play acts with him for her own entertainment. But he is afraid that she is getting more brazen with time. He indulges the hand that feeds him, as that's his only glass of milk for the entire day.

"Come near my Sanjeevni Booti, infuse some life into me. Your friend Thappa is too drunk by night and blown in the day to work on me" giving him demure, loving looks. "I can also feed you, besides giving you milk daily" says Rupa.

"I only need the milk that I get from Nandi. You know I'm a father...going to be one. How can you behave like this? That too first thing in the morning, we all have a hundred tasks to do. You will get us all fired from employment, and no one in Lajpat Nagar 1, 2 or 3 will hire us as Sahib knows each and every owner by name." retorts Sanjeevni.

"Why are you boiling over, even the milk has more patient effervescence." replies Rupa. Acting hurt in her eyes and a put-on evil smile on her lips, she still grins back.

"Lucky is the woman, who has wed you, and will mother your child. There is not one loyal man in this neighborhood, on either side of the lawn, street or bed-room. You stupid Rajput, you have turned my mood off, and stunk it like Thappa's morning produce. Now entire day, every word '*Nirmalajee*' says, is going to hurt like her heels biting the grass off the drive-way."

She mocks him, acting like the all-important memsahib she is herself not, knowing she's lost her candid thirty seconds with '*Booti*'.

As he walks out, she attempts to pinch his derriere. While he is startled, he grooves on his black shoe heels and recovers. He walks a little away, sits on a large oval stone, used like a seat by all of them. He makes short, hurried sips at the hot milk while tucking his shoe-laces into themselves at the fat-base of the shoe. He does not like his laces to hang loose, neither wishes to trip on the gravel part of the driveway during duty hours. From his seat he looks up at the terrace to see *Nirmalaji* look at him very knowingly as if she has always suspected something fishy going on. He turns a bit red around his ears and hopes that the change in his complexion is not visible and looks away from the memsahib.

He notices Thappa has come out of the bathroom-cum-toilet, relieved, yet with a painful expression on his face. He meets his eye-contact and blurts- “Bhai Booti, my fissures are increasing and this mad woman, does not stop putting laal-Tikkha masala from the market in our food. I should have married ma-Kaali in my sleep and remained a bachelor. She does not let me sleep at night, nor shit in the morning with peace” cries out aloud the Nepali.

He mumbo jumbos something about making a pilgrimage, someday, to ‘*Pashupatinath*’ temple.

Rupa neither meets his look, nor glances at ‘Booti’. She’s done with both the men for the day and starts moving around efficiently to manage her own tasks. She gets ready to move into the main house from the back-door kitchen with the boiled milk in both hands held with her towel cloth. She has access to the worker toilet *inside* the house, in the guest bedroom on the lower floor of Malhotra Niwas. It was her only condition to accept work here as a full-time help knowing that her memsahib can be both bitch and bimbo. She however concedes to her conscience, that Nirmalaji has her heart in the right place, pays well and manages her hygiene across all her monthly cycles.

Rupa finds Nirmalaji quite agreeable heart of heart, but the house too big. It needs to be dusted, swept and cleaned repeatedly to keep the dry dust off the marble surfaces, Rupa curses her own fate and Mony Sahib's large body weight. Every cloth to be ironed is one and a half times the width and length of a normal human being. She is ready to face her day's labor. The hard life of every domestic help in Lajpat Nagar.

At 10 am in the morning Mony Malhotra gets out of his house with a straddle of a Punjabi stallion. Feeling proud of himself with the knowledge as he is getting out of his bungalow, to his shop – that he was prince when dad ran it. He is now the reigning king of a dying empire. His pride is slightly dented with worry. Two public listed companies have entered the eye-wear business and his own shop has lost nearly twenty percent of all old clients, with few new customers being acquired. His Nepali cook's wife carries his four-tier heavy tiffin and passes it to Nirmalaji. The food is prepared by Thappa, packed by Rupa, while the fresh juice is poured out in the morning by Nirmala herself. That's one job to be done herself, as she needs the orange peel rinds for her limp face skin and under-eye bags.

The wife folds the day's two business newspapers, neatly into a roll that fits under the husband wife paunchy cuddle.

The papers pass over to the armpit huddle of Mony as Nirmala Malhotra smiles affectionately and they walk out together. Nirmala stands in her night-gown at the door of the house, waving with boredom, knowing that she can expect him back by 7pm sharp and no newness in her life. He descends his heavy-set frame into the SUV, and lo behold Ramlal comes into visibility after his master shuts the car door, just in time. Sahib lets loose a short fart. The newspapers come in use to swat away an imaginary fly inside the car cabin.

Nirmala has four hours to kill before her 2pm late-lunch kitty appointment with her own old gal-pals in Rajouri, but she hates to go across to that side of the city despite the numerous fly-overs in Delhi.

She knows the city has changed, and cannot bring herself to accept it. She is not happy with the prospects of the city's future. Having supervised Thappa's potato wheat-based ghee laced parathas for her husband, she has eaten two herself with four dollops of butter. She is ready for her afternoon nap at ten in the morning.

Sanjeevni has set himself up at the house gate. He opens the bronze and black mix gates and first salutes, and then waves at driver, car and sahib, as the car passes out of Malhotra Niwas.

Nirmala lets Tiger out and the dog lazily struts his booty, walking towards Sanjeevni.

Life, as you would know it, is no longer exciting for anyone, as the action moments of the day are over and everyone goes their separate ways.

Only Sanjeevni is left at the gate cabin, with Tiger.

Sullen, yet hopeful, he looks at the screen of his mobile phone, and hits the first number on his fast-dial contact list.

Jyoti must be waiting he thinks, as she is about to start her daily chores in Nawalgarh.

4

TIGER THE LOYAL FRIEND FROM SIKAR

Monsoons of 1983

Tiger was born to a stray migrant father of the Labrador breed, in Sikar. One of the working officers with the British Army, had brought his loyal friend from the United Kingdom and was fond of using him to smell out small pieces of detective work during the partition days. This loyal friend was the great, great, grand-father of Tiger and had been an expert at water fowling during his Scottish days. Their ability as a breed to carry game or accompany hunts was due to their soft grip of their mouths.

They remained loyal to their masters. These genes existed in Tiger.

Tiger's maternal grand-mother had been in Sikar from time unknown, perhaps migrating from some royal roots of Rajasthan when the fort was being built. She had proudly paraded around the area of the Sikar fort from where she travelled to the '*Harshnath Lord Shiva*' temple with her masters. As she was not allowed inside the temple, she had met her match at the steps of the temple. This was due to another visitor carrying his male canine pal. The male canine was luckily the descendant of another European Labrador breed from Jodhpur. Tiger's mother was in such a way born in Sikar and adopted by the local Station Master's father, who had some connections with the local Jains. They were the community who had financial arrangements with the Royal family of Jaipur.

Tiger was born in this domesticated scenario in the Jain vegetarian house of the station master of Sikar junction. He knew the whereabouts of all the bridges inside and roads outside the station, being quite hyperactive as a pup.

He had played for two years on both sides of the rail tracks, but never jumped off the platform. He would always follow passenger human feet and developed his own sense of smell all over the station. He was fond of snacks and wheat biscuits that visitors shared with him.

Tiger's favorite spots were the red post box outside the station building in the shade to avoid the sunrise in the morning and the roof of the tea stall inside the station after noon. The laziness gene of the Labrador breed was part of his DNA. He rarely barked, except a faint yelp when the train chugged into the platform blowing its horn, or when the engine whistled whilst pulling out the Sikar Express from the platform.

Tiger's ancestors had been around armchairs and at the feet of their Scottish and English masters, during the penchant of the British love affair with Indian tea. They had grown used to seeing leather shoes, boots, stockings, socks over fair skin, and some form of carpeting on which their own coat would also get warmth. The status and position in the house, was similar in India for his immediate grand-parents, except the brown skin tone, devoid of stockings and socks at the eye range for the Asian Labradors. Indians managed to insert their coarse skinned feet into shoes and sandals more directly, perhaps due to warmer weather akin to sweaty skin.

Tiger too loved the aroma of tea, mixed with sugar, milk and ginger. Especially when the beverage reached a boiling point crescendo before being brought off the stove to pour in small glasses.

He would peer over the reinforced asbestos roof of the tea stall and watch the customers sip from small muddy glasses, and savor the steam flavor on the roof.

His lunch would be two *'rotis'*, mixed with milk that was provided by the tea stall owner to the station master. By four pm at late noon, Tiger would meander toward the desk of the Station master ready to go home and nap below the visitor's chair, which usually stayed empty.

Before exiting the railway platform with his master, he would pee at the plastered wall corner behind the ticket window and observe the '*paan-stains*' and plaster them with his own short jet output.

Not really territorial, he would wait till the station master would move hastily with files to walk home. The station master would come and stand around the same area, and plaster the wall with his own betel nut leaf stains, projecting the spittle aimlessly. The wet spit spray would land in new and old areas of the textured ticket window wall with a new spray of maroon red.

This habit irked Tiger, though he did not dislike the smell of the stains, nor fancy the old orange rust ones. He looked down upon the stains on his master's jaw, with green threads and brown strains stuck between the four incisors. He never saw them in any other normal adults all over the crowded railway platform.

The '*paan chewing*' somewhere an inherited Austronesian migrant habit, apparently never impressed Tiger, who was the descendant of British migrant Labradors.

Tiger and his ancestors had never travelled toward South East Asia, so their prejudice was also limited to the geographic arc of migration they had experienced. The same chewing habit had been exported to the Persian area, by Indian occupants who were themselves migrants.

The station master was being pious in his habitual consumption after meals, as it was known that Lord Krishna consumed it as per the *Shrimad Bhagvatam.* It was a habit he had picked up from his own Bihari retired colleagues, who were inspired by both the Mughal dynasty queen, and the new singer *Noorjehan* popular now on the other side of India.

The ticket-window wall had borne the brunt of all the employees sputtering wetness, since independence and never been painted.

There was also the residual glue of film posters that had been pasted, ripped and re-plastered from the Raj, Dilip, Dev era, down to the Shammi, Rajesh, and now Amitabh times that Hindi films had unleashed on Sikar. This vile field of remnants aroused a strong displeasure in young Tiger, who was seeking new boundaries to change the foundational development of his canine senses.

New betel leaf-stains, mixed with cheap glue from posters were not going to be enough.

Sanjeevni had set foot out of Nawalgarh to expand his horizons and increase the potential of an extra income for the joint family. He knew his two brothers would till the land and he being the eldest always had a share in the inheritance as the records with the registrar office and district collector records needed his thumb imprints.

In 1983 India had won the Cricket Prudential World cup in UK at the mecca ground of Lords.

The cricket final had been viewed all over India and had created a sense of hope and infused ambition across states, that made people restless in cities and villages they lived in.

Big city professionals made serious attempts to start sending their children overseas, especially to London due to the colonial hangover. They aspired to become doctors or engineers.

The village habitants dreamt of city life, with its modernity and hope of increasing per capita income. Everyone suddenly wanted to live double lives, with extra sources of income, if it was possible.

The movies also presented the orderly overseas world to promise riches, in the form of diamonds, gold, or smuggling that was arising from imported goods, even though the ones doing it were the cigar chomping villains in the Indian movies. India had already experienced an Emergency and people's freedom being curtailed had not worked during the forced sterilization program.

The victory in a new area, that too sport, after the victory in war over its unfriendly neighbor a decade ago, bolstered the confidence of every Indian.

The train he had boarded, had stopped at Sikar Junction, on its way to Delhi Railway station.

Sanjeevni had initially been influenced by Maya's family trading roots and thought about Bikaner, but ended up buying his extension ticket for Delhi.

Tiger had been befriended while buying milk at the railway station from the tea stall owner.

Sanjeevni had poured a small amount in his saucer and offered it to Tiger. Sitting crouched in his camel pose, Sanjeevni appeared animal like in posture, attracting Tiger to come up close to lap up the milk from the saucer.

It was a novelty for the young strapping Labrador all of three years of age.

Tiger lapped it up before the remainder in Sanjeevni's own glass was finished.

Tiger's mother was herself eight years old and had another set of puppies to look after. His mongrel father had mated with her a month before the three puppies were born, meeting his fate on the tracks when an engine had run him over in his sleep at night.

Tiger was visibly affected, with the sudden absence of his father missing the paternal care in the initial months. He never shared his grief with his mother, who had earlier lost two of Tiger's siblings. She was in full motherhood mode, with her new set of babies and Tiger had moved on his own as a loner at the railway station, distinctly detached from his own family.

The station master's father had also aged and there was no one to shower love onto Tiger. He felt devoid of family, and knew he was fatherless.

Sanjeevni patted him on his head for a good ten minutes. The smell of human emotion and fragrance of sweat and human odor of travel felt sweet to Tiger.

Sanjeevni eventually got up and turned back to embark upon the train, when Tiger had jumped on playfully, following him.

Sanjeevni had lived on a farm, where the blend of human with soil and bull made him open enough to embrace love from whichever species he received. He had himself just left home.

Tiger was true to the Labrador breed as they were known to vanish if they engaged with someone new. Tiger was also not really territorial and the platforms, and noise of trains had now become part of the boring scenery for him. He was willing to be separated from his Station master owner without much fanfare or saying goodbye.

The scent that had attracted him, was the earthy smell from Sanjeevni's clothes and the fragrance of fenugreek seeds from his hands. The act of pouring milk in the saucer, that was meant for human consumption, had the same scent of the tea that he had often seen the tea-stall owner brew. No one before Sanjeevni, had accompanied Tiger in sipping the same milk from a cup and saucer together.

Sanjeevni had not realized what attracted him, but in his own separation and sadness he accepted Tiger as his partner in those moments. He understood that Tiger was eager to travel. Tiger was prepared to be the escape artist and vanishing pet par excellence due to his boredom with the limitation of size and landscape of the Sikar railway station. He had switched his loyalty permanently to Sanjeevni in the fraction of that second, in the love and manner of care in which he had fed him the milk.

Tiger leapt on behind Sanjeevni and climbed aboard, executing as humanly possible a feat, that a dog could achieve on his own, following his new master onto the train.

He had been raised as a vegetarian dog, as his masters had been Jains. The food Sanjeevni carried with him; curds and green vegetables with the black lentil was a new fragrance he discovered on the groovy train.

It was a new experience for both, and Tiger was yearning for the new as much as Sanjeevni.

Sanjeevni named him in that lunch break.

Tiger had a dull yellow coat of fur, more cream then white, but the unidimensional Sanjeevni took it to be pure.

"Here white Tiger, you are brave to follow me, a man who himself is new to Delhi and does not know his fate. We will both be kings of the new jungle."

Tiger had looked up all three years of age, with his droopy ears and sleepy eyes giving an endearing loving look to Sanjeevni.

It made Sanjeevni forget the pain of moving out of Nawalgarh and reoriented his thoughts.

If a dog could leave his home, for a stranger and trust him, he could surely call upon himself to extend his horizons to Delhi for a better future.

Even the Mughals had come to take a seat in Delhi.

He was himself the son of Khazanchand, who had willingly been loyal to the interests of 'Hindustan.'

Sanjeevni thought to himself that Tiger was a stray.

He had found him at the tea-stall, which was mostly just a pre-lunch hangout joint for Tiger. The station master had not really cared, as getting older himself and approaching retirement, his disdain toward the many pups that his father's loyal friend produced, had drained him enough.

In that journey that day, Sanjeevni had made a loyal friend.

He taught Tiger to eat slowly, and from the base of a newspaper on the train, as there was no bowl or saucer. Sanjeevni shared his own food at face level with Tiger. Tiger had always been at the feet of the station master, who used to throw food at him in a bowl, creating a splash in the old remains of the morning milk. It scared the pup making him run a bit away from the food, before suspiciously devouring it. Imagine eating out of a liquid white explosion of milk. He would gamely have to lick off the spots of milk that tasted dusty, outside the saucer from the musty floor.

Tiger watched keenly, as he saw and emulated Sanjeevni, morsel for morsel. He would bite and chew slowly as Sanjeevni demonstrated.

"You are my lost brother Tiger. Want to sit and eat huh? You must have been a Royal in your past life, re-born as a dog?"

As Tiger looked on, appearing to actually smile and wag his short stout tail, Sanjeevni affectionally slapped and held his face in both his hands and played with him.

Tiger was ecstatic. He furiously licked Sanjeevni's large hands over and over again. He had never been physically loved and attended to and could sense his journey on the path of loving a new family had just begun. He could create that space in his heart, for new territory and a new person easily as the scent and attention it got him in return was heady.

He leapt onto Sanjeevni to lick his hands again, but turned around and sat instead obediently for a nap of a lifetime.

The human and dog embrace complete, the nature of empty vacuum of their past lives, was suddenly full of love.

5

MAYA'S ILLUSIVE DREAM

1950-70

Maya wakes up to the smell of dawn, the soil is moist from yesterday's paltry rainfall. Yet the weather is dry today, the air lightly dusty. Maya looks toward the well behind the house from the kitchen window. She wants to get a feel of some sense of moisture as she drinks water using her right hand, while her left hand holds the tap of her earthen pot in a shuttered position.

She places the water on the flame of the stove, and shreds ginger, places it together in an accurate hundred grams measuring bowl, with sugar, and the granular tea leaves.

In a few minutes, her tea boils over and is cooled off with the milk she pours in it from a stainless -steel glass, that has an inscription of her father's name on it, 'Lal Chander Rajput'.

The tea mug, the '*kullad*' is kept ready with a net strainer that will hold all the processed tea and wet ginger shreds. The ginger appears infested with polka dots of sugar, while the tea powder appears like lice stuck on strands of hair. This soil like mix, gets trapped in the strainer. Maya smiles to herself, her shadow falling onto the brown surface of tea steaming hot in the mud container. Everything the color brown, soil like and earthy.

Maya enjoys her first cup of tea as her morning wake up concoction at seven in the morning. The early morning sun rays invigorate her and allow her to get some time for herself in the first couple of hours of the day.

She enjoys her privacy and her own me time to dream in full wakefulness. Toppling the coir bed outside the veranda, she drags it to an off-center position from the main door of the house. From there she can see the main gate of their property, and behind the house too.

She places the tea '*kullad*' near the right foot-base of the bed and throws a large crimson red patchwork sheet over it. She settles down on it in a sleeping Buddha reclining position.

She realizes with every passing day she is the living uniting existence between Hari and Jyoti and keeps their unit all together as a family. She reaffirms to herself, she has two more sons to settle into matrimony, with the eldest yet to return to his own householder status.

Hari is just about fifteen but looks like eighteen. Hari is at the same age that Sanjeevni was when Hari was born, and now Sanjeevni's son was to be born around that same time for Hari to experience childbirth.

These are enough reasons for her to want to stay alive. She is also excited at the prospect of herself becoming a grandmother. She has seen so much time, and people pass. The prospect of a new arrival in the family rejuvenates her.

"Ah, the circle of life, so many come, so many go. How tired Mr. Time must be? I am in this shape with time ticking unrelentingly, will I get to see all my grandchildren?" she mumbles to herself. It is a habit she gathered in the 1980's after Sanjeevni had left for Delhi, as her inner voice began talking to herself.

She stares at the solitary mango tree behind the well, where she had planted the seeds of half a dozen mangoes. She had perhaps brought them from Chittorgarh, during her first visit to this land. She thinks of walking to the tree, and talking to the tree, but instead chooses her own company that she enjoys more.

She observes silently the tree, in the eastern direction, same as of the sun. The tree casts a large shadow upon the well keeping the water cool inside during the first half of the day.

"Hello '*Surya Dev*', another rise for you, eh? So, Mr. Time pulls you up and again gets you out of your bed?!" ...she nods vertically, acknowledging with the lift of her eyebrows repeatedly, as if the sun, is communicating, showering her exclusively with its countless orange tube lights.

The sun rays as if in response to her eyebrows, radiate on her coir bed and establish a crimson network below the bed.

Her father's nomenclature for the morning sun, has stuck on in her head, as many Kshatriya dynasties and Raghu families of Rajasthan, consider themselves '*Suryavanshi*', spin-offs of their descendants. They all consider even *Surya,* - the sun, as God.

The '*Chandravanshi's' or Yaduvanshis* were the descendants of Lord Krishna and believed themselves to come from the Lunar Dynasty, as was Khazanchand. His grandfather worshipped the Lord, as the only God.

Maya's thoughts shift from Lord Krishna's crown, images of Baby Krishna, to her solitary mango tree leaves.

"How parched are they like me? They appear soiled with dust", she acknowledges to mother nature and thanks the tree for casting a shadow so *well over the well,* almost perfectly at this hour without jeopardizing the fruit.

The tree extends only till part of the distance toward the water source and the mangoes tantalizingly hang in mid-air from the branches, loading them with enough weight, yet light enough for the branches to stay inclined upward. The position of the tree and its foliage still shelter the well from the sun and partly filter the dusty beamed rays via a green prism toward her abode's roof.

Her knowledge of the benefits of the mango leaves, is now known to her very late, since she has lost Khazanchand, to excessive sugar.

"I salute you my dear Khazanchand, for the perfect placement of the seeds. Despite my argument with you then, to sow more than six, only one correctly planted seed by you has given me fruit! Yet the fruit was mine to enjoy and was from my mango. Just like I have given you three blessed sons from within."

She appears proud, even pompous in expression - and in full glory in her morning tete-a-tete with her husband. She imagines her husband, looking back at her at nearly the same age, at which she is now. The age gap that had existed, had been abridged with the passage of time. He politely corrects her, without rebuke, that he was just about 55 when he passed, and she still has catching up to do. As Maya has gotten older, age and numbers have become worth counting for her.

"You are still young" he seems to say. He casts his look all over her reclining position, grinning. He seems to slurp next, with light yellow color on his hands, and the seed in his mouth, cleaned out of any element of orange. She remembers him, deliriously enjoying that mango, as he is sitting before her in his white kurta, with a dark pink turban, the right color to wear on a cool night under the stars and the white moon.

Tears swell in her eyes, she picks up the tea and takes a big swig at it, blowing hot air off the surface, to give her face a hot flush, aborting her emotions. She daily remembers her husband, quite fondly at the start of the day.

It was he who had bought a dozen of mangoes with her from Udaipur. She is unsure though, as she still contemplates, if it were those seeds that gave fruit via a sapling at the land that grew to a full tree. Perhaps it was her choice of mangoes from Chittorgarh. She misses his presence to really argue with him, like any wife would playfully do, having lost that right by virtue of his absence. She has lost that banter. The last six from the mixed two dozen were eaten by all her sons and one of them was used by him to plant the solitary tree which bore fruit eventually.

"All the fruit has been for me to enjoy alone, the mangoes and your sons. What did you get? Only the joy and pride to father them. Here, I share this tea, with every sip, these moments...and those that have long passed, I relive them again, to cherish with you." The mangoes from a certain location, were giving their water-well good cover and shade, that too in her own heaven on earth. Elements of sunshine, water, land, earth, soil, she thanked them all mentally, her late husband Khazan, and mother nature, - 'Prakriti.'

She prays that they all continue in the same cycle to protect her entire family always. The presence of that tree makes her feel rooted.

Maya annually estimates a load of seventy to eighty kilograms of mangoes from the tree she has selectively cultivated. She cannot spare more water from the well, to grow any more trees, so she does not expect to cultivate an orchard. She has over the past decade fostered the tree, like her two absent sons who are not with her. The mango tree has been showering its share of care and concern upon her. She does attempt to start speaking to it, and ends up speaking to herself.

Changing the elbow support below her neck and chin, she happily anticipates the visit of her eldest.

Sanjeevni is due to return to Nawalgarh.

Her thoughts usually flicker toward him, after she is done with Khazan, momentarily. She decides to wait, to pluck the ripe mangoes with Sanjeevni's help as he loves to gorge on them like his father.

She intends to make him visit the Indian Hospitality Resort before he leaves back for Delhi, to deliver the fruit pulp for their storage and obtain a contract for mango pickle from the store manager. She knows she must make a separate set of two jars, one for Sanjeevni to carry back for himself, and another for his employers at Malhotra Niwas. Maya works to retain all the blessings and connections that her family has obtained, by nurturing them, with whatever means her land can offer.

Her attention shifts, as she steps out toward the clothing line, she takes in the smell of the earth to which she is attached, for it is here that her husband left her, with her three sons, before he passed on at a young age of fifty-four.

She sharply recollects the summer of 1976.The heart attack, the only first one he gets, is fatal. She knows of so many women in Nawalgarh whose spouses have survived three.

She rues his youthful years, and feels sorry albeit briefly, for herself, to have met him late in life. She married him in 1955 when he was thirty- three years of age, and she just twenty a wide gap of thirteen years.

Then his handsome rugged looks, appeared so solid and adroit, appearing long standing. She had no misgivings then as the age gap was taken as normal as long as the families could agree on the terms.

Her skin tone was accepted by the wheat complexion man himself. He had a good vision toward life, a sense of minimalistic speaking and more doing. Khazan was a doer, always hungry to learn. and try new things and explore the invisible paths in life. One such choice had brought them all to Nawalgarh.

"The sugar must have eaten into his heart and the salty fried food he enjoyed in his life delivered him a double whammy" she mutters to herself softly.

It is because Sanjeevni is expected back and he is the eldest male of the house. It reminds her of her own vulnerabilities and future health. She knows she will soon enter the spectrum of time, from when she will be repeatedly made a grandmother, as her two younger sons were yet to marry. She was in her forty's when she lost her husband, and now was in her fifties.

She swears to herself not to pamper her first grandson with sweets.

Sanjeevni was just twenty, and Ashwini around fifteen when she lost Khazan. Hari was at an age, when he could have been led by Maya's father if he was around, to the nearest sweet shop, but she thinks he's been better off missing those indulgences. Hari has missed the benefit of both his father and maternal grandfather's pampering.

Hari has grown up looking up to Sanjeevni as his elder brother and Jyoti as the *BhabhiMa*. Hari was born on this land, in 1971, when the India Pakistan war was at its peak. They had tried one last time hoping for a girl in 1970 and landed themselves into a black-out due to the war, when she was ready to deliver Hari. She remembers the much concern on Khazanchand's brow, extremely worried for her to get the mid wife to come on time. He was nearing age of fifty when Hari was conceived and the prospect had made Khazanchand feel young, romantic all over again.

Maya had immersed herself in that rekindled love and bliss of fertile matrimony.

Khazan's worries had changed to a youthful energy, playing with Hari. He would do all his chores, including feeding him milk from new sterilized bottles that he used to personally wash in fresh water and ash. He would place the bottles near the mandir in his house near Lord Vishnu's frame and ring a bell in the evening, signaling to little Hari to wake up. He would then carry Hari in his arms, pace around to feed him the bottle of milk.

It invigorated those years of Khazan at home, when he had re-started his vocation on the land as a farmer.

Toiling by day, Khazan playfully enjoyed the bliss of married family life in the early evenings. His morning gazes at the still youthful and energetic Maya would put her in a swooning stride in the kitchen with the two elder boys. All of them in their white kurta shirts, looking like the mirror images of their father.

Sanjeevni had Khazan's forehead and chin. Ashwini had his shoulders and long arms like the Hindu God Vishnu. It was Hari that had all the features. Hari's limbs were identical to his father and that led to a similar posture and walking style. If you would just glimpse at Hari quickly you would think it was Khazanchand standing there, with the same wavy hair and gait. Back then he was yet to grow into an adolescent before which she lost her spouse. Khazan used to love her in dark brown and deep maroon attire. She had kept those two colors for her clothing and not the white that orthodox widows usually followed in those days.

She would imagine him standing there often. He was attired in his white kurta shirt, and a pink turban. She wanted to correct him to wear the red or yellow one, because it was daytime. His words rang in her ears as she sipped her tea.

She remembered how he would always come close to her ears, and pantomime on the songs playing on the radio. He would repeat the lyrics of all Raj Kapoor movie songs as they played on their Murphy's transistor. He would stay up late nights, talking to her softly, about the stories of his past experiences in Sialkot and the move to Solan, as they lay in bed after dinner. She would patiently listen to him repeating incidents about his work at the armed offices, of the bygone days before he had retired.

He had a memory of his father telling him about trains coming from Pakistan, with dead bodies of Hindus, and how they reached platforms of stations in Amritsar with blood flowing out. As the platforms got soaked in blood, police officers had to wear boots and wade through these blood rivers to identify the bodies with relatives. Khazanchand had himself not seen these scenes, but he repeated the story told to him by his father very often after his retirement. In a way, he was thankful that he had managed to move out to Solan earlier to the partition of India and Pakistan.

In her solitude, it was just a matter of synchronicity for her, to play the same images in her head, that he had so often spoken about. It was not a dream. Many unique events had really taken place with his father, and now they were carried by her in her container of memories. The memories appeared like an illusion, but she lacked 'that' someone with whom she could experience or share those thoughts with.

It was up to her now, in her own solitude to recreate or abandon thoughts for her lone self. She observed herself, that her feelings led her nature sometimes and flipped her toward loneliness. This created a wedge between her contentment and otherwise gracious self.

As her tea was over, she commenced thinking about her late spouse's life.

Khazanchand Singh was born in 1922 into a farmer family of a *Rajasthani Jat* father, and a *Yadav Chandravanshi* clan mother. The mother's clan had migrated to Sialkot from Rajasthan in 1912. Maya had received the full story from '*her Khazan*' and she remembered it conveniently in parts, like individual episodes of a television serial. She often repeated trailers of a few clips to Hari, so that the roots of the family were recorded and stored in the youngest member of the family's memory, to have a sense of history being passed on in the form of attitudes, and attributes.

Khazan's parents had immigrated with his mother to Sialkot from Rajasthan when both territories were under undivided India. His maternal grandfather ran a sweet shop in Sialkot and wanted Khazan's father to expand the business by breeding cows. His plan was to run a private diary from their large home in Sialkot.

The famine in Rajasthan in 1921 near *Jhunjhunnu*, made Khazan's father abandon his employer's small farm on the outskirts and migrate to Sialkot.

The farm's employer *Karorimal Rathod*, a bachelor, was himself migrating to Nawalgarh, with his cattle to start operations for a small dairy there. Karorimal had a small piece of land he had purchased during his good days in Nawalgarh, as his mother's in-laws had a haveli there.

Khazan's father thus easily accepted his grandfather's offer, as it appeared to him that running a dairy family business was more lucrative over his current employer who was shutting shop.

Khazan's grand-father's sweet shop was called '*Doodh & Boondi*' and was in the main commercial street of Sialkot. This loosely translated to '*Milk and FriedSweetenedFlour*'.

The place had earned itself the reputation, of being the best sweet mart in Sialkot, especially for its dry *fruit barfis, khoya,* and all varieties of *ladoos,* including '*besan' and 'motichoor'.*

'*Doodh & Boondi*' was two streets away from the four room, double story house that was eventually gifted by the grandfather to Khazan's father.

In 1921, as a son-in-law, Khazan's father had accepted the migration based on the plan to participate in his wife's family business. He had humbly accepted to living in their house, as she was their only daughter and his father-in-law was ageing with no heir.

Khazan's grandfather was only interested in his own shop and had enough space there to live and reside if he so wished.

Khazan's paternal grandparents were no more since 1918. Khazan was raised with a lot of love and affection by his mother. She was the only child of her family, and Khazan, the only male child of his. He had the luxury to walk to the shop with his grandfather personally holding his index finger every morning.

The chubby Khazan, with apple pink cheeks hanging on both sides of his face, a sparkle of sweet jalebis in his eyes, would walk briskly with a heightened pace, as he would near the shop. His long, wavy hair, would curl around the back of the neck and around the chin. His mother would personally groom him, combing his hair for a long ten minutes, as she loved his silken locks.

A cherubic child, still small in height, chubby, wearing the '*pathani*' suit and kurta with two pockets full of almonds, well-groomed with talc and skin rubbed with cream, oil in hair, looked every inch the heir to the successful grandfather.

On certain days, the doting grandparent would reach out to the '*Shahtoot*' hanging loose from the mulberry trees lining their walking path and share them with his grandson. This would be done after methodically polishing, cleaning and tasting them himself. The colored kerchief in the evening would be hand-washed by the grandson. They were an interdependent team due to the walk to the shop.

Khazan would observe other merchants setting their wares for sale, especially the dry-fruit shops setting up almonds and pistachios. His grandfather would buy the fresh stock of both from his neighboring shop, run by his long-standing friend- Sajid Khan.

Khan was the only importer in the city for nuts and other dry-fruits and was the descendant of an Afghani family from Kabul. The special sweets prepared for marriages needed sourcing of figs, walnuts and other nuts, for which 'Khan Bhai', alone had access to the Afghan merchant trade. The town's entire scale of trade of dry-fruits ran from the side of '*Dhoodh & Boondi*', giving Khazan's grand-father a steady stream of visitors and buyers from Khan's shop.

Both Khan and the grandfather were garnering business and conserving wealth like hungry squirrels hiding their nuts, while the son-in-law was also accustomed to milchig it at the home dairy.

Khazan would enjoy his rich breakfast of samosas or bread paneer pakoras, fried in the new oil of the day. His grandfather would show him how the sweets would be made in the kitchen by the two workers who resided there.

It was a mid-scale operation, but Khazan's view from his height made it look deliciously colossal to him. A child at his height of three and a half feet, watching sweets on display through glass showcases, each piece larger than the other, stacked in neat piles like rectangular and square bricks in a pyramid.

The complete pyramid looked like a brick wall of a small house, and yet was something he always counted up to 10-9-8-...3-2-1. '*Fifty-five barfis*', he would proclaim proudly displaying his count and simultaneously contemplating their consumption entirely. Little did he know then, he will not live past that number.

Like the teasing pause he would take at fifty-four before proclaiming loudly the apex number to stop his count, fifty-five would be the number, which he would not see his life ending at the pre-cursor of fifty-four.

Khazan felt elated and extremely delighted at the prospect of sitting at the cash counter every day with his grandfather. Shiny coins collected for every sale were passed to him. Some were round like the *ladoos,* and some diamond shaped like the *barfis.* The aroma of sweetened milk, butter, ghee, various flavors of fruits, fried *'puri' and 'besan'* would mix in the air, with the fragrance of incense sticks that he would light near Lord Krishna's idol behind the cash counter.

Khazan would look up to his "Nanna" who wearing a clean starched white kurta and dhoti, both folded up halfway, would pray, do bhajan kirtan in a quick sixty seconds, and rattle the brass little bell. That was the sign for people outside the shop on the street to recognize the opening hours of business.

The grandfather would push up with his left hand, the *'steel kadda bangle'* up the right arm and commence the day's display of pyramids of '*barfis' and 'laddoos'* as speedily as the kitchen would dish them out.

The mouth-watering proposition was too good to miss for the young Khazan. He would get to play with the one '*anna*' copper nickel coins, the two anna silver coins, and the quarter anna copper coins that customers would use to pay his grandfather.

Khazan would act as the chief collector, neatly keep them in four separate bowls of steel, after counting them in heaps of tens. When he had collected one hundred it was young Khazan's responsibility to insert them in a plastic packet and seal it with a thick dual layer white thread which was also used to tie the *'mithai sweet boxes'*.

The 'Nanna' would have his loyal free labor, and the company of his favorite family member with him through the day. He believed he was teaching family business skills to his grandson, besides feeding and entertaining him. It left Khazan's mother free to do the household chores while Khazan's father would toil with the cows for the milk, and supply the fresh daily produce by eleven, to be served at the shop. The said milk would be used to serve cool in the summers mixed with butter and cream, topped off with shreds of pistachio nuts to all customers in the market before lunch at noon. In winters it would be used to serve hot with more dry nuts and hot piping samosas.

Subsequently, the ample home supply of milk was used to curdle for the next set of sweet preparations after two in the afternoon. When not counting the coins or the pyramid's individual bricks, Khazan's entire day was spent looking at the photo frame and idol of Lord Krishna in the large mirror afront the cash counter.

The reflective imagery of butter from the earthen pot, with milk and cream soiled on Baby Krishna's hands and face, was what Khazan felt had flown from the idol, all over the shop and into his heart and subconsciously his soul.

Khazan's "Nanna" would send him off by four to play with his friends at home, when his mother would come to pick him up. She would deliver some leftover food for his grandfather to eat his rather late second lunch at the shop and escort Khazan back home. Khazan's reward would be two large pieces of white *barfi* before leaving the shop, covered with silver foil.

Khazan would wait the entire day for this reward, as he would eye the '*vark*' when it was laid out on the fresh 'barfi' platters at the start of the day before they were cut into little diamonds and placed into a pyramid.

It would make each individual brick, and his favorite sweet, '*the great Indian khoya barfi*' - appear even more ornamental and delicious for consumption. He would salivate mentally, and stich his lips tersely twitching them, before mouthing the two pieces voraciously. The mornings were no different.

The 'Nanna' would start the shop's operations with feeding his grandson before a single customer would be served from the shop. Khazan was the solitary loyal customer to get the morning fried snack, on the dot of the stoppage of rattling the bell before Baby Krishna's idol.

In the late afternoon, the 'Nanna' would keep the bundles of coins ready for his daughter to take back with her in the afternoon, when Khazan would leave with his mother, feeling nourished and enrichened.

Getting off the three soft cushions from the cash counter, Khazan would embrace his 'Nanna' and touch his feet at the same time, making the grandfather teary eyed and emotional, yet delirious with joy and pride.

Khazan grew up in this environment from his age of six, till he developed into a serious school student. His hours at the shop were then reversed for the evening slot when he would especially enjoy the hot milk in winters, laced with dry fruits. He enjoyed the colder months diet more over the sweet lassi and butter milk of the summers.

Khazan's nanna was a '*Vaishnavite*' and believed in the philosophy of goodness. Goodness in thinking, speaking and acting. He also believed that there was a connection of milk with Khazan's ability to father children in future and ensured that he got his staple diet freely at both home and at the shop. This was an easy endeavor for a man running a business both of a dairy and sweet shop.

Khazan had always seen the finished product on the sale side of the shop and never aspired to manage or govern the kitchen. He was happy to enjoy the fruits of another's labor and simply savor the sweets and all goodies. He was a taster and not a creator. On the side, he had mastered the art of counting and understanding the financials. As he grew up, he discussed the sum of all weekly gains of the business with his 'Nanna'. This gave him a sound practical accounting knowledge and made him feel confident on monetary transactions of larger values.

He developed the knack of grasping the larger picture and staying away from day-to-day business operations.

By 1940, Khazan had grown to the last year of his teens.

India was seeking freedom from British rule, the struggle gaining momentum. His father was now manning the sweetshop, while his "nanna's' photograph adorned the same wall where the old baby Krishna photograph still hung well framed.

Khazan's father had done away with the use of dry-fruits and the relationship with Khan-bhai, from the adjoining shop had deteriorated. The Muslim league in India had commenced the grumblings with the Indian National Congress, and it appeared that people's opinions all over the country, had started getting divided on religious lines.

Khazan had decided for himself not to join the family business as he could see his parents manage well with the addition of half a dozen workers. He sat with his father once a week, like he would with his 'Naana', and visited the shop in the evening on weekends.

Khazan had observed that the British Raj, had started hiring young lads, to govern the operations of its forces and its people. He saw this as a life-long employment independent of location and a way of exploring the country entirely via travel.

His visions were growing outside Sialkot.

After finishing his intermediate studies, Khazan took up employment under the Punjab Regiment, with the Military accounts department when the British Raj was marshalling inductees before the partition of India. He had a childhood mastery over mental math - counting and '*Ganit*' as the arithmetic part of mathematics was called in those days.

His immediate senior officers were ageing Indians and all of them were recommending him in after office discussions to move toward the heart of India, or toward Calcutta on the first opportunity.

The prices of everything had increased.

The one anna price of a 1930 '*pau barfi*', was now the price of a daily newspaper. Many events in the country were routinely published, including in the weekly newspaper 'Harijan' that was edited by R V Sastry under the auspices of M.K. Gandhi.

Gandhi's efforts at keeping the country united had developed cracks with the ambitions of both Nehru and Jinnah wanting to be Prime Minister of their own independent country. The Indian National Congress philosophy was inclusive and secular, and that of the Muslim League hung onto its religious beliefs.

In early 1947, at twenty five years of age, Khazan was instrumental to move his mother and one willing resident aged lady worker to establish the same business under the name of 'Punjab Sweet House' at Solan in H.P..

He had made the selection based on the collective decision taken by his senior retiring from service, who had relocated and settled his father Shri Gurpreet Singh at Solan.

The Sikh family had chosen to open a provision store and live in the shop house above, in the commercial street of Solan. Many defense personnel and their support staff moved together. Khazan's choice was automatic and final. Or so he had thought.

His father refused to move, as he believed, in keeping the business income alive from '*Doodh & Boondi.*' This caused immense grief to Khazan and led to intense discord between the father and son.

Khazan's father had no external view outside his own inherited business. He had already made one successful migration into Sialkot from Jhunjhunu in his younger years. He was not affected despite his wife having left as she had keenly understood the challenges on Khazan's shoulders and moved to Himachal.

Khazan's father sought time to sell some of the cows of the dairy business as an excuse to stay back, and continued his life as usual. Muslim buyers of cattle however were only buying cows or bulls for their meat alone.

As this was against the cultural values of Khazan's 'Nanna', Khazan's father had turned acrimonious toward his neighbor Khan Bhai. Religious and cultural beliefs were suddenly making neighbors go after each other's throats.

In the first week of August 1947, Khazan came back from Calcutta where he was based then for his work with Military accounts, to urgently fetch his father and wanted him to move back to India the next day. The communal situation all over the country was explosive, and he feared the safety of his mother too at Solan. He knew from internal sources that he had very less time, to protect the safety of his father.

A late evening argument ensued and his father told Khazan to get out and leave the house, as he was willing to stay back and burn with the riots and rioters that were breaking out everywhere.

Khazan's father could not believe and accept that the same '*karmbhoomi*', where he had worked and delivered all his good thoughts, good actions were now turning ugly after twenty-five years.

Khazan started the day early the next morning to catch a bus for Jalandhar in Punjab. At the first bus-stop, Khazan was deep in thought while sipping his cardamom flavored milky tea. He watched before him an entire family with three generations, open their packed snacks to eat together.

"What have I done?" he bitterly regretted to himself. "I have failed to convince my father. I must go back for he will not be able to survive the riots" he grumbled to himself. He paid the tea stall owner and crossed the road to go back to Sialkot in a bus filled with Muslim refugees going the other way again. All traveller eyes of suspicious looking passengers stared hard, casting aspersions upon him. Some even questioned his brazen foolishness, and spoke to each other with aggressive posturing by fellow passengers doubting his motivations.

Upon reaching the bus-stand, Khazan had headed straight to the shop in the commercial street.

He knew the business operation hours of the street. Upon reaching there, he noticed the neighbor Khan Bhai, with a group of onlookers, arguing loudly with his father. Breaking up the fight between the two, Khazan took his father into the shop. Khazan used to sit with Khan Bhai and his own Nanna as a child so had earned that respect from Khan.

Making him sit, he told him. "Father, time is short, have faith on me, do not argue. Please listen. I am just going to take you back with me."

Khazan's father broke down and sobbed for a full two minutes. After recovery, he looks up from his circular glasses and asked, "Will you take me with you everywhere you go? Its better you leave me at Solan with your mother. I made a mistake I should have gone back and always stayed with her. It is my indecisiveness at first and then taking a wrong decision in that indecisiveness."

"Father, this is also my '*janmbhoomi*', but we will have to leave, just like we leave Guru Nanak behind. It is important, as a person on the move, to remember Guru Nanak's teaching to us. Lord Krishna is everywhere. We will just follow the values of Nanak and my 'Nanna' wherever we go. The place is not important. Being alive and living a life of safety is important. The creation of Pakistan is happening on religious lines on this side of the country. Leaders who shape India have decided that all religions and philosophies can co-exist together. That is true Hinduism, as we already have so many Gods there is no argument. Everyone can have their own God. I have already moved Nanna's pot of gold weighing two kilos. You have the remainder one kilo. We will sell gold and live if we have to in the initial few years. Do not worry. There are a larger number of people with taste and food needs on that side of the country. Your hands will still feed millions."

Khazan had also met a young Maya's family at Solan. Her father had also folded up his trading business and migrated to India. They were *Rajasthani Rajputs*, but traders and lived across the street from Khazan's mother.

Ensuing the shift of his father to Solan in 1947, Khazan's mother fell gravely ill that December. Maya as a youngster would visit their shop daily, to buy the required milk for her own parents, and knowing that his mother was ill, would help entering their household to do the kitchen work for Khazan's father. This started in December of 1947 and continued for the better part of the following years.

Gradually her hand-made Aloo parathas and tea, would perk up Khazan's father's breakfast. On this initial visit in 1947, Khazan had only seven days of leave, and few days were lost in travel, to and from Jalandhar first to Sialkot, then Solan. He had to rush back to Calcutta the next day after dropping his father off at Solan. On his return to Calcutta, leave was impossible as the situation of refugees pouring into the country from both sides was huge, and he was made to work on sections of people come in from East Pakistan.

Over the years from 1948, Khazan would make a short inquiry, via a weekly phone call from his official facilities by calling on the neighboring '*Sardarji's*' provisions shop. This would be to enquire on his mother's health. As time elapsed and work became more overwhelming, he would walk to the New Market area at the corner of 19 Lindsay Street of Calcutta where the fashionable tailor of 'Gurpreet & Co' would allow him the use of his phone.

Sikh businessmen were industrious at their work, and also courteous to allow people a service if they were their customers. Khazan would get his trousers stitched from the tailor and use the benefit of calling to the shop at Solan. His parents occupied the next-door shop of '*Singh & Sons*', and lived atop the commercial establishment themselves. This was the same Sikh senior retired member of the work team from

Calcutta, who had now been posted from Calcutta to the redefined state of Punjab.

Yet, Khazan always felt relieved that his parents had the senior "Papaji" of this colleague there, though older and aged, his presence next door had a very calming impact on his parents. It was also his same colleague who had introduced him to the tailor shop Sikh gentleman in Calcutta.

As his mother was bedridden, he could only speak to his father, with whom he was able to chat during the evening hours every Saturday. Khazan's father was by now mostly in an affable mood, having re-established his business. Except Gandhi's assassination period of uncertainty, he worried only for his wife's health.

By 1949 Khazan's mother generally always complained of aching body and bones and any amount of warmth in the winters did not help her to feel good. Solan was at the foot of the Shimla hills and Khazan's father kept urging him to get a transfer from Calcutta to Shimla, so that he could be nearer.

Khazan's colleague and Papaji's relative had been transferred to the southern command in India and Khazan had lost his foothold to get any transfer. He was the only old hand the East India office had for accounts, who knew the history of cases of new immigrants who had come into India. To help the cause of such refugees, Khazan had himself become an unwillingly marooned one. He was now stuck in Calcutta.

Three years had passed since partition, and Khazan was not getting leave to visit his parents. He used to send the occasional monthly post card from Calcutta P.O, with images of the Victoria Memorial and *Chowringhee* Lane with photos of Trams. Some cards would have two images of Park Street, or the Howrah Bridge cut in two halves with trams on the other half.

On one of the post cards, he obtained hurriedly from his tailors, was the cover of the movie '*Barsaat*' a new Raj Kapoor and Nargis starrer. He scribbled words for his educated mother, after he had thought deeply at night.

"Unattainable" he wrote atop the center top of the postcard. He scribbled the date 15'Aug'50, very sullenly, as images of his Nanna, his growing years, and his Sialkot home, school and mithai shop flashed before his eyes. He wanted to write something that did not delve on the past but could explain the situation to his mother, and yet had to be done optimally in the confined space of a post-card.

UNATTAINABLE

"Physical is ephemeral, Mental is mindful.
It is the spiritual that is unattainable.
Life is short and you still get to stretch it.
Take it in your hands - Wrench it.

We all go through changes in life,
With a fair bit of evolution since birth.
If we look around not much has changed,
Yet eventually everything about us does.

Try to spend as much of time,
Thinking of 'good' memories.
Call back the 'good' moments,
Remember the temple bells and churches that ring.
Listen to lots of music, it is always 'hope' that happiness brings."

Khazan's intention was to share the post-card as a symbolic love image of the two stars, for his parents, coupled with his carefully crafted words, very legible on the card. The 'unattainable' post card reached the Solan shop. It was glanced at by Khazan's father in September of 1950. He had intended to take the card upstairs, later in the evening for Khazan's mother.

The sweet shop kept him busy, and he left the card in the drawer below the cash and change register.

Khazan's father did not entirely read the "unattainable" and did not absorb what he did. He absent-mindedly left the post card, below taking in the pictorial image, thinking that his son was trying to nudge him to watch a new movie released in Gaiety theatre in Shimla. He was not one to understand much of poetry. He was also not a film buff and was yet to ever see any movie since partition. He was partly literate with paltry beginnings he had managed to read numbers and only a bit of the 'devnagri' script.

His simple joy was to listen to music.

The post card remained there for a few months. In December of the same year, Maya visited Punjab Sweet House at ten in the morning from next door, as usual to cook lunch for Khazan's father. The kitchen and the dining room was behind the shop, from part of which steps went upwards to the toilet and bedroom upstairs. She cared about the family as elders and was not their worker or helper. She would call him "*Baujji.*"

At fifteen years of age, she was an expert of the rolling pin and would help to make their daily breakfast. She would also set the curd in a large bowl for them to consume through the day and at night, as doctors had suggested it was good for Khazan's mother's calcium intake. This was avoided in winters by Khazan's mother and his father would sell the excess in five bowls via his shop. He would use this as a tip to Maya to have her fun with 'her' money.

That day of December, Khazan's father had to go back upstairs with his wife. She was in exceptionally poor health and groaning as the winter had advanced. Despite medication use for two days, her body, limbs, and specifically her left foot ached.

Baujji requested Maya to run the shop for a few hours in the morning after which she could lock up and leave for him placing two chairs outside the shop indicating an early closure. The traffic of buyers was anyways thin.

The weariness of age and the onslaught of the winter was gradually ebbing the health and mood of Khazan's parents. Like any other child in the armed forces, their only son, was serving the national interest, not theirs. This was taking a toll on Khazan's mother.

As Maya cleaned the cash counter and took stock of the loose change, she inquisitively opened the drawer below to rustle up and clean the papers inside the drawer.

She chanced upon the 'unattainable' post-card.

Her first brush with 'Khazan', came in the written form. She was a year away from being on the cusp of sweet sixteen and was to appear for her grade ten examinations in the following year.

Upon discovering and reading the post-card that afternoon, Maya read and re-read the card a dozen times. She noticed his blazing signature going upward toward the corner of the post-card, as there was no space at the bottom.

He had ended saying lovingly yours, son – K---z----. she could only decipher the alphabets K and Z. The rest looked like the jalebis at his father's shop.

She had seen him three years back and even exchanged small mumblings in his first visit when he escorted his father. But she had not been introduced to him. She turned over the ravishing Nargis photo, as she barely looked at Raj Kapoor. Men with pencil thin moustaches, did not impress the young girl. You either had to have thick whiskers like her father or none at all.

She looks at the four anna *Bhuvanesvara Stamp of India,* and the mark "POSTAGE" on the left corner. She observes the temple shrines on the stamp very intently. She tries to read the date of the post office circular franked stamp and discovers the date of 01.09.50.

There were no customers that afternoon.

She wondered why someone would send a post-card and not write anything personal to his parents, yet scribble long philosophical quotes.

She hazily recalls his attire, the khaki-colored trousers and blue shirt look in his last visit of August 1947.

He had long wavy locks of hair, slickly combed at the back of his head then.

Little did she know, that this tall 'babu' as his father called him affectionately, would be sending a post-card to Solan.

She scornfully placed the post-card back. As she goes about the chores in the shop she thinks about the card, the entire afternoon.

She reads it repeatedly, to gage the handwriting enough number of times.

She eventually interpreted and understood the deep hope and love the card held out for the mother and wanted to immediately share it with '*Maaji*' but had to wait till evening when Khazan's father would step down.

Maya twitches her nose, as the heady memories and the ensuing conversations come racing back at Nawalgarh. She can see herself, sitting at Bandstand Bombay, and reminisce her past from Solan to Nawalgarh. She pulls herself back into the flashback.

At four thirty that evening, Khazan walked to the '*New Market*' tailor shop, in Calcutta, a packet of "*moodi*' in his hand. The evening snack he enjoyed was a mix of peanuts and puffed rice with lemon juice, Bengal masalas and lightly boiled gram.

It was a cool day in Calcutta so he lazily put his left hand inside the vest he wore below his blazer, and dials "*Singh & Sons*" number on the old-fashioned instrument of the tailor shop. He had to hold the speaking piece in his hand as he moves the left hand out of his pocket to catch hold of the separate corded ear piece to his left ear.

After being put on hold for twenty seconds by "Solan's Papaji' from the provision store, he hears a sound rustling up the phone on the other end, with clanging bangles.

"Jee, Hello! Hello!" he heard a nightingale chirp inside the tailor shop he thought.

Gurpreetji in Calcutta looked up at him and observed his poker face.

"Why the surprise?" he asked.

"Ahem...I'm not sure, is this Solan?" said Khazan, forgetting he had just asked Papaji to call his father from next-door.

"Well, this is not Calcutta, that's for sure." Maya spoke confidently.

She saw Papaji, look up, from his writing of books, his bushy white eyebrows arched, as he lowered his thick rectangular spectacle frame. He watched intently as he knew Khazan had called.

Though Maya came from the opposite side of the street, it was Papaji who was the immediate neighbor of Khazan's parents. Papaji had been requested to keep an eye on his parents, and he had found only Maya alone at the shop that day. Before he could prepare Khazan, Maya had reached the phone instrument, leaving Papaji busy with his count of inventories of the yellow '*Dalda*' oil boxes.

"Excuse me?" asked Khazan.

"Well, you are excused! Just by me. I am not sure '*Maaji*' will excuse you. You have left her here in the cold weather and she is keeping poor health. You have never visited them for three years. Yet you call only weekly in the evening. Is this your way of fulfilling your responsibilities?"

At fifteen, girls are usually chirpy and feel free to talk to strangers without feeling awkward or shy.

Maya was no different.

Except that she was dishing out a strong reprimand, with a reminder about the passage of time.

She was raised by her parents with a sense of the future and a keen observer of the virtue of present time, not just the past value systems. With her confidence, she had no hesitation of the events to be interpreted any differently.

She had been promoted today itself by Khazan's own father in the line of duty and the first thing that came to her mind, was out on her lips. She was not one who was going to be late in line of duty, nor in speaking the blunt truth.

"And who do you think you are? My grandmother? Where is father? Why has Papaji, put you on the call?" retorted Khazan a bit tersely.

"If I was your grandmother, I would have pulled your ears hard when I would meet you next. Thank your stars I am not."

A gap ensued with silence on both ends.

"And by the way, the physical, the mental and spiritual are all possible together. Life is long. Maybe you interpret life very wrongly!"

Papaji at the provision store of '*Singh & Sons*' now put his pen and paper down and pulls his glasses off, to wipe them with his kerchief.

He looks back at the girl, as Maya pulls her dupatta over her right shoulder and waits for return fire.

There is none.

Again, silence prevails.

"When are you returning to Solan?" asks Maya.

"Er...when I get leave." replies Khazan.

"Apply for it urgently. Before it's too late".

Maya's conclusive reply was a blunt cut.

She had already bled him with a few incisive queries earlier.

Her sardonic comments on his post-card were the final stroke.

He just ended the call and looked up at the tailor inside blankly. Quietly, Khazan leaves the tailor shop very sheepishly.

As he strolls out before New Market's imposing structure, he wonders why his mother had never written back, nor replied to his post-card.

He only relied on hope himself as he was bound more to his duty and work, rather than his family. Now his conscience had been pricked, and the invisible blood had settled at the bottom of his heart making it feel heavy.

Suddenly, Calcutta city seemed bitter and cold. He understood the concept of time well, and the phone call taught him to respect it.

He was in Solan by the next weekend. He had managed getting his leave by giving an ultimatum to his seniors that his mother may not make it any longer.

When Khazan reached his parental home in Solan, they were not expecting him.

•

His father broke down first as he embraced him at the entry of the shop. Khazan took full two minutes to break the hugging grip of his father, who nearly hung onto him. He patted his father on the back and stepped upstairs to greet his mother.

When he entered her room, he saw three layers of blankets and a coal based '*sigdi*' by her side, keeping the entire room warmer than what was needed.

His mother's eyes were open as she transferred her gaze from the ceiling to Khazan and tears rolled from her right eye, first on her pale face, then sideways on the pillow.

Khazan was clean-shaven, with a crew cut, and short sidelocks on his face, highlighting his square chin and strong jawline.

He rushes to his mother's side, on his knees to wipe the tears off her face, finding it difficult to not allow his chin to quiver.

"Son, it has been a long time since I could see you. We need you to be here. It's not hope, but health that I do not have. My life is coming to an end. It's so nice that I could see you today before I depart. You will understand this only when you have your own children"

"Mother do not start all over again. You know it's not as if I do not wish to settle down. My work does not allow me to. We have to change cities and shift all the time. Some of the postings are in locations I have yet to see myself. It just so happens that post partition I am based in Calcutta for now" responded Khazan.

"You are a migrant vagabond or are you with the army?" claimed the mother. "I only pray and thank the Lord, that you are not a solider."

"So, you got the post-card? Did you listen to any music.? I had left the radio atop the mantelpiece here, but I observe father has kept that in the shop downstairs. Music helps to heal Ma" says Khazan with a sense of persuasion.

The mother pleads. "Maya read me the post-card. We read it a dozen times together. I do get your post-cards. But your father has become forgetful, he has tucked some of them away for himself in the shop below. He reads them again and again quietly and does not tell anyone what he understands If it was not for Maya, I would never receive all of them."

She points to the drawer by the bedside which he opens and finds his scribbled cards.

"Who is this, this Maya? The cards were for you alone. Why did you read them with someone else?" he shoots back.

"She's my postman, cook and like my co-shop-owner. Will you make her my bahu? No one can care for us the way she has. Not even you, with you being away. She comes from a good family, and who knows, I may not live forever as I know, my life is short".

Khazan's mother in the first engagement of thirty minutes after three years of absence, tries to offer a proposition to her son.

"Mother, I need time, for promotions. Without that they do not allot a living quarter to personnel. Where will I keep your bahu? Which girl will wait for so long? I have not even seen her or a photograph of hers."

"You had seen her three years back when you brought your father from Sialkot via Punjab."

"That child?"

"It's been three years. She's grown up."

"Maaji..."

"Khazan, she has read your post cards more often than me. She has read them aloud to me, as if she has first read them to herself. She can say the words without looking down at the cards. She has waited for you as much as me."

Maya had the resilience and patience of a tribal Rajasthani woman in her spirit. Stoked by her father's adventurism and the free manner with which he had raised his daughter, Maya was accustomed to wait. She was a waiter par excellence.

Maya had waited all her youth for her father to return from his trade trips, when they too lived in what was now Pakistan, and erstwhile undivided India.

They too had relocated to Solan. She had waited for her father to come this side of India in Himachal, as his group traders had told him before partition that his wife and daughter would await them in Solan. Her father had taken two years to return, after independence. Many family members in this way did not know where their loved ones were, and if at all they were alive.

She was thus an experienced mature child woman, who now had seen '*Maaji*' wait for her son.

Maya had experienced a lifetime of waiting, watching her own mother wait for her companion, and now had been fast forwarded to the life of a mother awaiting her son.

These experiences of her life, would come to good use for her in her maiden youth, eventual middle-age and pre-fatal death age. Her horoscope had predicted a long life for her till the century would turn to the next one.

Her mother had trained her to build resolve and virtue as two traits that a woman must have. Her father had given his spin to create the independence of character and compassion of experienced traders.

Khazan's mother had admired these traits from up close through her sickness and aspired to have her as the daughter she never had.

During those sessions by the bedside, Khazan's mother had emptied her heart out and told the stories that later Khazan would go on to tell Maya in his retirement years. Only the perspective was of different age points for Maya, and the story tellers view had been a tad bit different.

In Solan, she got the full mother's view via Khazanchand's mother. When Khazan repeated the same stories to her in Nawalgarh she had a son's view. This certainly helped her define an understanding of how sons thought.

"Let him at least freshen up, he has just come today". Khazan turns to find his father at the frame of the door.

"Step down in the afternoon, she will be in the shop then at three today. Papaji next door told me about your conversation."

Khazan maintains a silence.

His father continues, "I also approve of this girl, as she has been able to get you back and finally reunite our family. We have been living as if our family has been in partition for three years. Whenever I asked, you always told me you are not getting leave."

Khazan's ears turned a rose pink, as he is now confronted by his father also to commit to this girl for marriage.

'*Who is this woman?' he thinks.*

"Okay let me at least see her, hopefully she is tall enough. It is important to me to judge her height, and to know she is not deaf. I already know she is not dumb, for she has worked her ways into both your hearts."

The same day at three in the afternoon, Khazanchand stepped down. He was fresh and warmly attired with a hand-woven royal blue sweater over a white shirt and khaki pants. It is quite the combination of the local school uniforms in the district.

Maya was in the shop below and watched the street outside developing a reflection of his khaki trousers, disembarking from the steps.

It was like a mirror image reflection of someone descending from the residential area, visible to her in the glass doors of the shop.

The '*halwai*' worker inside is frying the hot samosas on one large frying pan, while the counter on his right has jalebis stacked up.

The shop environment makes Khazan self-conscious, as he has never really had the need to speak to girls of that age before. This is different from the similar shop experience earlier in Sialkot. He is thirteen years her senior and approaches her with a childlike curiosity, though it is she who has the infantile spirit and innocence.

The samosas are well cooked, the batter golden brown, the potatoes and masala firmly held together by the batter over it. As the worker removes six of them from the sizzling oil, droplets of fried oil, leak through the large spoon with many holes.

Khazan's heart feels like the scorched hot samosas, with blood running through his veins a bit faster like the mercurial oil. He feels trapped like the potatoes, with the masala. She the masala in this situation.

She does not turn. She allows him the full view of her long hair, fully open, down till the top of her hips.

He watches silently, the cooked samosas as the worker cook removes the next six of them soaking wet from the frying oil. He goes into a repeat emotion of heart felt connection to the samosas. He looks around the shop, all three hundred and fifty square feet of it, standing at the corner edge where the staircase from above has brought him down into this oily hot mess.

He feels like that part of the batter, that is left stranded, overcooked longer in the frying oil, burnt a dark brown, but is not part of any of the samosas anymore. He has sailed into his own frying oil, feeling the heat inside the shop, as the small ceiling fan is only over the cashier counter, which she occupies.

He remembers his childhood and slips from present to past for a few more hot frying moments.

He remembers the three cushions his "nanna" used to seat him on, in Sialkot's "*Doodh & Boondi*"...

"*Khayenge, will you eat?*" she questions, both in Hindi and English, without turning back, she disturbs the human silence, with more oil frying, ear shattering noise coming from the samosa frying zone. The worker pauses for a second, looks at him and holds the spoon in mid-air before deciding if he wishes to eat the samosas already out of the oil, or those that are swimming like burnt crusts of his heart inside the oil.

Khazan remains tongue tied. He cannot see the sweets, as the countertop is angled in his line of sight, and is like a long table, running till the end of the shop, where she is standing. She is looking outside and now gesticulating to someone outside the shop.

Khazan walks forward, and a bit toward the worker chef de la samosas, when he gets the full view of the person outside the glass façade.

Its Papaji in his blue turban pointing at the samosas and showing three fingers to the girl with long black hair, who apparently maybe Maya, inside his father's shop.

Khazan's heart could explode he fears, drowning the shop with hot oil from within, scalding everyone and all the already soaked samosas could cause further mini explosions of their own.

He is yet to answer her, as he has not registered her query. He remains paralyzed. She sweeps in one movement and turns, with effect, toward the worker and tells him, "Place three on a paper plate with tamarind sweet syrup, as Papaji eats it without the green chilies on the side."

Maya's reflex movement makes her look at him as if she is admiring the continued scenery inside the shop, alongside all the fritters, food shelves, fried sweets and syrups on the shelf in front of her. A casual glance of a common kind that reduces him to a nobody in his own parent's shop.

The wall before her has a large mirror she can look at, which gives her the side profile view of Khazan. Due to the reflective nature of mirrors, they are placed to make most shops look double the size and create a sense of more space. She can look at him, without really looking him in the eye. She knows the vantage positions of the shop and which spot, creates the correct angles to view.

As the worker leaves the shop to deliver the samosas, Khazan walks up, as if to confront her with an opening remark. He opens his mouth, as if to say something and she turns back, behind the cash counter, to put on the radio.

"*Ghar aaya, mera pardesi*" she sings, to the tune of the yet to be released new film Aawara being promoted by Raj Kapoor's new studio on All India Radio. The movie was to be released in 1951, post Barsaat, the movie that featured on the post-card, and its promotional songs had been followed by Maya in Solan on the radio.

The sudden singing cuts his intention of saying anything and he dumbly just stares on, first at her, then the sweets lined up for the day in the store inside the glass counter.

She stands behind the counter and looks at him, observing there is no moustache. She dislikes unshaven men.

'How unruly. No respect for women. Good, he has at least groomed himself before stepping down, or coming back from his Calcutta' she thinks to herself.

All India Radio, breaks into the K.L. Saigal special from the movie about *Taj Mahal's maker 'Shahjehan', 'Jab Dil hi tut gaya, hum jeeke kya karenge'* Loosely translated as: 'Now my heart is broken, what will I do by living on'

"It appears that Saigal Saheb has not much hope" she condemns with her opening.

"Well, you surely do, it appears. You seem to like it here, in the shop." He finally finds his frozen tongue.

"It's my job, not duty. I get paid by your parents." she retorts

"Well, any other place in Solan, you like equally?" He looks at her quizzingly.

Finally, he is relaxed, a conversation is happening, and he wants to dramatically shift it away from the phone call kind conversation he had earlier from Calcutta.

"There is the *Sankat Mochan*, a makeshift Hanuman temple, but it's at Shimla." comes the flat reply. She goes back into the cash register, sifting papers and cards, some his post cards that he can see and recognize.

"Oh, a Hanuman *Bhakt*?" he asks.

"I have faith in Vishnu and Lord Krishna too." As she looks up to the framed old photo and idol from Khazan's Nanna' days of Sialkot.

"Lord Hanumanji has a deep following here. There is a rumor, or you can call it more of a myth. As you are an optimistic believer, that *Hanumanji* flew to the top of the Shimla hill, and rested his one foot there, before he flew onward to the '*Gandhamardan*' hills to get the Sanjeevni Booti for Sri Ram. Sorry, for Ramji's brother, *Laxmanji*."

"This *booti,* it has some magical cure?" He seemed perplexed, as he had never read the *Ramayan* and broadly knew of Lord Ram as one of the kings of Ayodhya, who was so popular that his idol was worshipped in temples. Though he had no dislike toward any of the Hindu gods, he had no special status or like for anyone except the real Lord, childlike in his eyes, - Baby Krishna. At times this bothered him, as he could not care less, and there were times he remembered with reverence his childhood days in Sialkot.

For him, the lord was the way he looked in the framed photograph in his "nanna's" shop in Sialkot, which now rested above Maya's head.

The *Sanjeevni Booti* had magical powers as it was known to infuse life back in someone who had anxiety, or nearly lost their '*praan*' – i.e life due to stroke or an attack by virtue of difficult circumstances.

"I thought '*Maaji*' can benefit so I have asked our family priest, Neem Baba to arrange and get the herbs from his counterparts at the foothills of the Himalayas. Some of them are wandering mendicants, while some are genuine priests attached to the proposed Hanuman temple there. There are forests nearby. They want to build the temple shrine there as it has a large number of monkeys there, so the myth is taken as the final truth by the people of the hills". Her attempt was to educate this man, such that sometimes drastic situations needed desperate measures.

As the conversation was about his mother's health, it became easier for Khazan to treat her like any other person and talk for several hours with Maya. He did not notice the '*to and fro*' movements of the workers or the customers in the shop. He kept listening to Maya that afternoon, and was brough to speed on matters of the Solan commercial market, the prices of vegetables, milk and the characters of all the heroes of the *Ramayan* and the two workers inside their Punjab sweets shop.

She had found someone to show off her knowledge about a scripture she had recently read. That afternoon, Khazan realized that Maya was merely an embodiment in spirit, body and mind, of the philosophies of his maternal grandfather- the '*Vaishnavite*' Nanna.

His 'Nanna's concept of Hindu dharma was, that they all had their Gods and loved all of them, and yet did not dispute the existence of many goddesses too, that others had faith in. Largely he also noticed, that by action, she was really speaking good, acting good and doing good by way of her work.

All this while still studying early mornings in school till noon. She came across as an industrious innocent girl, confident of herself, and someone who Khazan could respect as his equal.

He thought this was different from the women and girls of that generation who usually found themselves in a subservient position to men in society. Khazan liked this sense of independence of thought and yet the love and affection she sprinkled naturally on his parents.

After a fortnight, a trip was arranged with Maya's parents and Khazan's parents to the hills where *Sankat Mochan Hanuman* temple was being proposed at Shimla by road.

A minibus was hired and the workers of the shop with *Sardaar Papaji* from next door also accompanied them.

It was a Sunday and a family environment was struck, first inside the bus, and then later when they all sat to eat the langar lunch inside the '*Bhandhara*' area.

After the lunch, Khazanchand's mother, pale though she was, sat on the cement seat at the entry of the temple shrine area, and motioned toward her husband to distract Maya's parents to speak with them privately.

The proposition of asking for Maya's hand in marriage was in principle accepted by Maya's father, on the condition that she be allowed to complete her studies.

Khazan's father accepted as he knew there was time for Khazan to also obtain his residence allotment.

Khazan knew that their alliance was being struck, while tying the straps of his sandals, he had part of the left foot still wedged outside.

He looked toward Papaji, who also gave his blessings silently with a calm message in his eyes, "*You will not get a girl like this Khazanchand*" seemed to be his communique.

Khazan looked at all this as divine intervention.

He looked up at the skies where there would be future temple spires.

They had obtained the herbs in the visit and there was a new sense of hope in his mother's eyes. It was extremely relevant to him, that his mother also liked Maya so much.

As he spoke within himself, he noticed the stress on the word 'also' he had just uttered in his mind. Khazanchand believed, that it was important for him to seek the fondness of the girl, who he found to be very young. He was nearing his thirty's and she was barely just fifteen.

"Do you know what they are talking about and planning?" he pointed toward his parents. Without much shyness, she looked up at him, and said, "Yes, my father has kept me updated; but I know you will give me time. Time to grow up a bit and time for you to also visit here more often. Till then, I can give a hand in running Punjab Sweet house!" she proclaimed.

He laughed out loud. As he had his hearty laugh, she took annoyance to his demeanor and kept asking him, "What is it? What?"

There was no shyness. She was simply being candid. And that innocence was what he fell for completely at that instant. He wondered how a young girl could be so mature, when it was her hand in marriage that they were seeking.

He was a tall man, large frame, mature, with a heavy shave on his chin. She was just smack in the center of puberty, and still to learn how to wear a sari or handle the affairs of a housewife.

She was ahead of her times, and that was something he had taken notice of. He reiterated to himself the real bonus was the natural affection she had for his parents. He was like the side dish, to the main sweets and food that his father's shop churned out for her.

His reminiscences of his childhood, how he had taken for granted his 'Nanna's' shop and business, flashed past his mind. He decided to concede his heart forever to Maya and told her so.

He fleetingly missed his 'Nanna' and thought of him smilingly himself, with a beaming smiley image in return from the grandfather looking at him from atop the hilly skies.

A cool breeze was blowing. He moved his head, to rest some locks of hair from the left side of his forehead to the right.

"Don't worry, I will keep your heart within mine." she retorted. "Get us a good house wherever you are posted next. Then we will see, what is the hurry? I am already in your house."

"Not really, you are in our shop," he said lovingly.

Those were good times. India was beginning to find its feet, and many relocated migrants were being able to re-start their lives and gradually take care of their ageing folks.

The marriage date was set five years away, with both the families mutually accepting the same. It was done to wait and give the girl time to grow up and also complete her inter mediate studies.

The age gap between them was not entirely uncommon in those days.

By the winter of 1955 Maya was married to Khazanchand.

She had relocated with him in the new year 1956 to Calcutta. In the interim period of those five years, many visits were paid by Khazanchand to Solan and they walked the hills together, without ever holding hands. They would often take the local contractor's bus to the hilltop of Shimla and walk around the '*Ghanta Ghar.*' The British had built it on the Ridge in 1906 to mark the silver jubilee of Queen Victoria, and Maya always exerted her impression on the colossal nature of the structure.

Khazanchand would just nod to her silently as he was not exactly a fan of the British imperialism in structure and aesthetics, but he knew he had no choice like many Indians to accept these as their imprints on his soil.

They had developed a bond, as partners before they became one.

No one knew them in Shimla and he was visiting from Calcutta.

The *Sanjeevni Booti* had cured Khazan's mother completely.

His parents went on to live long and bless the couple, when they married and play with their two boys when they were born and later visited Solan.

6

KHAZANCHAND THE GUILTY SON

(WHO FATHERED THREE PRECIOUS SONS)

He felt deep in his heart, that he had married early.

They had Sanjeevni in 1956, within the first year of wedlock.

Khazan had the choice to make; he knew he had to continue living in Calcutta and continue the service under the supplies section of the army.

There was excitement and good news in the newspapers that year.

Sanjeevni too learnt to rattle and roll. The couple had initially chosen the boy's name due to their experiences in Solan and the Shimla proposed temple location. Khazan's mother had become independent and had stabilized with the medicant's herbs.

As a baby in his seventh month, Sanjeevni started making attempts to stand with some support. He would hold the support of the sofa and armchairs and walk holding support, fall a dozen times and stand up again and again.

During one of the weekends at home, Sanjeevni was placed by Khazan in the baby crib they had set up, which also doubled up as a play pen. Khazan and Maya sat in the balcony enjoying the flowing trees and spare human traffic on the streets of Alipore road when they heard a resounding crash. The whole pen was built on a frame cage of steel rods, with blue see through netting on the sides and a thick cloth base.

Sanjeevni had stood up on his feet, and pushed the pen downwards, with himself in it, knocking himself out of the play pen, and was crying out loud. His hunger for milk had woken him up, and he had landed squarely on his forehead and created a bump for himself on the front of his skull.

During his growing up years, Sanjeevni sought his little freedoms especially from any kind of constraining in his play areas. He liked to step up, walk or run and never feared striding up footsteps, never bothered to look back. He would even attempt jumping multiple steps down, with large jump strides, with no fear for injury or hurt.

His parents soon understood, that Sanjeevni was fearless to try new games, or events, which he was always willing to undertake with childlike curiosity.

He was always ignoring the risk or fear behind outcomes that he never knew were pre-existent taken as usually natural risk by adults.

The family had moved to a bigger three-room house in Hastings and lived there for four years, when Ashwini was conceived in 1960.

Ashwini, was someone Maya groomed, and played with as her little one. She had expected a girl, but he was born a handsome eight-pound baby. He had fine features, long limbs, and curly hair as a child.

Though both the parents and grandparents on both sides had straight hair, Maya was besotted with her '*ladlaa*' curls and fair complexion. He also had the ability to keep his eyes open for long intervals, blinked very less and slept peacefully at night in one go till eight in the morning.

Maya had managed to wean him off very early and get him used to *Farex* formulation powder that was popular due to Glaxo and the earlier presence of senior British officers and wives in India. Glaxo had introduced the product in 1934, to help British wives to manage their children's dietary habits and the product was being pushed in all colonies.

In this way Maya and Khazan learnt to parent their children with some trial-and-error effort, with one thing working on Sanjeevni and another on Ashwini.

Though he never completed his graduation, Khazan's intermediate qualifications had been enough for him to keep his job, when Independent India's armed forces retained their stationed staff in Calcutta.

The department of accounts was realigned first under the Finance and eventually much later under the Human Resources Ministry.

The couple had enjoyed their continuity of stay in Bengal, as the city had a lingering British hang-over. They often walked with their first child from their simple Alipore abode toward Park Street over the weekends, till they reached the Esplanade.

When the family had grown bigger, and so had Khazan, it was K C Das in the early evenings for their fill of '*rosogullas*' on Saturdays when both kids were around at Hastings.

It was Das that had invented the *Rasogulla* which had become nationally famous.

It was much after so many years being stationed in Calcutta, that Khazan in those days discovered Krishna Chandra Das to be the inventor of the '*ras-somalai*' that he and Sanjeevni had become fond of. He would buy many tins of the vacuum packed '*rosogullas*' and father and son would devour them at home over the weekdays sitting on their dining table.

Khazan had discovered the wet, Bengal fash-ioned sweets that he had never experienced in his Punjab and Himachal days. Ashwini as a baby would look on bemused, happy and high on Farex for-mulation with his father and brother drinking the transparent sugar syrup, after gulping what looked like two white milk balls. Ashwini never developed the taste nor asked for the sweet, hanging on to his milk bottle for dear life.

As Ashwini too grew up, Sanjeevni continued with his Punjabi Medium school at Alipore. Over the weekends Sanjeevni would usually play and practice hockey, a sport that had gathered popularity in India. Though it was injury prone, Sanjeevni played for the sake to play and enjoy his carefree days at school. An injury from a high-speed penalty hit to his little toe on his left foot, broke his toe, but not his spirit.

He had grown in height, and with large feet of UK size 9, he would wear a size 10 to give space to his toe on his left foot. This would make Sanjeevni slide his right foot a wee bit as he walked with a slow gait and yet no one would know that his thick socks allowed him to wear the bigger shoes he sported. With more focus on playing hockey, rather than studies, the elder boy enjoyed his days in the green fields behind his house, practicing penalty shots. The younger son was more inclined to watch movies like his mother Maya, who was a music buff and enjoyed the visit to the cinema.

Ashwini would mostly stay indoors and listen to music coming out of their transistor radio on the pickle shelf in the kitchen.

As time passed the four of them would find themselves inevitably together on the weekend in a cinema hall. The family would on alternate weeks, walk toward the Paradise Cinema at Bentinck Street and enjoy their staple of weekend Hindi Cinema. The Raj Kapoor, Rajendra Kumar starrer in color, "*Sangam*" was their best film experience in those years.

It was 1964 and Khazan spent the wee hours of the next Sunday morning debating love, friendship and companionship with Maya.

The boys were busy with Hockey and radio. It was the last week of the month of June of 1964 and Khazan spoke about the dramatized and fictionalized elements of Hindi Movies, which could never exist in their lives as they were true rationalists.

Maya had latched on to the turning point of a love letter in that film. She rued Khazan's inactivity in the expressive department and ribbed him endlessly to write a make-believe love letter, as though she was his only love interest.

Her efforts did not meet with much approval, as he always knew them to be unsustainable. She had called him 'Mr. Unattainable' often due to this and he enjoyed the reference to the old postcard on which their alliance was struck and after so many years still hinged.

By 1965, Khazanchand became deeply philosophical.

Like any father of two children and a married man, he sought answers from life for a higher sense of purpose.

He began short walks towards the Rama Krishna mission after work and became preoccupied by Swami Vivekananda and his books on Vedanta.

He would pick up second-hand books from the road sellers on Esplanade and Park Street, and soak in all the words written by a young Swami Vivekananda in those books.

He was impressed by the energy and clear-cut philosophy in those writings and like any other man of his time, taken up by the fact that this man had preceded him just less than sixty years back on the same planet earth in his own country and city.

Yet his father and mother had no clue of his existence or his writings. There was no spiritual leadership within his own family or any sense of direction. Some of his sayings and quotes hit him hard, and amongst them three were his favorites:

1. Truth can be stated in a thousand different ways, yet each one can be true.
2. External nature is only internal nature writ large.
3. You cannot believe in God unless you believe in yourself.

He would take the family all the way from Hastings to Gol Park on Sundays to visit the Ramakrishna Institute, and when Maya would argue, he would retort telling her to be pleased that he has not taken them all the way to Kanyakumari to meditate on the rock.

He would leave the children to loiter with Maya in the green area of the mission and immerse himself lying under a tree in the garden with books on Vedanta and Philosophy.

He read voraciously and sometimes repeatedly about Vivekananda's vision of Hinduism and his ascent and self-discovery due to his guru Ramakrishna, on whom he named all his missions.

He understood anew the concept of humanity and service to mankind due to these books.

Khazan remembered his own father from the experiences of Swami Vivekananda who was known in his pre-monastic life, as Narendra; born into a wealthy family, Swamiji's life had dramatically changed after his father's death. Khazan took note of the changed life of Narendra, from a spiritual crisis to an awakening.

He realized himself, that he had affixed his own emotions more to his own maternal grandfather and had lost the opportunity to become closer to his own father despite them all being in India.

He could never truly explain to himself, why he had not moved his parents to Calcutta, other than commercial means. He had set up his father in Solan, to join his mother to run his past legacy business, which was not really an inheritance. He could have moved his father to his city but had perhaps abstained from that action subconsciously to enjoy his own freedoms entirely.

He was also always unsure about transfers from Calcutta but had ended up staying on year after year. Yet he felt no sense of belongingness to Bengal.

He would think often to travel to '*Shantiniketan*' to see the other Guru's abode, but never got down to doing it. Yet listening to Rabindra sangeet in the shops he felt paralyzed in bliss to walk on and stayed glued to the spot.

He preferred Satyajit Ray movies over Maya's Hindi movie fascination, especially after watching the '*Appu Trilogy*'. He had first watched *Pather Panchali* when he used to live in Calcutta alone, and identified with the character Appu.

Though he was in Bengal, he knew he would not last there forever yet there was a bit of Bengal now inside him, which would remain forever. Bengal was the confluence of cultures, taste, and sentiment of a New India that he was getting to experience, with a context and connect to the past India that he was leaving behind like the staggering population of the country. It made him think about things he had never thought of in the past.

Accommodation was also a challenge, as Khazan himself shared a room in a low rise shophouse in Alipore, before he moved with Maya after marriage to rent an apartment from a Jain family leaving for Delhi. Jain business families had decided to move in the late 1950's towards Delhi to shift their attention to the new capital as Calcutta had started losing its significance in government contracts being awarded by the center and this had hastened with the Indira Raj after Nehru's daughter came to power in 1966.

In the meanwhile, Khazanchand was completely bowled over by Vivekananda's address of 1893 at the Chicago conference at the Parliament of religions, where he had held his own amidst many religious speakers. He found this new discovery on one of his many trips to the mission in 1966 and it changed his perception about religion, atman, soul and life philosophy completely.

He was deeply impressed that a man like Vivekananda had come so much before his time, left a message for the world and exited the world so early at an age of 39.

During these years Maya would often find her Khazan distant and reflective in deep thought.

In one of their walks along college street, Maya bought her husband books of Tagore. The noble prize winning Gitanjali and novels like 'Gora' and 'The last Poem' by Tagore won him back from the precipice of worldly renunciation to the path of romance and eventual surrender to matrimonial duties.

Tagore had written The Last Poem when he was an ageing poet, while younger authors were attempting to establish themselves in his shadow in Calcutta.

The poem at the conclusive end of the book, had a lasting impact on Khazan and brought him back into his householder mode completely.

Maya had succeeded in making him look up to a poet rather than just a monk. She had pulled him back from completely shunning the material world to immerse in her own love. Her devotion to him was already complete.

In marriages of those times the role of a wife, to take control of the relationship, steer, lead and stabilize seldom came.

She realized in those years, how important it was for her to express and show the deep affection she had for him. Maya worked on Khazan to make him understand without reading any of the deep texts that he had read; 'that being good, required him to act and do good for people, whoever came in his life' - and by virtue of that he would at least contribute that much to life at large.

Maya justified to him that he would not be able to free himself from his children's responsibilities and he should not be depressed with poverty and now corruption that he was witnessing around him. She led him to act to the best of his ability and do his '*karma and dharma*' correctly.

Maya opined and shared her philosophy that they had acted correctly in sync with time, as 'time' was their second companion besides each other. They had done their duties and his knowledge of a monk's morality should not be allowed to affect his thinking as a householder.

She used to profess, "Time, waits for no one, and yet is your only permanent companion". She also reminded him repeatedly about the *Bhagvata Gita* messages and what Khazan's own 'Nanna' would say, "Speak good, do good and keep good thoughts"- the message of a '*Vaishnavite*'.

When Khazan was in his late twenty's he had aspired to work for a decade or two in a fixed income role, where he could feed his future family in flood or famine. He had seen partition and experienced migration. He had heard first hand many stories from his colleagues at work who performed relief work for refuges in Delhi's Lajpat Nagar colonies.

In 1968 with Ashwini reaching eight in age, he broached the topic of leaving the services with Maya.

He had contemplated renunciation so relocation or restarting life was not a fear.

Maya was all for an early retirement and a move back toward the northern borders of India herself, as she had no belongingness to Bengal. By 1967 both Maya and Khazan had lost all four of their parents in Solan. This had set Khazan thinking about his own time, and how much was left of it.

The parents had been able to see both their boys. The deaths had happened one after the other for different health reasons as Doctor's and mendicants, and some practices at that time were rolled into one.

Their parents had no access to good health care of a big city.

By the summer of '69, Maya would feel more devastated in the evenings than Khazan.

He had gotten used to live first by himself, detached from his parents, and then with his own children and wife – his immediate family.

She feared his renunciation and detachment from herself and the children. She was looking for an urgent hook, back into the past.

The couple had made multiple trips to Solan in the 1960's, each time alone, taking turns with their children back in Calcutta, while one spouse attended the last rites of one parent at a time.

A decade was looking like slipping by and the real main concern was to feel 'settled down'.

Initially Himachal was thus a default option to retire to; due to Khazan's family sweet mart business, and the known neighborhood.

Maya did not know, that Khazan never liked to get his own hands dirty in the kitchen side of the business, as he had himself worked with '*sahibs*' at his own office work and only the financial side of the family business all his life.

In the Durga Puja that year of 1969 in Calcutta, Khazan and Maya Singh, attended with their children the '*pandaal*' adjacent to K C Das's shop.

They noticed, for the first time in years the same *Sanjeevni Booti* was used aside the entire frame of Durga idol decoration with flowers.

In the music and manic flow of people, they could see the women of Bengal, dressed in their red bordered white saris.

They recognized the symbol of the hills, the herbs, that had cured Khazan's mother were before them in the sanctum area, where the priests stood, with one of them fanning the idol and the other offering the fruits and '*bhog*'.

The *Sanjeevni Booti* herb simply lay attached to the temporary wall in large bundles around the Durga idol.

"*Was 'Durga' ma and Khazan's mother signaling something*?" spoke aloud the couple in bed that night. They both looked at each other as they felt and said the same thing.

The couple had never thought of visiting Darjeeling or Shillong, though those places had been considered after reading Tagore by Khazan.

The choice to again migrate to new lands, off center from the center of India, did not appeal to them.

In the winter break after Durga puja, a trip was undertaken in December to Solan. The family reached their family shop and old home with light luggage, feeling bone chilled cold. This reminded Khazan of his mother and her prolonged sickness due to the weather.

The couple struggled with the key sets to open the iron door locks and *Godrej 'navtal'* locks on the inner wooden door.

Opening the premises of Punjab Sweet house, they find upon entry, their mirror of reflections turned into a rusted blackened mirror on the surface.

This was the spot where the workers would fry '*jalebis*' and samosas in the shop, and that had seen their first meeting.

The trip was short and in three days they realized the energies of the home and by lanes had changed for them, though the streets had remained the same.

Their neighbor was a new Sikh family at Papaji's old provision store and home structure. There were dull signs of *Coca-Cola and Cadbury's Double Decker* chocolate, as the signages had partly extinguished, yet not entirely faded with time on the store's jaded walls. The business had been re-hauled to an auto spare parts one as many residents had invested in scooters to go up and down the valley.

Many of the products that Papaji sold were no longer available in the market. Larger format restaurants had opened up and people preferred sitting there in Shimla and buying back their monthly supplies from the hill or Chandigarh.

The other shop owners and occupants did not know where Papaji had disappeared.

The current auto business owner had purchased the store from the second buyer who had opened a liquor shop after purchasing the shop from Papaji.

Khazan's colleague had lost touch in the myriad of the southern command where he had been posted years back.

Everything suddenly appeared very impersonal.

Khazan had never really lived and stationed himself in Solan over the years; he was always the 'outside visitor'.

The old street across where Maya lived, had become stuffy with many two wheelers parked in the tight narrow back lanes of the row of houses on that side of the street.

The scooters blocked the entry of those houses, while the auto-spare part owner's shop decorated the periphery of shop-houses on Khazan's side of Punjab Sweet house.

The lane now looked like a parking lot of scooters.

Wires hung on some wall surfaces loose, from antennas over terraces as everyone was glued to the government channel '*Doordarshan*' on their personal sets of black and white televisions. No one stepped out in the evenings to chat or walk, as the Hindi movie on Sunday was the only treat to watch.

They had enjoyed the same place a decade ago with all the basic essentials of life, clean pure air, water and a family bond that had brought them together. Those family members had gone away forever. The place and home had served its purpose.

On the penultimate night before leaving back for Calcutta, they agreed to sell the property to their neighbor Sikh family who needed the next-door shop for repairs of scooters and stocking of more spare parts. They asked them to draw up the papers and send the same by registered post to Khazan's Calcutta office address.

That night Khazan had a hazy dream.

He could see himself opening his bank account with the State Bank of India (SBI), upon moving toward Solan, Himachal Pradesh when his parents had needed funds for his marriage.

Standing there outside Punjab Sweet house, he could see himself in the dream questioning that as he knew he had a bank account now at the Union Bank of India at Camac Street, off Park Street in Calcutta.

Khazan could see images of Ashwini as a toddler when they had just moved into their Hastings house. Yet he could not explain why Sanjeevni was walking with a cow first in Sialkot then at India Gate in Delhi in the dream.

He had heard stories about Lajpat Nagar from his co-worker refugee families but had never been there himself.

What was Sanjeevni and a dog doing there?

He could see Maya near a mango tree, much older in a dessert, where there was water in an oasis, and Maya appeared parched, but there being no one around her to offer her water.

He could not understand the dream.

It was causing him much restlessness and stress.

He was trying hard to remember his own parents, but could not recall their names, nor see their faces in the dream.

In the next instant he could see his 'Nanna' offering him a piece of white barfi dressed in his starched white kurta. Despite stretching his hand out, he was not able to reach the piece of sweet.

His 'Nanna' kept egging him on. Khazan asked his 'Nanna' – *"Where are my father and mother?"* ... repetitiously. He received no answer.

Khazan woke up from his dream in sweat and Maya has to calm him down.

She re-confirmed to him that they were in Solan at his parent's place and they were to leave in a few hours for Chandigarh to go to Calcutta via Delhi.

Perhaps the talk of all these places the previous night had conjured up the dream.

Khazan retold Maya the dream, with Ashwini at the foot of the bed listening intently. Sanjeevni was still asleep below their beds, on the foot stand side and Maya could see that he was in his own dream world as he smiled.

Perhaps a young boy's adolescent dream thought Maya, and acknowledged the same to Khazan, to distract him from the past where he remained embedded.

Maya had taken her own understanding from the entire week's incidents and realized that Khazan had a sense of guilt of not being with his parents for so many years.

He had to stick to his bread and butter as he had to fend for them and his own family. The income from the sweet shop had never remained predictable and was merely a vocational set up for Khazan's father to give him some sense of activity in India. Their safety to extract them from Sailkot was the goal then.

Next morning, the couple agreed that the old place in Solan brought back disturbing nostalgia and they had moved far too much toward the eastern part of India.

Pakistan was on both sides of the border and if Maya had to still live near the new Muslim country, she felt she should be closer to where she had her own roots.

Khazan had no roots or heritage attached of his own in Calcutta.

...sitting at the veranda of her Nawalgarh home, Maya could hear the Shiv temple's bells in the background. It brought her back to her present, breaking her own daydream.

As Maya rubbed her eyes, images on a wide and colorful canvas of the past places she herself had lived in, flashed by in her greying brain cells.

It was a new day and her memories of her youth came back to her in a gush.

She feels the nape of her neck with her fingers, missing the stroking of her husband's nose on that empty neck. She can see her youngest son standing and walking on his own big feet. It reminded her of a morning, when they had just chosen this piece of earth to live on, with their first two sons.

These fathers and sons.

They had dominated her life.

The guilt trapped Khazan and his precious three sons.

7

KHAZAN THE INDULGENT HUSBAND

1970 New beginnings

Upon return from Solan, the couple waited to let Sanjeevni finish his grade eight school in the summer of 1970.

That year, after nearly twenty-eight years of working as a clerical senior accountant, without any degree, Khazan retired from national service.

He was just forty-eight years old.

After Khazan completed the formalities of his official paperwork that summer, he took the family to the Kalighat temple and Victoria Memorial one last time.

He hurriedly aborted the future plan to visit Shanti Niketan and Belur Math, that he had harbored since his Alipore road days and replaced it with a visit to KC Das one last time.

In a fortnight from then he moved the family in two phases to Rajasthan, from Hastings, Calcutta.

The first phase, was a planned semi-vacation which was left to Maya to decide on.

Maya had always loved the hinterland and she started by telling him to let go of unnecessary possessions before she could help him to empty the Hastings house. Her gold and that from Khazan's parents, the important photo frames, Baby Krishna's frame and Lord Vishnu's idol, some of the old post card correspondence, folded photographs of Maya's own parents were locked up in four metal trunks.

She packed in muslin cloth a select few of her important clothes, the Himachal bridal attire, and her collection of Bengal sarees.

He agreed with Maya's choice and they zeroed down on Rajasthan.

They planned to show their two young boys the forts and palaces of India.

Initially they visited the state due to Maya's temptation to uncover her own family history.

Once there, in the end of summer Maya explored deeper, exhausting some of the financial resources that the family had saved up for years; as she believed in doing a proper recce. The intention was to ascertain strategic features of the town they planned to live in.

Khazan knew he had funds in his SBI Himachal and UBI Bengal accounts and the Provident Fund yet to be enchased.

His superiors were sad to let him go without much fanfare and a farewell dinner had been hastily declined. He was neither an officer, nor a ranked soldier, as the quasi-employees hired by the British defense ministry before partition of India were gradually being let go off, as mere aged accounting clerks. This way the Indian Army and HRD ministry would be able to hire younger trained recruits under the plans they had with the setup of the NDA by the mid 1950's, and trim their own wage bills due to rationalization.

There was no scope for such middle-aged employees in the British-free scheme of things, and there was a natural displacement of such migrants who had come along with the British empire dreams into older parts of Hindustan, which were now marginalized in a new India.

Khazan had outlived his vision to explore outside of Solan and Sialkot and felt free, yet experimental all over again.

Maya first insisted to travel towards the fort city of *Chittor* to show her sons the valor and history of Mewar and the largest fort of India as well as Asia.

Khazan had no parents in tow, and no baggage, since the sale of the Solan property had gotten him new funds in his bank account in Himachal.

He knew he would access that later to close matters there completely and handover the property papers after the Rajasthan trip, to the new Sikh family there.

There were no roots anywhere. He had last migrated during partition and it looked that India was going to stand up on its feet after all, under the *Prime Minister-ship* of India's first Lady, Indira Gandhi. Coca-Cola had been told to leave India. India would prepare its own beverage drinks in the future and people were going back to sugar-cane juice with a vengeance in the hinterland.

Though he had rich memories of his parents with the backdrop of Solan, he had never really spent his own time there. The cold weather in their older age kept Maya and him wary of considering any other options in Himachal.

For the first time in his life, he could indulge her and himself enjoy the newness of places at his own pace. This was to see life as it was, as he was unaccustomed to during his work years, where everything around him passed by like a haze in a huff.

Little did the migrant in him know that they would become permanent residents of the state forever. He was an Indian by taste buds, and now more so by virtue of having made a choice to live inside this country since 1947.

He keenly understood that he was neither an immigrant, nor really planned to migrate anymore. He wanted to drift and float like a butterfly.

Like most migrants from North west frontier and the old Punjab, many older 'Hindustanis' had migrated towards the warmer climate that India's lesser harsh winter provided.

Khazan had survived his only posting in Bengal for a longish continuous stint and had gotten to see both his sons grow up from a toddler stage during the ten annual Durga festivals spent there.

Yet the eastern culture of Bengal and the fishy food never met the senses and palate of Khazanchand & family. Except the Bengali sweets, everything else revulsed his appetite in particular and churned his intestines.

Hunger inducing fragrance to the locals, was distasteful smell to the *Singhs.* Their oil, was always too mustardy, and it was in their food, it was on their hair, and in the air everywhere. He would only miss K C Das '*rasagollas.*'

The family's genes were accustomed to ghee and wheat, the aroma of powder, meeting the rolling pin and after a few artistic spins made to meet the pure ghee in the wheat's bloated form, to hiss the hot air out of one small freckled gap on the edges. They loved this aroma versus rice and curry. Khazan was accustomed to eat from his tiffin with colder dry vegetables and a wheat-based diet with curds. This helped keep his accounts dry in the case of a food accident at work.

Maya would serve sensibly the morning's cooked dry vegetables in the packet of used bread packaging paper, which he would relish later at his work place. She would herself hurriedly eat the 'double roti' slices of bread for her own meal with lentils at noon. She cooked the choicest of pulses, one color or thickness for each day of the week, making it fresh for lunch, and re-used with a '*tadka*' of ghee for dinner. It was the only meal that the entire family sat together and ate at night.

The boys would get packed tiffin in ice-pail carriers, with steel enclosed pyramids inside filled to the brim with their mother's *daal* and father's dry vegetables and curds.

Each of the parents ate with only one of the things while the kids got two. The diet was deeply North Indian.

That was all that Khazan was leaving behind in Calcutta. Memories.

He had felt that way in Solan and Sialkot too.

He had memories of eating at their makeshift dining table and their set of two wooden chairs, built higher specially for the children's height, with a light green leather top. Those would be deserted forever, with the oval *'Sunmica'* sheet covered dining table that doubled up as his desk on Sunday afternoons. They did not have much trouble leaving this behind, as in the case of Solan.

As Maya wished to dream and explore, Khazan revered the beauty of his still young wife. After being a mother to two children the exquisite beauty she offered now in her thirty's, made Khazan want to re-start life all over again.

The middle-aged migrant in him had met the young vagabond gypsy in her. They had a sense of belonging anywhere in the country as India was theirs. They respected their freedoms and could now choose where to live.

They travelled with a sense of abandon, as if they ran the government and yet humbly felt an ownership as people of the country. He had moved from Sialkot to Solan, to Calcutta and back to Solan via Chandigarh, before eventually exiting Calcutta permanently.

In each of the locations they lived, he had seen her in the local state sarees of the region. He always bought one for her diligently in the Diwali week.

Her look, with the kohl bordering her eyes lit them like live smoldering ambers in his. The two concentric red circles over maroon centered dots on her third eye, between her sharp natural eyebrows made him shift his gaze between her eyes, eyebrows and that crimson tilak, the '*bindi*.'

There was a grace in her body movements, as she heralded her two sons and walked with pride with her family.

It made Khazan want to buy all the Kota maroon and brown sarees from the shops of the street market in Chittor.

He was hoping that time would allow him a chance, to watch her do her '*shringar*' and recreate their romance of youthful days. This possibility in retirement, with all the time on hand, quite increased his fondness for her. He admired her poise and watched her moves while walking for so many hours in the hot sun during the holidays in Rajasthan.

While she never broke a sweat, small beads of water would settle on the tip of her nose, which he came close, and flicked away with his right thumb – often teasingly, winking at her.

His state of mind and condition was that of a new lover, of new found love. A pleasing calmness came over him when he looked at his two sons in tow.

He imagined another addition to the pride of lions he saw in his sons' gait and believed that there should be a much-missed illusive daughter in his arms.

Maya too wanted the same since so many years.

He would bid his time, to catch her, when she also wanted to be caught so that the love could be of mutual interest, and not that of her lonely submission to him and his selfish needs.

Khazan tested the tenacity of his family on this trip. He knew they lived in a new India, post-partition and understood the nature of what to expect as the struggle for necessities became crucial.

He had sought sixty days to see India and left his belongings in four trunks at Hastings at his friend's two storied place. He would mentally count those items sitting in his friend's attic in Calcutta, with a plan to fetch those later. He had gifted his friend the dining set, including the two children's chairs as the friend had girls of similar age.

They thus travelled, seeking to see the forts of *Chittor and Udaipur* sharing the stories from their limited knowledge with their sons.

They decided after the first week in Rajasthan, to randomly travel towards the city of gold - Jaisalmer. They had carried along four dozen raw mangoes from the commercial streets in Udaipur and Chittor and mixed them up together with a plan to eat them along the way.

It was past memories of her father's trade, the nature of the Jain temples and description of markets inside the Jaisalmer fort that beckoned Maya.

She replayed those travel tales she had heard stories about to her sons.

This made her want to see the city herself.

She wanted to ensure that the illusion created in her mind, was not just a fabrication of events intellectually misled by her father.

Train travel was slow and inter-connectivity of towns and villages for the last mile at times was by foot. The family seldom got to hitch rides on slow carts driven by bullocks on uneven non-existent roads, as those farmers themselves had larger families or goods they were carrying.

They often passed women with large loads on their heads, including numerous pots of decreasing size going upward from their heads.

It reminded her and Khazan of the *Changar* women of Himachal, whose men had the least significance. Here the men wore large Rajasthani *bandini*, striped, or plain turbans.

The rainbow of colors welcomed the children and Maya to experiment with a plethora of options themselves with clothing.

Every ten or fifteen kilometers they covered they noticed the style of wearing the '*pagri*' – the turban, changed. As the harvesting season was near, they witnessed more of the '*panchranga*'- multi colored turbans atop all male heads, with large black whiskers of the farmers and white beards of the elderly. The grey and white hair cut a strong contrast to the colorful turbans atop the erect unidimensional heads.

With two large '*mashks*' for her company Maya had since her maiden days loaded them with fresh water. They were now carried diligently by Sanjeevni and Khazan on the trip. She had acquired a third one from a '*Kasbba*' during the first leg of the holiday in Chittor's market, but the goat skin lining inside did not keep the water as cool as the earlier two she had inherited from her father.

Chitrakut as the fort city was known in historic Mauryan times, was cooler than Udaipur due to its expansive spread on the hill. She had bought the third *mashk* as she silently still harbored the desire for a third child, hoping to pass on one each to all of them.

Little did she know that the folklore story of water spouting in the reservoir of Chittor was attributed to Bheem, and that she would yet again conceive a third son, who merited the comparison due to diet and strength in later life.

All through the trip. she had her eyes equally set on Khazanchand, as much as he; often meeting his gaze with her raised left eyebrow, questioning his intentions tantalizingly.

It mostly led to her rolling over the child in the middle of the night in the make-shift bed, and lying in Khazan's arms till morning.

At dawn she would go back to her separate position before waking Ashwini up, who was positioned to sleep between them.

As they travelled across the Mewar kingdom they had followed Rana Pratap's horse 'Chetak' path, across villages and streams, and slept easily in new beds every night. Tired and exhausted by the long walks and warm weather, they were thankful they had kept luggage down to the two minimum '*peepas*' they carried.

She kept the third '*mashk*' close to her side for Khazan to sip on and often mixed water with her own concoction of cool sandal like paste of powdered almond, saffron, *gokshura and ashvagandha.*

Ashwini was ten and she hoped that her magic potion worked further wonders for Khazan and for her. She silently hoped to have her dream of a daughter come true.

Rajasthan's '*jharokas*' were everywhere in their culture, in homes, palaces, over horse stables for sun-cover and even in the layered '*boonda*' jewellery. The women adorned their ears, with a cascade of silver ornaments that had larger puddles of layers as they hung from their naturally made large ear-lobes. Maya wondered if God had specially designed Rajasthan women ear-lobes, or they just became longer carrying the permanent weights. The earrings were so shaped, such that each puddle *or jharoka*, had small dots of water droplets appearing to hang from those puddles.

While the desert was not such a wet place, the imagination of the royal gold smiths was vivid and wise.

Her mind meandered toward her own wild imaginations with Khazan.

Each morning he looked more in love as he gazed at her, following it with a morning embrace and poking his nose into the nape of her neck, while caressing her with his fingers at her back, over her blouse strings.

All the pores on the skin of her arms stood and the back of her neck felt knotted with muscle and hair both sore. She missed his morning fingers, their even stroke and balance of power, by the evening hours of their travels. Tirelessly she waited daily, till dawn.

Maya's mother had taught her the art of saving gold in her pre-marriage days and the principles behind acquisition, storage, and holding power.

Her father had the tribal women '*boonda*' earrings brought back from each trip though the ornaments on their side of the future India's national border was mostly in silver during her adolescent years.

Each night, Maya painstakingly removed her own earrings, and kept them aside, and again collected them in the mornings to wear them again. She ensured they did not interfere with Khazan's daily love pecks.

Due to her father's trade access, he would get designs converted to gold and made by the goldsmiths in Jaisalmer who supplied the same to the ministers and Jain financier families of the royal family.

It was always her father she remembered in the art of desert weather survival.

Be it for water, or for her unique inherited gold treasure, she had learnt from her father and his caravan of camels and carrier rider boys how to walk on sand dunes, keeping her strong back upright, and lips moist with head covered from the blazing sun.

This would be practiced in this trip repeatedly, without letting the garment slip from her right lip. Her mother had taught her to manage the '*mashks*' and prepare the potion she prepared daily now for Khazan.

She wondered, which of her parents had made the more ever lasting contribution, as she used the tips from both. She had as a young girl child, grown immense fascination for the ornaments her father brought as a sign of love and affection for her mother from Jaisalmer due to the barter of goods.

Maya's skin had become tough with age, but it had always remained a lovely coarse light brown, cooked over the years of natural sun bathing as a child on camel rides.

Her mind still functioned like an oasis in a dessert. Memories that were so fresh, cooled her inner being and these articles she had collected over a decade helped her connect to her own family's glorious trading past. The skin could again feel the severity of the sun, not yearning for shade as much, like the rest of the family.

After Udaipur and Jaipur, they had eventually meandered toward Nawalgarh, near Sikar on the fifty first day of their two-month plan.

They had intended to find Karorimal, the employer of Khazan's father, who had migrated there with the cattle trade to set up the dairy, when Khazan's grandfather had made his father move to Sialkot.

They also knew there were age old havelis that were a popular tourist attraction in that region. Maya hoped still in her heart, to find a connection, that would lead to belongingness and a sense of roots for her Khazan.

During that holiday, Hari was conceived.

On that trip they encountered the event of discovering the farm land – and Hari's *'janmbhoomi'* – i.e. the birth-place, the plot of two acres of land.

That is where the family lived eventually. It so happened that it was being readied for sale by Karorimal's son.

They had stopped by for a meal near the Shiv temple in Nawalgarh, when they found out the only bullock and cattle raiser address from the temple priest. The priest named him as *Sudarshan Rathod*, and the family name matched that of Karorimal, which Khazan had recollected from his father's stories.

Uptill then he did not recollect the family name Rathod.

It so turned out that Sudarshan was the name of the bullock merchant in Nawalgarh, and he indeed was the son of Karorimal Rathod, the deceased employer of Khazan's father.

They met him at his single story haveli, a few kilometers walk from the Shiv temple.

Maya touched the small Nandi sculpture as she entered Sudarshan's home courtyard, prayed to her in her ear.

She then worshipped all her Gods in her mind and thanked Lord Shiva, Vishnu, Ganesha and Hanuman as she entered their '*dahleej*', the main door of the Haveli.

It was heavy like the trunk of a stubborn elephant, as she estimated the two dozen ornamental decorations on both the open half-doors, while stepping in.

She imagined that you could hide the carcass of any corpse human or animal on the pointed bolts of the door, and blast it like a furnace, but the door would still not open if it was in locked position on the inside.

Sudarshan welcomed them warmly, insisting that they eat a full meal with him as it was his meal time. He displayed photographs framed on the living room walls to Khazan with respect and humility. He displayed a long-forgotten photograph of Jhunjhunu and how their place looked before his father Karorimal had moved to Nawalgarh.

After a meal of '*daal-batti-churma*' and over eating '*immartis*' the heftier version of jalebis, just more orange and saccharin sweet; Sudarshan informed the Singh family about a plot of land under his upkeep which was on sale.

The afternoon made Khazanchand relax and feel at ease with Sudarshan as if there was a relation with his family, though he could not see any photograph on any frame of his father's employer Karorimal. The thought came to him in his mind, to frame photographs of his own parents, and relocate the trunks from his storage boxes in Calcutta, his 'Nanna' with the Punjab sweet house frames of Lord Vishnu and Baby Krishna, once he settled down.

The humble behavior and welcoming spirit, with business like skills of Sudarshan reminded Maya of her own parents. Sudarshan's wife Sulakshna had been a wonderful host and offered tea after the courtesy rest post the lunch meal.

She insisted that the family stay with them for a few days, if not weeks as her own children would also get company. Though the elder daughter was preoccupied with her own friends, their younger boy was happy to have Sanjeevni and his own age group Ashwini with him. Sudarshan offered to help them walk and identify that piece of land. It was a few speedy paces from the haveli, and it meant having a known family close by to both parties.

Much to their amazement free of any encumbrances, yet fenced with a bamboo elongated H like structure, they discovered the land to be bordered at the other end in the north eastern direction with a fifteen-meter high *Gulmohar** (**peltophorum*) tree on the extreme right. There was a large natural well, off center from the extreme left with no trees around it.

The *Gulmohar* tree was in its full glory due to the summer, with its bright orange yellow blossoms. The flowers shone like a hundred and eight 'Sudarshan Chakras' of Lord Krishna.

The Singh family had found Rajasthan very welcoming wherever they went. Their host was also named Sudarshan. It appeared to be like a divine intervention in their life to discover them so easily and be led to the piece of land.

Sudarshan's haveli home, was built in the style of Khazan's old Sialkot home where he was born. It had color paintings of Krishna and Radha on all ceiling and wall surfaces and in the courtyard and the balcony like veranda above even on the first floor. Though the haveli apparently was over three hundred years old, the color of paint and beauty of the Krishna rasa dance, was still alive as if just performed yesterday in Vrindavan.

Sudarshan's kind, yet purpose driven respectful behavior, the well-fed meal and the rekindled romance between Maya and Khazan made them exchange loving looks with each other.

Their love too was in full bloom like the tree they admired on the land, mirroring the emotion of Lord Krishna for Radha.

The link with Krishna, appeared that the Lord was following Khazan since his 'Nanna' days. Khazan had broken free from an old work life into a new sense of love, hope and abandon - it had stoked the flame of Maya's desire and a sensibility between them both, which she never wanted to lose.

That feeling of eternal contentment and love was no longer an illusion. The land was real, and before their eyes.

The tree and the well enriched the land and certified its virile fertility.

It showcased the lands feminine personality and the masculine imprint of the water well's stone structure like a '*Shivling*' protruding from the earth, with the child like existence of the *Gulmohar* tree on it. It was like their own reflection in time on the land and it radiated more powerfully than the sunshine on that day.

The land appeared to be just over two acres in size as assessed by Khazan and he immediately recognized it to be shaped like an auspicious '*goumukhi*' plot. It started like a traditional cow's mouth, and grew into the digestive track of a cow and ballooned centrally like the stomach, ending broadly at the rear.

Maya stood on the dusty south west end of the dry road and gazed from the narrow gate like opening of the land. She could feel the fragrance of the flowers yet on the tree and stay glued on that spot forever in admiration.

The well in the corner and the light green grass in the center made her feel comfortable to use the scene in her inner eye to feel she could settle down there. The fragrance came from the tail end of the cow shaped plot, due to the yellow poinciana.

She could feel the new life churn inside her, as if Hari was taking shape. Ashwini standing by her side, watching the serene view silently for a few minutes, blurted his prophecy, "Mai, it appears like we have lived here already."

Their houses in Solan and Calcutta had a small patch of grass outside, but Calcutta streets, Durga pujas and the noise never had any serene comparative to where they stood now. Khazan turned quizzingly and looked at Ashwini.

Sanjeevni spotted the bore-well, from which water would be drawn in future, sensing a moistness appearing in the light wind.

Sudarshan walked by and stroked the dark hair on Sanjeevni's head, and spoke, "This land is immediately livable as there is ample water table reservoir beneath. Some of the oldest members of the city used to drive water from here, before they made their own homes. The well is built in such a way underneath, that it refills the water table."

Ashwini's hair tuft had been moved by the frail breeze over his left forehead eyebrow, the urchin like look on his face, stemming more from his vest and open shirt collar than his expression. He looked up at Sudarshan, and swung his neck roguishly to settle the hair strands back to their oily puff origins atop his head. It was a more noticeable gesticulation than what Khazan would do to settle his hair atop his forehead with less guile. This gesture was always seen as an auspicious sign by his mother and Khazan knew in the look she had affixed on her face, that Maya had found a place to settle down.

Khazan was willing to ditch the urban, for the semi-rural setting as it filled them both with a sense of calm and made them want to get anchored there. Maya loved Rajasthan over East Hindustan's metro, Calcutta. Khazan's work had made him travel in pre-independence Hindustan and later post partition Bharat.

Maya had never adjusted to Calcutta, and though she liked the food in Solan, the Calcutta home had provided her with a gas cylinder and two stove burners. The neighboring home aromas would get mixed in the air in her own kitchen to make her feel sick by evening.

She aspired for continuity, permanence and longed to have a place she could call home. Nawalgarh gave her that solidity, and a time warp continuum.

Since the weather was similar and terrain steady to walk – she was transported back to her own child hood village memories with her folks, making her rediscover her youth.

Partition allowed her the security of Khazan's family first and then Punjab Sweet house followed with Khazan's own secure employment. It had made true, their migrant family choice to live in Hindustan.

She was seeking a culmination now into the comfortable smaller town life. Like any other wife, she had achieved to set up her family, love her husband back, and had wanted space, her own farm and a place where her children could play, grow and extend themselves with nature.

The thought of it all and a sense of past family experience, had attracted her to the plot they eventually bought in Nawalgarh. She thought that to be her security, the land would suffice with the gold she had, and she hoped that with Sanjeevni and Khazan having farmer's blood, they would be able to sow and reap some wheat crop to start with.

The aroma of wheat from their own land, being cooked on their own stove and '*sigri*' in the kiln was something she could conceivably imagine. It appeared retrograde and backward, but actually the environment appeared more pure, clean and the setting rich to her in heritage minus any nostalgia. The freshness of the soil was like the newness of their future that lay ahead of her children. Farmers were being given importance in the new India Nehru's daughter was building.

Maya was willing to bury her gypsy desires and felt the churn of the new baby in the making inside her again. The land had appeared equally fertile to her and Khazan, due to some moisture in the soil. The presence of the deep bore well was the real gift of Lord

Shiva, as if carrying the Ganges there for her. It was pre-constructed by the earlier occupiers a century back and their descendants guarded it on behalf of a city politician in Rajasthan. The politician was now wanting to spread his state wings to the center stage of national politics and was migrating like the seasonal birds, albeit never to return.

The land thus fell in the lap of Maya very easily, as the honest merchant and Sudarshan as caretaker struck a deal and Khazan eventually emptied his SBI Savings from Solan. He christened the place '*Moh & Maya*' and unabashedly requested Sudarshan for help to engrave that on a cement wall, with granite and marble setting, so that the name would stand the test of time.

It meant 'love was an illusion', what it really reflected was an end to Khazan's hunt for material gain, as he had found love, with Maya in his own household. He had redirected his fondness for her by securing her the land she loved.

Maya decided to stay back in Nawalgarh at Sudarshan's haveli as his wife's invitation was open. In those days staying with relatives and old found family friends like them was the accepted norm. She stayed back with Sanjeevni, and Khazan went back with ten-year old Ashwini to pack his belongings in Calcutta and join them in a week. He gave an order to the local ironsmith and mason, to construct the main body of the house in the shape that Maya had drawn with her '*sindoor*' on a piece of paper using her index finger at night.

He gave it the natural extensions of the veranda, based on his Sialkot memories and the structure of openness of Sudarshan's haveli. They only wanted a one floor one level house and nothing but a wide terrace above. It would serve as Sanjeevni's future bed below the open sky.

By the time Khazan and Ashu were back, Sanjeevni had helped his mother paint the brick fencing and the bore-well with a bright blue and chosen to adopt Nandu and Hariya from Sudarshan.

Maya had conceived Hari and discovered she was carrying Khazan's third child, but was yet to reveal it to him.

A relationship as neighbors and city goers was struck permanently with Sudarshan's family and they relied on them for small cooking vessels and steel plates to start their house in a week of Khazan's return. The toilet and bath area were built in three days and Maya was ecstatic to move into her own house with her red feet of *'alta'* over the altar. She was now carrying Hari inside her, about four weeks pregnant.

The town of Nawalgarh also kept her in her own state of Rajasthan, and on the other side of Jhunjhunu where Khazan's father had started his own life, before his migration to Sialkot.

The circle of migration had completed and ended with their generation.

At least that is what they thought at that time.

8

TRAIN OUT OF CALCUTTA

KHAZAN & ASHWINI (1970)

After the tiresome job of packaging all their goods and dispatching it via booking it on the train cargo, they wait on the platform to board the train back to the center of India.

Images flash by Khazan's memory and he silently remembers his folks. He can see his 'Nanna' in every old man at the platform, as he looks upon his ten-year old boy.

He is amazed that Ashu and Sanjeevni do not miss their friends and have not resisted the change.

Ashu is busy licking the chocolate off his ice-cream bar. He has never resisted his father calling him by his pet-name, and is acting every inch the child he is. The bustle of Calcutta's railway station, the noisy coolies and the crowd has no impact on him.

"*So blessed were children, they have a clean slate and no memory baggage to think of.*" Khazan ponders to himself.

Ashu looks up, jerks his head to the right to get the hair falling on the left of his forehead back upright on his puffed locks on the right side of his head. His left hand was smeared with the broken chocolate from the bar and the vanilla portion of the ice-cream was now clearly visible to Khazan.

Ashu looked at his father with a perplexed expression, half-heartedly offering his ice-cream to him.

When his father declines, Ashu asks, "If you are sad, you can buy a new one. I can share that one with you!"

Khazan smilingly asked, "Do you wish to have a full second one for yourself?" As he watches Ashu nod, Khazan smiles with a guilty expression, pulling out two coins from his flare pant pocket, to hand-over to the Railway snacks counter, and hollers, "Another of the same one."

He points at the child with not much change in expression. The stall owner throws the coins into a part open wooden drawer and dryly pulls out another '*choco-bar*', in its brown and white paper.

The bar has been an iconic favorite with most children of that age as it packs a punch with both, the milk and cold inner core of vanilla, with the coating and layering of thick hardened chocolate on the outside.

Unlike Sanjeevni, who grew up on a part diet of cashew barfi and jalebis from Punjab Sweet house in Solan, that too selectively controlled by Maya during his holidays, Ashu was an out and out ice-creams devouring child.

The state of the vanilla ice-cream was similar to Khazan's life, so he thought, staring at Ashu. Melting away, albeit tastefully. It brought back a sense of joy in Khazan to watch his son.

As coolies hollered and passengers negotiated and haggled for lesser last-minute payments to the T.C. and railway duty officials, a light smoke immerged from the new ice-cream in Ashu's hands as he peeled the wrapping off the second one.

There was excitement, belligerence and ecstasy on Ashu's face. He had never experienced a double treat as this was happening in Maya's absence.

The chocolate had melted from the first ice-cream onto his hands. The second one was being dug into by Ashu, with vanilla icicles drooping from the stick onto his hands, thankfully not soiling his clothes. The white part of the ice-cream still held much promise, for taste and coolness with much to nourish and give refreshment. Khazan looked on optimistically as the second ice-cream was fast disappearing into Ashu.

He took the barren first stick his son has licked dry and threw it into the waste bin with an aim, making it fly as if it is on the path of a propulsion rocket.

He recognizes that he has to ditch memories of the first life he has led as fast as the first ice-cream stick and move on, like his son, onto the second.

Ashu's face starts reflecting a sense of satisfaction and for the moment relief, as the final drops of white milk from the vanilla stick now melt into his mouth in the Calcutta heat.

The father affectionately tastes the ice-cream in his mind, feeling less anxious for the onward journey.

The father son duo, have observed the loading of their cargo onto the bogey of the same train they go ahead to embark upon. Ashu is a bit worried if the baggage of trunks and their contents would be safe. His father holding his hand quickly nods reassuring him that the Railways can be trusted to deliver the goods.

Each time Ashu is lagging behind on the platform, the father walking briskly ahead softly jerks and pulls his son's hand, walking on the platform. Jostling for space with other passengers at 'Howrah station' Khazan is making sure he does not loosen the grip on his son's sticky chocolate creamed palms.

Prior to boarding the train today, Khazan had taken his son to the hobby shop the previous evening at Park Street. The idea was to get him some collectible toy to earmark the stay of the entire family in Hastings.

The hobby shop had some exquisite vintage cars, aeromodelling planes and a large collection of stamps, coins and old notes from the British era. While Khazan ignored the philately section, he had himself lingered into the narrow alley at the coins section, having set Ashu loose to choose the toy he had wanted to pick up.

Ashu looked up at the toy vintage cars most over half a century old as if from some Britisher's Christmas past. Ashu spent considerable time on his own pondering the choice to make between the models. He reviewed the planes hanging from the ceiling and shortly admired the Spitfire, Concorde, and Mosquito models, before settling his gaze at the Vauxhall, Rolls, Daimler and Chevrolets.

Eventually, he had settled for a 1935 Rytecraft British "Scootacar'. This prized possession of Ashu is wrapped inside a large amount of shrink-wrapped newspaper and plastic covering, along with few hard-body suitcases that are piled over six other bags, four metal trunks and the three '*holdall*' sleeping bags that the family has accumulated in its Calcutta stint.

Many shoes, old office papers, sandals and Swami Vivekananda books have been discarded by Khazan and an equally large number of them are tucked away into the sleeping bags. Khazan has only a small school canvas bag which he has carried since his own school days when his mother would give him the lunch tiffin. It is greased from the old Sialkot shop with ghee on surfaces where he would keep the bag after school. Khazan holds onto the broken re-tied knotted strappy concoction of what is left of the bag.

He boards the newly commissioned "Rajdhani Express" mail cum passenger train with his son.

Khazan and Ashwini have ahead of them a spectacular journey via train, for their return from Calcutta's Howrah Station to Delhi junction. They intend to connect to Jaipur and then onward to Nawalgarh by road. The journey becomes an adventure for Ashu to embark on, to gain experience for his own eternal future when he will be man enough to travel.

So, the father thinks.

He has earlier on few Solan trips given Sanjeevni the same experience.

A boy should know how to '*wrap up*' and come back home.

Khazan internalizes a bit sheepishly, acknowledging that it was a tad bit late for himself. Hence the father's indulgence with the toy car and ice-creams.

He had missed time with his own father through his youth, due to his boisterous 'Nanna' and in the later years, spent most time separated from his parents.

Khazan stands at the door of the train as if to wish goodbye to the seventy-year station. The same was built by the British, with their imprint on the outside façade.

Khazan knows that he is gradually leaving behind everything colonial, the city, the responsibilities, the earlier role for settlement of refugees, the structural edifice of Calcutta. Khazan watches the tracks merge and separate as if originating and drowning like snakes from each other, thanking the British in his heart, for some semblance of infrastructure created by them, even if they were for the benefits of the East India company.

As he watches the snake like tracks, he feels he is on the ladder going up places on the game board of his children – snakes and ladders.

It is from where he has made at least half a century of trips himself during his years of work to visit his parents and to access the initial onslaught of refugees from East Pakistan.

He remembers the bridge over the Rupnarayan River at Kolaghat that connected Howrah to Kharagpur, and onward road trip to the IIT College he had wished at one time for Ashu to attend.

This move to Nawalgarh, was retrograde, and in retrospect, not entirely moving the children forward, as much as moving to a soft spot for the two spouses themselves.

Khazan argued with his inner voice on unseen sights he has left behind in Calcutta, and struggled to agree, that the land on which the new house 'Moh & Maya' was being built in Rajasthan, will now be his last calling.

He quickly realigned his thoughts on Maya, and his elder son, to transfix himself into a trance like condition.

It was not as if the train would reverse its path to take him back to bare Calcutta now. That life was over, with his work, as he acknowledged to himself, he was not really from there in the first place.

Where did he belong? Would he and his family keep migrating and travelling this way all over India?

That is what he had romantically wedded his imagination to, when he had left his parents and come to Bengal. Much had changed from 1947 to now, India in 1970. His wedding at the premises where Sankat Mochan temple stood in Himachal, had never been revisited by him again.

His two children's birth, and racing memories of gorging on *rosagullas* at K. C. Das, watching technicolor movies, raced past his mind.

The 1500kilometer journey left Ashu fascinated, forever impacting him due to the view through the grills on the train windows. He was travelling by train recently, a third time, after the vacation trip earlier with his mother and brother. He had slept through most of that journey, and the year before when they had visited Solan.

This was a '*man*' trip with his father, where he was keeping vigil, to also check on his goods, the flask of tea, the spectacles on the mini-table and the vintage car, at every platform the train stopped. He had enjoyed his ice-creams.

Ashu also had the opportunity to witness some fellow-passengers of Chinese origin, who seem to be relocating from Calcutta to Delhi. He observed the features of each of the passengers in neighboring booths as he went past them, to the railway toilet in his bogey, falling and tossing himself through the narrow alley of his compartment.

He recognized each and every passenger by the end of the journey via their eating habits and alighted with those he had befriended at platforms where the train stopped. A few passengers offered to share their curry and rice with him for their day meal, as they liked his affable and easy-going nature.

At nigh there was the smelly, metallic water mixed with the *Binaca* toothpaste he used, and the '*baidyanath*' oil on his hair, created an odor on both his limbs which he would remember for years till after the journey.

That and the toilet phobia he had developed disappointed him during the journey. The moving train jolted him repeatedly, as he stood and attempted to aim and piss looking away at the only remnants in the toilet of excreta and waste on the metal board toilet 'hole' that he witnessed. The toilet compartment rumbled noisily passing by other trains going the opposite way. It made his piss deflect off all surfaces that it should not have landed upon.

The toilet is something that Ashu ends up deeply despising about the train journey.

At the platforms he moved away from the compartment door as far as possible, thinking it would bring him the unwieldy aroma.

Upon embarking the train at some platforms, he is short of correcting all his fellow passengers when his father stops him. He inquisitively asks his father about the squint eyes of the Chinese and the oily skinned fellow passengers coming from Orissa, Calcutta and Nepal, and the probable reasons why they too are all travelling northwards.

The train cuts across *Asansol, Madhupur, Jasidih, Gaya, Patna, Mughalsarai* and eventually chugs into the *Delhi Railway* station.

It has been a journey of sensory and visual treats and punishing olfactory as the train passes by West Bengal, Bihar, Uttar Pradesh.

At one of the stations, Gaya, Khazan stepped a few meters away from the door of his compartment to buy some food from the platform and himself eases out at the railway station toilet, hoping for better hygiene and cleanliness.

Ashu, not noticing whether his father is back, embarks upon the train, to find himself alone in the duo's compartment. As the train leaves the platform, for shortly being shunted, a new engine is replaced at the head of the train. Ashu begins to worry that his father has missed the train.

In his short blue kurta shirt, with Lucknow embroidery, he twitches upon the ends of the white *pyjama* he is wearing. A tear in his eye, and fear in his heart takes over. As the train has left the platform, Khazan has boarded the train three compartments behind his son's, and attempts to walk through those to the compartment where his original bunker belongs.

Khazan stands before the compartment and watches Ashu twitching his eyes and folding the corners of his Kurta with the other hand.

Lo behold, upon re-uniting with the father, Ashu hugs and embraces him, without any words and the father understands that Ashu felt he was left in a lurch.

"My Son, I had gone to fetch some food for you. Will I ever leave you alone like this and not embark upon the train?"

"How was I to know?" Says Ashu angrily, "You should have entered the train on time. All kinds of things came to my mind. I thought you were missing Calcutta so much, that you have taken a train back from the opposite platform."

Khazan remains surprised with the abandoned perspective of Ashu's thinking.

He had recognized at one level Khazan's own sadness for his separation from the city, yet at the other level felt that a father could leave his young son alone.

He ruffles Ashu's hair and sits together to enjoy their grub, wiping the solitary tear from his son's right eye. They both eat silently.

After the travel from Delhi to Jaipur, Khazan and Ashu catch the state department bus from Jaipur. They commence their day by eating their morning breakfast at LMB- Laxmi Mishtan Bhandaar in Jaipur's jeweler commercial street – 'Johri Bazaar'.

Khazan is nostalgic, as he watches the spread of sweets, sitting at the break-fast table, tucking away '*bhaturas and chole*'. He makes Ashu taste '*tikki-chole*' next and tops it off with two glasses of lassi.

They reach Nawalgarh the same afternoon. At around 2.30 pm with the Vintage car atop the tempo they have rented, Khazan alights outside '*Moh and Maya*' with Ashu and eagerly looks for Maya and Sanjeevni inside.

Little does Khazan suspect, that a fifth member of the family too is on its way.

9

HARI'S BIRTH

Nawalgarh.
1971-75

Hari was to take birth in March of 1971. The planning had been done.

Over the second half of 1970, Sudarshan and Sulakshna were also supportive of the family. They became aware of Maya's pregnancy during Diwali celebrations of 1970 and they ribbed Khazan who was again going to be a father.

The children rarely joined the banter. The two couples had become close. It was a time of celebration and newness for the entire family, as new occupants of '*Moh & Maya*' and the family expecting a fifth member.

The challenge of the unknown and the simplicity of the residents of Nawalgarh was something that appealed to the hearts of Khazan's family.

Sanjeevni truncated his education and had become a support help to his father to till the land. Ashwini would assist his mother inside the house, as he preferred to avoid the sunshine, and help in chores that would usually be relegated to women.

Maya would often curdle the milk, share the butter with her 'Ashu' and have the rest herself.

Khazan and Sanjeevni would tend to the mango sapling and draw water from the well, keep the newly built toilet on the other end of the land clean and feed the baby bulls Nandu and Hariya.

Sanjeevni would be able to play with Nandu and get work done by him. Hariya always ignored him and tried to shun going to the plough to get bridled. Sanjeevni would often pull the plough from one side, with Nandu on the other side, challenging each other, their strength and direction. Nandu would be happy to camp at any part of the periphery of the land, where shade was possible from the *Gulmohar* tree and in later years under the mango tree.

It was Hariya who stayed near the house structure periphery, as if in anticipation of the birth of Hari.

As their family was growing after a decade, Khazan was a bit overwhelmed with the situation. Maya was neither shy, nor apprehensive. She wanted so much to have a girl but the protrusion of her stomach and size of the belly with the child made all ladies of the neighborhood and the town house midwife predict that it was going to be a boy.

Maya had decided to give birth in her own home, as the comforts of hospital and rest could be equally attained there. Sulakshna had promised to cover for their family for food, cooking and taking care of the children. She would continue till after the pregnancy.

Maya would miss her mother-in-law like in every other pregnancy, but more this time due to her own older self, having her third child at thirty-five.

The child was taking birth in a household of men, none of whom knew how to manage kitchen affairs and none understanding Maya's anxiety. Yet she kept her patience through the period.

Maya would insist that the family eat their meals together however modest.

The *dal* made at the start of the day by Sulakshna, would be attended by Sanjeevni to get off the stove in time for lunch, and reused for dinner.

The water arranged by Khazan from their well, would be converted to all the three '*mashks*' one each for the two boys and one for the father. The rest of the water would be converted from the pails, to the potted contraption in the kitchen for the remainder part of the day. Maya would make Sanjeevni assist Sulakshna to boil the milk she would fetch from her house dairy, set the curds, and clean the cooking areas thereafter.

There was a sense of purpose and hectic household activity that bound the family together inside '*Moh & Maya*'.

On the few occasions that Jyoti would join her mother Sulakshna, Sanjeevni would abruptly leave the house and join his father outside on the land, leaving the mother daughter duo to do their work.

Maya would look at the irony and history repeating itself, with her in bed and two other women work in her kitchen, remembering Khazan's mother's times in Solan. Jyoti's future in the family was yet to be decided.

The night when her labor pains started Maya's water bag broke around three hours after mid-night. She had to nudge Khazan to wake up, in the wee hours of the morning, to go and inform Sulakshna.

Khazan awoke to a bit of panic within himself. He did not expect his child's arrival at that time of the day and had to rush, running to their house. He walked Sulakshna back, in the wee hours before dawn to '*Moh & Maya.*'

He had forgotten the family cycle in his compound, and that was well enough because the wooden seat contraption he had built on the carrier behind the leather seat, had cracked under Maya's weight a few days back.

As the mid-wife comforted Maya in the inner recess of her bed-room, Khazan sat outside in silence on the lowest step of the veranda with Sanjeevni, while Ashu was in dreamland. It was a unique experience for the two men of the house as Sanjeevni had no past memory of attending an event of this kind, during Ashu's time.

"Baaba, was it like this when Ashu and I,… I mean were we too born at home?" queried Sanjeevni.

"No *betta*, we were in Calcutta both the times and in the comforts of a small maternity clinic where all deliveries used to happen. It was a small clinic around '*Taltala*'. The only similarity is that as in Ashu's time, your Mai still wants a baby sister for you."

"Why Baaba? Are we sons not secure guarantee enough for mother? How does she know she will have a daughter for sure?" probes the boy.

The father and son foreheads are both lit by the partial illumination of the moonlit sky and brightness caused by the light from the bulb on the entrance wall of the house.

One forehead has lines of worry, another lines of query.

"No son, it is not like this. A mother loves all her children equally, whether son or daughter. She carries them for nine months. You may feel at times while growing up, that one is a favorite over the other, but it is not so. You will always be the eldest and the one being born, will always be the youngest. If I am not there, the '*turban*' will be on your head, to be like a father to them. To provide stability and to care. Till I am there I am there for you, when I am no more, you will be in my position, with no father to look out for you. But never make your mother choose between any one of you."

"I understand father." replied the son.

Though he was just sixteen himself, he had grasped the emotions of his father, missing his own father and yet relegating to the son his position, relinquishing it easily, even if only upon his absence.

Khazan spent a few minutes explaining his own loss and how he had to perform the last rites of his parents, going up and down from work. The fact that he had missed his parents active old age years made him glum and quiet again.

"I will not leave you father, to be alone." comforted Sanjeevni again.

In that moment, the worries of Khazan diluted and ebbed. He looked at his young son's face, looking back at him keenly. He understood, that his son was at the start of his own life, the very beginnings of promise and hope.

He kissed his son's forehead.

Sanjeevni embraced his father and they both sit together for a good thirty minutes.

Though Maya had chosen the option of not going to Jaipur, she had in the penultimate week developed swollen feet with the weight she was carrying for nine months and a fortnight. The delivery had gotten delayed.

The mid-wife would always comfort Maya that she was carrying a tall baby and it would take time for him to take complete form. That night, by the time the mid-wife had appeared with the relevant equipment and her help, the baby had taken a turn, with its head in the upward position.

The night stretched on, and twilight was now visible to Khazan seated outside.

Maya would cry out every few minutes with the pain of the contractions.

Ashu was in deep sleep, oblivious to the drama in the house, and to the emergence of a new life.

Khazan and Sanjeevni sat before the photo frame of Baby Krishna, the stone idol *of Lord Ganesha* they had acquired from Calcutta, and in turns stared at them and the poster of *Lord Vishnu* on the wall.

They would then shift their gaze toward the portraits of Khazan's 'Nanna' and parents on the wall, that was on the other side of Maya's room.

Each time she would cry in pain, Khazan and Sanjeevni would look up at all the Gods, appealing, cajoling sometimes even promising them treats, sweets and all future sacrifices of fasts they would undertake and food items they would stop eating.

Hari took over two hours, to come to a natural position, with the umbilical cord wrapped around his head.

Their prayers were answered at 8:50 am in the morning, when loud cries were heard. The stress of the situation had put Khazan to sleep, but Sanjeevni was awake. The mid-wife had asked Khazan for time and his faith and trust to allow the baby to encircle back on his own and take birth via natural passage.

Hari was born a healthy nine-pound baby, with a condition of polydactyly. He had six toes on each foot and a small sixth index finger on his right hand, and an extra left thumb on his left hand.

When the mid-wife brought the tall baby '*bheema*' child out, she found to her amazement, the young Sanjeevni looking up at her, with a finger on his lips. She placed the heavy child in his lap.

As Sanjeevni looked at the child, bewildered with the entire experience of having waited out the entire night, he counted the toes and fingers and looked up at the mid-wife.

The child, narrow slits for eyes, completely calm, had very small hands, but with definite well-defined fingers, each distinct from the other. He felt each of the six toes on both the feet and placed his right palm below the two feet.

Hari's feet disappeared into Sanjeenvi's fate lines on his palm.

The child kicked into his eldest sibling's palms, as if pushing away Sanjeevni's fingers, making him realize the child was about to stretch. A whimper of a yawn took place, and Sanjeevni gets to witness the small pandiculation, realizing the miniaturization of the event by the tall baby.

Sanjeevni whispers to the mid-wife, "The baby is so tall, yet everything is so small…is my sister?" not being able to recognize whether the child is male or female.

The features too small, the nose a bit pudgy, yet the size of head, as large as 'Bheema's mace, the legs long and arms outstretched, as if asking for an embrace.

The presence of life on his lap, in small movements, is observed by Sanjeevni silently. He enjoys the exclusive privacy with the baby and places his right hand on the baby's chest, as if to comfort the child.

The process calms the loud thumping drums that seem to be playing out from the baby's heart, after a long night of twists and turns for survival to burst into life.

The mid-wife replies, "No, he's your *Bhai*," indicating to him he has another brother.

Sanjeevni witnesses again, from head to toes, the wriggling body, heaving, moving up and down due to the shortness of breath and realizes the baby appears exhausted, yet not relaxed.

"My brother appears tired already in the morning." smiling back at the mid-wife.

Life, is a struggle from birth.

Hari had just performed life threatening crawl and all kinds of stunts, to see the light of day. A long exercise at birth itself. Neither hungry, nor cranky, he fell asleep in his eldest brother's lap, as if the cross-legged boy is a continuation of the mother's belly.

Sanjeevni feels protective. He notices that his small talk has disturbed Khazan, who had fallen asleep with his back to the pillar wall.

The father looks at his grown-up son resisting the closure of his heavy eyelids. His sleepy eyes barely staying open, part due to tears and part due to his own exhaustion waiting. His vision shifts toward his new born son, his form and size are absorbed as the father can see fully the intensity of love and affection of the elder sibling.

He lets Sanjeevni cuddle and pat the baby to sleep. Khazan gets up to look for his wife. But first, he stops before his new born child and Sanjeevni. He blows kisses in the air while touching both the cheeks of the new born with his right thumb and forefinger and blesses him in his mind.

He is partially troubled with the son's late coming and has overheard the mid-wife telling Sanjeevni the sex of the child.

Khazan was a paranoid mess at night, and is a relieved person now.

With tears coming out of his eyes he walks up to Maya who is lying in her own sweat, in her bed, with legs upright, yet fully awake.

"We have a fourth male member in your house. You are tired Maya, sleep." Khazan lowers his head and bows in obeisance to the lord, before taking Maya in his arms.

He was thankful that Maya was healthy, post the birth and was amazed at the miracle of the supernumerary digit finger, toes and the extra thumb.

He there and then whispers "Hari" in Maya's ear, as if the child had miraculous powers even before birth.

Hari grew up, in the months ahead, consuming more milk than what Maya could deliver. She would have to arrange for more milk from Sulakshna, to keep his hunger at bay. Sulakshha would feed Maya the *'ghee and gond' ladoos,* while Maya would feed Hari three times in the morning till evening and twice more before his sleep at night.

He would awaken in the middle of the night to have two more feeds. The child consumed more than the elder siblings and Khazan would look at Maya wryly, as she would blame it on his genes.

"No one in my family, ever consumed this much of milk in their adult life in months, how much this child consumes in a few days. These are your *'halwai'* genes. You sweet-mart smart people. He is comfortable with creamed milk, as if he has no interest in diluted or my milk, just never satisfied."

Khazan observed a new line of complaints coming from Maya which had never been the case in family life till now.

"What to do?", he said, "You have been making us travel all over Rajasthan, here is your Hari, born a hungry prince. Whatever you were eating in those days, *parathas, dal batti, lassis, halwas*, all were gobbled up by you hungrily. Hopefully he will have strength of Bheema, like the folklore of '*Bhimlat Kund*', at Chittorgarh where you ate so many mangoes and carried many back here."

"He is getting round like a mango himself. We should have named him Bhimu then." She loved her child, even though it was not the daughter she had wanted. She fed him affectionately, but she felt exasperated by the number of '*Langots*' to dry and clean each time.

Home-made cloth diapers were the only solution she had, as their use helped to avoid skin rash. In every forty-five minutes he would give her a ready squirt and she would spend the better time of the day drying his reusable cotton fabric nappies, and the rest of the time feeding him. This caused her to take longer than desired help from Sulakshna, who happily extended it.

Sulakshna would also play along and keep her visits ongoing.

The two had become steady friends. "He is your lucky charm Maya, it is very rare in thousands of children, for a baby to be born with extra fingers and toes." Sulakshna would say. "Don't worry so much, eat your *ladoos* and get your own strength back. It's going to be a challenge lifting him"

“His father will do the heavy lifting not me. He has already broken my back over nine months. I worry more for his shoes and what children will say when he goes to school.” The anxious mother always finds a new reason for worry for her child.

The days became weeks and months and the family witnessed its second monsoon on the land. The lovely days, with more moisture in the air would end with light rain evenings. A few grey and rare white pigeons came to rest on the terrace of the house.

As the couple had designed the house to be a single storey, Sanjeevni and Khazan would go upstairs after evening hours, as they loved to sit and talk after dinner.

Ashu would spend time relaxing around Hari, and Maya would wind up her kitchen as soon as she could.

Khazan would share intimate details of his work days with his eldest son and both would reminiscence the Calcutta sweets, Victoria memorial and the Hastings home days.

Khazan had willingly let Sanjeevni give up his school and help him on the land. They had harvested their first Rabi crop of their land and had obtained a bountiful of wheat and sesame. With Sudarshan’s help they had provided the wheat to the only resort in the town and had obtained a large profit from their hard work.

It was the first time Khazan was living a non-urban life and in the prime of nearing fifty himself he felt reassured of his decision to have migrated back to the hinterland.

In the past year Sanjeevni had gotten accustomed to sleep on the terrace and would come down only in the mornings.

Ashu would keep Hari company after he had turned six months, and Hari would sleep soundly with his legs resting on Ashu.

While Sanjeevni was more the father figure to the brothers, Ashu's attention shifted to Hari, while Sanjeevni's to Khazan. This created some space between the two elder brothers, like a time-off.

It was Maya who still lacked her female companion. It had kept the couple together and not weakened their bond, as their new life at '*Moh & Maya*' had revived their spirits.

The couple in these simple ways thrived on newness.

The following year, Ashwini had expressed the desire to continue his studies.

It was agreed to dispatch him to the 'St. *Xaviers School*' at Jaipur city, where the English teacher was known to the store manager at the Resort in Nawalgarh. He had agreed to provide the shared living quarters as a spinster and Ashwini left that year from home, to continue with his school education.

He had urban trappings, and the parents understood the need for him to progress for his own future.

Maya let him go with a heavy heart.

She understood him to be the finest and sharpest in the family, a quality that none of the others had. Maya knew, that Ashwini had a hunger for fulfilment of desire which could be used to hone his skills in the pursuit of knowledge.

As Sanjeevni had silent loyalty as his underlying dominant facet to his strong character, she was satisfied that her family structure of four residents would continue.

It would still give one child a chance to make a different future for himself. Both the parents also deeply respected the quality in Ashwini to look outside their current location he was in, and restart life elsewhere. So he had both their genes.

Maya also thought, she could spend time concentrating in raising Hari.

Both Ashwini and Sanjeevni had only acquired one parameter each from their father's personality, as Khazan had both, desire and loyalty in equal measure.

She wondered what Hari would grow up to become, and was preoccupied that year with the baby about to start walking on his feet by December.

The India Pakistan war had broken out in December, and there were an amazing number of blackouts till India broke off east Pakistan into Bangladesh, after the Pakistan Army surrendered to India.

Ashwini's plans the next year to go away thus came with circumspection mixed with optimism of a fresh start for the next generation.

As three years passed, Ashwini would return in the summer and winter breaks to be back with the family. As the child had broken the shackles of family life when he was quite young, movement and travel came very naturally to Ashu. He figured his freedom and independence had taught him so many new things, and given his life and part of his upbringing, a totally different meaning compared to the other children of the family. He still loved his family, but was not shy to pursue his own goals, and yet remained calm, and grounded. But he appeared distant physically and aloof when present, a price he was willing to pay for progress due to migration like his parents.

Sanjeevni had also observed the change in Ashu, becoming more '*English Sahib*' kinds and Khazan would tell him to ignore making any comments on him in his presence.

There was no kind of competition between the siblings, nor any sense of superiority in Ashu.

However, the pattern of movement of Ashu's travels and Sanjeevni's permanence in Nawalgarh led to a varied sense of events and exposure for each of them. Naturally, their perceptive impact on their minds and behavior had changed forever, yet the elder sibling always made the effort to keep the familial bond intact.

Ashu felt that he was really only learning the English first hand from his teacher, with whom he lived permanently after school hours. He learnt good convent spoken English, as the teacher taught him the correct use of adjectives, the perfect grammatical use of clauses and the benefits of written legible handwriting. This enhanced his control over the language, and refined his grasp on prose and poetry.

It did not however change his ability to express emotions correctly, or write anything substantial himself.

Ashu grew up on a diet of William Wordsworth, Charles Dickens and Y. B Keats, mixed with a small measure of J. Nehru, M.K. Gandhi and Tagore's writings. The colonial Indian hangover was all over the text-books and Ashu lapped up everything he was given to read. He would come back and share stories about what he had discovered during his school days and Sanjeevni would give him a patient ear.

Sanjeevni would refer to the old stories and poetry he had read about from his Calcutta days by Vivekananda, Premchand, Tagore and B Bose.

Gradually over various trips of Ashu to '*Moh & Maya*' the brothers realized they were followers of two different times of India, and would agree to disagree. Their relationship matured with mutual respect, as Ashwini understood the work Sanjeevni did with Khazan, that was something he was not interested nor capable of.

Their only common pass time was something they carried over from their childhood to the terrace of '*Moh & Maya*'. It was playing seven tiles, *or 'pitthu'* piling up seven stones on top of one another, in the center of the boundary area at the front of the house. They would toss a coin, then take aim with the ball, and score points with each other based on the number of stones scattered.

Whenever Ashu found a flat stone in his Jaipur school compound or around the cafeteria, he would discreetly pack it for his post examination vacation to carry back home. Ashu's holidays were the period, when Sanjeevni would also get a break from his land duties, but they continued sleeping the way they were habituated. Ashu indoors and Sanjeevni atop the terrace, outdoors.

This impacted their subconscious choice to live in different places of India, in their own adult life.

In 1973, a movie called Bobby released.

This movie had a deep influence on Ashu.

The hero played by Raj Kapoor's son, Rishi, called "Raja" falls in love with Bobby, a girl who is a poor catholic.

The theme of the movie was centered on love between two different sections of society, and the couple eloping and running away from their homes eventually.

The movie was written as a story by renowned writer cum director - K. Abbas. The music of the film would blare from practically every railway station Ashu's train stopped at, as well as the radio in their house, the transistor from the Punjab Sweet House days.

The writer of the story designed the script to cater to Raj Kapoor's desire to save his studio, and make an Archie comics inspired story, with an adaptation that displayed why even a rich man's son only aspires for love.

The song, "*I do not ask for Gold or Silver, I ask for love*" shot in a fisherfolk set up in Bombay's '*koli*' fishermen colony showed a different side of India to Ashwini. The only way to experience it in those days was films. The song was deeply etched and engrained in Ashu's heart.

'Love' became the center of his existence. To seek it and to experience it, he would go to any lengths. It gave a new shape to his sense of desire, outside the context of his own family. He was only just a teenager himself but he could not help but crushing over the heroine, 'Dimple' who played Bobby.

His romance with the silver screen and life in a city like 'Bombay' had started and gradually it became a consistent dream in his mind. Ashu would visit the cinema, even in later years in Jaipur with his friends, to listen to songs of Bobby outside the theatre, while it ran successfully for months in matinee shows.

Sanjeevni in 1975 discovered the movies of Amitabh - the other big influence of the 1970s. *Deewar and Sholay* were released in the small circuit house cinema, and Sanjeevni was enamored by the silent, brooding 'Angry young man' as Mr. Bachchan the star came to be known.

Coming back home from the movies, he would practice and recite dialogues to the night air at the terrace. He would enact the rolling act of an action scene on and under his bed, as if a non-visible villain had shot him. Both the movies had left an underlying simmering anger in the audience, whoever had seen them, though they had no parallel to their own lives. Sanjeevni liked the raw anger and had about just started to shave himself. He would keep his shirt and kurta buttons open, like his role model and tie a knot on the shirt ends to capture the essence of the coolie played by the hero of '*Deewar.*'

The psychological impact of the movies was that Sanjeevni understood he would at some time lose his life and that he did not want to fall into any wrong doing to lose his mother to Ashu, when they would grow up.

There was time for that..., yet it was Ashu who developed a fever after watching the movie together with the family. He spoke to no one, and no one said anything to him the next evening by when the fever went away. It was understood, that they each had love for the other, and Maya kept her silence, busy with her chores to pamper Ashu, as she knew he would be away after the break, back to Jaipur.

He was now in his ninth grade and it was important that at least one child of the family attained the highest form of education.

Sanjeevni understood, that Ashu was there for two months of the year, and all his favorite dishes of *'saag, dal, and papad'* would be made for him repeatedly.

The father and the elder son, kept themselves happy with the butter milk and the lassi that they would get as their continuous form of diet.

Hari would regale in the curds, rice and creams he would get to devour, besides his milk guzzling, half a dozen times in the day.

Somehow though they were five members, the family would spend time together in twos. They would naturally gather in groups also in twos.

Maya would be with Hari, bathing him, and reminding herself of all the naughtiness of Lord (Baby) Krsna, and how mother Yashoda may have had to tolerate his pranks, and yet could never punish him.

She would love the cuddly nature of Hari's limbs, and embrace him just before he would collapse to sleep, powdered, after his pre siesta milk dose. He had long limbs and yet soft and pudgy arms which his strong bones carried well.

His frame was large for his four years of age. She had adorned him with a golden '*kadda*' in his right hand. He would sleep with her, with his back resting on her one side.

If he would sleep with Sanjeevni, it would be only after dinner, before Sanjeevni went up for his own terrace bed under the open sky.

Hari would mount Sanjeevni like a race horse and make him go all around the house on his fours after dinner. He would then expect to ride on Sanjeevni's belly, making him turn around, while wanting the elder brother to rock him pushing his buttocks, till Hari would fall sleep.

Every night he would himself go to Sanjeevni, after dinner for an encore.

These would be nights when Maya and Khazan would catch up with each other, or simply listen to AIR (All India Radio) in the background. On weekends they would listen to Ameen Sayani's *Cibaca Geetmala*, and songs of the 1970's with the occasional chart buster of Rajesh Khanna or Shammi Kapoor playing in the background.

Hari appeared ambidextrous to Maya, as he would use his left hand to clutch at the milk bottle and the glass beaker of water. The beaker had a sticker of Joy ice-cream and was a tinted brown plastic material, thereby not showing the color of the liquid that she would give him. Due to over consumption, she always feared stomach aches for him as he would rarely burp after having his milk, in his half a dozen daily doses. She would mix some concoction of pudina and lemon in the water, and make him sip from this beaker when he was not greedily consuming milk.

When not playing "*pitthu*" or discussing movies that the brothers had seen, Sanjeevni would spend time with his father asking him all kinds of questions on his past life. He would let Ashu get time with Maya and willingly help and step out more often with Khazan sometimes even eating their lunch together in the fields.

Khazan would tell him his childhood mithai shop stories, about Sialkot, Solan, and how his parents would dote on him. The stories would inevitably refer to his own childhood memories about his own 'Nanna'.

Sanjeevni realized that his father was fond of his grand-father, more than his father. It appeared that paternal affection rode one generation above, and skipped the in between generation, as Sanjeevni's own grandfather in Solan also used to dote on him. By the time they had gotten together, Sanjeevni could see Khazan still being obsessed about his own grandfather.

Yet, Khazan would spend more time with Sanjeevni, describing his own childhood, rather than giving attention to the boy himself as his father. It was rare, that both Khazan and Sanjeevni, as father and son today, but as children in their own formative impressionable years, they had spent time growing up inside a mithai shop.

They had enjoyed sweet delicacies patronized by their kurta dhoti clad grandfathers. Sanjeevni noticed though, that Khazan would wear only Kurta shirts, and never sported a moustache, mostly working in his lightly stained dhotis in the field.

One afternoon, he confronted his father with a series of questions.

"In your life, have you been most fond of your maternal grand-father, your 'Nanna'?" he asked rhetorically, yet hinting the reply himself in the affirmative style of asking the question.

"Did you ever feel like making a business livelihood out of Punjab Sweet house? Why did you not stay back in Calcutta itself?"

Khazan sat patiently listening to his son and often ran his fingers through Sanjeevni's hair.

In all answers of his father, he found rational, logic and some form of deep love for Maya. Yet he would rarely see him openly express his love for Maya.

Sanjeevni said this to his father too, several times.

He was answered by Khazan in such immaculate details as a father, that he was satisfied to know as a son, that his father was really a content man, happy to live this life at "Moh & Maya" in order to move back toward the western center of India.

The 1971 war had led to some migrant problems again and the family had just moved out of the east in time. His father shared intricate details of the property they lived on.

"We made the land deed in your mother's name. Our family never owned things directly, we always kept the house for the women, as men rarely led long lives. Here, even the name of the house that's why, is in your mother's name and the affection we all have for her. She is the only lady of the house. She came into my life due to my parent's blessings and she took full responsibility of them and all of us till date. Her ability to perform household tasks and feed us is secondary. Her ability to find strength on a day-to-day basis and love all of us equally, is her primary quality I admire." Khazan confessed to his son.

"It is her, I love the most, as it is from her that I have sired all three of you. You all came later. She came first in my life. I definitely respected my parents, and my grand-father really doted on me, but it is Maya who is devoted to me. That's why, I love her the most. Today the love I have for all of you sons, is also out of a sense of responsibility, as I was entrusted your lives by the God's and it is me who has brought you on earth. I'm merely a temporary custodian."

Pat came the next question, "I came in your life before Ashu and Hari. So do you love me more than my brothers?" questioned Sanjeevni.

"To a certain extent that is true. I expect more from you. That is also a form of love." his father takes a break to see that Sanjeevni is absorbing his replies.

"You are more like my friend, and also my son. More of a companion now, than your mother. As men age, they lean more on their sons. As sons age, they wean off their mother and lean more on their father. My father was not there when I needed him, nor was I there for him, when he needed me. It is fortunate, that we are all together as a family here. I did not stop Ashwini to go, as he needed to for his own growth. I need you to understand do what you wish as you grow in age, but never hurt your mother. It is the minimum you can do for her, as she has given you a life. I have just given you food and work."

"Yes father, I understand. You have also given me the most time. I deeply value it. There were days I watched in silence while you kept reading books in Calcutta and listened quietly when you and mother spoke during our travels. I do understand that we needed to change our place of stay. I do not miss my friends from school, I just miss playing hockey in Calcutta. I will remember every word you have said.

For me, your words are my books. Mother now has Hari. Yet Hari is as much mine as yours. I was there that night…I could hear mother in pain when he was born."

"And what about Ashu?" asked the father with concern. For Khazan, really all three boys were equals, but the age gap was too much so he was secretly aware, that it was Sanjeevni to whom he felt the closest.

He could open his heart and talk to him, and spend time with him as his working companion on the fields. Sanjeevni had such a natural love for animals, be it the birds on the terrace or Nandu and Hariya, he would lovingly feed them and also cradle Hari in his arms.

Khazan had along with himself sealed his eldest son's fate, by choosing the location where life would unfold. After realizing that Sanjeevni was most attached to both the parents, and not so much to his Calcutta friends or life there, Khazan felt he had given his eldest son, a chance to break free from the pressures of urban life.

The sense of abandon, on one's own land and a knowledge to grow one's own crops was something he was hoping to give back to his children for the future generations again.

The cities were more developed but the life where they lived had a more tranquil quality that added peace, and as the son had come to experience, time to their relationships.

This kind of time, would not have been possible in Calcutta, had Khazan kept working. This way, though he was not, his choices were working. He had lesser worry and more time for his children, who experienced a different way of life from Calcutta and Maya could raise them with a superior diet and quality food. Overall, they also felt a sense of belongingness to their own roots.

"Ashu is like my friend. Hari is like my son. They both collectively to me, are what you say, I am to you." echoed Sanjeevni straight from his heart.

Khazan embraced his son as they got up from their lunch position.

The meal time was over, and the dal stains had crusted under the sun into dirt grids on the stainless-steel plates, with the few rings of curd forming white clouds in between.

It drew a pattern of a dull sunny day in the plates though their palates and minds were overtly satisfied and bright after their discussion.

Khazan spoke "May Lord Krsna bestow upon all fathers of India, an eldest son like you. Love is not divisible. Love is something that multiplies inside our hearts for all. You are blessed by Lord Krsna who could give all the 'gopis' of Vrindavan the feeling, that he was simultaneously with each one of them. They were so immersed in their love for him, that each of them thought of him in their hearts, and felt he was with them. You have that quality as a blessing from the Lord himself. You have answered spontaneously and made my heart swell with pride. I am proud to be your father" says Khazan emotionally.

His son Sanjeevni has been with him since that day when Hari was born.

"*Pitaaji*, I am so happy here. Happier than what I was in my classes in Calcutta. I did not want to grow up and become a *babu*. If you had not taken the decision in time, today we all would not be here. I would never get to see this life. After all everything in life is just an experience, it comes to an end. I have recognized from our travels to Solan and stay in Calcutta that nothing remains the same. Yet we seek some permanence. As long as our family is together, there is no more joy than that. I will never go from this place, our land, as I will live with you and mother all my life."

"Ha ha ha, oh ho", laughs Khazan gleefully. "It is just a matter of time, my handsome. Your wife will come into your life, and then shall begin your strife! Enjoy these days, before you enter your *'Grihasthashram'* as these are the best days of your life - that of bachelor hood."

"I will like to eat the mangoes of this land, father. Perhaps travel like you but only to return. Will you keep me here with you?"

"Off course son, but listen to yourself. You know life is just an experience, it comes to an end. The land is your mother's and after us, everything is for all three of you, you brothers. So, remain united and give each other strength. That is why family is so important. We cannot take our land up with us."

"Neither can I, father." Sanjeevni was smiling peacefully back at Khazan.

Khazan is content that the son has received his knowledge, while displaying his own natural wisdom. Khazan wonders about the righteousness ingrained in Sanjeevni and from where it really is arising.

He sings some blessings, first to the lord and to his son in his mind. Khazan walks with his son, while his son carries all the collected steel plates, to walk toward the well.

They draw some fresh water out and have their fill after the meal. The weather remains dry, unlike their parched throats.

Ashu would spend all this time with his mother Maya indoors, like a duo, inseparable in love. He would idolize his mother for her looks and openly shower praise and butter her up. Upon being asked, his mother would get replies about the movies he had seen at Jaipur in the previous term and the description of the entire story of the movie.

Ashu also shared with his mother the good practices of the catholic religion and those of the English teacher, in following and thinking about Jesus.

He would draw parallels in the story and imagery around Jesus as God and Lord Krsna and debate with Maya on who was the superior supreme force.

Ashu had come to realize the multi faith religions of the world, by way of stepping out in the world and would question why his mother would not display an image of Jesus on the walls of their house.

Maya would rattle the names of all Hindu Gods and offer her versions of listing out all the Gods and how her numerous Hindu Gods were superior, and how they were all vegetarian eaters.

Ashu would point out the lambs in the images of Jesus. Maya would point out the cows in images of Krsna. Both the mother and son accepted the imagery of God as a shepherd.

Maya would argue that death was glorified with the cross and the suffering of Jesus. She felt he was an import onto the culture of India and poor Indians who had converted by the early Jesuits who came to India. Ashu found her logic very un-inclusive and un-Hindu to think this way. An international God was also God, like the domestic one for him.

To Maya, playing the flute '*our Lord Krsna*' would silently stand cross legged as a good shepherd. Hindus never converted others. You had to be born as a Hindu, into the philosophy of inclusion.

She began to see a parallel develop in Ashwini's behavior to that of Khazan who had become philosophical after the exposure to Vivekananda's

Vedanta. She worried that it was too early for her son in life, to develop a bent of mind that would not remain open for long years ahead of him. She knew the church as an institution had done good to bring under it many deprived souls in India, who had suffered in the existence of casteism that was Hinduism's bane.

The beliefs in Hindu Gods, had still sustained and was the internal and external imagery that the worshippers and temples used to keep faith alive. Religion was another matter and the general population had been left to make their individual choice, which is what Hinduism originally stood for. It never forced itself upon the people as faith was passed down the generations in form of tradition, rituals and culture. The young generation was now not willing to blindly follow the same.

Ashu would argue the participation in the Mahabharata war and the killing of his own uncle Kansa. And so, it went on.

Maya realized over various visits of Ashu from Jaipur that he had developed a sense of his own judgement and was growing up before his age. She also knew he had developed a sixth sense, which he used to judge small events and steer himself clear of debates with his father, or elder sibling.

Ashu only engaged and argued with his mother.

If it was not about religion, it was about love shown in the movies, which for old fashioned Maya, was getting too bold and showy. "It's the seventy's Ma, for *even God's* sake. We are the land of the Kamasutra and Ajanta Ellora!"

"For which God's sake Ashwini? Please do not bring me a fish and mutton eating Catholic as my daughter in law. Our eating habits will collide, and there will be explosions in the kitchen."

Ashu could never understand this selectiveness of diet and food habits.

Ashu realises his mother is upset as she uses his proper full name. He continues to rib her, "How will I live with you? *Booti Bhai*, Sanjeevni is there for that. I will live my life independently Ma, with my Catholic and international habits wife."

He spoke in a teasing manner, testing, yet simultaneously cajoling his mother. "Even if I love you so much, I have to love my wife, after I am married. Father also stayed away, did he not?" was Ashu's retort. "And if she does not fight me or you, my wife will end up fighting with brother's wife. And I would not want that."

"Oh ho, you have lots of future plans already in your wise head. Grow up first and support yourself properly. With your desire of visiting the movies, you will end up being broke and your wife will starve!" Maya got back.

"I am not like your milk guzzling little one Ma. I have simple needs and still desire to live like a king, not spend like a prince." There was lightness in Ashu's tone, so Maya let him go on.

"I have learnt to live by myself and am already quite independent. I only observe and pick the good habits of my English teacher, his poise, equanimity and modern traits. Some of their practical habits, like breaking bread together, having a sip of wine and expressing their love in poetry or prose appeals to me"

"As long as you do not imbibe their religion, it is okay. They have been converting our poor by calling them to the churches."

"Why what is the harm, if I do? Though I do not represent the poor. But the poor who have been abandoned by our own religion in the name of caste, upper, lower, are so poor, they need the bread and food the church supplies. They do not sleep on a hungry stomach, and this ties in with what Swami Vivekananda used to say - uplift the poor. To me the instrument and mechanism is not important as long as people get uplifted. It was happening during the British era too. Everything they did was not bad for India. It only increases the diversity of India."

Ashu's love for the Indian movie Bobby, and the union shown in the movie, had impacted him strongly in his impressionable school days.

"Who can argue with you son.? As long as you have peace and love in your heart...." Maya is interrupted by her son again.

"Why do you doubt that? I just have slightly bigger aspirations like father. Religion is irrelevant. Loving humanity is more important."

"Your father spent his entire work life away from his parents to serve the country. It looks like you intend to do the same." Maya tries to evoke a response with her evocative plea and yet prods the evasive Ashwini.

"Patience mother! Let me complete my studies, I will get you wherever I am posted when I grow up and you can always live with us."

"Not with your dress and skirts wearing Catholic wife!"

"Oh Ma, *Bobby* is just a movie character. Though I do love her! But I am confused now with '*Julie*.' Have you heard the songs? Kishore Kumar has sung for you – '*Dil Kya kare...*' what can my young heart do???"

"You are incorrigible!" the mother says acceptingly, "Foolishly romantic too."

"Ma, hear the songs of *Julie*, and tell me, if you like them more over *Bobby*. I am not able to make up my mind. *KishoreDa, over Shailendra* which will be the voice of the future playback singer?"

"Why do you not ask your father?"

"He does not understand romance and love. You should now that better."

"*Badmash*! Don't go about trying to take your father's place. How do you know what is in your mother's heart?"

"I know Ma I can see it in your eyes. So often you asked Pitaji to pen something for you. Has he done that?"

"Have you Ashu? If you are the poet of the family, why don't you?"

"I can sing for you," he goes about to sync his voice to sound like the title track of '*Juile*', replacing the name with "*Maaaajji, I love you!*"

"Practice your flirting with someone else not your mother!" she hustles him and gets up to switch off the transistor radio that Ashu has been using as a decoy.

Khazan and Sanjeevni enter with smiles on their faces. They keep the plates for washing around the water area.

As time passed, the year 1976 had come rolling in with this repartee the two boys had privately with the mother and father.

Khazan appeared to successfully harvest his sixth season of wheat and sesame. The sesame oil used in cooking, and the natural sun had given enough energy and bright sunshine to make him feel healthy and fit.

Yet quite another thing was going on inside his body.

The years of fried food and sweets had continued and the unknown medical precautions of that time led him to ignore pains on the left side of his arm, chin, and legs, assuming them to be the workload of the fields in the day.

He would twitch his left chin, while working in the fields, rarely observed by Sanjeevni.

Nandu and Hariya had grown like Hari, to be strong companions and Sanjeevni had just started increasing the work load for himself.

Khazan was now fifty-four. He would remember the count he would indulge in to number of *'Barfis'* in his 'nanna's store, and recollect himself adding up the piles in the pyramid as a child to 'fifty-five.'

That afternoon after Sanjeevni and Khazan had completed their tete-a-tete and Ashu had entertained and lightened up Maya, the two brothers went upstairs to play seven tiles. Khazan decided to lie down alongside Hari who he usually played cards with. Hari had finished having a smaller than usual glass of milk, as Maya had weaned him off the bottle. He had an iron clad grip on the plastic tumbler from which he had just finished. He would hold the tumbler between his lips as if to pull it upwards, with his face looking up at the ceiling. It had become his new trick and Khazan would look at him, smile and egg him to engage the trick on a repetitious cycle.

That afternoon after lunch Khazan intended to play cards with Hari. While lying on the bed where Hari and Ashu slept in the outside room, Khazan hit upon the novel idea of using playing cards to make

Hari recognize numbers, pictures and colors and differentiate the suits. He spent an hour making Hari memorize the cards.

The hearts and diamonds would be collected by Hari, who loved the red cards, and Khazan would keep the darker spades and clubs. With the joker clutched in his left-hand Hari collected two cards with his right, both fives, both red.

It showed fifty-five. An age, Khazan had yet to reach.

Khazan collected two aces and a queen of hearts in his hand, and dropped all the three cards. He suddenly grimaced, with his left side of the face and chin beginning to twist further onto the left, his left eye, grimacing with pain.

A surge of fear, anxiety and a deep pain went through his chest. It ached and it constrained him, not being able to say a word. His face flickering like the light from a bulb that momentarily gives the last few sparks of light before it goes out completely.

Hari let out a gurgle of laughter assuming that his father is merely pantomiming the act of the joker card in his left hand. He shows again the two cards of five. The red diamonds suit, with the red hearts suit.

The call had come prematurely. '*Is his time up?*'

Khazan thinks of Maya, will she be okay without him if he was to go now. Who will take care of her? Sanjeevni comes to his mind. He looks back at Hari even though his pain is intensifying. The face further holds a sombre grimace.

Hari again lets out a yelp of giggles. Maya is inside the inner recess of her own bedroom folding sheets. She thinks the father and son are busy as usual. She has kept water on her bedside and is about to relax for her afternoon siesta. A nap she so deserves at that time of the day.

With four men in the house, each needing their fix, the curds to be set thrice a day, twice for consumption, once for butter milk, and the planning of storing the boiled milk for Hari's consumption there is a lot to do entire day, exhausting her by lunch time. The rest of the day is spent planning the next day's vegetables and dals to be cooked, and the favorite menu that Ashu would appreciate, and one that the father and Sanjeevni do not decline. These thoughts preoccupy her and Khazan is hardly on her mind. She is permanently planning ahead for her three sons catering needs of food, diet, milk or affection.

It is endless.

She rolls her eyes, looking at the Idol of Baby Krsna and only falls short of asking Yashoda, '*What kept her going?*' She slides into her dream as her eyelids are about to shut.

A second wave of the attack intensifies. Khazan is now visibly choking with pain. His breath is running short, as he is unable to inhale.

The fear cycle runs a blinding knock on his senses as he drifts towards the edge of the bed, still holding his gaze toward Hari.

Hari's eyes light up further, expecting another stunt from his father. Usually, he mimics a fight sequence and falls off the bed. Hari is paralyzed, awaiting the next act from the father.

Khazan, on his part now begins to think of Ashu, who he can hear from upstairs shouting playfully. He faintly hears the voice of Sanjeevni replying as he thinks Ashu is the one leading in the game and challenging the elder brother to push himself harder. Sanjeevni replies something to the effect of him willing to lose to his brother.

Khazan now is going reddish purple on his face. His movement has stopped abruptly with his left side completely frozen. The left side of his face does not move, but the right side shores up a small half smile. It looks funny, and at the same time blissful. His eyes reflect a serenity that Hari has never seen before.

Hari raises the two cards in his right hand, showing them to his father, that he has matched the two fives, expecting encouragement and more laughter in return.

Khazan looks back at his third son, his family complete, and prays for the Lord's final blessing upon them. The pitter patter of his two sons above the thump of the water beaker that falls from Hari's hand on the bed, disturbs Khazan's final thoughts.

As one side of his face is frozen, he is unable to breathe deeply from his mouth.

He is hit by a third wave of pain. It is like a crescendo. It lifts his chest off the surface of the bed like a tornado about to hit the earth. He remembers the scenes from Solan and Sialkot. He recollects the visit to the Shimla temple site. The days at the Calcutta Ramakrishna Mission briefly flash before his eyes.

His entire life starts passing by in his mind, as he observes so many fleeting pictures calmly.

Khazan moves his right hand, despite the pain, with huge effort, to turn aside two cards from the closed pack of cards strewn all over the bed, like fallen leaves from a tree. He looks at Hari in the eye.

Hari is now silent, in anticipation, watching his father, wondering why he is moving in slow motion. Khazan's right thumb turns one card and shows a King of the diamond suit, and the index finger in another three seconds, turns the Queen of hearts suit.

Khazan's pain is intense. He thinks of a form of a baby, a girl they never had perhaps, but someone somewhere in his family would have eventually. He cannot see the face of the girl very clearly.

He remembers Sanjeevni taking the new born Hari in his lap. He remembers the expression on Ashu's face devouring the vanilla ice-cream in the *chocobar* at Calcutta's railway station platform. There is a train leaving the station in the background.

There is a clanking of noise from the engine of the train. He looks up to see Maya, in *Punjab Sweet House* store.

He is at the foot of the steps inside the Solan shop. She is yet to turn, she is young and her hair are open, ending just above her hips. '*Turn, turn, turn...*' *he says to himself.*

Hari throws the joker from his left hand down. To pick his next two cards. He has enjoyed and is thrilled with the act the father has put before him.

Khazan is now at the edge of the bed, head hanging with the right shoulder from one side of the bed, with his left leg and part of the body still not moving off the bed.

Hari picks up two cards from the pack, both are aces. Khazan can see the image of Maya in his eyes as she has turned around in the Solan shop.

She is waving back at him from the gate of '*Moh & Maya.*'

He looks up to get one last look at Hari, his *own Baby Krsna.* The form of the lord, innocence and truth in Hari's eyes is intact like a shrine holding an idol.

He realizes he has not embraced Hari since morning and moves forward collapsing in Hari's lap.

Laying there motionless, staring back at Hari in his lap Khazan passes away.

Hari rocks his father as if to sleep, placing the two cards on his chest. He places his left hand, on the left side of his father's face, as if to straighten it. Thinking that his father is also taking a nap, Hari cradles him in his lap.

Khazan was found as if fast asleep in Hari's lap when Maya woke up that evening to her misfortune. She cried out loud for Ashu. It was a shrill piercing cry that could be heard till Sulakshna's home.

Ashu leaves the ball from his grip and is followed by Sanjeevni running down the steps, to find their father in Hari's lap.

Hari is lightly caressing his father's crooked face with his left hand and his hair with his right. His long cross-legged limbs and sweating arms, soft pudgy hands softly still caressing his father. He has been doing that for over forty-five minutes non-stop.

Khazan's head, in Hari's lap face upward is serenely looking upward at the sky. The two elder boys, fall at their mother's feet, held tightly in her embrace.

Ashu hugs his mother tightly.

Sanjeevni is held in his mother's embrace.

His hands, tightly holding his father's feet.

10

DEGREES OF SEPARATION

1979

Maya awakens, at her usual time at seven thirty. After drinking water, she goes about her movements brews her tea, dries the wet clothes on the clothing line and picks up the dried ones with her other hand.

She is not that ambidextrous, dropping the dried clothes into the dust on the floor. With eyes transfixed into the past, she picks them with much frustration as she realizes the countless errands she has to now do alone as a widow.

She is unable to move on and think of her future without Khazan. She knows she has to. She takes the transistor out to the veranda, places it on the window sill on the outside of the house and turns the knob of the radio to the 'on' position.

"*Ek din bik jayega, maati ke mol....*" blares Mukesh with Kishore from the movie Dharam Karam. The radio jockey, the famous anchor Ameen Sayani is in a punishing mood and does not appear so iconic anymore. Every song that he introduces these days makes him appear quite sardonic.

"*Uff... Raj Kapoor!*" she thinks of the melancholic actor, reflective of her own mood. She knows very well, he was Khazan's favorite his movie songs composed by Shankar Jaikishan written by lyric writer Shailendra, more poetic and touching, were his staple diet. The current song, more a 70's tune by R.D. the new beat master of filmdom, comes to an end and moves to the "*Jeena Yahan, Marna Yahan...*" as if sealing the fate of Maya to continue living, till death at '*Moh & Maya.*'

The singer Mukesh, sounds like rattling off a king's scroll slightly pompous and over purposeful, reflecting Raj Kapoor's ideology and Khazan's order.

Before the song can move to the next tune, she anticipates, "*Jeena Isika Naam hai,..*" visualizing Khazan humming it to her, wearing his trade mark white dhoti over his short dusty kurta and entering the house with the steel plates with Sanjeevni. That is the last look she had of him. There was still so much to talk, discuss and decide and fate just snatched him away from her.

She stares at the curtains hanging over the entrance '*dahleez*', stitched from her older sarees an innovation suggested at that time by Khazan. Maya can no longer explore, travel, migrate or move elsewhere. She wants to run away. She feels marooned on the land, without Khazan and straightens out her crimson saree, another Khazan gift thinking to herself.

"*Shall I change the curtains and switch to white myself, I must stabilize my thoughts. The boys are still young.*"

Sanjeevni was only about twenty. Hari still under six. Ashu was chasing his far away dreams. Her thoughts guide her, though she feels like a sunken ship. Her ship has two anchors, one old and one too brittle to hold her pulling her back into reality.

She digs herself out of the shallow sea of pity feeling like a ship laden with a cargo of memories. She attempts to sink her feet into the soil while she feels the hull of her ship of destiny, its welding tearing away open, pulling her like a wreck with pithy in a new direction.

After Khazan's pre-mature death, Sanjeevni had picked up the cards from the bed on which his father lay. He had pocketed the cards, straightened his father's body and lifted Hari into his arms, to reorient the rest of the family members.

Ashu and Maya had sat on the ground at the foot of the bed, numbed into paralysis, stone-like, in able to act or think. Sanjeevni had pocketed the joker and the king of diamond suit, and placed the queen of hearts at his mother's bed-side drawer on the heap of post cards and letters she had collected from the Calcutta and Solan days.

The King of Diamonds, he placed under the Lord Vishnu glass frame, at the lord's feet, above the marble temple structure they had inside the house. He had placed the two cards of five, left open by Hari into an old kurta shirt pocket of his father. This kurta was kept as a memory by Ashwini in his section of the '*Godrej*' cupboard that stored the clothes.

The ace clutched tightly by Hari in his right hand, was not released by the young boy, as he understood with grief all around him and his mother's shrieks that something was amiss. In days to come Hari would understand that the games he would play with his father were forever over. He began playing the game of memory and matching card pairs with Sanjeevni. Hari later had kept the Ace card under the used matchboxes of "Ship" brand on the last shelf of the Godrej Almirah in his out-room which was the play room with his father.

Sanjeevni had discovered in this same steel cupboard that he, Ashwini and Hari shared with Khazan, a note book which had some scribbled writings, and torn pages. It was called Khazan's notebook. In it he discovered a letter he had written, addressed to Maya.

For nearly a week, Sanjeevni secretly guarded this letter but eventually read it to himself late at night under the oil lamp at his bedside.

"Dear Maya,
I never thought, I would be able to love someone.

The partition had scarred my emotions and I witnessed so many displaced refugees,

at the work place.

I could not love anyone till then. Till you came along and displaced my heart in Solan.

I have lived without it since then, as it is in your possession, wherever I am. You taught me to love and the family we created of our own, took me to an experience beyond parenthood. It gave me more than what my own father and mother had shown me, from whom I only took love.

The experience with you, taught me to give and shower love. The care you took of my mother will bring us together again in our next life, as due to your Karma, we will owe you.

Your children will now grow up before your eyes and some will fly from the nest.

I have written a small piece, the "Degrees of Separation" for four of you. Something you always wanted.

Alas, it is not exclusive for you, as I have also included my love for my sons; as I see them merely as an extension of you. You will now have six more eyes on you. Do share the piece with them at opportune times of their life.

Lastly, all the boys have our genes. Some have traits that are worth appreciating and some that need smoothening.

I have performed my role with Sanjeevni over the years at 'Moh & Maya.' He is the most responsible and sensible one. I am also very sure he will give love to Hari always, performing the same role with him.

Perhaps Ashu will only receive from you as it is not easy for me to give him my influences, he is already a lot like me. I have only given him material comfort, but to Sanjeevni, I have given some spiritual and philosophical foundation. The games I have played with Hari, maybe forgotten forever, but the child's eyes have sparkled and moreover he has learnt patterns and counting.

I have never advised you but I do have one thing to say – "Do not love someone so much, that 'you' get hurt easily yourself.

Also, do not love yourself so much, that others do not get a chance to love you."

Yours frying,
in oil,

The Samosa man.
Khazan Chand Singh.

Sanjeevni moved his thumb over his father's signature upon reading the letter and closed his eyes. He looked onward in the note book not finding other pages referred to by the father, presuming that Maya had torn those pages from the notebook.

It was a year or so, by the time he could speak to Maya about those pages on the first death anniversary of his father. After the puja was performed, Maya brought out the pages and handed over the "*Degrees of Separation*" to Sanjeevni.

"I do not need it anymore" she said, dryly "I have it memorized. Perhaps your father had a premonition about his departure." She retained her calmness but there was an everlasting look of sadness in her eyes.

The last rites of Khazan had been performed by Sanjeevni, with Ashu emotionally observing his elder sibling as he clutched on to Maya. They both wondered who was consoling who as the death had taken a toll on both mother and Ashu. While they both were very close to each other, the male member providing the spine to their relationship was gone.

One dwelled on the marital bliss she had experienced, the other on the paternal blessings and joy he had jointly experienced, with no worry in life.

It was after Khazan's death, that Ashu discovered a new sense of closeness to Sanjeevni, trying to fulfil the potential of a male bond he missed creating with his father. Hari just went on innocently with his games playing with the eldest sibling.

It was Sanjeevni who was held lone responsible for the land as well as Maya's emotional outbursts. He never had the space or time to outpour his grief, and just had to let it dissipate into the soil of the farm, toiling hours under the sun. He mostly kept quiet in those years post twenty-one and over worked himself often to stay outside from home.

He would eat his lunch alone a tad bit later than rest of the family alone under the *Gulmohar* tree, and go upstairs to the terrace to brood alone. Sanjeevni believed that only time could heal everyone and allowed it to pass like a kite meandering loosely in the sky.

The ensuing year after the death led to Ashu spending more time in Jaipur city, preparing for his prelims and then his board examinations for his grade X. He would often amble along at LMB at Johri Bazaar remembering the journey back from Calcutta with his father, where they had taken their morning breakfast before starting for Nawalgarh. His resolve, was converted to strong intention. He wished to shift a school and move towards Bombay or Delhi. He believed that his Xavier's stint had now outlasted time and with his father not there, he was yearning for a bigger change.

Maya was unyielding and would have none of it.

The mother and son would battle in each term break and vacation, and he would return, forced to continue in Jaipur. Sanjeevni would listen quietly to the noise and din of the arguments taking no sides.

In every visit toward the end of the trip to 'Moh & Maya' the duo would clash, often with Sanjeevni acting as a mute witness. He would remain standing, a silent spectator. He could see his mother, intensifying her struggle to control Ashu and the second son making an even bigger effort to break free of her grip on his life and choices. Ashu would walk out of the house and the main gates and go for a walk in the sun for a couple of hours and return silently by lunch.

The more Maya tried the more he would attempt to seek liberation. The dynamics of the three had changed with Khazan's death. Sanjeevni stood his own ground, blankly staring at the walls of the room trying to seek direction from his father's soul. He would stare out from the veranda at the fields and the water well. He received no magical prophecy, and silently watched Maya's spectacle unfold, letting her play the more vociferous parent. He knew Ashu was better off that way and he would be better off playing the role of a confidant rather than offer any opposition.

Maya had Sanjeevni to work on the land almost alone with Nandu and Hariya and they lived off their field. The surplus little including wheat and sesame to convert to oil, would be supplied by Sanjeevni to Sulakshna and the family bond continued, albeit under tokenism.

Sulakshna saw in Sanjeevni a strong shoulder to rely on as she knew their own finances were dwindling to take care of the large haveli. The planned orders received at the start of every harvest season, would be sold to the new company that had taken over the old resort – rebranding themselves as "*India Hospitality Resorts*" with mother and son walking the long walk to the store manager.

The store manager's relative had now moved out of Jaipur and Ashu was on his own securing his accommodation at the outhouse of the *Rambaugh Palace*, with an estate manager of the royal family. Thus began Ashu's experience within an aristocratic setting, giving some realization to his lofty dreams. As his stay advanced over the months, he saw the option of the hospitality and hotel industry to secure his own future around the same hotel group. This also calmed the environment back at home and everyone gradually simmered down. Ashu was happy doing the odd jobs at the hotel.

Khazan became a part of a photo-frame alongside his 'Nanna' whom he used to look at. That would not be possible now on the same wall even if Khazan's eyes could squint to look alongside. The children now looked up at the wall at some point of time in the day and mostly took invisible blessings from their father, as they passed by the outer room.

On one trip in 1979 to '*Moh & Maya*', Sanjeevni invited Ashu upstairs and sat Ashu down at the terrace after their dinner.

Sanjeevni's bed was ready for his night time dreaming under the sky.

Ashu had completed his intermediate studies and was now unwavering in his determination to move ahead to another city. Grade twelve was the highest level that Sanjeevni had studied. The eldest brother knew that the scales were about to tilt, and yet he had to carry on selflessly carrying the family responsibilities at '*Moh & Maya*'.

The same year, Sudarshan had taken ill and their family dairy had collapsed before their eyes, with an older group of cows that they had to let go.

Jyoti's brother had been dispatched to Jaipur like Ashu for studies and with no male family member being able to taking responsibility on the finances, the family's pecuniary position had begun to slip. Sulakshna had stopped visiting Maya as both the ladies in absence of their men, were now entrenched in running their own households.

Both the brothers had different priorities and their relationship was neither like friends nor like real brothers. They both had become distant in the past two years. Sanjeevni had waited so that Ashu could mature a bit to share with him the message that Khazan had laid out to them.

"So, you are back now, I presume forever?" led Sanjeevni; he was polite to his younger sibling wanting to explore the option of evincing support and help. He could make good use of two additional hands he would get on the land, or use Ashu's connect in Jaipur to build some new markets.

"No bhai, I wish to continue my exploration. Mother does not understand. My teacher had told me about a place called Goa in western India which was a Portuguese colony. I am keen to study history, and understand the reason that brought Vasco Da Gama to India. He came first to Cochin, and then to Goa.

I am intending to move out of Jaipur, but not back to Nawalgarh"

As this response was unexpected in the realm of possibilities that were anticipated by Sanjeevni, he was visibly surprised.

"Hmm...," he thought aloud for a few minutes.

Silence ensued.

Usually, the fields in the early evening would have male mating crickets sing out loudly, and almost always ignored by the family, as if they were part of the background score music of a movie playing in the town hall cinema.

A hungry cricket, chirped out loud that night calling it's mate by the rubbing of its feathers. It was taken as a healthy sign, not just of anticipated rain, but also a change of course and luck for the family. Sanjeevni thought of it as an omen, perhaps an impending romance in it for his brother, whose case the cricket was pleading.

Sanjeevni decided to bring Khazan's vision into play. "Father believed in the concept of self-study and self-exploration, much like Tagore. I read some of the books father had brought back with him from Calcutta, but they were in tatters so we let them go last year."

He assumed Ashu would want to study further, but wanted to take a break in between, to travel and explore the country. He understood from past stories shared by Maya, that Ashu had the same nomadic spirit as their mother. Sanjeevni had only read Tagore amongst all the authors that Ashu had read about and used it as a starting point to find some commonality.

"Bhai, I know our finances are limited but mother does keep referring to the gold she had saved up for so many years. These are the years we need it to survive and spend. If you are not able to arrange more money, do not worry, I will do some odd job, as both my hands work well inside the house. There are many tourist spots in Goa, and I will find something to earn my keep. If I do not succeed there, my reputation will win me something back at Rambaugh Palace, and I will return to Jaipur."

"I can afford to send you a few thousand rupees a month. I have saved up some from sales in last three years of wheat and the mango pickles mother and I process annually. Why don't you go, explore and return as soon as you finish by Diwali? I can finance you for a year or so easily."

Sanjeevni decided to surprise Ashu with a kind offering rather than build a conflict in the family. He had realized it was important to set Ashu free, before one could rope him in.

Ashu got up from his Sai Baba pose and embraces his elder brother. "Bhai, you are like my father now. I promise I will never let you down. You have understood me so well. Perhaps if I discover a richer future, I will ask you to join me."

"That's not possible Ashu. I cannot leave mother alone here ever." Sanjeevni breaks away, walking some steps pacing back and forth. He appears disturbed and perplexed.

Ashu waits silently for a few minutes.

"So you will live their life then?" Ashu bites his tongue, its pink tip partly visible between his lips. Like a satisfied snake, he has let out the venom, but his conscience comes alive burning him with his own sting, as the words had come out, unconsciously.

"It is my life as well Ashu. Why do you sound so selfish suddenly? What has come over you?"

"Nawalgarh is not the place for us to settle down. All three of us can make our own future. Sudarshan Kakka is older, and unwell. Father is no more. Is that the way we too should meet our end? Ma's attachments here are to the wrong past memories of *Babba.* It was their idea of life to lie low. We are young, at the start of our life. The small things she is transfixed over, cannot feed us all our life. There is much to be discovered outside Rajasthan and we can make our life better, with more progress, amidst modern amenities that big city babus have."

Ashu spoke softly this time. It was a pragmatic appeal, not an overarching speech, as he wanted to persuade his elder brother to change the direction for the entire family. The elder brother realized he had to change his approach, and with some tact.

Sanjeevni only understood farming, and knew it was sustaining them with a livelihood. He also knew his mother would not leave the land, stubbornly attached as she was to the soil, the well, the mango tree, and the fruit that the land bore. And honestly considering himself in the situation he too did not want to leave.

Ashu continued his appeal, "There is a hidden culture in our country. We do not understand it but it is there for us to discover. People from all countries have visited, invaded, and even robbed our country, and taken what they plundered, back to their own countries. Ships were used to travel the high seas." He waited to let Sanjeevni digest his appeal.

He continued, "I want to be able to travel and see the world. Maybe I will meet someone with whose help, I can join the merchant navy. I do not wish to live the life of a farmer decided by my parents and thrust upon me."

"There are so many cities in India, we cannot see them all Ashu. There are many places in the world, will you want to be so far away from us and dock at every port of the world? There is no end to this adventure and yearning for more. Yes, the choice is yours for your own future. But do understand, nothing was thrust upon us. It was their vision. We were their dependents. I have seen father come back from Calcutta, feeling tired and disillusioned with urban life. He was already a '*City Baabu*'." Sanjeevni gave a pause.

"Then why did he quit everything and take us back to the hinterland? We can learn from their experience. There must be some emptiness in the city life." Sanjeevni's tone was passionate yet not pushy.

He justified his bliss and also valued his own life, unfolding as it was at its own slow pace. "We have an open sky to sleep under, enough water on our land, and a large field to feed us. What more can we find outside '*Moh & Maya*' that we cannot find here?" explained Sanjeevni.

"I also have struck a contract with the store-manager, with whose help we had sent you to Jaipur. I am committed to supply them mango pickles and wheat every year. Once we go away from here, who will manage our land and keep it secure? Who will till the land? Who will supply our produce to the India Hospitality Resorts.? How will mother and Hari be taken care of?" Sanjeevni knew he had set up an agri-produce, supplier, buyer mechanism and had toiled for it.

He had a hook into the resort to off load his supplies there itself, without having to go to the city. He stood by his mother with an allegiance he had received in inheritance from his father. Loyal, like Khazan, he knew he had taken his father's position and Maya would be worse off it, if they both travelled.

"You can use my cycle, to market your produce to other shops and traders" retorted Ashu. "Our parents planted our flag here. Maybe I can plant my flag some-place else. Should that choice not be ours? Why did father not settle down in Solan over Calcutta, or in Calcutta itself over Nawalgarh? The main city is Jaipur. I do not get the sweets or savories I can eat at LMB, at Johri bazaar, or C K Das of Calcutta, here at Nawalgarh. There is one 'Shiv' mandir in our town, there are so many in Jaipur, or in Varanasi and in Himachal. Why not live there?"

Ashu did not realize as he spoke, that his mother was a Lord Vishnu follower and despite Hari being born with a serpent like umbilical cord around his neck, they had not named him Shiv. Yet, Ashu displayed his sense of knowledge to seek other alternatives and thought other cities may provide a better living experience. The desire to explore was galloping like an unbridled stallion.

"So, you do not intend to live permanently in Goa?" asked the puzzled Sanjeevni.

"No, not at all." said Ashu very flatly. "Who knows today, where I will land up? I will like to decide based on my circumstances and not by way of pre-conceived notions. Today people can immigrate out of our country, why should I think of any one city inside our own country. It is very limiting."

The elder sibling was now in a quandary. "Ashu, you can afford to dream on and live to chase your dreams. For me this is my life. I do not have your dreams. My parent's life, is my life. You are different. You should finish your studies, then I will finance you. First come with me to the '*India Hospitality Resorts*.' Tomorrow I have to provide them with the provisions, the harvest is complete. The money we get, you can use for your exploratory travels, but return you must by Diwali. Finish your graduation as I did not get to do that. It is not a regret but the lack of a complete education can become a limitation more than the choice of a city to live in. It will cripple you later."

The elder brother, speaks with concern, and good intent writ all over his face. Sanjeevni's brown eyes stare into Ashu's black ones.

He leaves Ashu perplexed, and to think deeply for a change. Ashu decided to bury the matter there.

"Okay Booti Bhai. I will go with you. I will complete my graduation from Jaipur itself. But after three years, do not ask me to return to this land. I cannot find a good woman here that's for sure. Any romance in the air for you here? Pitaaji was set in his ways in life. We have still to get set."

Sanjeevni evaded talking about his own life and took only the second half of the question. He respected the fact that he was in no position to influence Ashu on matters of the heart, which he himself was yet to decipher.

He had a clear picture about Khazan.

"Father was patient and committed. He was an eternal optimist. His way of expressing love was different. He wanted to be with all of us, as he had missed doing that with our grand father and mother. He came from a simple time, with childlike memories of his own youth, that he had to leave behind in another country. He could never go back to his place of birth, and he had no childhood friends due to that. His work colleagues were from other cities, and they all went back to their native villages or stayed back in Calcutta. He was not from there."

Sanjeevni waits for Ashwini to digest all this information. He continues to open his heart, hoping he can open Ashu's mind.

"He had a clear vision of his life. He wanted to re-start anew. You are right, we are young now, but he had to make that start, in his middle age. He was blissful through his last days, and so content. He shared so many memories with me over many meals. He loved getting his feet into the soil. He would pat the bullocks Nandu and Hariya affectionately, as he would to Hari. He would get Hariya close to the veranda and get Hari out to show him that it was Hariya with whom he had worked, before Hari was born. He made Hari befriend them. He made me understand that I had to look after mother and you both. He gave '*Moh and Maya*' a real meaning here. He showed us how to live with love. You call it being set, but you can use it to settle anywhere in the future. Maybe God just called him upstairs very early. I sleep here every night looking up at the stars and the moon and I hope he is up there somewhere, looking at us." Sanjeevni in this soft and reassuring manner gave a past perspective to his brother, filling him with respect for their father.

"So *bhai*, you believe in fate and destiny too?" Ashu spoke cautiously, neither mocking his brother nor anymore pinning him against a wall.

The two brothers were now in a free-wheeling conversation and the younger was acting in doubt and distress, yet with the same curiosity Sanjeevni used to express with Khazan.

It was the eldest son's turn, to display maturity and explain all over again.

"What other reason can you explain his death before fifty-five?" Reasoned Sanjeevni.

"His diet, his food habits, and never a visit to a doctor." claimed Ashu. "Perhaps also the choice of our location, if we were in Jaipur city, maybe he never needed to work in the fields and take the strain for the shift, and would have merely considered a visit to a doctor to show himself."

Sanjeevni finally grasped from where the problem of staying back at '*Moh & Maya*' arose for Ashu. While the place was a reference point of love for Maya, it was that of digging their roots in a place for Sanjeevni. It was where Hari was born to the soil, making it his '*Janmbhoomi*'.

Sanjeevni did not want to separate Hari from it as Khazan was separated from his, but he understood that Ashu did not uphold the same value to the land, as they three did. There was something different in it for each one of them, as their perspectives differed.

"Ashu, he worked a hard life. Now he wanted to spend time with his own family. He got a chance to do that. After his death, I discovered a letter written to Ma, and a small poem too. Here it is, do read it" shared Sanjeevni, removing a folded paper from his pocket.

"You must also know, who your father truly was. Mother took a year to share it with me after he was gone. I have taken two years to share it with you."

Ashu disbelievingly looks at the ruled notebook papers, and takes it toward the wall that has the door of the terrace and stands under a bulb, flickering with insects.

DEGREES OF SEPARATION

He is he, and I am me,
There is not much, similarity.
Father and sons.
She in her own way,
Is mother to three
But she too,
mostly thought uniquely.

Like the sun's original ray.
She let the boat on the surface of water, just lay.
Watching us both, father and sons play.
Like a church where some fell, or turn grey
... and some just simply liked to pray.

He could barely balance his own feet,
As his six toes got wet.
My youngest son, the 'ace' of my pack,
Had both arms outstretched,
his hug would grow to a smack.
It felt like treats to be with him,
When it rained pitter and patter
he would be grim alone, yet not matter
to him.
For a lottery was to be won
that would keep him happy and trim.

Asleep, my Maya, with her middle son,
Both cuddled, they lay like lazy cats.
While father and elder planned the farm yields,
I could speak gaily to him, in the fields.
Yet my eldest is not me, nor I am him,
But somewhere as friends we came down to a team-slim.
He is my 'joker', my dharma,
While Maya's 'Ghulaam', is the middle one.
Set him free,
as it is his karma
The sun rays will be his Shakti,

While Hari is Krsna's personality,
he will settle with only bhakti.

Water flows, from one to another,
like love of the family.
It collects itself from well, to your home vessel.
Maya, my only passionately loved angel.
As if a blessing from past life, my most pretty one.
Moh and Maya, makes me swell with happiness,
My heart soar with bliss.
There comes a separation,
Albeit a short one,
There is no real end.
Don't seek the past, the present is the only continuous
We should live in the moment,
The future only then rapidly unfolds upon us.
How you lived and loved,
Will return to you.

We will reach our mend,
As only time will make us bend
As life and love flows within us.
It is in our children's lives, and before us.
I pray, they too find love.
They will need it more, than us folks
Preach nothing else, but 'pure love'
For there are no real degrees, that separate us,
Me from you, my love.

A time will come my children,
When she, my Queen of hearts, will be with me,
None of you, will feel like King.
And he will be with her, yet the favorite one,
The youngest will be afar South, beneath us
Then a time shall come, when a wafer-thin margin separates them.
A girl will come along, on the steps of a Basilica,
And take you towards the coffee beans arabica.
This trade has been on since Maya's time immemorial
Love often ends feelings mercurial.

He is like salt, you cannot eat without him,
You cannot live with all life excesses, minus him.
From the joker, 'the booti' the infuser of life.
Save him. And you all will be one.
You will all kiss each other lovingly,
Or die with divinity blessedly.

There will be just no, None.
No degrees of separation from being one.
No degrees of separation, between us.

Ashu, looking at the words, read and re-read the same, a number of times. His tears welled up but none came out.

He looked up in the moonlit night to find Sanjeevni upon him.

"Bhai, what is all this? I cannot understand some of it. And the end parts, none of it."

"It appears like some sort of message from him, in hints and riddles. Some of it is just his verse and rhyme, but some of it appears like it is a prophecy. As if warning us in some way, that we must be together as a family. Yet he guides us, to live in the present. It is very difficult to find a balance of a sole meaning from his writing, but based on my time with him, I know he doted on mother. Yet mother feels let down a bit by not just these writings, but by also his being snatched away from her."

Ashu looked into Sanjeevni's eyes for more and nodded in affirmation for him to continue.

"It has suddenly transfixed her attention, on us and makes her cling to us, due to his absence. Earlier it was an obsessive desire to explore, briefly it was even anger to return to the hinterland, later there were moments of love between our parents, which I observed as the eldest, and now there seems to be detachment from everything." expressed Sanjeevni.

"It is difficult for you alone, to keep our family together *'BootiBhai'*. Maybe father just penned things down based on his observations of all of us here. Do not be so serious and intense. Live your own life too." suggests the ever-effervescent Ashu.

Bubbling back to the present, he attempted to derive no special meaning from the work. "It is just a piece of work, like memorabilia he has tried to leave for mother. You are interpreting it to be a prophetic prediction." Ashu himself had one keen eye on the future, and one on his current present state of being.

There was in Ashu a more direct sort of love and romance ingrained in him. He sought pleasure, not pain, and wished to explore his youth, not dig his past or delve on his parents aged past.

I have written something myself too, shared Sanjeevni.

"Let's share it with mother, so that our collective memory will record the correct events, and the memory of our father. To me, he was a true friend I could turn to, when I would not understand the reasons behind decisions, he would painfully sit and explain things to me."

"Bhai, it will be too much for me in one night..."

"Read on Ashu...it is important for me. The earlier one was important for our Ma."

Ashu unfolded the second piece of paper, it was on the letterhead of 'Indian Hospitality Resorts', the hotel room stationary, which he pulled out from the same hotel envelope.

"Baaba": our father

He never looked for appreciation,
He loved us all, never one to boast.
He just went on quietly...working,
For the ones he loved the most.

He seldom spoke of his dreams,
His needs being very few.
Most of his own worries,
Went unspoken with us too.

He was someone we could all turn to,
Though unsure himself, if he could do the same,
For his life went through twists, n turns.
Till he left us here settled and true.

-Sanjeevni

"Where is all this coming from, Bhai?" Ashu dazed, looks up at Sanjeevni.

Sanjeevni is silent. Ashu remains silent.

The night crickets suddenly fall silent, as if waiting on the brothers. He puts his arm around his shoulder and offers.

"Let us all step down and sleep together below. I will accompany you tomorrow to the resort."

The next morning, Ashu wakes up, to find Sanjeevni and Hari are asleep in the outer room. He observes Maya quietly, acting as if he is still asleep.

She closes their bedroom door, the common sitting area where they congregate and eat, is merely partitioned with her old Rajasthani curtains. They were her old Kota sarees at one time.

Ashu remembers it was Khazan's ingenuous suggestion to convert her sarees into curtains.

He watches his mother slip out to the veranda, with the transistor in hand to start her day. After her tea is consumed, he can listen to the music within… from the Raj Kapoor movie Dharam Karam "….*sawal gori, leke, tere mere mann ki dori…….Ek din bik jayega maatti ke….*" *It is the song which Maya was listening at the start of the day yesterday.*

The eternal romanticist, Ashu listens to the same number, with only ears for the romantic lines. He filters the '*dharam and karam*' of it away. He knows only Raj Kapoor's son Rishi, and not the fact that it was the father who had directed the son in Bobby who was singing now in 'Dharam Karam' which was the next RK Production.

He has understood last night, what his father and now Sanjeevni has impressed upon him. But he had acted ignorant with his elder brother.

He always knew love is the only way.

Khazan too had just reconfirmed it.

Ashwini carefully folds and keeps his father's select playing cards, including the two fives, of diamond and heart suit, and the *Degrees of Separation* prophecy which Sanjeevni has handed to him at night.

He neatly packs it into his leather folder, and saves it carefully to carry it wherever he would go until he settled down.

He did not know then, that he would in his later years, read that prophecy, again and again, and again.

11

JYOTI & THE PEACOCK

1981

Jyoti has come to settle around nine in the morning, near the kitchen work area. She has had her bath, and her wet hair over her right ear lobes comes out of her saree over her head. The locks of hair rest nicely under her chin. There is freshness in her face, and yet the sweat due to the heat inside the house, starts to trickle down her fair neck

She sits on a mid-size stool so that she neither crouches nor stands for long, to do her own work. She helps Maya cut and chop the vegetables. Today her task is to break the fenugreek leaves and the coriander leaves using her bare hands, separating them lightly from their stalks. She picks the clean ones and places them aside in a large utensil which is usually used to knead the wheat with water. The unclean ones are brushed by her bare left hand index finger and thumb with a light rub.

It reminds her of her adolescent days in the garden at Indian resorts where she used to assist her mother Sulakshna.

As Sanjeevni and his mother Maya used to visit the resort to sell their powdered wheat and millet, they used to linger and talk. She can still visualize that scene, when the shy Sanjeevni used to stand alongside gaping at the lawns rather than talk to Jyoti.

After eighteen months of periodic visits, each being only once a month Jyoti had seen all the plain and checked shirts that Sanjeevni wore. As he never spoke, she could see him plainly looking the other way and notice the days he even repeated some of the shirts. He had still not mustered the guts to look her in the eye and talk.

Upon arrival at the resort, he would acknowledge her presence with a dry nod, as both the mothers stood and spoke.

Maya had observed Jyoti closely and would always from afar inspect her hygiene and sense of attire. This was not known to Sanjeevni who would simply look down at her feet, silently admiring Jytoi's penchant for changing her nail polish every month.

Jyoti had no personal sense of romance or love till then, other than what she had observed in Indian movies like Mr. Natwarlal and Ram Balram.

The commonality with Sanjeevni was the impact that superstar Amitabh Bachchan was having on both of them from his bigger than screen image as a movie star. Her idea of love was the one the village belle and simple girl had for the star in those movies. Maya knew that she was the only daughter Sulakshna had, and observing her sense of neatness, started speaking to her while she plucked small flowers from the garden. The resort manager used the same flowers every morning to welcome new guests and the additional flowers were used by Jyoti to string a garland of marigold to welcome future guests in the evening.

In the second year of the visits to the resort, Maya had an extended period of ill health for a couple of months. This placed Maya in an indisposed condition and led her to appoint Ashu to go along with Sanjeevni to deliver the monthly wheat to Indian Resorts. It was the summer of 1980, and Maya felt Sanjeevni had grown in age as he was nearing twenty-five and could now deliver the goods himself, count the cash and walk to and from the Resort. Ashwini had managed to buy a second-hand cycle that he would use to loiter around and that was used to load some extra sacks. The cycle was pushed by the smarter younger brother.

Though Sanjeevni had the brawn to carry the load himself he was thankful to cover the two-kilometer distance with comfort of the cycle. They reached the resort sooner than usual.

Fate is the best friend of lovers for it causes collisions by accident when the future has a beloved in store for you.

Jyoti's mother was not tending to the gardens on that day and Jyoti was the only person present on the premises.

Acting as the liaison between the head cook and the gardens fresh produce of vegetables, Jyoti chose to make Sanjeevni and Ashu wait for their turn for a good half an hour.

The impatient Ashu was silenced by Sanjeevni as the elder sibling felt he was the more responsible and experienced out of the two.

"How long does she think she needs to make us wait in the sun? We have already spent half an hour loading and carrying the wheat here!" says Ashu.

"It is okay, relax, we will need to take our goods further to the Jaipur market then which will be more inconvenient. It is better we dispose if off here." responded Sanjeevni.

Jyoti was within ear shot and could listen to the brothers debate the subject, she calls out to Sanjeevni, gesticulating and asking him to alone come forward.

"Come here, and see what your mother had delivered previous month!" she shouts, posing in a commanding way. Jyoti is bare foot. She has been waiting to see Sanjeevni alone someday and with the elders not being around it gives her an ideal opportunity to play a prank.

Ashu observes silently and does not yet smell a rat, this being his first visit.

Sanjeevni speaks, "Do not blame our mother. We are the ones who process the wheat and get it in this powder form. There is no question of any mistake as we do it ourselves and grind it inhouse. What is really the matter?" he asks looking straight back at her, and not her eyes anymore.

Jyoti quickly covers her head with her saree, and plays along, "There are small stones and '*kankkar*' in the wheat. Are our guests supposed to eat pebbles? How can you farmers take it so lightly?" she quips. She hands him over tiny granular sort of miniature marble like stones.

"These stones may have been added by you from your garden. There are similar ones on your feet right now. They are from your own resort garden and not from our farm. Our soil is more fertile for crops and does not grow the flowers which are here. The pebbles come from your own soil which requires your wetter and muddier soil" responds Sanjeevni.

"Oh ho, so I am the culprit? Someone really loves his farm and his mother at the same time. Where is the scope for such a man to love a woman of his age?" says Jyoti teasingly.

As Sanjeevni goes redder in the face Ashu takes this as a signal to come forward pushing his cycle. Its pedals start moving more furiously than the pace of Sanjeevni's heart, as the cycle's chain falls loose suddenly.

"My Flower-like-sister, why are you harassing my noble brother? I promise this consignment has no such issues and you can check it. Maybe '*BootiBhai*' can help you to check through the wheat? Strain it. If the old one has issues, why don't you call the head chef and we can inspect the wheat together" says Ashwini authoritatively.

He maintains a cool exterior and calm disposition.

Jyoti knows her trick is caught by the impish younger brother and looks at him squarely, "Looks like your elder brother does not have a tongue, or he cannot think fast enough on his feet."

"Maybe both sister and maybe that is good for you, isn't it?" returns Ashwini. Ashu waits till Jyoti reasons, that with another man, the situation could have become a heated argument.

As Sanjeevni relates to what is going on, he starts to say something, but then stares at Jyoti's face, finding her yet demure looks gazing back at him. He realizes that the light orange color kurta shirt he is wearing is similar in shade to her peach sari and the nail polish adorning Jyoti's feet. He simply freezes.

A peacock appears from behind the storehouse of the kitchen in the back lawns of the resort and first attempts to stare at the trio, and then turns its back on them.

"Lo behold there goes a pretty bird" says Ashu, as if to break the impasse and create a diversion for the unmatchable couple.

Both Jyoti and Sanjeevni take turns to admire the peacock and then each other from top to toe.

It appears to Sanjeevni that he is looking at a woman for the first time in his life. He has never observed Jyoti so minutely before, her hair, her eye-brows and her large eyes. He is lost for words and just dumbly stares on.

Jyoti now self-consciously re-adjusts her saree over her head and begins twitching her toes in ward as if attempting to conceal them. She feels that she has painted herself in the corner and is running out of time. Yet with nothing to say except offer his gaze upon her, Sanjeevni begins to turn the heat on, by looking at her unconsciously and stares at her behind.

He finds her, abruptly turning away and walk toward the store room of the kitchen. Ashwini is just about five steps behind Sanjeevni, but nearer than before, and is still balancing the wheat sacks on his cycle.

Sanjeevni shifts the weight on the middle-bar of the cycle and is about to rest, when the peacock seeing Jyoti turn toward the store flinches, and noisily shrieks and attempts to fly over her, taking flight in the direction of Jyoti.

Jyoti replicates the shriek, louder and more vociferously than the peacock, turns one hundred and eighty degrees backward in a reflex and runs toward Sanjeevni.

Seeing both the bird and Jyoti literally fly toward him, Sanjeevni flexes his thigh muscle for a moment and digs himself harder into the ground of the lawns. He is taking a posture to pull the plough further into his farm with Nandu.

Seeing a change in expression on Sanjeevni's face steadies the peacock's flight, while re-assuring Jyoti, to continue running toward him. As she had walked away in a huff some distance had come between them, and now running that backwards it was a matter of few seconds that she would be upon them.

The peacock hearing Jyoti shriek, keeps flying a path, a bit higher than its gait and grace would usually permit, and aims to target a branch on the tree that has the white 'Krishna Kamal' flowers radiating on it. The branch is protruding off the tree and is diagonally above where Sanjeevni is standing.

Ashwini was even more startled with all this. He found to his comic relief his first journey to the Indian Resorts, very entertaining and yet intriguing to see this vague chemistry between Sanjeevni and Jyoti.

There was this peacock incident now unfolding before him.

Ashu observes Jyoti's move and that of the bird from behind Sanjeevni, and takes note of Sanjeevni's posture change and coming to grip with the situation.

In ten seconds, Jyoti collides into Sanjeevni's right arm and occupies the pulpit of his chest and the bird settles on the branch above. Its impact of landing on the tree leads to some of the passion flowers to fall. The peacock has appeared as if to equip cupid to spread its magic on the couple.

Jyoti's eyes are tightly shut whilst the peacock showcases its feathers in full form, acknowledging the radiance and surety of Sanjeevni's calm presence. It ends up showering more flowers doing its delicate dance perched on the branch. The peacock has oscillated on its two feet, in a 1-2-1-2 *chachacha* sequence performing to Ashu's delight.

Sanjeevni feels her feminine grace and can sense the perfume from her well-groomed hair. He can feel her soft body in his chest and does not know whether to comfort her, embrace her, or hug her.

In his unsureness the peacock lets out another cry, and Jyoti further grimaces and hides in his arms, as innumerable passion flowers fall over both of them.

The same flower is known to act as a calming herb for locals to cure anxieties and seizures and hysteria, yet has no calming effect on the woman working in the gardens of Indian Hospitality Resorts.

The same flowers with marigold have so often been strung into a garland by her, but today each flower touching her skin, makes her feel more anxious. She shifts her own balance from one foot to the other fearing the shrieking peacock.

Ashu, from behind, seeing the expressions that Jyoti displays, reaches out to his brother by offering a simple statement, "Well done Booti Bhai, the bird could have scratched her." He observes the chachacha dance that both Jyoti and the peacock perform.

Sanjeevni knows the trap laid out by the situation and Ashu's presence and turns Jyoti around. Using the same arm, he places her more off center from his chest and tries to look her coolly in the eye, and then spins around to face Ashu who is even more sangfroid.

"It appears Ma's Lord Vishnu has presented us with a golden chance to save a woman from fear, and cure her anxiety, let us not make fun of it." Sanjeevni's words are to appease and yet mollify Jyoti.

"Sure brother, not at all" quips Ashu. "I was hoping you had the width on your chest to also comfort me if I was to run to you?" He speaks cheekily, pointing to all the three sacks of wheat he is finding difficult to balance on the cycle and nods his hair from the left side of his forehead toward the right, seeking some help from his sibling.

Jyoti walks tip toe towards the cycle, a bit crimson faced and cautiously takes one wheat sack away breaking her hands locking embrace of Sanjeevni.

"You say too much", pinching Ashu's nose as her bangles clang along her right hand.

Sanjeevni scratches the back of his neck and still observes her from behind not knowing her expression. He has comforted her all this while but not been looking at her.

As he looks up to gaze at the peacock in its full splendor, he points out, "It is just a bird and much smaller than any one of us, why fear mother nature, instead admire the beauty it offers in humans and birds." In trying to get a word from Jyoti he makes little sense to himself and the other two.

Jyoti now pleads to Ashu to help her with the cycle, turns without looking at Sanjeevni and walks behind Ashu.

She neither acknowledges nor reconfirms the sentiments of Sanjeevni. She just leaves him standing in the middle of all the flowers, as Ashu's cycle tires go all over them. Jyoti ensures she side steps the flowers.

Sanjeevni bends down, picks up with both his hands as many flowers as he can and fills both his kurta pockets with them.

He has never loved mother nature more, than this day today.

In 1970, when the land for 'Moh & Maya' had been purchased Aswhini had accompanied Khazan to

Calcutta. Maya had stayed back with Sanjeevni at Sudarshan and Sulakshna's place.

Two dozen workers were put to work on the site, to quickly make the skeleton frame of the house. One team focused to start the process of masonry for the inner ceiling, roof, cementing of the veranda, and the other for dragging the electric circuits from the junction box of the state electricity department inside the plot.

Since Sudarshan knew both state department people and the local community of workers he had assisted Maya to speed up the execution of the drawings that she had approved with Khazan, for the structure of the house.

The periphery of the property, with the well had been finished, and Maya would walk to the property site daily with Sanjeevni before the end of the day to watch the workers wind-up, and check the progress. The children were huddled up together without a choice at Sudarshan and Sulakshna's haveli.

This had led to sharing of some space of *Sulakshna's daughter – 'Jyoti's'* room. It was handed over to Maya for her comfortable stay and use of attached bathroom facilities going one level up via a private staircase.

Maya would frequent the area only in the mornings and then spend the rest of the time chatting with Sulakshna, or jointly cooking food for the children at the intermediate level which had the kitchen.

Many sesame laddoos and lime drinks with sugar, called as *'shiquanjji'* by the locals, were prepared for all at home.

During these hours Jyoti would have to revisit her own room, to collect her clothes and use the bathing area after Maya had used the same. Maya was given the preferential treatment as a guest of honor to use the bathroom first. This became a daily adjustment for Jyoti to make.

Sanjeevni with Jyoti's younger brother Raj would spend the early hours after waking up till noon, playing with *'latoo' tops* and a spinning thick yarn, teaching him to swing the rope in a jerking action. This would allow the top to spin on its nail's axis. The boys would ignore Jyoti completely during their rope tricks.

In clock-work precision like the top, Raj would go for his bath, after Jyoti would come out. She would spend time drying clothes on the clothing line atop the terrace. During that time, Sanjeevni would walk to check on the *'Moh & Maya'* construction and walk back with his mother after the daily survey.

The setting of the terrace of Jyoti's house was such that it was the highest level, and would over look all other terraces that were at a disadvantaged height compared to Sudarshan's haveli structure. She could see Sanjeevni walk back at an even kneel and pace her chores, so that she would still be at the terrace when he would come up looking for her brother. Their terrace was naturally on the third level, versus the others who were at either the one and a half or second floor height.

Sanjeevni would linger around the terrace but never spend time looking toward the side, where Jyoti would dry clothes for herself and her mother.

On one such occasion, without hesitation or any sign of shyness, Jyoti simply walked up to Sanjeevni.

Sanjeevni was just a couple of years older than her. A paltry moustache appearing above his thin lips, gawky, and awkward, Sanjeevni nearly did not react. He sees Jyoti approach him but just dumbly stares back at her.

"Who me?" he seems to say by play acting, when he can see her stand before him.

"Who else is there on the terrace you *dhappu*? Come here take a look at this vessel and help me" Jyoti had been assigned with the task to separate *small 'kankkar'*-dark colored like stones from the raw pulses.

It was that day of the week when 'black daal' would be made for lunch, mixed with kidney beans and butter. The '*maharani*' *dal*, famous in north of India, was the end product which Sanjeevni loved, but had never seen in raw uncooked form.

He had never spoken to a young girl till before this, and was bemused. With a hockey stick back in Calcutta sitting in the green grounds of his school, he saw many children play, come and go, but he never had sat with a young sweet girl like Jyoti.

Neither had he lived in the company of the same sweet kind of girl at home ever before. In this stay that still appeared like a school vacation to him, he knew there was no turning back to Calcutta. Sanjeevni had indulged in all kind of past times including kite flying with Raj and loitering about the terrace. He had never participated before this in any kitchen activity and looked at Jyoti with raw unexpecting and clean eyes. Jyoti enjoyed this as she could see he was a simpleton and he would not get half her jokes or pranks.

Sanjeevni finally ambled across to her part of the terrace and stopped at an artificially created boundary and nodded his head upwards to seek further direction from the girl.

She beckons him to come forward and squat and herself plonks down on the terrace concrete.

He comes to sit cross legged, before the girl, who is sitting with her legs tucked below her hips on one side. Her hair still not entirely strained of water, are tied inside a damp towel to keep them semi wet, so that the sun overhead can dry them gradually. He notices the Sikh-like-turban style and smiles more to himself than at her.

"What brings your parents here of all the places to settle down?" she asks.

"Your mother says your father has gone to Calcutta. I had heard Bengal is quite the place, with influence of culture, music and poetry. If you are all not from here why reside in a dusty sand field, where you will have to grow your own crops?"

She separates the dal, with a dividing line for him to use one half of the dune, her own dunes are cut into two, one set clean, and the other still needing sorting. She quickly throws out some tiny grey pebbles in the corner of the terrace that she has managed to locate from her unclean dune of dal. He watches her dexterity of her fingers and attempts to speed up his own sorting.

"Well, my grand-father was a farmer, so it is in our genes. He used to work for your grandfather. Perhaps its mother's desire to be closer to her roots." There is silence for a few seconds.

Jyoti looks up at him and urges him to continue.

"She is quite an explorer. The hope of newness and the chance for me to live and sleep under the open sky, is very exciting. I like the pure air here, the sand on the streets, there is a different kind of dryness in the air which is easy to breathe. Besides there is no stink of fish anywhere."

"Hmm…so any smell here you like?"

He continues, without really replying to her.

"Father was keen to drift back and try his hand at farming, so father and son can work together." As he completes, he finds some small stones which are light brownish color and passes them to her. She throws them on the same side of the terrace as she had earlier.

As he tries to create his own mound of the brown pulse his hand brushes against the fingers of her right palm. She uses her left palm and knocks his hand badly as if striking a stroke on a carrom board.

He yelps.

He looks up at her, a bit cross, but no words come out. He just looks at her, her radiance blinding him like the strong sun behind her. He admires her eyelashes, without really looking deep into her eyes.

She looks at him impishly and roars, "The stones and dal, not the rings of my fingers you smart guy."

"Oh, so you think I am a smart guy? Looks like I have made quite an impression."

"Your mother has taken my room, and you are sprawled on our terrace the entire morning. I would like to have you out of my house quickly." she whispers softly, changing her tone and tenor.

"Not quite the good host then. You don't seem to be like your family who are such warm hosts. Or are there stones in your heart and dal in your food? For our family if guests visit, they are like the avatar of God"

"My lord, I have my board exams coming up. I desperately need to study!"

"Oh, I do not know about that. I was never a good student. I would be happy raising cattle like my maternal grand-mother. A fresh glass of milk in the morning, a lassi in the afternoon, and butter milk to sleep at night." Sanjeevni is lost thinking about all the tall glasses of milk he would polish off at Solan and the stories his grandmother had told him.

"Why don't you become the milkman of Nawalgarh?" sarcasm dripping in Jyoti's voice.

Sanjeevni does not get it, thinking she is genuinely suggesting a potential profession.

"Not a bad idea, is there a dearth of dairies, when your father is blessed with such a large one?"

Sanjeevni knew the history from Khazan, about his grand-father and it appeared to him, that there was some dynamic of history getting recreated. He took everything that Jyoti said on face value.

She gives up and takes the entire vessel away from him, to do the work herself.

"What??" he quizzes.

He cannot figure what has upset her, so he simply sits cross legged with her.

The afternoon sun passes over them and Jyoti packs the excess quantities of the '*daal*' into three large containers and the small amount to be cooked that day in a large bowl.

That same afternoon, Sanjeevni was served fresh wheat rotis by Jyoti hot from the kitchen 'tandoor'.

As Maya sat at the table with her son Sanjeevni was served by Jyoti, who had specially rolled them and coated them in ghee.

Maya's rotis were served to her by Sulakshana.

As Sanjeevni bit into each of them a resounding crunch or two were encountered by him in each roti, as his teeth continued gnashing them together with the rest of the morsel.

As it all got mixed with his food, it was too late to separate the gravel, from the vegetables, and the saliva in his mouth.

Maya looked at him to enquire if everything was all right, and Sanjeevni gamely smiled and continued munching.

"Jyoti makes lovely food too, but its early for her to cook the dal on slow fire." says Sulakshana.

"It's good Mausi. She should focus just on the rotis. They are appropriately colored with the black freckles on top..." grudges Sanjeevni, hiding his criticism from his expression.

"...and stuffed with black stones within" mutters Jyoti to herself.

They are seated on the eight- seater marble dining table with the children at the head of the table on two different ends, and Raj with his mother at the center with Maya opposite.

Jyoti glares at him with devil in her eyes.

She is just having her fun with her first male visitor to their house, and enjoys the clash of yin and yang.

Confident and keen to complete her education, she is never too happy with her mother discussing her culinary habits. She is not interested in the kitchen matters at all, like these senior women she thinks.

As she chews on her food slowly, she wraps her left finger, with her hair dangling from her left ear and scowls back at Sanjeevni while the two mothers are lost in their banter again

That day at the India hospitality resorts, as Sanjeevni got up picking up the passion flowers and pocketing them in his kurta, he remembers, that he thankfully no longer has the gawky pencil thin moustache, but *'dhappu'* that he was he had forgotten to connect the pebbles and stones story to the old '*kankkar*' prank Jyoti had played on him.

It took Sanjeevni some time to figure out the feelings within him and to recognize that *Ms. Yin had snared Mr. Yang and that their yin and yang had gotten intertwined.*

12

SANJEEVNI LEAVES NAWALGARH.

The 1980's

It was the summer of 1982.

Songs of Amitabh Bachchan movies blared one after another on the radio and playback singer Kishore Kumar had become his default voice. The star had a string of releases in the past year, with hits like *Naseeb, Barsaat Ki Ek Raat, Lawaris, Yaraana, Kaalia, and Silsila.*

The movie audiences lapped up his movies as if there was no other hero in town.

"*Chu kar, mere mann ko, kiya toone, kyaa ishara....*" a melody from Mr. Bachchan's Yaraana was doing the rounds on the family radio. Dinner was being laid by Maya at her regular pace inside '*Moh & Maya.*'

The family now had a small fridge in the kitchen and the curd set earlier in the afternoon was removed from the chiller by Ashu to assist his mother.

Sanjeevni's romance had blossomed on the watch of Ashu, who knew right from the start where it was headed. He would share a rapport with Jyoti during their Resort visits, and pull her leg, about not being able to evince much of a response from Sanjeevni.

Eventually it had been Ashu, who had played cupid, and brought the matter before Maya that evening, over dinner.

"*Rang jamake, aaye hain, chakkar chalake jayenge…*" blared on the radio from the soundtrack of Manmohan Desai's magnum opus. Ashu looked at Sanjeevni seated before him, who innocently stared back.

"Ma, Booti Bhai is old enough to be married." A blob of curd dropped from Sanjeevni's spoon. He looked up quizzingly at Ashu.

"I know son, but you know your brother he does not have any interest in marriage." replied Maya.

She looked up at Sanjeevni, while the T.V. had been flicked on by Hari. He was more interested to watch the color visuals on television's '*Chayageet*' songs, a program that had become popular.

"*Mere angne main, tumhara kya kaam hai…*" blared Mr. Bachchan's voice. "*Jiski biwi chotti, uska bhi bada naam hai….*"

"Hari either keep the Tv on low volume or switch off the radio" said Sanjeevni a bit irritated.

Hari gets up a second time, in between his dinner, and turns off the radio kept above the kitchen fridge. The transistor is the same radio equipment that Maya used to listen to from their *Punjab Sweet house* days. It had been relegated for Maya's use as the brothers, except Sanjeevni, preferred watching television.

Ashu spoke again, "You will be surprised ma, Bhai has eyes for girls these days."

"There is no such thing", replied Sanjeevni curtly.

Maya watches Ashu intently goading him to go on. Ashu is having some simple fun, ribbing his elder brother. He is keen to hint to Maya, that the time has come.

"I had thought that I should speak to the store manager at the India Hospitality Resorts. His sister's niece is of marriageable age he mentioned, before I stopped going to the resorts. I can ask Sudarshan Bhai to intervene and introduce us" says Maya innocently. She is talking to Ashu and exchanging looks with Sanjeevni who is silently eating his third roti.

"There is no need mother" comes in Sanjeevni coolly. "I am just twenty-six and there is ample time."

"Half your age is gone, and the other half will also pass by like this. By the time I am fifty-two at least you should have made me a grand-mother." Maya has been counting the years since Khazan's death and is worried that she too could be at the end of her own life.

Heart of heart she was thankful that her two boys had grown up before her husband had left for his heavenly abode. She looks up to Goddess Laxmi's photograph in the 1982 calendar that hangs loosely from the doorknob of the kitchen cabinet.

"Your other sons are there, why don't you wait for them to take the plunge?" retorts Sanjeevni.

"For that we need you to clear the way" explains Ashu. "Mother holds on to her sequence to settle us, in the same order she gave birth to us. I have no problem if you wish you can talk to Sudarshan uncle for me."

Maya stares on dumb struck.

"Jyoti *didi* will be too old for him, mother" replies Hari, tongue and cheek.

Sanjeevni turns crimson.

"It is the chilies…mother how many have you put in the *daal* tonight?" he says deflecting the topic without taking a position.

Maya stares at Ashu. He winks.

Hari has his mouthful with rice in his hand.

Both the brothers point toward Sanjeevni who has gotten up hurriedly to wash his plate and keep the bowls cleaned up at the side of the kitchen sink.

Maya now understands and it slowly sinks in. She goes about bobbling her head with a big, "O" as if suppressing a yawn between her lips.

Sanjeevni lingers and keeps his back turned to Maya.

The mother waits as she cannot see his face and judge his emotions.

"Where will we all stay and how will we fit in this house...?" Sanjeevni turns around, "…if I were to get married?"

"Oh, is that it?" questions Maya. "You are ready to tie the knot then? I will make the arrangements you do not worry about that."

"The terrace is open for you Bhai! The sky's the limit for you remember?" Ashu pulls his brother's leg risking to mock him even further.

Maya decides to pin him down.

"Are you keen specifically for Sulakshna's daughter?" she looks at Sanjeevni.

Both the brothers look up at their elder sibling, stalling their food as their eyes pierce him for an answer.

"Her name is Jyoti" says Sanjeevni, exasperated. "If we take no dowry and you are fine with the girl, only then I am fine."

Maya is elated. "Oh yes I am fine with that girl, she has already been coming to our house so often since childhood. So, you have had your eyes on Jyoti? Why did you not tell me earlier?"

"Nothing like this mother, it is just that you are also comfortable as she has been visiting us from Hari's birth time. You know her mother, and her father is unwell. So, there is no question of give or take. I will agree, only if she comes to our house with her few pair of clothes." advises Sanjeevni.

"I also love the milk that comes from that house," chips in Hari. "I hope that will not completely stop?" Everyone breaks into laughter.

Sanjeevni married Jyoti in the winter of 1982. The marriage was held in a small ceremony at Sulakshna and Sudarshan's haveli at the same terrace where Sanjeevni used to spin his top.

The couple with all family members had just to walk back with the girl.

As Jyoti's father had been in poor health for preceding years, the dairy business had been curtailed down to just two cows for their own family.

It was the year of the Asian Games in New Delhi.

The sale of colour TV sets had gone through the roof in cities. Sanjeevni had already procured theirs earlier that year with some help from Ashu via Jaipur.

Suddenly the cinematic experience of full technicolor was brought into the household in Indian homes.

The family had enjoyed many movies on *Doordarshan* on Sundays and song sequences on the musical programs of Chayageet. For Sanjeevni, there was another reason of color in his household, as the vacuum created by his father's loss had been filled to some extent for him by the vivacious nature and vibrant garments of his wife.

Jyoti infused the house with her energy and small private jokes with Sanjeevni leading to smiles and laugher in '*Moh & Maya*' after many years. The musical notes floating in the air from the same transistor radio sounded so fresh, melodious and romantic to the couple. Each had found someone new in their life to divert their love energies into.

Maya was joyous for many reasons; her eldest son had got married and Sulakshna's daughter had come into her house. Maya saw it as some sort of karmic cycle and she felt it bode well for all the three brothers.

Maya knew that with a smaller age gap Jyoti would be like a friend and a lifelong companion to Sanjeevni.

Subsequent to the marriage, Sanjeevni had decided to visit Delhi in 1983 for more work as now all three brothers were at home. He wanted to complete the harvest, and show his brothers the details of division of wheat, sesame, and mangoes for the resort and their own home. He was also desirous to set up a link with Delhi's supply merchants to have some sort of direct trade in the city from the farm land.

Post the summer of 1983, India won the world cup of cricket in June. The entire nation had watched the victory on television. The Captain of India, a very rustic looking Kapil Dev had brought the sports trophy, the "Prudential Cup" home. It had acted as a trigger and created a burning desire to move to greener pastures amongst many men all over India.

Though India did loose terribly in the ensuing test series from West Indies, the ODI World champions title for the next four years was India's honor. It had made many believe that they too could travel for higher education overseas from urban cities. A certain restlessness overcame the country.

Ashu and Sanjeevni both recognized that with passage of time, soon Hari would be old enough to manage things at the farm. Sanjeevni migrated to Delhi in search of work in the winter of 1983.

He landed at the Delhi railway station, with one small bag, and a '*jhola*' strapped on his shoulder, with a copy of his marriage photograph with Jyoti, his few belongings and the water '*mashk*' which he had used from his younger years.

He had made Jyoti understand that the family would be able to prosper more, by continued cultivation of their land and that she should continue helping mother. The idea was to have another source of income from the city, that could supplement the farm income and some savings get created for the family. There was no promise for her to move with him, as he knew he was going into the unchartered territory. After celebrating their first year Holi and Diwali Sanjeevni had set foot out of Nawalgarh.

On that first evening at New Delhi Railway station, he had encountered a taxi driven by a Sikh turbaned driver, who had driven him around India Gate and then taken him to South Extension. At Bengal sweets Sanjeevni had evinced interest to work for a "mithai' shop and the Sikh gentleman, who himself enjoyed his snacks and tall lassi with cream, had recommended, "South-Ex". After eating his early evening dinner there, Sanjeevni had bravely asked for some work, from the owner of the shop.

"Do you know how to work in the kitchen?" asked Pran the owner. It was merely a coincidence that the owner's name signified life, while Sanjeevni's was symbolic with the herb, that reinfused it.

"I can only wash the dishes" replied Sanjeevni. The Sikh driver, who had stayed back to enjoy the meal with his customer witnessed the conversation. "But I have worked the fields at my own farmland in Nawalgarh. I can do any hard work in the sun."

"I cannot keep you with your Labrador pet dog. He will chase my customers away. And furthermore, I have no space to host you to sleep at night." replied *Pransahab.*

The owner of Bengal Sweets was a simple Marwari businessman practical and keen to help, but pragmatic too. The Sikh Gentleman, was about to offer a few nights stay at his '*taxiwalla*' dormitory when Mr. Malhotra, from the next table interjected.

Mr. Mony from his optician shop had earlier walked across, to enjoy his evening samosas with his neighbor Pran and was waiting on him. He had overheard the entire conversation and observed Sanjeevni's tough built and rural honesty, with frugal belongings. He was also attracted to Tiger at the feet of Sanjeevni outside the shop, not moving an inch.

Tiger was without a leash or collar at the neck, yet ready to his command, he could see the dog's loyalty to the Rajasthani man.

"Will you work with me? I have a small vegetable garden, growing cauliflower and fenugreek at the back of my house. I could do with some additional security too, as there are some buffoons who throw stones on my car from across the street."

"Sure sire, how kind can you be? Will you be able to get me some space to sleep at night? I can work through the day and just need the open sky to sleep under."

"You can sleep on our roof. It has a part terrace extension built over our bedroom and is shaded due to the water tank that is raised. You can sleep under the tank in the summers."

"Sir, you are God sent," said Sanjeevni. "I am habituated to sleep under the stars. How will I ever thank you Pransahab? Your food has nourished me and your shop has been so lucky for me to find this Saheb."

"Mony Malhotra is my name! How much pay do you desire?" asked the pot-bellied Mony. He had wrapped up, dunking his samosas into the sweet tamarind *chutney* and gulping them down. It was time to leave.

"Sire, enough to save and send back a few thousand rupees to my mother." Sanjeevni had calculated that he would actually also sell the wheat, either to Praan Saheb or some other contacts via the Sikh Taxiwalla he had befriended.

He could not ask for more on his first night.

It was getting late, so Mony Malhotra agreed to his terms and Sanjeevni agreed to move his belongings into Mr. Malhotra's car. He bid goodbye to the Sikh Taxi driver sharing Mony's address with him.

Mr. Malhotra had pointed out at his shop opposite Bengal Sweets.

Mony had made Sanjeevni keep his belongings in the boot of his car, and asked him to hop in with Tiger. The three of them, driven by Xavier, the driver sped off towards Malhotra Niwas.

That night, Sanjeevni rolled out his military style '*holdall*' – opened the makeshift mattress '*bistar-bandh*' and sprawled out on the terrace of Malhotra Niwas. Thus began the continued sleep below the stars for Sanjeevni, and he looked up at the moon.

The terrace was equipped with an old pocket transistor that the Nepali cook Thappa at Malhotra Niwas and the driver Xavier used to share.

Flicking the radio onto the *All-India Radio* channel he was amused at his luck, listening to the 1977 hit number that his brother Ashu was fond of. "*Chand Mera dil, Chandni ho tum...*" from the 1977 blockbuster *Hum Kisi Se Kum Nahin* sang to him as if Jyoti had wished it upon him.

He recollected 'Chintu' *Kapoor* the Bobby star and remembered how Ashu was struck by the film when they were young kids. He could visualize his younger brothers gorging on the vanilla ice creams during the interval of that movie they had seen together.

He could see the radiant moon beaming back at him with beady eyes that appeared like Jyoti. The innocence of the smiling moon was reflecting a silver light upon him at the terrace like the joy that Hari would give him and created the same cool presence like that of Maya. He could feel his mother was still around him, due to the terrace and moon setting and found his attachment and fondness for his family tug at his heart.

Smiling back at the moon, he prayed for all his family members and delved into his sweet dreams, rolling off into dreamland.

13

ASHU'S TRAVELS

The kharif harvest of 1984 was bountiful. Ashu was exhilarated at the profits the land had made the family. He had held ground for the family in his eldest sibling's absence, commanding Hari around the land. Sanjeevni had convinced the family to apply for a telephone line at their '*Moh & Maya*' residence and sent enough money back for Maya to run the house for another year.

Hari was now just 13 but he looked like an eighteen-year version of Sanjeevni. He was taller and broader than Ashwini. The television had only Hari as its sole loyal viewer as other home occupants had lost interest to sit together before the *telly*.

The movie *Sharaabi* had released in the May of 1984 and was a roaring hit all over India. Jyoti would wait to listen to the song, "*Inteha hogayi, intezar ki...*" over the radio and Ashu would rib her about Sanjeevni's absence.

Jyoti felt her married life had fallen into waiting for eternity to end, for her to be able to just see her hero, her husband. Songs of the Subhash Ghai movie '*Hero*' resonated with her and she remained glued in the evenings to the same transistor radio that Maya would hear in the mornings.

In the Indian film industry other heroes like Dilip Kumar, Rajesh Khanna were still managing to get work, but it was super star Mr. Bachchan who towered above all, with his movies being awaited with the maximum anticipation.

In 1985 Ashu conveyed over the phone conversation he had with his brother that he had decided to follow him to Delhi. It had been just a couple of years after Sanjeevni had left. In the month of April that year the elder brother received Ashu at the New Delhi Railway station. Maya had thought, that Ashu would return after meeting Sanjeevni at his work place. Sanjeevni knew better than that, as he had witnessed Ashu's restlessness earlier.

Ashu had already completed his graduation a few years earlier in History and quit his work for the hospitality chain at the palace. Prior to return to Nawalgarh he had commenced work as the assistant estate manager of Jaipur's royal family. After that stint he realized he was not fond of the life inside palaces and forts, as he was witnessing the same scenery. He came out of that experience richer, with a small belly and began to sport a moustache.

Upon his arrival in Delhi, Sanjeevni had decided to take Ashu to the same snack shop in South Extension hoping that '*PranSahab*', would be as lucky for Ashu.

PranSahab was yet to commence work at the shop.

"Bhai, the time has come, for me to move onward" said Ashu as he sipped a cup of tea.

"You have just reached Delhi, and you are already making plans?" says Sanjeevni a bit heatedly, while drinking the hot milk in his steel glass. He had taken the day off and was hoping that '*Mony Saheb*' would also get to meet Ashu in the afternoon.

"No Bhai, I have an onward ticket to Bombay, by Rajdhani. I had bought this with help from my friend Javed Jaipuri. I have to catch the train before four in the afternoon today."

Sanjeevni fell silent. He knew, he had already stalled Ashu's progress and travel plans earlier. He also knew that Hari and Jyoti were now back home with Maya at Nawalgarh, and he was alone enough to take care of their needs, besides the land's bountiful crop that did the needful.

His money was being saved by Maya and she still had some gold that was being held by her for Jyoti and the future daughter in laws.

"It is your wish Ashu, it is just that I never expected this so fast. I thought, I will have someone of my own with me in Delhi" said Sanjeevni dryly.

"Brother, if I had told you, mother would not have let me come." replied Ashu. "You all are too conservative for me. I just wish to explore. In the end, we can all meet at Nawalgarh."

Ashu had a bent of mind towards the film city of Bombay right from the start. He was intrigued by what he saw in the films and especially the romantic songs he enjoyed.

For Sanjeevni music was just the background but for Ashu the romance he witnessed in the songs of the Hindi movies was intoxicating.

When he would watch or listen bewitched, it was like the air he breathed had been diluted with '*bhaang*' the Indian hemp plant. It had mind altering properties that was drawing him toward Bombay since childhood.

At the same time Ashu was also a bit more educated than Sanjeevni and he had cast his ambitions a bit higher. He was used to aiming for the stars, and enjoyed the sense of adventure having left Nawlagarh for Jaipur. He was keen now to expand his circle of influence.

In comparison Sanjeevni was more rooted to the north as he needed to stay closer to Jaipur, and Jyoti.

Both the brothers enjoyed their jalebis.

Sanjeevni had them with milk and Ashu with his tea.

During that afternoon Sanjeevni was hoping either Pransaheb or Monty Malhotra would surface, and they could convince or lock Ashu up at Malhotra Niwas with him. Sanjeevni felt a tad bit hurt and recognized quietly to himself Ashu's ability to surprise him. He had no choice but to respect his desire to chase his selfish goals that he alone drew up and later simply announced to the elder sibling.

Sanjeevni felt in those moments, that a chapter of their lives was coming to an end and perhaps a new one for Ashwini would commence, on his own accord. He also thought what his mother Maya must feel, with both of them having moved on and being left behind only with Hari and Jyoti.

The two brothers fell silent for a while.

The radio behind the payment counter interjected Sanjeevni's feelings and blurted out the song "*Lalla…, Alah Tera Nighebaan...*" from the movie Abdullah. The song had starred his father's favorite, the forgotten and now ageing hero Raj Kapoor. Sanjeevni reminded himself that though his paternal concern was similar to the protagonist in the song, he was not Ashu's father. He had to control and stall his paternal urges and concern for his own wife and family.

In this way, the first detachment between the brothers began.

It was a strange setting, as the pandit like sales clerk behind the cash counter, sat with sandalwood on his forehead, two large portraits of '*Jagannath of Puri*' behind him. Light smoke from the '*dhoop and agarbatti*' infused a pleasant smell of jasmine and rose around the entire shop. The Urdu words in the lyrics of the Abdullah song took Sanjeevni's memories back to his father.

Sanjeevni remembered the sessions he used to have with Khazan at the fields and felt he was falling short of giving any direction to the independent minded Ashu. He could see that Ashu had now grown up in his own mind and he neither sought advice nor looked up to him as a father. Perhaps that was the real challenge.

The younger sibling saw only a friend in the elder, not a parent.

Ashu did not feel accountable.

"May the lord Jagannath, May Allah, guard you wherever you go…" blurted out Sanjeevni. He felt the family going through a further split, which was not the intended long-term plan of action when he had come to Delhi. However, he recognized that his '*Moh*' toward Ashu and the '*Maya*' of joint memories they had since Calcutta, Solan and Nawalgarh days had already come to an end when they left their mother behind and set out in the new world.

"Do not worry *Booti Bhai.* My path is different but our destination is the same. All three of us are united by our mother. We will return some day to '*Moh & Maya.*' "

Ashwini had noticed his brother's distraught sentiments and tried to offer a futuristic assurance, which Sanjeevni knew to be untrue.

"Which day will that be?" asked Sanjeevni rather dull and sad in that moment.

He could see his brother charter a separate path.

"I do not know brother but whether Lord Krsna, Jesus, or Allah, their eye will be upon me, and I will try to use their divine guidance, as my third eye." Ashu's reply had followed the trajectory of the song playing on the radio.

It amazed Sanjeevni as he always felt, that even the music was interpreted differently by Ashu.

"Bhai just remember, our '*Jannat*' our heaven, is in our parent's abode. It is where mother is, where the mango tree they planted stands. It is where we can see our farm and the *Gulmohar* tree in spring. It is where the well serves us water. If we charter a path too far and wide away from our roots, it will be very difficult for us to wind our way back." The elder sibling restrained himself, as he did not want to chide his younger brother, yet knock the senses of a persuasive argument to remain close despite the distance that was now going to be further created. Sanjeevni had thought, by his having the option to fold back to Nawalgarh, he could have always reunited the family quickly, but with Ashu also stepping out, perhaps in a few years Hari would have the same temptation.

"It is not just heaven I seek, for that we will find after our life ends, and we will meet father up there. It is my '*Mannat*' that I follow, my wish. My desire. It beckons me to answer its calling. I cannot live with despondency when there is more to life elsewhere. We are merely spending time on mother earth, and if destiny and luck has its way it will reunite us. If it does not, it will only be, because we are meant to be elsewhere and fulfil our *karma*, and perform our actions elsewhere. If we do not stretch ourselves and our imagination, we will never see and uncover new paths."

Sanjeevni is noticeably silent now and Ashu waits till his message can sink in for his elder brother. He wanted to make his elder sibling understand that rather than being fatalistic, it was perhaps better to go out and seek what is in store for one's life and create to some extent one's own destiny. Ashwini did not at that age want to rest on the laurels of his parent's abode and he never saw a full-time career in farming as his calling.

This meeting was pre-ordained by Ashwini to explain himself so that his elder sibling gets the visit as a mark of respect that he deserved. He was not sure if the effort taken by him to take the break in Delhi and specially meet his brother had been worthwhile.

"Come Ashu, let us go then. We should reach Delhi station on time. I appreciate you have made this journey and broken your journey to meet with me, to inform me personally." Sanjeevni realized that there was no stopping his younger brother.

Ashwini smiles and picks himself up with some zest.

Upon entering the Delhi railway station, Ashu offers to stop with his air-bag and buy Sanjeevni some milk.

The elder brother declines.

He is not up to it.

"Do not be sad Booti Bhai! I am not leaving you forever." He hugs his brother and Sanjeevni sheds a tear.

The embrace weakens him momentarily and the piled-up tension of another separation brings back the Calcutta memories for both the men.

They are standing near his compartment. Ashu turns back impromptu, to the railway cart and commands the vendor selling '*Joy*' ice-cream, "Two large cups of Joy please!"

He silently remembers his own father Khazan rather fondly, without any melancholy. Ashu gulps down the vanilla as if sharing the ice-cream in presence of his brother, and in absence yet remembering his father. It rekindles his spirit.

The engine whistles like an alarm clock egging them on into action for their final separation.

He realizes as he sets foot on the train, that his hands are sticky with vanilla, but he loves that fragrance on his fingers. He remembers Khazan at

Calcutta station, and bids good bye to Sanjeevni standing at Delhi Platform.

Together in that one moment, he bids goodbye to both.

The train lunges forward and in a few seconds abruptly comes to a stop a couple of meters ahead. A part of the train has shot off the platform, while half of it, still hangs on, as if not willing to leave Delhi station.

Sanjeevni has turned away, walking back towards the exit unaware of this happening. He leaves the train in the background and takes slow measured steps with tears in his eyes.

In the foreground of Ashu's vision now is a rather tall man, with wavy hair, black fat frame of spectacles falling a bit crooked on his youthful face. He has grey hair on his temples and sidelocks and appears out of nowhere, wearing a large white robe, its sash swaying in the wind.

The '*Padri*' side-pushes some coolies and attempts to embark the train. He urges Ashwini to step inside very politely, and places the singular suitcase he carries on the entrance spot, where Ashu's feet had been plonked minutes earlier.

All this hurried activity happens in a minute and the priest is now straddling the door of the train. He quickly closes the door, clamping its levers to lock it from within.

Before he knows it, Ashu is trapped inside the train, and cannot lean out of the door anymore.

The train begins to inch forward, out of the Delhi Railway station. Ashu can no longer look at the end of the train and is hurtled inside the air-conditioned train compartment by another fellow passenger lady. She has to cross him, despite her big buttocks and manages to nearly choke him with her bag, as she moves ahead of him brusquely. Her big bottom forces him sideways and her air bag knocks some air out of his breathing passage.

He is simultaneously hit by the blueness of the Rajdhani train and the increasing cool air draft. He observes many other passengers inside and the railway catering department clerk, taking orders blocking their passage.

"Move in my child" says the father from behind him, very much like a priest summoning you for a confession, calm and soft mannered.

"The train was about to leave and it appears it waited to just allow me to hop on. Father Roy Tanglewood D'Costa! You can just call me D'Costa like my friends" says the priest, offering his right hand for a shake to Ashu, the left clutching the suitcase bag. "I do play the guitar well, as my family name would suggest, but I am not from Rhode Island as the friendly name indicates."

Ashwini takes his hand and tips his head down, flicks his hair back, and pops the word out, 'Father...' out of sheer respect. As he says it, he smiles, thinking he had just bid adieu to his father and brother and all their memories. They seem to have hopped back on the train in the form of this priest.

Ashu finds the seat 26, close to the door in the second last compartment.

The priest his fellow passenger is at seat 25.

They both have been allotted the seats by way of lucky draw, a prevalence of destiny for single travelers in those days in the passage of the doorway.

The priest's allotted seat above Ashu's on the side of the passage, separating the four-family compartment.

Father D'Costa appears about ten years older to Ashu, but is nearly fifty.

His boyish looks do not deceive Ashwini.

"Sir will you be able to climb above?" quizzes Ashu.

"Off course young man, with my priestly robe, I have pants underneath and I should be able to hoist my tall frame. I can fold my legs to sleep, if they slide side-ways, do knock them back in." he laughed, and spoke lightly, enjoying the situation he is in.

"You are travelling till Bombay, father?" asked Ashu.

"Well off course, I will not get off at Rajasthan mid-way at Kota, or wherever this train cuts across. Though I would love to see Rajasthan, I will get off at the final terminus of Bombay Central and be onward to Bandra. What about your young self my lad?"

"Same here father." replied Ashu.

"And where are you from?" asked Father D'Costa.

Ashu explains his Nawalgarh background and the fact that his mother is there, while he was in Delhi to meet his elder brother.

Father D'Costa takes it as a common place event, and moves the conversation further. He folds his legs, the right over the left, pulls out a kerchief from his priestly robe and starts to clean his glasses.

"Why Bombay?" probed Father D'Costa.

Ashu keen to speak of his dreams, checks himself to be brief and posts a query back at the father, "To discover life anew sir. Do you work for a church father?"

Ashu till then had seen a priest like D'Costa only in films like the *1977 Amar Akbar Anthony*, as mostly priests wore their black robes. He is curious on the white color of the robe that father D'Costa adorns, unlike the movies, yet he does not want to do something foolish, or speak anything about religion, for he knows not much about his own. Neither does he attempt to voice aloud that the white robe brings to his mind, the superstar Mr. Bachchan who has adorned the same in the climax of that movie.

"Hmm... you seem to be well versed in English. Well, I used to work for St. Scotts School in Bombay, it is attached to the church in the same suburb. I am now with the Pure Hearts Boys School. I was trained at Kerala and moved to Bombay in 1978." The priest has cleaned his sparkling spectacles and sports them on again.

He continues, "You know, Bandra is a small quiet fisherman village, around the *Chimbai* fishing colony, and Bandra Fort. It resembles in many ways our European villages, so I decided to settle down there. You will be amazed to know that I am just returning from Germany. I managed a once in a lifetime trip to Rome and on the way back had stopped by to watch the Pakistan v/s Germany finals at the world hockey tournament. Pakistan beat West Germany 2-1, while Great Britain beat Australia. We Indians are nowhere in the top four."

The priest puts the kerchief back in his robe side-pocket and pulls out his bag, to pour himself a drink.

"Oh Father, you drink?" asks Ashu bemused and bites his lower lip for having thought aloud.

"I do not join those who drink too much wine or gorge themselves on meat, for drunkards and gluttons become poor and their drowsiness eventually clothes them in rags. Do not drink wine, which leads to debauchery, be filled with the Spirit."

Ashwini looks on silently, as Father D'Costa has a very small sip of the golden liquid, out of the big gulp he has poured himself into the steel flask glass.

"The Bible does not forbid drinking. It only warns about excess because it is immoral behavior or abuse led out of drunkenness that we must shun. I do not encourage it if you have never tasted it. I am used to a small one in the evenings to keep me warm like medicine."

He further justifies, "I am a single man and human after all. She has been my only companion since my Kottayam days. I have a doctorate in Moral Theology and believe one must enjoy whatever one does. I play soccer and hockey with my students in the day and seldom enjoy a drink alone at night to get a good sleep. The rains in Bombay can be noisy and one should stay warm in the season. I need some shut-eye tonight in the train too, as it rocks me like a baby in a cradle. Just make sure I do not fall from atop. Ha, ha, ha" he laughs and brushes off any seriousness you expected from father D'Costa. He is not solemn and dark, instead is bright and sprightly in his moment. He had an anglicized laughter, elegant, pointed yet brief. It was more an extension of his speech.

"I will sleep upstairs, don't worry sir" said Ashu, offering his bed with responsibility.

"We are both of nearly the same height, and I am younger."

"Oh, that will be kind of you, I accept your offer. But you must accept mine. I have helped to build the extension of my old school into a college and it is near my home in Bandra. I suggest you stay over the first night with me till you find your bearings. I am sure you are new to Bombay and till you make your new life, you are welcome to stay with me for a fortnight. Precisely fifteen days. After that either I will kick you out, or you must help me on the college building project and work there to assist the church."

Ashu is pleased to know the mixed range of activities this kind yet modern man is involved in and his easy-going manner is so charismatic and transparently flamboyant that he is attracted to the father as an elder. Dinner is served in the steel cut out plates, and Father D'Costa dives into his fish curry dish, while Ashu has the vegetarian one.

"Have you never tasted meats?" asks Father D'Costa. "It is good for its oil. That's the only meat I eat, otherwise I am a vegetarian like you. In fact, I do not like eggs at all. I dislike their smell when they are being cooked. I believe, fish is the further most from the human species, so it is okay."

This was typical small talk as part of the journey throws passengers together at meal times inside the speedy '*Rajdhaani*' train.

Ashu thinks about his family beliefs and convenient yet practical morals of the priest. He can see both the benefits and pitfalls by way of observation once he has set out of home. He tells himself to do as he likes and be tolerant of friendly people who like what they believe in. "Sir I believe, we must not eat anything, that has a mother." Spoke Ashu, with soft diligence, copying the priestly style without the experienced tone.

"My grand-parents would not eat onion and avoid garlic like the plague of their times. More over anything that grew underground would be avoided. With every generation, we became more tolerant and changed our eating habits based on the taste of the tongue, but as a family we rather desist and keep away from all living species."

"Plants and fruits too have a life" retorted the father to continue the debate.

"They ripen and fall sir. If fruit is not consumed as God's gift, it will just rot away and decompose in nature. Whenever I visit my home next, I will get you mangoes from our farm." Ashwini kept it short and brief as he believed in a bit of diplomacy to go far in life.

"Live as you like young man. It is the choices we make, that make or break us. Always do what you are yourself comfortable with. You are welcome to stay with me and explore the neighborhood of Bandra."

The next morning there is a quick service by the attendants who bring fresh breakfast from the pantry car and clear the trays hurriedly afterwards. Due to this there is an aroma of parathas and upma mixed with blankets and pillows soiled with hair oil, and the fresh breath of toothpaste, each time the passage door opens and shuts, engulfs the passage.

It takes the train thirty minutes to terminate, despite entering the busy intersections of Bombay stations early in the morning.

Ashu looks out of the frosted windows and gushes at the suburban trains. They seem to whiz past at double the speed due to their own and the Rajdhani's express speeds crossing each other in opposite directions.

The distance from his family now has widened and Ashu thinks about the '*choices we make that make or...*' as Father D'Costa had put it last night.

Eventually, they alight from the train at Bombay Central and without any help from the eager coolies offering their services, they step out of the station on their own. Both of them pass through the narrow passage of a grilled area on the platform that separates the train from the hustle bustle of the city.

Ashu looks back at the train and the infestation of passengers like roaches headed in different directions for other exits on the same platform. The train hisses and huffs in sobriety, tired for having made the long journey much opposite to the priest who with his new found day has a spring in his step.

Father D'Costa exudes a sober freshness with his black slick hair combed back in waves. He confidently hails the first square top *Fiat Premier Padmini Taxi* which awaits passengers in a serpentine queue of more taxis behind it.

Ashu is thankful to have met the priest on the train as he can hear the yelling and observes the haggling of fares on the other side of the road, where new passengers are alighting to catch the outbound trains.

Both the passengers sit at the back of the compact cab with their bags atop the steel grid carrier on the taxi's roof tied tightly with a nylon rope. Ashwini intently observes the '*carrier*' atop taxis ahead of theirs and notes its similarity in design and shape, but difference in size and utility, to the *carrier* they had fitted behind the leather seats of their cycle in Nawalgarh. He tries to calculate the number of sacks of wheat they could transport with such a mechanism if he had a Bombay taxi back in Nawalgarh.

"That's the Maratha Mandir cinema, where Sholay has been running in a matinee show for many years. Do you watch '*Hindi*' movies?" asks the cab driver.

Father D'Costa gesticulates to Ashwini to take over the conversation as he attempts to take a brief nap.

As the taxi crawls ahead of the traffic signal, it leaves the thousand seat theatre at the back, and cuts into one of the nine-roads of the "*nau-raasta*" and tapers down *Mahalaxmi* station toward *Worli*, a local village.

"Where does Rajesh Khanna live?" asks Ashu to the driver as their banter continues.

"At *Carter Road*, I will show you. We will be in Bandra in a few minutes. There is no rush on Sundays and usually traffic is trim" speaks Father D'Costa, keeping his eyes shut continuing to dive in and out of sleep and yet keeping track of the conversation Ashu attempts to have with the '*taxiwallah*.'

Ashu is self-absorbed, looking at the different shape of each and every taxi compared to the bulkier ambassador in Delhi that had ferried him "Is everything here as cramped as the cabs?" asks Ashu to the driver.

The cabby explains to Ashu that both the compact models are called 'Fiats' due to their engines, the only difference being the front doors of the older cabs opening front to back on the front compartment. Those vehicles were called '*dukker*' fiats. The new cars had both the compartment doors opening like wings from the front and center.

"Ha, ha, ha!" came the anglicized laughter from D'Costa. "Well, not my church, nor my school. You must visit both the St. Scotts and the Pure Hearts School and participate with my students for football or hockey on Sundays. It is our fun day next week and you will see a lot of space in those grounds."

The taxi arrives at the apartment which Father calls his home, a quiet lane behind *Chimbai*.

Father D'Costa opens his apartment door, with a key from a chain of crosses, and Ashu is brought inside with plain kindness.

The house inside is spartan and as uncomplicated as his fellow passenger from Delhi. He is amazed by the priest's open heartedness to bring with him a rank stranger to his house. Perhaps his life story of education in Jaipur and studying under the English teacher there has impressed Father D'Costa.

The priest orders him to fetch some fruit buns to enjoy for lunch with butter and directs him to go outside and explore the local bakeries. He hands out some twenty and ten rupee notes generously to Ashu. The father explains to him to give him thirty minutes so that he can sweep and clean his flat on the inside and open the windows of all the rooms facing the back of the compound to eliminate the mustiness in the closed flat.

Ashu steps out within minutes to discover the suburb he has been excited to see and explore. It is a similar fishing village as was shown in the movie Bobby, and it is Ashu's first day in Bombay.

As he walks the periphery of the sea-face at '*Chimbai Gaothan*', he is bewildered with the closeness of short building structures to each other.

He walks by a huge cross built on a base red cemented stone. As he moves out of the lane onto the junction he observes a simple white lettering on a black background short hoarding over the compound wall of the church, with the quote, "*I will walk by faith even when I cannot see.*"

As he reaches near the gates of St. Andrew's Church, some elderly couples walk out after their morning mass dressed like 'English' babus. He asks them for directions toward Bandra Fort and is told to slip along sideways and walk on the other side of the church compound.

The church building is simple, creamy colored with some blackness of rain and ruin.

As he reaches the other-side he smells the fresh salty sea and takes some deep breaths. He feels excited and exhilarated as the wind blows on his face.

He swings his head from left to right side, to rest his hair locks off the left side of the forehead in his trademark style. He had last had a haircut a month ago and his hair falls at the nape of his neck, covering both the ears. Entirely the trendy super-star haircut to sport in Bombay, Ashwini walks like the stars he has seen on the silver screen.

He keeps his faith as the church hoarding has forewarned him, and with confidence walks alone. The sun in all its glory says hello to greet him to the sea shore at eleven that eventful morning. It's a breezy day than usual, the vastness of the Arabian sea hits him as he walks closer to the rocks. He had missed seeing the sea-face at *Worli and Mahim,* the station taxi taking the more industrious route via *Dadar and Matunga's* interior artery roads.

He walks along the Bandstand, as it is famously known, staring at high rises on the other side of the road. He reaches a round, circular, gondola like structure, at the mid-point of Bandstand, and can see an old British built structure with Victorian pillars on the opposite side. He walks up to the villa. He reads the name "Villa Vienna" as he approaches the old structure, it is lying amidst some stray grass in open ruins, with a spoilt, spent garden from afar. It appears to be an abandoned old Parsi house facing the sea, yet with not much height, the land automatically giving it a vantage position.

As Ashu ambles on, the road converges and moves like a rail track tapering toward Bandra fort. He recognizes the spot to be the location for the confrontation scene of Ramesh Sippy's Shakti, starring the duo-Superstars, the reigning Amitabh Bachchan, and the outgoing senior Dilip Kumar. The movie had led to a spat at home with Maya, who felt *DilipSaheb* was superior while Sanjeevni had rooted for the brooding, silent, rebellious son, played by '*lambujji*'

The Bombay-ness of the city is now before him, imposing buildings in the backdrop from the Bandra fort are visible to him, as is the Arabian sea on one side, and the land-kissing shoreline of South Bombay on the other.

He observes some hidden lovers at the rocks above Bandra fort and some at the road side below. He wonders about the folklore of the churches and the stories he has heard about the Portuguese occupation and handover of the city in dowry to the English. He looks on agape at the sun, and how different the ball of yellow looks through the hazy clouds of Bombay.

He is not tired from his travels and the scenery before him infuses a new vigor. It prompts him to continue his march backwards and recommence the walk back.

As he descends from the Bandra fort, he randomly turns right and walks up a road from the bottom of which he can see a hill above. He passes numerous hospice and old age homes, peering into them from the gates.

Atop the hill he lands himself at another church '*The Mt. Mary's convent*' and is amazed to know from visitors that it is an all-girls school. He climbs up the stairs and pays a visit opposite to the Virgin Mary. As he turns around and looks at the shrine below, he recognizes the spot as the famous scene of *Amar Akbar Anthony*. He recreates the scene in his mind for a few minutes and them ambles back using the other parallel side of the road.

He descends the hill from a short burst of steps, towards Mehboob Studios.

As he reaches the gates of the studios, he is given to understand that *a 'Chintu Kapoor'* starrer called *'Saagar'* is being shot for some mixing work inside for a musical and love triangle movie.

He is keen to go into the studios to get a peek at his favorite movie star Rishi Kapoor. The gateman pushes him away and denies entry, leaving Ashu severely disappointed. He notes to himself how close he is to the place where stars visit and shootings happen.

Ashu crosses the road and sits on the pavement bench from where he can quietly watch the guard. He waits for nearly forty minutes but is sad to see the security guard glaring back at him, not leaving his position at the iron gates.

The guard, a proverbial Bombay 'watch-man', raises his cap in a mock salute to Ashu.

Gradually coming to terms that it is only his first day here, he gives up the place on his bench and hops along back toward Father D'Costa's residence.

It is nearing lunch time and he chastens himself to buy the buns that the priest had sought from him.

As he runs inside toward the ground floor flat in the apartment block, Ashwini can hear children chattering and laughing. As he enters the open door, he is shocked to see a dozen kids huddled together, looking up at Father D'Costa who is seated on the dining table.

The father has a book on his lap and is concluding a prayer, "*In the name of the father, the son, and the holy spirit, Amen*"

The priest then hands out a huge basket of buttered buns to all the children at his feet, after blessing them with the holy 'Trinity'.

Ashu is amazed to see the children huddled quietly together. They are all of uneven age, some in their early fives and sixes, some nearly eleven-twelve. They do not wait for any sermon as they hungrily bite into their food. In their hands are earthen cups with large handles, for them to clutch onto.

"It's a watery vegetable and lemon coriander soup. That's all I could cough up so quickly, since our building gardener *'Gangu Telli'* brought me the coriander from his house pot. Will you like some?" he asks Ashu, observing him standing, staring at all the elves like children, who in turn are smiling in glee like *Snowwhite's dwarfs.* The children have infused a magical and happy mood in the apartment that was musty and lying locked a few hours ago.

The kids are all dark-skinned, tanned from generations of fishermen who have bred them with their fisherwomen. "They are the sons of this soil, just like you are from Rajasthan. They can barely afford food in some families as the unseasonal rains are upon us again. For a short two weeks fishing is not permitted during these times. I seek their attention and will get them admitted to my school. Hopefully by the time they grow up our college wing will be ready. I am raising funds from all students in the classes, to get donations and charity from their parents work places. We have managed to raise a few thousands. It looks like a pipe dream, but I will get there. I built the entire new children's school building near the canteen in the same way."

Ashu is amazed at this new world before his eyes. The compact three-storey building structures he has passed on the way to Father D'Costa's home, have small balconies with western dressed women in skirts standing in them. They appear half Irish, half Parsi, to Ashu. He is not sure if they are Catholics or are dark skinned Hindus converted to a new religion. They appear to be united in this land called Bombay.

He can see that the children understand the language of hunger, and respond to it for some free food. As the children finish their paltry meal, Father D'Costa commands his students Ramu, Michael, and Peter to play some music.

The two children pick on some records, whisper to each other their choices, and settle on the same one. It's a record from the Nasir Hussain movie, "*Zamane Ko Dikhana Hai*". Before Ashu realizes it, Peter has placed the needle of the gramophone onto the vinyl of the record, and the trumpet like structure belts out, "*Dil Lena Khel hai dildaar ka….*" By Rahul Dev Burman. Another tune, of another 'Rishi *Chintu Kapoor*' movie.

Ashu goes over the cover of the vinyl record and stares at the images of his star with fondness.

"Are Rishi Kapoor and Amitabh Bachchan making all the movies these days?" thinks Ashu to himself as he misses the point the song is making. Perhaps Bombay is all about films. He can see Father D'Costa enjoy and pantomime, play, act and dance with all the children in the room.

Ashu is impressed at Father D'Costa's life. There is much to learn from the man and his ways. The ordinary man sipping a bit of drink in the train, is here a priest amidst young children at home, like a teenager with short jives and moves. He has the neighborhood kids from the fishermen village nearby in his house. It is as close as it can get to real life '*Bobby*' for him.

A few months pass as Ashu gradually discovers the entire suburbs of Bandra over the weekends. He encircles Carter Road and passes by another fishermen's colony at *Danda* that appears predominantly '*Maharashtrin*'.

He watches children play under-arm cricket, as undisturbed fish dry all over on the open grounds, their nets acting as boundary. These are the grounds you can see from the terraces of the Golf Links societies where old Parsis and new residents settle in before the year turns to 1986.

After a few weeks, Ashu shares some news with his brother via a post card that he sends by registered post from the '*Chuim Village*' post office. He tells him that he has found work at the canteen at St. Scotts and St. Andrews and is also helping a Father D'Costa raise funds for the college building, as he continues to stay as his guest in the long term. He has managed to get some repair contractor work in the church annexe to Pure Hearts School at the

Santacruz premises for repairs of both the school and church benches.

Ashu has survived to make a living in Bombay and has his hands full with Father D'Costa's numerous charitable agendas. He tries to portray a sense of independence and yet downplays his news to not make it sound too flippant.

As fortnights elapse Ashu becomes a proud Bombay resident.

He stops by at Carter Road to pick up an occasional cigarette at Sea Spray, one end point of Carter Road, before the road slopes upward toward Pali Hill area. He has attempted to walk toward the 'Otters Club' but randomly turns before Rajesh Khanna's *'Ashirwaad'* bungalow side on Sundays going uphill. He observes that yesteryear actors Rajendra Kumar Dilip Kumar, Dev Anand and Sunil Dutt too live there. He has often spotted the landmark Mercedes Benz or VW Van, coming out of Dimple Theatre at the foot of the hills. It is where all movie screenings happen before their actual release.

Though Ashu is enamored by the film word, he is clear he has no creative skills and he has to find some sustainable work that can permanently help him to settle down in Bombay. He has loved the city by the Arabian sea with its' weather and the vibe of Bandra. The movie *'Saagar'* he heard about during its filming at Mehboob Studios has released. He finds his escapades by the bed of the sea that occupies a large volume of the Bandstand area, standing by the Bandra fort very enchanting and mesmerizing. He often contemplates getting a job in the studios, but can never get past the '*watch-men*' at Mehboob Studios who seem to block his fate and entry into the movie world.

He is aware that his yesteryear movie flame, the real life 'Bobby' has moved out of her husband's house and is now back at being in the movies as an actress. He has been reading many film magazines for fun and gossip. The attraction of watching the actress Dimple on the silver screen is too much for Ashu to hold back on.

On a Monday morning, 5th of August, Ashu is the second member in the line for the opening of '*advance booking*' at Gaiety Galaxy Gemini theatres at Bandra. The three theatres are on the western side of the railway tracks. These cinemas get audiences that recognize the pulse of the nation's public and Ashu has his heart racing as he gazes at the publicity posters outside the booking window.

The booking window, an old style, stone and grill prison cell kind of room, is lying locked on the outside of which a queue awaits the commencement of ticket sales.

He has told Father D'Costa he is away for an early morning walk at Bandstand and asks for the day off. He is actually at the cineplex queuing up to buy the Friday evening show after work when the movie releases. The cinemas are located down the road from Pure Heart School at '*Swami Vivekananda*' Road and he knows he can walk it in a few paces or even run in to catch the evening six pm show. He has mastered the streets and lanes between these Catholic churches, missionaries and swami named roads of 'Santacruz', a suburb connected to Bandra by another called 'Khar.' He has not been too adventurous going onto the other side of Mahim creek which has its own mix of mosques, churches and temples. He does take note, that Bombay seems to have many pious and religious places and people perhaps need their Gods around them, to bless them on the go. The city and its people are never still and drive the energetic pace of the city peppered by religious institutions.

He is queued up to buy a ticket in the 'Balcony' class, as he refuses to be in the lower or upper stalls.

In the booking queue there is a talkative girl behind him chattering non-stop with her younger companion, who is ahead of Ashu. Ashu realizes he is sandwiched between them, but is not willing to let go of his own spot, lest he lose a ticket or two in the backrow.

They are both apparently there in queue for their favorite movie star, Rishi Kapoor.

"Why do you not let me come ahead, I was just parking my moped, when you have come in between. You can still get your tickets." says a girlish voice to his male stubborn back blocking the passage with a firm posture.

Ashu turns behind.

He is speechless to see a Sikh girl quite clearly a '*Sardaarni*' he guesses, due to the length of her hair and her features he observes. She is dressed in a Punjabi salwar kameez. The girl ahead of him, is a chubbier shorter version of her companion.

"Look, Amitabh Bachchan is the bigger star at present. You both should await '*Mard*' when it releases later this year" says Ashu. He has been reading the trade weekly '*Screen*' and keeping track of the movies yet to release in anticipation as if he is a distributor.

He does not know the correct way to react so he ends up saying something about the future movies to release and build a conversation.

"Why don't you be a *Mard*, and step out of the line then?" retorts the beautiful girl. Her eyes sparkle and sets flaming sparks flying everywhere around Ashwini.

"Excuse me I am here to watch *Saagar* too. The only reason this movie will work, is due to Dimple's comeback and the music by R D Burman. Your hero is too chocolate faced!" he continues to rib and irk the girl.

"*Kiran Didi* he has been spying on every word we speak" says the younger girl.

"Everyone in our queue has heard you two loud-mouths" retorts Ashu to chubby girl.

They are all distracted as a pack full of three containers loaded with '*Guru Kripa Samosas*' from Sion on steel trays are whisked away up the steps from the frontage of the cinema where they stand in queue.

As the ticket window opens, Kiran from the back passes hundred rupees notes, to her younger friend ahead of Ashu to buy ten tickets.

As Ashu's turn is next, he buys the first ticket of the next row for the same show, Friday six in the evening.

After he is done, Kiran picks up the next nine, on the same row and same show.

Ashu and Kiran exchange glances at each other.

Both walk away silently.

Ashu stops at the corner of the by lane and watches the two sisters, astride the Bajaj Moped overtake him as if he is an unknown pedestrian. Kiran looks at the rear-view mirror and catches Ashu's reflection and takes note of his hairstyle.

"Another Amitabh fan and a copy-cat" she thinks to herself.

On the 9th of August 1985 at six in the evening, Ashu is a bit late and still outside the cinema.

He runs up the cinema's old marbled stairs and hastens his way inside, after the ticket checker cuts his ticket stub into half.

Moving briskly, picking up two samosas and a '*ThumsUp*' bottle for himself, he enters the cinema and looks for his B1 seat number.

It is the first seat in B row.

He finds Kiran seated at the second seat, with a row of nine girls her age on the same row seats from B3 to B11, leaving seat B2 empty between his, and hers. The row above is Kiran's chubby friend from the queue, seated with ten other children dressed in frocks, denim pants, and floral tops with matching color pumps in their feet.

"Everyone wants to be Madonna!" he says to himself.

He sits aside Kiran and realizes she takes no note of him as the movie is about to start the empty seat between them creating a slim sliver of space for both of them.

As the R D Burman tune and song "*Oh Maria*" breaks in Ashu is mesmerized and stares at his favorite actress Dimple on screen with his mouth wide, gaping open.

Kiran steals a glance at him from her side seat and observes Ashu's hardened features. His profile, his long nose, and strong jaw, stand out in the lights thrown on the audience from the song.

Not really a chocolate boy, more a vanilla man she says to herself.

She digs into the choco-cone that she has in her hands and looks on to enjoy the movie. From her perspective it is very clear. Rishi Kapoor must get the girl, not Hassan his competitor in the movie.

As the movie breaks for the interval, Kiran is taking orders from all her friends to step out and buy snacks for all of them.

The younger girls and friends remain seated.

Once outside Ashu comes back to the ice-cream counter seeking his own vanilla ice-cream, and watches Kiran struggle with the popcorn and other eats with her younger companion. Kiran is grappling with the samosa packets herself and is placing an order for the chocolate ice-cream cones. The two girls are also trying to hold onto half a dozen *Simba* wafer packets as Ms. Chubby appears to salivate.

Ashu wonders, why the rest of the girls have not gotten up.

He offers to Kiran his willingness to help.

Kiran looks up at him, from top to toe.

Ashu is dressed in his working white shirt and blue denims and the bottom of the shirt is knotted, while his shoes are the Bata canvas type shoes with slight mud on them.

Kiran is herself glowing in her skin Punjabi hairstyle and shining clothes. Her hair this time in plaits is tied up neatly, with a small '*bindi*' on her forehead.

"It's my Kiran Didi's birthday", chips in Ms. Chubby. "Please help na" she says appearing suddenly sweet and friendly.

"Oh, Happy Birthday, I hope you are having a good one?" asks Ashu and wishing her at the same time with a clairvoyant smile.

Kiran dumps all the samosa packets on his two outstretched arms and walks away, holding the popcorn and ice-creams herself.

She cries out to the ice-cream vendor, "His ice-cream treat is from me. I will pay after the movie."

Ms. Chubby follows with four packets of popcorn, which Ashu assumes will all be eaten by herself.

Ashu winks at the ice-cream vendor and points at the cup and *choco-cone* with his two eyes and asks the vendor to send it inside for delivery at the "B1-B3" seats.

He walks away too.

As the movie commences post-interval the ice-creams arrive. Ashu passes the choco-cone to Kiran, nudging her very delicately.

She looks at him irritatingly briefly missing her scene on the screen.

"Happy Birthday" he whispers back to her. "You seem to like 'chocolate–heroes and ice-cream. If you had told me on Monday, I would have stepped aside and let you buy the tickets first" he attempts to copy Father D'Costa's style but ends up sounding more like imitating Rishi Kapoor.

"Thank you", she hisses, as Kiran snatches the ice-cream cone, scratching a bit of Ashu's fist with her painted nails.

Ashu enjoys the deliberate banter despite its aggressiveness.

Kiran blushes a bit despite her own forwardness.

The songs that follow break into a deeper sense of romance, leaving both Ashu and Kiran glued to their seats.

Ashu wonders what Ms. Chubby at his back must feel watching the love story unfold before her. He decides to stay well behaved and yet concentrates on his partner at hand not daring to look at the back at all, lest he upset his friendly neighborhood.

All through the movie and the melodious songs, they both steal glances at each other.

His attention and life obsession has moved away from Dimple on screen, to his *Bobby* alongside.

14

ROLE REVERSAL

It was 1988.
Hari was nearly 18 years old.

Sanjeevni now had to return to Nawalgarh as Jyoti was due anytime.

In the last week before Sanjeevni's departure, Rupa's Nepali husband suddenly died due to an intestinal and pancreatic problem that ate up his heart.

Thappa collapsed in his sleep during a light shower of the monsoons.

Mr. Mony Malhotra took care of his last rites and put paid to everything.

At the end of the week, Rupa was more elated than sad as she sought her own freedom. She had to conceal her real feelings and remained silent as far as possible, and spoke only when spoken to.

She wanted to explore the country, for it had been nearly a decade that she had not had a break from Delhi's extreme climate and her housekeeping duties. It was a job she did now exclusively for the Malhotra's but her initial start was through the grind like any other domestic help in Lajpat Nagar.

For a few days Rupa had her mood swings and felt empty from inside. Malhotra Niwas had reallocated all duties of her husband to Rupa, so her work had increased.

All the outside house duties for purchase of Groceries were given to Sanjeevni.

Sanjeevni himself longed to be back in Nawalgarh for a few days, but he waited till Hari reached Delhi as his arranged replacement.

The plan was to keep his seat warm with the help of his youngest sibling, as if the job at Malhotra Niwas was a permanent government job. Sanjeevni also wanted to continue the grains and wheat trade he had established with PranSaheb and the temple priest at the corner of Lajpat Nagar.

Jyoti's relative worked at the customs office in Delhi and Hari was being escorted in comfort along with him. In the mean while on the same day, Sanjeevni was packing two bags in the makeshift sleep area he had on the terrace as Rupa looked at him forlorn, with sad eyes.

He was her only hope, as she had never set outside the Malhotra Niwas in Delhi for the past five years. Her '*Nepali*' husband was no more and she only anticipated further getting embellished in the household quick sand.

Sanjeevni's departure was ensuing like the loss of the last family member she had, though she knew he always maintained his distance from her and only respected her as a close co-worker.

Over the years this had increased Rupa's respect for him. Sanjeevni's departure would eventually leave her alone without '*her own*' family. She had to continue her work to watch for the Malhotra's who were expecting their son Sonny from overseas. The comfort of sameness and routine was going to break and Rupa would find herself alone to manage the household. She was anxious and at the same time excited to meet Sanjeevni's brother. This was the set up in which Hari was entering.

Hari was to reach Delhi with Jyoti's relative by noon. He had been busy with the scenery from Jaipur to Delhi as that part of the road was new for him. He kept himself tuned to listening to songs on an audio tape, that was used on the system 'deck' of the Jeep he was travelling in. Each time the jeep hit some road blocks, the tape would often bounce inside the system deck and Hari would 'eject' and 're-insert' the same to continue with the music. The contraption of the 'system deck' was mounted loosely with red and blue electric wires running from the handle bar Hari held, toward the steering wheel of the Jeep and disappeared into the bonnet ahead for the power source.

He had listened on a loop to songs of Feroz Khan's movie - "*Aaj phir tum pe pyaar ayaa hai*" on side A of the tape. On the reverse side of the tape, side B was the song from Hatya "*Main pyaar ki poojaran*" which Hari heard on a loop.

He thought about the meaning of those songs falling off the speakers onto the jeep's seats rather than into his comprehension. As he hummed the tunes Hari was numbed by the city's crowds and dense cramped low-rise structures in Delhi once the jeep was in city limits.

The musical tunes stayed with him but the deep meaning of the words was lost on him.

It was 2pm when the Mahindra Jeep pulled over into Lajpat Nagar.

As the jeep came to a halt, Hari could see Sanjeevni standing eagerly at the road outside Malhotra Niwas.

Sanjeevni was ecstatic and beamed a broad smile to his kid brother. Hari waves from the open door of the jeep pleasingly. Hari has a serene look on his face despite the journey. He knew he had little understanding of the city's ways and had no ability to imagine the duties of Malhotra Niwas's inhabitants till it unfolded upon him. He remained relaxed.

He had come as a replacement to his brother for a purpose of sibling duty and there was no anxiety about the work duties to be performed. He had not dreamt of the most unexpected person on the periphery of the household – Rupa, a young, unfulfilled widow who was someone he would now get to see for the first time in his life.

The two brothers embrace and Sanjeevni takes him hurriedly to the terrace, to show his sleeping arrangements. After the quick orientation of the premises from the terrace and small talk on '*Moh & Maya*' and its occupants, Sanjeevni explained to him that he had to rush down back to his own duty.

Within ten minutes of meeting his brother he comes down the steps hurriedly to man the main gate.

In the meanwhile, Rupa was lining up the food on the '*thaali*' – *the steel plates* prepared for the new guest in the Malhotra Niwas kitchen. It had been planned that Hari and the jeep driver would get one clear day of sleep and Sanjeevni would leave for Nawalgarh the next day.

The jeep had to return to Nawalgarh, as the driver and its owner was a native from there.

He was to leave at 7am the next morning till when Hari could sleep, re-adjust his sleep cycle and understand from his elder brother the workload.

As Sanjeevni ran down, Rupa ran up the steps with a large glass of milk and five rotis as had been communicated by Sanjeevni for his younger kid brother. He had made Rupa understand that his kid brother could eat like Bheema and had provided separate grains grounded wheat and bajra to Rupa, to make food separately for herself and Hari.

Hari looked up, and saw his lunch ready to devour.

The demure Rupa with her sari, tucked in on one side, *wheatish* by complexion and mischievous by eyesight, bent down to keep the food.

She looks directly into Hari's eyes. "Would this suffice, or you will need more? Your brother says you could eat twice of that, but in the city, this much of food will be difficult to ingest and digest."

As he looks at her and admires her, he checks her out, starting with her eyes, top to bottom, down to her curves. Hari has really never seen a woman outside his house, besides his mother and *BhabhiMa*.

Rupa has not put the usual red round '*bindi*' on her forehead. Her white sari with the red border, hair slickly tucked behind her ears, with a large white flower in them, makes her look the simple bubbly girl that a man like Hari would admire.

To see someone who is not dressed in the authentic Rajasthani way and instead is dressed in the Bengali traditional way, appeals to him right away. Yet he looks down bashfully and handpicks two fat black ants. He side-tracks them, changing their path.

"Why did you not kill them?" asks Rupa.

"Why should I?" replies Hari. "They mean and do no harm, especially to me, and neither can they bite. I used to play with such fat ants as a child. They would remind me of the black Ace cards my father used to play and make pairs with me."

"Used to?" asks Rupa. She admires his fine looks that appear craftily shaped with a chisel. She can see his towering height by the nature of the long legs and length of his feet as he is seated crossed-leg on the terrace floor.

She finds him even more handsome and desirable than Sanjeevni. She is open about her fleeting affection as her eyelashes dance like a butterfly.

"*Yet like the elder sibling, this dumbo also cannot see my feelings!*"

He is a decade younger version of his elder brother and appears to have just started shaving, his clean skin, barely green with hair growth, is more tanned reddish, than brown. His long limbs resembling Lord Vishnu and his conch shell like eyes, resembling Lord Ganesh.

Rupa is hardly into any kind of worship or spiritualism but she finds the resemblance uncanny with Gods on Calendars displayed in the Malhotra household, with their Optician shop advertisements.

Rupa was always transparent and clear of heart. She had been fooling around with Sanjeevni, but always kept a distance as she knew he was married. He would rarely talk with her and if so, not more than a few words in weeks.

Today seeing his younger sibling, barely all of eighteen she falls in love on sight and the chemistry hard to resist. Every minute she waits on him to finish his food she feels he is simply irresistible.

Hari does not realize that Rupa is looking at him with those eyes. "We lost Papaji many years ago. I was still a child. We used to play 'pairs with playing cards.' *BootiDa* is more my father and less of a brother." He puts a morsel in his mouth and finishes quickly as he gulps it down his long neck.

He continues "He has taken care of me since I was young and has now brought me here to let himself go back to meet *BhabhiMa.* I was never keen to come to the city, as I am very happy at home, but stepping out I realized today is fun to explore a bit near-by. I spent the entire journey listening to music in the jeep that dropped me here. I have always heard music sitting with Ma at home or on TV after dinner. Working here should be easy, as it is like a home. Booti Bhai has told me, that there is no difference between our home and this one, and we should not look upon ourselves as servants. We are doing good work in our own house and if we treat this like our own house, then the desire to work nicely is always maintained steadfastly to serve our employer."

Rupa watches him finish off the lunch, drinking the milk in one big gulp. She admires his biceps and forearms that bulge with blue color arteries and veins from under his full sleeve turmeric colored kurta. His sleeves are pulled up and tucked into the elbow area, highlighting the sculpted muscles.

She has not digested his thoughts as much as admire him.

Suspecting a new visitor Tiger breaks onto the scene, entering from the terrace door and lets out a short bark.

Rupa bends to pick up the steel plate and bowls. Startled, the bowls fall back off the plate, onto Hari's squared up legs and leave a long strain of left-over '*dal*' and curry on the shirt kurta.

Rupa embarrassed on her clumsiness, feels bad, "Ooi Ma, I am so sorry! This Tiger startled me."

"Come here my boy" calls out Hari to Tiger, who licks off the spilled stuff on the Kurta shirt and the remains left are more of Tiger's saliva than the dal that fell off the bowl.

Rupa takes note that Hari does not even shout or scream but just blinks his eyes looking at her.

His eyebrows twitch pleasingly, saying through his eyes, that it is not something worth apologizing, He showers his love onto Tiger as Rupa turns away and beings to walk toward the terrace door.

"I have *BootiBhai's* bedroll, I hope you will get me the food everyday twice as Bhai has promised? The salt was a bit more. It is good to eat less salt says my BhabhiMa. I also have brought some jaggery and peanuts from home, which I can share with you for break-fast, but I will need a glass of milk with every meal. Will that be possible here in the city?"

Rupa, glances back and imitates his eyebrow twitch and blinking her eyes, looks at him as if she is admiring him and nods.

It is now Hari's turn to feel bashful and he blushes a bit.

Rupa winks and steps into the terrace open door and disappears down the stairs.

The next night after work is over inside the Malhotra household Rupa goes to her own empty room. Her ex-husbands clothes and belongings have been tucked away by her inside their old canvas bag and she pushes it away under the make-shift kitchen sink. She had given Hari his dinner but had skipped the milk glass.

She now places the milk in a large utensil and mounts it onto the cooking range, while turning to slow gas and goes for her shower.

Hari has ended his shift and walks up the steps brushing off some flies and rolls the bed onto the open terrace and lies down under the misty sky.

The stars are not visible, but there is a mild breeze and his wet hair, settle like flowing locks behind his head. He switches into a white kurta he uses to sleep in and has moved into his village dhoti, looking like the missing moon in the sky himself. He radiates a shine from his face that hits Rupa as she steps onto the terrace.

Rupa meets him mid-way at the terrace and hands over the boiling milk. She herself has a smaller half-filled glass for herself, held partially by her red bordered Bengali Sari.

He beckons her to sit on the floor at his level, by tossing Sanjeevni's two pillows, one to sit on and one for a back-rest.

She raises her left eyebrow, while he assures her, "We can chat for a while."

Rupa sits down and they both look at each other for a few minutes.

The silence is not awkward. Though Hari has never been around other women, besides his mother and Jyoti, he feels comfortable around Rupa. He encourages her to talk and she speaks.

"I have been living here for past nearly ten years in Lajpat Nagar, the *Malhotras* are a kind family. However, I sometimes wonder, will my entire life go like this? I came from Calcutta due to work, but sometimes I feel wasted and tired with all the house work I do, it is for someone else..., ...and it is not even my house."

"Have you ever travelled nearby? *Chittor, Jaipur, Mathura, Dwarka, Haridwar, Kashi?*" asks Hari, names of places he has heard from his mother. The very gypsy like demeanor is there in all Maya's sons and it comes out with interest for travel and city names to explore.

"No!" she replies in a single word.

"Is there something you seek from your life? We are young, there is a long way to go." Hari speaks softly in a senior advisory sort of way. Though it is he who is newcomer and novice in the household, Rupa does not seem to mind.

"I really do not know. Though I never had a plan, life seems to be drifting in a direction which I do not like"

"Let *BootiBhai* come back to his duty, I will take you to Nawalgarh just to meet our mother. You will feel a sense of tranquility under the trees there. You can eat good food with *BhabiMa* and me. When the *dal* is being cooked from scratch, or when the vegetables are being cut, and my Nandu is locking horns with Hariya, the simple landscape of our fields just before the rains…it is very peaceful and relaxing. Let's hope we can be there by next season. It will blow away your sadness"

Rupa is keen to know how he seems to know or guess about her inner quiet melancholy.

"I never experienced family life. Baba used to hit ma and she would barely have time for me, after all the damage he did to her. I can never overcome the fear, nor the hatred I had for my father."

"In my case, on the contrary, Ma has all the time in the world for me. They loved each other and Papaji passed away in my presence. I still remember the funny faces he made as he fell on the bed we used to play cards on. I thought he was entertaining me then, but later when I grew up, Ma told me he had an attack. They were really fond of each other's company that harnessed their love a lot."

Hari removes his wallet to show Khazan and Maya's photograph clicked in Udaipur before the city palace.

He continues "They were my world, and now *BootiBhai and JyotiMa are my idols.*"

"You are so fortunate", says Rupa, knocking off a tear, from her left eye with her right-hand forefinger. She gets up, her toes bent inwards as she outstretches an arm to seek his glass.

"I hope I did not displease you Rupaji. I do not know very well how to talk with women. I am sorry, that your parents could not spend time with you. It is a wealth... you cannot earn, nor lose. We are indeed fortunate to be blessed with our parents' presence and love. We have learnt how to love each other because of that and stay together as a united family. Your mother did give birth, so remember those impressions of her." Hari speaks with maturity and with a sense of personal understanding as he too had lost his father early but the remainder family members presence mattered for his stability.

'*Grief is for those to handle, who are left behind on mother earth.*' He thinks to himself and does not speak this sentiment aloud.

Rupa takes the glass from him and turns away, walking abruptly back to her abode as if she can hear his sentiments. She goes toward her room at the back of Malhotra Niwas. They both go back to sleep in their respective arrangements as planned.

At five in the morning, as the day breaks, Hari shifts his balance and makes a turn to his left. He realizes his left arm, is in embrace with another arm and can feel the length of hair, and thinks that Tiger may have come upstairs.

He tries to open his two eyes, but only the right eye opens with the left sticky with early morning laziness.

His right eye vision gives him an eyehole impression of Rupa, asleep, with light kajal extending out of her eyes, like the stem of a mango leaf. Her hair is open, on one half of her head. The other half is tied up into knots crisscrossing each other like a braid, yet loose.

She is dressed in the same Red and white Bengali sari and it is draped all over her, as if like a sheet, coming lose. Her feet are coming out from below with no nail polish.

Her left toe has a broken nail while the right toe has a longer than usual nail. He is a bit petrified with the situation he finds himself in and at the same time in awe of the female bodily form so close to him.

He can see her breathe in slight soft movements of her body.

He unhooks his left hand slowly, so that she does not wake up and tries to move away from her, inching slowly towards the terrace boundary wall. He is perturbed and slightly aghast, at the same time a bit worried, and wonders why she is here? All this while he inches slowly away.

"Is she planning to get us both fired?" he thinks to himself.

He places his right-hand thumb and forefinger below her tiny nose and finds her even breath, exhaling peacefully.

Rupa has spent the last week neither mourning nor being able to come out of the dread of her life. Her living quarters seem to absorb her.

She was merely ten years old when she commenced work here and on a lark was made to marry Thappa when she was barely fourteen, a year before Sanjeevni arrived.

Now she too was barely nineteen and already a widow.

Mrs. Malhotra did not do much to console her as she had her own plans to visit her sister once her son, Sonny came down to Delhi.

With the last rites of Thappa, Mony Malhotra too felt he had done his duty and with Sanjeevni gone, Rupa really had no one to be able to even have a simple conversation since a few days before Hari arrived as his brother's replacement. She had taken note of Hari's diet and beyond that Sanjeevni too was in no mood to spend time talking to her as he was keen to make his own travel out and had also some sadness in him seeing Thappa go.

A physical body was less in Malhotra Niwas and both Sanjeevni and Rupa did not know how to show that concern to each other.

Rupa had not much anguish but there was a slight amount of confusion in her, on how to go about her life ahead. The marriage was one of convenience to legitimize their using the same premises to live.

Hari watches Rupa sleep and smile while in her dreams.

She can see her vivid dream, as the clouds turn orange and the sun also wakes up, as if to peek at her quickly Due to the position of Sanjeevni's bed laid out in the east, Hari is seated now with a backrest of the terrace wall in shade.

He watches from the boundary wall and the initial rays of the sun, start to hit Rupa, spraying a golden hue and shine on her face. The morning light falls upon her skin, dyeing her sari into a yellow bronze look. She looks like a Goddess, blissful and admirable in her posture, with a serene glow emanating from her.

He continues to admire her silently as the sun radiates powerfully now its full sunshine. He moves away, stands up and looks at her from afar. He straightens his hair and stretches himself, ironing out his white kurta with his bare hands.

He spots some long hair of Rupa on his left shoulder, hand picks them and throws them off the side wall of the terrace. He spots Mr. and Mrs.

Malhotra's balcony below, and side-steps that to throw her hair off.

He smells his left hand, to get the fragrance of her hair. As he turns to look at her, he finds her awake, eyes open lying straight on her back, staring at the clouds above.

She turns her back to him and lies down in silence, her feet hidden by her sari now.

He looks at her back.

She again turns toward him and lies down on her side. She keeps looking at him with a wry smile but does not say anything.

He waits and looks back at her.

Blank, bemused.

She checks him out top to bottom, blinks her eyes, repeatedly.

He admires her.

She smiles.

After a few minutes of them both looking at each other, she gets up, folds his bed and walks away.

The previous day, Sanjeevni has started the day early, running to the gate of Malhotra Niwas, waving to Hari atop the terrace, while stepping into the jeep. Tiger is snapping at his feet. He wants to join Sanjeevni his initial master from Sikkar Railway station on this trip.

Only Sonny Malhotra is at home, as Papa-Mony is away with his wife to her sister's house at Chandigarh.

The duties hand-over, training and knowledge shift has happened from Sanjeevni to Hari the previous evening, including the finer nuances of the household car washing and morning milk gathering process.

Sonny feels a very large sense of gratitude toward Sanjeevni. He has spent time, watching Sanjeevni run from temple to gate, tend to the mother cow at the temple, follow a life of discipline and worship and yet never let one thing out of place from their large home interiors. He has never seen Sanjeevni step in, or step out of line with his parents and is now re-assured, as if a baton is passed in a relay race, with tall and strong farmer Hari, his brother to replace him.

Sonny nods at Sanjeevni, to allow Tiger to join in. "SaahabJi thank you!" says Sanjeevni humbly.

"Tiger is your find Sanjeevni! He was always yours, show him the countryside! And do return, don't stay back forever with mother and wife, I will miss you."... he breaks for a reaction from Sanjeevni who continues to stand with folded hands before Sonny.

"... and lastly, thank you Sanjeevni. Do send us a photograph from home, and tell us whether you had a baby boy or girl."

"SonnyBhai, it will be a son, my mother says so, so it will be so!" he shouts, as the jeep reverses in the lane to do an about turn and speeds off.

The driver Khemu Singh, offers to play music and pushes the audio cassette into the tape stereo system of the jeep, fitted below the metallic steel dashboard.

"*Main pyaar ki pujaran.....mujhe pyaar chaiye*" blurts the music from the 'Hatya' tape. "Khemu, it is a transistor?" quizzes Sanjeevni.

Hari had referred to this song without much understanding of what was in store for him. Sanjeevni thought to himself, that Hari has to quickly grow up. How much longer will he be able to stay away from Jyoti?

"No Bhaiya, now these are audio cassettes... one can play them on two sides. Should I switch to *Dayavaan*?" Khemu driver hits the switch button, and off goes the same number that Hari had heard yesterday on the way to Delhi. Sanjeevni really enjoys the tune and the melody of the *Laxmikant Pyarelal* song.

"Nice!' echoes Sanjeevni, dreaming of his wife.

He imagines her sitting, all plump and heavy, cross legged before him eating her food, with smoldering angry eyes, blaming him for the state she is in.

Sanjeevni smiles with a stupid grin as he can well imagine how his reception will be back at Nawalgarh.

The vehicle makes its pit stops once it hits the highway and by the time he is at the outskirts of Delhi city, Khemu has picked up six other passengers who are headed toward Jaipur. Khemu driver allows Sanjeevni the space at the front carriage of the jeep all by himself. They stop directly at Jaipur, after a non-stop drive on National Highway 48 for four hours they stop at Ashwini's recommended Laxmi Mishthan Bhandar at Johari Bazar. Here Sanjeevni digs into his food and a tall glass of lassi paying for Khemu's meal as well.

All the other passengers disembark in Jaipur as they do not intend to go ahead and Sanjeevni offers to drive and relieve Khemu for the onward journey.

Sanjeevni is keen to experience the highway to Sikar and Tiger is happy post his milk and roti paratha meal, to sit back at the jeep alone by himself.

Sanjeevni is keen to see Maya and Jyoti's reactions when they see Tiger. The journey is under three hours, and by the time they cross Sikkar, they have heard the *T-Series 'Hatya-Dayavan'* combination a dozen times.

Sanjeevni hits the tape eject button, to semi-dangle the tape out of the stereo and stop the music.

As the jeep revs into third gear, Sanjeevni attempts to over-take a grass hay laden trailer, driven by a farmer riding a tractor. The trailer is tied to the tractor, with a steel hook and clamp, a primitive kind of apparatus, making the length of the trailer and tractor combined a bit unpredictable.

As Sanjeevni revs the jeep into fourth gear, it takes time to raise speed and his jeep is yet to overtake the trailer entirely, with the tractor, acting like an engine, is still ahead of the jeep with its linkage apparatus.

On the other side of the road, oncoming at fairly a slow pace in the distance is an approaching Rajasthan state government bus, seemingly a bit far off, but looking menacingly loaded to full capacity, tilted a bit onto its left side. The driver of the bus gives Sanjeevni the head-lights.

As Sanjeevni feels he has time, he does not hurry to hit the pedal, but to his shock, finds the farmer atop the tractor, pick-up speed at the same time rather than allow Sanjeevni to overtake.

This causes the jeep, to only go side-by-side to the trailer. Sanjeevni suddenly finds himself in racing speed, but still some distance to overtake to overcome the entire length of the tractor linked apparatus, and in seconds, finds the bus not too far from his own vehicle.

Sweat breaks out over his sidelocks and from his temple.

Sanjeevni realizes that he has mis-calculated the length of the trailer-cum-tractor.

It is a submarine like length vehicle equivalent to overtaking two vehicles at the same time. The hay bundles are still in the rear-view mirror of Sanjeevni's jeep when he finds the bus too close upon him and estimates a crash.

Sanjeevni hits the brakes and the jeep skids toward the right side of the highway, away from the trailer, but would still hit the oncoming bus, on its left side. The bus is already looking overloaded and would tilt any moment off the highway with its own weight, the bus bends further towards its left side as the driver attempts to control the bus steering.

The bus appears to come on like a bullet that Sanjeevni cannot avoid, making Tiger sense the danger. He lets out a bark that sounds more like a yelp.

The jeep is no longer in Sanjeevni's control. It is up to the bus driver to act as the tractor picks speed and zooms ahead with the trailer of hay bundle winning the race from Sanjeevni. Meanwhile in only five seconds Sanjeevni's jeep, his steering jammed is still skidding on the wrong side of the road, zooming for a collision course ahead with the red bus.

The God sent driver, veers the vehicle in three seconds after crossing the tractor and trailer, the moment the trailer passes, onto the wrong side of the road behind the farmer's tractor that has just passed.

This allows Sanjeevni's jeep to keep skidding, missing the bus, yet rolling onto the same path from which the bus has just meandered away from.

The jeep meanders onto the dirt path of the wrong side of the road and comes to a stop in a cloud of dust and screeching brakes, with its front fender kissing the kilometer milestone that the bus had just left behind on the edge of the road.

Sanjeevni spots the trailer still a kilometer ahead and revs the jeep back into first gear after reversing it back on the highway.

Tiger squints, expecting a confrontation.

Khemu looks at Sanjeevni, first exasperated, then relieved and now expectedly as Sanjeevni races on again toward the tractor.

In a minute and a half, Sanjeevni overtakes the tractor-cum-trailer, giving it a sharp cut as he overtakes the farmer showing him his hand outside the jeep angrily.

The two men and the dog in the jeep, sense, their meeting with death has been avoided for now.

Sanjeevni fiddles with the 'Joker' card in his front flap pocket of the uniform shirt that he wears during his travel. His one hand is on the steering and he leaves it for a micro second, as he now puts the jeep into fourth gear.

Khemu wipes the sweat of his brow. "Kya brother, out of practice?"

"No Khemu, just uncertain judgement. Becoming a father, I should not have taken that kind of risk. It will take time to change. I did not anticipate the length of the vehicle correctly and that bloody farmer started playing racing games, rather than giving me the right of way."

The incident remains in Sanjeevni's psyche, but he knows he's avoided a mangled death and pets

Tiger with his left hand, as he brings his right hand to manage the steering wheel. He thanks the God-sent bus driver in his mind.

"You both have just met '*Yamraaj*' and returned with me Khemu. You will both be my Khaas companions for the rest of my life."

As he switches on the radio, "Rah pe rehte hain, ...hum toh safar karte hain" from Gulzar's Namkeen comes rattling on.

Sanjeevni can feel some trembling in his left leg and feet.

He thanks all his good actions and karma as he wants to live to see the face of his baby and his wife.

"What would ma say? How irresponsible?" he thinks of himself.

"The days of the radio were better Khemu, one song after another with some interspersed dialogues. And no side swapping of tapes." he says to knock of his nervous energy.

The jeep reaches their residence, "Moh & Maya" at 4pm. Its early evening, and dust flying all around as he jumps out of the jeep, a pigeon comes and sits atop the canvas ceiling.

Sanjeevni hurries on, leaving his bags with Khemu to open the gate after he rubs his hand across *Moh & Maya's* stone edifice outside the compound wall, knocking off the cobwebs, and piled up sludge and dirt.

Tiger is unleashed, as Khemu unlocks the back door of the jeep, to run and chase Sanjeevni through the short driveway.

Sanjeevni's leather boots hit the pebbled pathway before the veranda of the house and both Maya and Jyoti push open the main door.

Maya is wearing her trade mark maroon wine colored sari.

Jyoti is dressed in a large Kurta shirt of Sanjeevni, peacock blue in color with a pink dupatta straddling across her large tummy. Both the women of his life, emotional, holding back their tears.

Sanjeevni holds up his arms. They both fold into his sky wide embrace. He tilts his head to the left to hit his mother's head, while his right arm, rubs affectionately Jyoti's back.

"I'm back and hopefully here to stay!"

Tiger joins in the embrace, running circles around them, as Khemu brings in the two canvas bags of Sanjeevni, with his *Mashk.*

Maya eyes the goat skinned bottle from the corner of her eye, wondering, how many journeys it has made with Sanjeevni, after all the ones with her.

The *Mashk* dangling from Khemu's shoulder is empty and jumps around as if it is yearning for water.

Perhaps it too is happy to be the bottle back home.

15

KIRAN'S JOURNEY FROM JUHU TO JAIPUR

Ashwini is strolling at Bombay's Juhu's beach. He has entered the beach at the side entry of the main promenade, after walking across the Ramada Inn Hotel's parking lot. He has just finished an early sumptuous south Indian meal at the nearby Shiv Sagar Restaurant and now wants to seek out the 'Juhu' beach before sunset.

Ashu loves the last few minutes of the sun, neither too bright, nor too dull, mostly golden orange, lighting up the sky on fire. The sun just before it sets off to sleep, leaves the sky in a mosaic of colors with grey strokes of the clouds that eventually overpower it and tuck it into bed.

He looks up, as it appears it is about to rain. There is a light breeze and the humid salty air weaves its path through Ashwini's hair locks, leaving them moist at the scalp due to his own sweat, yet some strands over his ears are wiry and dry.

He moves his hair puff falling on the left side of his forehead in his trade mark style of nodding his head from left to right diagonally.

It distracts and diverts the path of an onward crow flying low, which drops a struggling near dead fish in its mouth, landing before Ashu's feet. Ashu side steps the fish which is lapped away by the high tide waves and takes the fish back into the Arabian Sea. Ashu has wet sand on his feet and a smile on his face, thinking he has rescued one marine life.

He continues his brisk walk towards the string of hotels into the heart of Juhu.

He remembers his mother Maya, imagining her perhaps lighting her evening '*diya*' before the '*Tulsi*' in the courtyard stepping out to the veranda to listen to her radio perched atop the window sill. He can see her resting on her large *charpoi*, knowing fully well that she rests for those precious forty minutes before moving into the kitchen for the night meal. The only way to be with one's mother now, is in one's inner eye.

He remembers his elder sibling advise of not being so far away from home and misses Sanjeevni. He is now in Bombay and will be missing the birth of his nephew.

He knows from his mother that Sanjeevni is expected back this weekend and though he has them in his thoughts, he does not demonstrate by action. He rarely calls them, an oft repeated complaint of his mother. The STD ticking metered call rates from Bombay are too cost prohibitive and Ashu struggles for words on such calls. He is an in-person kind of guy who can talk and express his emotions freely.

As he approaches the boundary wall of *Sun 'N' Sand* Hotel, the backside periphery of which overlooks the beach front, he can see the long hair of a lady, dressed in a wine-red salwar kameez. Her hair is flying sideways in the direction of the breeze, the same direction he is walking in.

He tries to walk with an even pace and balance, despite having tailwind behind him and the soft clay like sand below his feet. He squints to observe carefully the familiar heart shaped face he had met at the screening of the movie – '*Saagar*', three years back. He observes her morose expression clearly as he walks toward the compound wall of the hotel, watching her sniffling into a handkerchief, which she uses to wipe her nose leak repeatedly. It appears like a tap overflowing with a cloth tied to it and yet water spouting, unstoppable.

In the backdrop of the sea, the setting sun, and the golden twilight, his mind races to recall her name, remembering her birthday and the ice-cream cones she had at the Gaiety theatre in Bandra.

"Kiran, ah, Kiran!" muses Ashu looking at the rays from the rusty setting sun.

As he nears the hotel façade, she picks herself up and becomes aware of his presence, a sole intruder into her moment of solitary misery. He waves at her, acknowledging her eyes, by shaping his thumb and forefinger above his own and pointing at the sea behind on the beach. His attempt at invoking their meeting at the Bandra theatre while watching the movie *Saagar*- the sea he points out to, is met with little success. She negates his mime, wiping her tears and snuffing out any facial expression, standing like a mannequin in mummery.

He moves his hand over his ear, as if asking for a clarification. She folds her one leg over another and pantomimes a flute, indicating the Krishna temple nearby, where she intends to walk and visit, on the other side of the hotel. He nods his head and walks through the passage after the Sun N Sand hotel, and between the Holiday Inn. As he walks a few paces, he sees her on foot, with a colorful umbrella stroll ahead of him. He runs a few paces to catch up with her.

So, "*Saagar jaisi ankhon waali*, pray tell me why is the sea weeping?"

She is silent, keeps walking on, ignoring his opener, but acknowledging his presence by slowing down her pace to his. It has been sometime since she last saw him at the Bandra cinemas.

They both walk a few steps till she says, "I am visiting Hare Krsna temple ahead, will you like to join?"

"Sure. Though I am not much of a fan. I prefer churches. I like their modern structures."

"Are you not a Hindu?" she looks quizzingly into his eyes, with her own watery ones.

"Are you not a Sikh? I'm just a human, 'Ashu', remember? What brings you here?" Ashu forgets his home memories and has shot off some questions to her.

"I live in Juhu. My father, *Sardaar Kirpaal Singh* used to work for the Sun N Sand Hotel. He is no more. He died of a heart attack while working at the hotel, wearing his uniform. He was a loved member of the hotel staff. The hotel allows me to visit on Sundays and I collect his monthly pension from the owner once a month. He had put some funds into a workers gratuity scheme, which has matured and I collect the monthly payout, so the owner is kind to hand it out to me, based on their hotel records on one designated Sunday of the month."

"Sweet. I am sorry about your father. How is your mother and your younger sister?" "Mother also passed away within a month from his passing. She was already suffering from blood cancer. That girl was a cousin sister and is now in *Panchgini's* boarding school" as she refers to Ms. Chubby.

"I am staying in Juhu with an arrangement due to the hotel owner and I have only one old paternal uncle as a neighbor and family."

Ashu is a bit surprised by the turn of events and the fact that Kiran shares so much.

Perhaps she is lonely.

The lovely young elegant and sprightly girl has been transformed into a calm, yet slightly melancholy woman with sad eyes.

He thinks of his mother, and remembers the sad look in Maya's eyes.

Kiran is wearing Maya's trademark colors too, with a dark kajal dot between her eyes. The vacant gazing look yet the poise and dignity in her walk makes him want to fly on a magic carpet right away to Nawalgarh.

He must seize the moment, he thinks.

There must be a divine reason for him to follow this woman to the temple, something he would not do on his own.

He thinks of Father D'Costa at the back of his mind, and tells himself he will share with Father this accidental chance meeting with his Bobby, that he was smitten by on the first day he set his eyes upon her.

"*God bless Juhu, the sunset and the hotels and restaurants which brought him there!*" he conveys to himself.

They enter the ISKCON temple together. Ashu is taken in by its marble flooring and the simple edifice of the temple, as he hands over his footwear to the 'shoe keeper man'. He looks up at the greying sky leading him to look at the spires.

"This land was a jungle. A temple was built here by the founder Guru '*Acharya -Srila A C Bhaktivedanta*

Prabhupada'. His love for Lord Krishna led him to author many books and take the movement of Krishna Consciousness overseas, especially to the western world. The people of churches, are devotees of Lord Krsna now" speaks Kiran gently. "They believe in the message Krsna gave the universe via his discourse in the Gita and have built a successful chain of devotees by way of imparting knowledge via a chain of '*Guru-shishya*' disciple succession."

She has taken her wine color dupatta and covered her long hair that were open. She evokes a beautiful mother like impression, pleasant and pious, yet soft and loving.

With no children around her, Ashu wonders, how women can appear so maternal, caring, and exude the divine force so strongly. Ashu still gazes at her empty eyes, the water in which has now completely receded. He spots a spark, a fiery awareness, a mix of desire and hunger.

She turns away suddenly breaking the visceral yet tender gaze she was reciprocating, keeping herself in the present moment.

"I like that, there should be give and take in the world. Their priests came to India and uplifted the poorer sections of our society with conversion. We can do the same." replies Ashu. He realizes he is concluding the same more to himself as she has run up the steps ahead.

He follows hurriedly to not lose her with the crowd.

"Yes, *ISKCON* is doing the same, by uplifting the consciousness of the people. The Beatles lead players were followers. It helped the founder guru that famous people adopted the belief" says Kiran.

"Can a belief be adopted?" asked Ashu.

"Let us talk after the aarti, it is going to come to a close." Kiran runs ahead to the steps after washing her hands.

At the left side of the main entry, there is a single water point with a long pipe going upwards and a small tap protruding like the number seven, which is the time of the evening now.

She enters the temple, with Ashu close behind. He is taken in by the splendor of the inner sanctum and watches mesmerized as the '*mahaaarti*' is carried out.

The eyes of the "Radha Rani" idol look to be replicated in the queen ahead of him, the same glow and glory in her skin. Ashu takes in the vibe of the temple and observes many priestly followers dressed in light orange, sandalwood yellow, and whites, bowing down in a full sleeping pose with their hearts to the left, towards the idols of Lord Krsna, Sri Ram – Laxman and Radha Rani.

The priests complete the ritual with offering flowers, prasad, water and the flame of the *diya*, and blow into their respective conch in unison. The vibration with the sounding of the temple bells is a well-practiced orchestra and symphony of melody and music to his ears.

He watches her from the side of his right eye.

He is distracted from God and is spying at her.

She is a picture of devotion, surrender and peaceful tranquility.

A tear falls from her shut left eye. He simply watches bewitched by her while she is in a trance. He is amazed how a young woman, in this city, living by herself, has independently talked to an acquaintance like him and led him to the temple, to this moment and shared her space, her few moments with her Gods with him.

It is quite unlike her behavior at the cinemas three years ago and he can observe the change in her enchanted state of being.

"Is she showing me the way? What is this connection that I feel toward her?" He is drawn immensely by her eyes and the movements she makes. Her walk has assured steps of a divine grace, so does the tilt of her long neck. He has worshipped the moment when she is worshiping, more than bow in obeisance to the Lord.

"Lord Krsna is the God of Love, he was worshipped by many Gopis", she opens, as she has taken around nine to ten minutes, the last few seconds of which Ashu has just bowed his head and stood with folded hands gazing at the people ahead of him lying prostrate near his feet.

"I know." He responds dry in his mouth. He realizes that the entire circumstance of the evening is now coming to a close, but there is a lighter feeling in his heart and a smoothened peace in his mind.

He is just there and no longer distracted.

He is with her in unison at this temple and nowhere else.

He looks on at the idols one last time capturing their image for his memory before he steps out.

After the aarti, she steps out, from the right side of the temple toward a line to collect her '*mahaprasad*'.

"You hungry?" he quizzes her.

"No, this is for my security guard at my apartment. Some blessings for him."

He comes to sit after collecting their footwear. He correctly keeps her sandals, on the right side of each foot, for her to easily wear the same, as she has prasad in her hands.

As he ties up his own Bata sandal straps, he observes some dry sand still stuck between his toes, rubbing them against each other, letting the loose sand fall from the inner sole of his sandal.

He stands upright.

"You should visit me at Bandra next weekend. I can show you the Mt. Mary Cathedral and the St Andrews church. They are my favorite locations to walk around in the evenings. I was at Juhu purely by coincidence as I visited this area of the city after real long. I intend to watch the last show of the movie

"*Akhree Raasta*' and strayed on to walk at the beach after buying my movie ticket. I just missed walking by this temple as I usually enter the beach lane directly from the Chandan Cinema, not noticing this place" "I have visited the Bandra churches and the St. Stanislaus Church as well. I even attended mass sometimes there in the evenings. They have a nice large compound where young boys play football."

"Which religion do you really follow? You seem to be a seeker of all faiths" pronounces Ashu.

"I am a *Bombayite.* I follow many religions. I believe what you believe in, I do not believe in challenging faith of others. During *Ganesh Utsov,* we are at the Parel 'Lalbaug Ganpati Mandal'. I was born to a Sikh family. The Gurdwara's at Delhi and Amritsar are special, but so are all shrines in India. The Gurdwara is special as I have my parental memories and the visits were around them. I have many friends at the Jesu Cooper school I teach at, who are Hindus, Catholics and Muslims. I am yet to visit the Haji Ali Dargah. Bombay presents us all with so much around us, that represents India's faith. We are usually born into our family and faith. We can choose all the beliefs as they are all a path toward the realization of God."

Ashu looks down at her feet.

Embarrassed at his ignorance, pleased by her goodness but most impressed by her passionate sense of a shared morality. Her humility in the manner of her speaking, the events that she has perhaps gone through due to losing both her parents, has changed her and that is evident to Ashu.

It increases her haloed magnetism and lures him toward her like a bee to its honeycomb.

"It is okay if you are impressed by the Church Edifices. My mother taught me this way to be. She was a good human. I strive to be just that. Humanity has its own forms of expression. The beggar on both sides of the street is living off our donation. I cannot check his religion before granting him his food or my charity, just because I am stepping out of a temple. If you step out of the Bandra churches do take note, the beggars seeking help outside sometimes are of a different faith." Kiran has spoken emotionally and as directly as possible retaining her soft voice.

"I do not know so much. I just follow my own heart." acknowledges Ashu.

"That is a good way to be. Do listen to your soul. Listening in to the '*Aatma*' the eternal soul, is the closest way to get to "*Parmaatma*" – the realization toward God."

"Will you meet me next weekend? I do not know why, but I sense a connection with you, which I do not feel with anyone as friend in this city. You shared so much and trusted a near stranger, I cannot impress you" urges Ashu agreeably.

"I know. You are a good human. I saw that at the cinema. God has willed we meet again. I will try next week. But no promises. These are my worship hours... If I feel from within and If I can, I will make it to the Bandra Mt. Mary church next Sunday around the same time. If I do not come, let it not make you feel let down and do go ahead yourself." She reassures, without any commitment. She steps out of the temple complex, gives him a wry smile and hails a rickshaw.

She speeds off without saying good bye.

Next Sunday, Ashu is all set ready to go waiting for a trigger to say action and dash he would like a hungry bunny on a hundred-meter Olympic race.

When Father D'Costa places his hand on his shoulder and stalls him at the door of his house, Ashu turns around with a poise like a swimming diver perched atop the diving board.

Father D'Costa is having kidney trouble and off late eats less but drinks throughout the day. "Son, you seem to be a man in a hurry, in love I must reckon?"

Ashu blushes.

"The same girl? Or meeting someone anew?" asks the '*Father*.'

No response from Ashu is forthcoming, as he is tucking in his shirt into the jeans he adorns.

"Hmmm, can you bring me two buns and a mutton cutlet or a patty when you return for dinner. Either or all of them for breakfast too.? *J Hearsch and Co or Amex* bakery next door, will do?"

"Will do Father!" Ashu rushes out before being put to any more tasks or queries. He is wearing his white *gola* shoes with red stripes, contrasting with the red shirt and the faded acid wash jeans below.

He nearly jogs to the hill before slowing his pace down atop the Mt. Mary steps to wipe the sweat off his brow. In a few minutes he is outside the church. His cardio activity, the jog and the anticipation to meet Kiran has set his heart rate ticking much higher than normal.

He looks to his right and discovers Kiran, stepping down the steps from Mother Mary's statue opposite the church in the open. She is wearing a peach sleeveless top and a dark denim skirt with a blue scarf around her neck.

Standing at the gate, he feels like much the *Anthony Gonsalves* he has idolized in the old movie. He admires her beauty from afar.

She crosses the road and meets him with a greeting by singing slowly the lyrics of the song, '*What a Wonderful World.*'

"*I see friends shaking hands, saying how do you do, they are really saying...*" she cuts off realizing the paragraph ends with "...I love you."

Luckily, Ashu is oblivious to the song and its lyrics.

The song was a hit in the United Kingdom when released in 1967 and had been re-released for an American success much later in 1988. It had made it to the top 100 in the billboard 100 of USA and had been used in the Muppet show and an American war movie on Vietnam that Kiran had recently watched from her video library in Juhu. The writer of the song had written specially for Armstrong as they believed in the ability of the singer to bring various races of the world together.

The song had brought Kiran together with Ashu in the setting of the church on one side and the Mt. Mary steps leading to Mother Mary on the other. The situation fascinated Kiran, and infused the contagious effervescence of Ashu into her.

The candle sellers alongside approached them and they both took one each, as Ashu in his charming chivalry paid for both.

"You seem in a better mood today, no less beautiful than last Sunday though." opens Ashu.

"I thought you had accepted you cannot impress me." retorts Kiran.

"Give me a chance, or at least a break" grins Ashu.

The Mother Mary statue inside gives strength to both.

As she is about to bow her head sitting at the bench, Ashu hands over sheepishly from the zipper pocket in his jeans a red flower to her.

She takes it in her hand and notices that all the thorns have been removed. The rose is moist and has a few water drops hidden inside its petals to keep the flower fresh.

She rubs her fingers softly over the rose and breathes deeply.

Ashu starts to tell her the story behind the broken hand of the idol disfigured by Arab invaders and the fact that the church has been rebuilt twice and attracts people of multiple faiths. It is a first visit for Kiran.

As they come out of the church, she speaks first. "Ok, where to next?" asks Kiran

"Since you have completed your worship, lets walk down toward the sea." There is a lovely juice shop opposite the bandstand promenade.

"Do you not wish to go to Bandra fort?" she quizzes.

"I already have many times before" says Ashu. "Let us have some fresh air and drink at the juice stall."

Kiran blushes due to the sun a bit. It is a warm sunny day with a light breeze, The sky is a bright blue over the steps outside the church and she looks one last time at Mother Mary idol there.

The hillock is about 80 meter above sea level and the vantage position on those steps had made the sea glitter like shimmering pearls when she was up there. She looks back at him, like an equal, with no unnecessary shyness or coy behavior.

She is as direct as him.

"Yes, I know, it is close to '*Rekhaji's* house'. They make swell '*Masala Pau*' and *chaats* as well. Come let us go." She is referring to the iconic and reclusive film actress who lives by the seaside.

They walk slowly downhill, hands not touching each other, yet fingers brushing the others at times. In a few minutes, they are there.

As they sip on two glasses of '*Cocktail*', a Sweet-lime and orange mix juice combination, Ashu bites into a spicy concoction of hot spicy vegetables on foldable white breads.

Kiran enjoys her *bhelpuri.*

Ashu tells her about the bakeries in the area and the items he has to pick for Father D'Costa. He hopes to elongate her visit as he fears she will hail a rick-shaw and disappear like last time.

They agree they will visit Father D'Costa together, as she is amazed to know of a priest with whom Ashu lives as a roommate. Her curiosity is piqued and so is her interest to see the bakeries.

Ashu acknowledges "Well, we are like Ganga-Jamuna another name for the cocktail juice we just had, I prefer these '*Masala Pau*' I have to fetch him his meal of buns and meat concoction he likes."

"Strange. You seem more mischievous than Father and yet being younger, you are the sober one versus a priest? This is a Bombay I did not know existed." says Kiran.

"Well, you may not know India by that same mea-sure. I come from a state of Rajasthan, where it was a mystery to me too in the beginning, when I met Father on the train. But he has given me shelter and is a very kind man, and that counts more than his occasional drinking habit."

"Oh, I have a history trip to Jaipur planned next week with the class 9 boys and girls from school. I intend to show them the real forts as all they see here is a Bandra fort which is in ruins" speaks Kiran. "I take trips to different parts of India every year before the independence-day in August."

"How come you fight the grief so easily?" He refers to the loss of both her parents.

"The children at school help. They infuse a new sense of life in me. When one of them greets me at the gates of the school every morning and wishes me, it makes me want to live all over again. They talk to me like their friend about the music and movies they enjoy. I lose my energy and the spirit gets distilled by the weekend but I am a different person on Monday. I am fine now. Last week the visit to the Sun N sand hotel sent back a gush of memories."

After two hours of strolling Ashu has confided in her all about his family past and roots and his homeland at Nawalgarh. She is taken in by the love he has for his family including his brothers and widow mother.

"You are lucky you have a mother, yet you stay far away. I genuinely miss mine."

"Why do you not visit with me you are already in Jaipur next week, Nawalgarh is the epicenter of over

500year havelis. Please come. I will take leave and also go home and we can all sit together and eat an authentic Rajasthani north Indian meal. My Bhabhi Ma is also a great cook and is going to deliver anytime soon, so *BootiBhai* may also be there. The only one we will miss is Hari."

"That sounds a delightful way to impress a Sikh girl." She flutters her eyelashes.

"Should I see that as a yes?" says Ashu suspended in suspense. His own trip is long overdue and he is keen to meet his mother now.

"I do not know, let us see. There are school children involved and I will have to seek permission after I examine if the havelis are worthy of a visit."

Kiran hails a rickshaw and hops on. She moves in on the seat beckoning him to join. "Let us visit Father D'Costa first."

They pick up the buns, patties and cutlets eventually from the '*McRonnels*' bakery instead of the others, and Kiran insists to pay for all of them, keeping the rickshaw waiting.

They get off near the gate of Father D'Costa's residence, where Ashu tips the driver to wait and shows him the Holy Family hospital cafeteria on the ground floor to visit for tea.

They both get in to the ground floor flat, which Ashu opens with his duplicate house key.

As the door opens, they find Father D'Costa sprawled on the orange sofa with a glass in his left hand.

"Welcome my dears, how delightful. This scoundrel has brought you to meet me finally. I could tell he is up to something."

"Father, she desired to meet you and we are just friends." retaliates Ashu.

"Yes, yes, everyone says that. Make sure you become very, very good friends, before you commit to this traditional boy. He is a scoundrel. But a very genuine man at that. I have never met his family but he is a gem of a guy, I can vouch for that."

"Thank you, *Father,* I wanted to know for sure about that. Nice to know from you. I only know this guy as a harmless fly. I am yet to see the scoundrel angle."

They both break into laughter, as Ashu enters the make shift kitchen to pour some water into the second whiskey glass and places the last two *'khari'* biscuits on a tea saucer. "I do not know about that, but I'm sure he will not break your heart. He does love you. Hasn't he told you that? Its writ all over his face.' Father D'Costa says with so much ease, something that Kiran has also seen and felt in her heart. Ashu has been struggling and bumbling with excitement with but been unable to say anything to Kiran. Ashu is bleeding a tomato red on his face as he enters from the kitchen into the living area and offers Kiran the flaky *khari.* He cannot control his embarrassment like a leaky tomato his ears seem to ooze the juice, as red blood vessels become more visible on both sides of his head.

Kiran is in splits.

Father D'Costa steadies himself and throws two ice cubes into his glass from the ice-pail on the wooden center table. The whisky is still quite golden in the glass.

Kiran wipes her tears both of joy and sadness, to meet a father figure, and enjoys the light moments and repartee at Ashu's expense. She gives him an expression from her eyes to relax and indicates that she is humored.

Ashu's stiffened ear muscles ease up a bit as he drags a dining chair from under the table and turns it around to sit in embrace to the back of the chair. He transforms from the bouncy bunny to a sleepy squirrel, its tail at rest.

"*Father*, you never asked me my religion." Seeks Kiran.

"How does that matter my child? I never really asked him his" responds the priest.

She is touched by his humane way of looking at life. She is actually amazed to know for real, that Ashu's story about Father D'Costa does come out to be true, and such a man does exist.

She looks at his simple two paintings on the wall.

"We all profess the presence of one God, in some form or the other, but truly he is within. Our mothers give birth to us. She is also within us at all points of time. I do miss my own too." *A father, who misses his own mother...*Father D'Costa shows his human side.

She is amazed about his understanding of not having her own parents without asking her any questions.

"May the Lord bless you my child and you may seek me and my time, anytime you are in trouble."

After twenty minutes and two glasses downed by Father D'Costa both Ashu and Kiran get up, bid goodbyes, and step out of the flat.

Kiran hails the waiting rickshaw to start its sputtering engine, pushes her long hair at the back and says a hurried goodbye to Ashu. Her mind is now more at rest having seen his place of residence.

"Meet me outside school next Saturday. Let us see what we can plan. And buy your train tickets to Jaipur first. We can travel by road from there." She mentions the details of her own bookings so that he can be on the same train.

"I will make all the arrangements from Jaipur, Do not worry..." retorts Ashu excitedly, jubilant that the trip till Jaipur seems sure for now.

"Bye" she waves him off.

The rickshaw whizzes away. He can see her peach top through the acrylic porthole kind rear side of the rickshaw. The sun has reduced its intensity as it is late afternoon and the brightness of his life is speeding away from him for now.

The tune of the song from his previous week's movie *Aakhri Raasta,* goes through Ashu's mind, "Lo ji shuru hogayi love story..." as he hums the tune, his heart feels light and his eyes dream on.

He flicks his lock of hair sideways, in his signature head movement from left to right.

Life feels right for now.

"Bring it on" he says, to no one in particular.

A week has passed by very quickly.

It is Saturday and Ashu is dressing himself up already with his socks on, his damp bath towel still around him. He wears his socks first so that his ironed clothes do not crumple when he has them on.

He uses the nail file of a nail-cuter to puncture holes in the Pond's dream flower talcum powder tin, making a large one in only two of the five prefabricated spots. The talc comes out in a hiss and fills up his armpits.

He pulls out the shoe lying under the bed, a tan color Lee cooper that has been polished the night before by him. The muddy Gola shoes lie in another corner of the room, left intentionally neglected. The light lemon color shirt contrasts with his denim blue acid wash jeans and he speeds up as he realizes he is taking more time than usual to get ready.

Ashu has booked his tickets to Jaipur on the same train from Bombay Central station, on which the students and Kiran are booked. He is euphoric to have been able to convince Kiran to let him join on the same trip; he is hopeful that she will also come onward to the trip to Nawalgarh over a weekend and will have extended the same for the school children.

The trip is scheduled for the next day.

Ashu spends time to bring out the notepad and scribble something for Kiran, as Father D'Costa is away for a visit to the near-by Holy Family Hospital for his health check-ups.

Ashu writes, thinking of the journey and his family.

He is also tensed how Maya will receive them if they both visit Nawalgarh together.

He reads and re-reads his note, seated in his towel and socks.

In the anticipation of love,
Time has travelled before me.
My heart is already there,
With you on the train to Jaipur.
I know you will join me,
To visit mother and my family.

He tucks the note with a tin box of '*Cadbury's nutties*' into a red cellophane see through paper and ties a bow tie from a stripped thin maroon ribbon at the top. The red tin box has the nutty nuggets ingrained on the box and can also be felt, jumping in the box like Ashu's aspirations. He rocks the gift back and forth like a can of soda that a teenager would like to spray on his friends in a prank. Ashu's heart beats harder now that the written note is trapped inside the wrapped gift, he can hear it jingling in his chest like the *nutties* in the tin. He rethinks the word '*love*' in the note a billion times.

He has written the note, remembering his father Khazan Chand and his note for Maya. He wants to convince Kiran to make the trip to Nawalgarh in the first two days of reaching Jaipur, so that the smaller havelis are seen before the gigantic forts.

It is raining like pin droppings, a stormy wind knocking the air out of Ashu when he opens the main door dressed in his leather shoes. He decides against changing into his *Gola* shoe and steps out with an umbrella, hope and love in his heart.

He walks across Hill Road, to catch a bus from near Bandra Station climbing on to a moving bus 222 on the red-light signal. He alights near the 'NMIMS' college junction of '*Mithibai* College' forty minutes later and begins to walk towards the Kala Niketan Saree shop. He looks at the numerous saris and resists the random thoughts to buy one for Kiran and Maya.

As he whizzes past the shop, he is thinking more of Kiran than of Maya. He acknowledges to himself that he has to buy a sari for Maya after the date. He has barely saved up ten thousand rupees from the entire years hard work, but he intends to take something back for his mother.

He ponders if he can seek Kiran's help and choice for the same.

He continues onward to the junction toward Prithvi Café, where Kiran has given him time for a coffee at1.30pm.

He is ahead of schedule, as she is always on time yet never reaches before her arrival.

Later he forgets the same as they spontaneously end up watching a play at Prithvi Theatre in the evening and return to their respective homes.

In Nawalgarh, Maya is equally excited that her Ashwini is going to return. She has received the intimation via Delhi from Hari, with whom Ashu spoke from Bombay.

The triad of places and brothers is intact and yet the information flows seamlessly to the mother.

Hari has called up Maya the previous night, taking help from Sonny Bhai, who has been rather kind and soft on Hari, since his parents are away for the month.

"So how is Sanjeevni doing in the village?" asks Sonny

"He is very happy sir, rejoined with his wife and mother" replies Hari.

"I heard you speak to your mother, earlier today, you seem to miss her too already." retorts Sonny.

Sanjeevni had called to speak to Sonny and thank him and then had requested him to allow Hari to speak to Maya, on that same call.

He was reassured by Sonny that Hari had settled well and there was not much work as '*Mony Paappe*' and mother were away.

Malhotra Niwas was much quieter and the neighborhood more peaceful.

"Yes sir, I have never stepped out from the village. I have come here to help Bootibhai that's all. It is an important time for the family. My second brother is also joining from Bombay. It will be a nice family re-union."

Sonny observes that his own aloof parents, have travelled as soon as he has returned from his Hong Kong, Korea and Singapore travels. He pines for family togetherness that is not to be found in his own family.

Rupa steps in with a cup of tea and hot pakoras from the kitchen and lays it on the center table before Sonny.

Sonny himself is quiet and deep in thought, when Rupa cuts in, "Sir, lunch will be at same time or a bit later?" It is already 1230 and past noon, she knows that Sonny will not have much of an appetite after the heavy snacks.

"Huh…?" asks Sonny, lost in thought, thinking of his folks, who are away on their holiday without him. He has the shop running at South Ex, with Dilip

Kakka managing the chores and there is nothing much in business to think about. He has tied up for the contact lens needed for the glasses and corrected eyesight equipment needed to conduct eye tests in their shop.

"Hari, I miss Tiger too. I have an idea. Pack your bags. Let us make a surprise trip to your home town. Will you be willing to travel so soon again?"

Rupa freezes as she has yet not turned back, but is waiting for Sonny's direction for lunch. "Sir, where you are going now?" She is referring to Sonny's arrival the previous day, a day after Sanjeevni has left, and is tired keeping track of everyone's food requirements and cooking as per their needs. "Don't worry Rupa, we will take you also with us. Jaipur is just a couple of hours from Delhi and after a lunch-break we can drive on. Papa's '*Tata Sierra*' is there outside. What more do we need? Food we will now eat tomorrow at Hari's place."

Rupa looks at Hari, gaping with her mouth open. Astonishment on the outside and excitement on the inside.

Hari blinks, looking back blankly at Sonny.

He cannot believe it.

Neither can Rupa, with the turn of events in the past few days.

"It will be a nice picnic, and we all can spend a week at the village. Here Rupa also needs a change, how many days of cooking she has done all the time.

I am curious to meet Sanjeevni at his home and surprise him, as he is going to be a father."

Hari is shocked, "Sir, you are pulling my leg…" "You are already too tall Hari. And don't you want to go? I will take Rupa along and go alone then!" laughs Sonny aloud.

His youthful spirit and light hearted way to suggest the plan, brings an opposite effect on Rupa, who is in tears.

"Rupa has lost her family, you are missing your mother, I am missing your brother more than my own parents. We will leave tomorrow early morning! But only on one condition, we will not tell them we are coming. Let us surprise them and see how Sanjeevni hosts all of us and enjoy the warmth of your home."

Rupa comes in, "Sir, I will pack my bags now in the evening itself. All the windows of the house have to be shut and the gate outside has special steel locks which are lying on the terrace. In how many days do we have to return?"

"Sir, at least inform your own parents..." suggests Hari.

"That will be wise" replies Sonny, who picks up the cordless phone and dials his Mausi's residence number to speak to his mother, informing her about the surprise in few minutes. He urges her to keep it secret from Mony.

The task is done and the plan is set.

Hari and Rupa leave Sonny with the pakoras and tea and move out of the living room.

Rupa, looks at Hari longingly, and brushes his hand, as she walks by.

Hari looks up at her and just gives an innocent smile. He cannot figure out what is happening, as its barely a week since his arrival here, and he is getting to go back with a free ride with his '*ChotteySahib*'

As Hari goes back to the gate to take his position, Rupa heads back to the small house structure behind the house. Sonny munches on his pakoras and has a large swig of tea, pleased with himself and his thinking.

Ashwini is at Bombay Central with his ticket, and small airbag. He hardly has any belongings inside the bag, and has much to struggle with his own belongingness to Bombay city, as he leaves it for the first time.

The presence of coolies at the railway station in their trademark bright red kurta shirts, reminds him of his many yellow and orange kurtas at home in Nawalgarh. It is due to this that he has packed more trousers and one jean, besides the acid wash jeans worn by him. He moves his head diagonally to rest the puff of hair from his left side back atop his head.

Kiran is late and he has gone to the platform number two, thrice looking for her pacing the platform up and down.

Her seats with her eight school children and one school assistant *Megha,* is earmarked and pasted on the notice board confirming the seats. The notice is pasted on the left side of the entry door of the bogey number B3, placing her at seats *18 to 19*, while he is in B4, on seat number 7.

He is one bogey away, and eighteen seats apart from her, but the two bogeys of the train are inter-connected with a foldable contraption, much like that of the musical body of a harmonium instrument. The metal plates on the base of the train shift when the train moves. He has experienced that during the days of travel with his father from Calcutta back and forth to Delhi. In those days, the jump would be exhilarating as a child, to experience some plain fun. Now it would be to just get a look at her, without the unsuspecting school children realizing it.

He wondered how he would break the ice with the school assistant and the children, but worried more about the present, as Kiran was nowhere to be seen. The departure was just twenty-five minutes away for the train to leave Bombay. His thoughts were not much occupied by his home town, as much as the delayed arrival of his love.

Kiran on her part, had started with a two-hour margin from Juhu.

Usually on Sundays the distance would have taken not more than an hour. But her taxi had bro-ken down just before Mahim causeway after crossing the Bandra Masjid. A mere no man's land, where no other empty taxis were available.

Just before the traffic signal and the puncture of her taxi's tire, they had crossed numerous empty taxis at '*Bandra Talao*', but she was late to make the shift.

She had two bags, both heavy suitcases that she could not carry and went on with the Sikh Taxi driver who assured her in Punjabi while replacing the flat tire, "*Assi phaunch jaange*" meaning - 'we will make it'.

The road side break, had allowed Kiran and the two school children she had picked up from nearby home at JVPD Scheme, to take in the ammonia fumes from the Mahim creak next door. The waiting experience took its toll on their young nostrils, making one of the children throw up the yellowish vomit, a melba of the morning eggs, toast and bananas his parents had fed him perhaps.

The Sardaar taxi driver had just finished loading the punctured tire at the back in the boot of the car and placed the bags on the carrier of the taxi's roof, when the rain drizzle started. Kiran insisted to keep one bag with her inside the taxi, and the other two bags of the children in the boot, making the tired taxi driver get off again.

He sat back in the car, his beard wet with sweat and rain giving Kiran a reassuring look that they indeed will make it.

As the taxi sped off ahead of Mahim Causeway, Kiran gazed at the Mahim Church and remembered Ashu's fascination for churches and spoke a silent prayer to Jesus. She knew they had forty-five minutes and on an empty Sunday, Dadar and Worli should not be much of a rush for their taxi to encounter.

The taxi spends five extra minutes at Shivaji Park and Kiran's heartbeat goes up with the *Gokulashtmi* celebratory plans at the road-side.

A set of young men were tying up the '*curdled pot of money*' at the street's junction with the pole opposite the Ganesh mini-temple at the cricket grounds.

She wondered if she would ever make it through this city of diverse Gods and decided to close her eyes, rest backwards and say her prayers to all of them. She had never been so eager for a history trip and the week ahead promised her to see Rajasthan, through the eyes of her new Rajasthani friend. She had completely forgotten about the other six school children who waited as eagerly, with their furious parents, at the Bombay Central platform with Megha.

As Ashu thought about all the reasons, including possible abandonment by Kiran, he noticed a Kwality Ice-cream vendor opposite his own compartment at the station. He fondly remembers his *Baaba* and the child like moments of devouring the vanilla ice-cream come back to him at the Calcutta railway station with Khazan.

He looks up to take in the views of Bombay Central and realizes it is not as imposing as the British structure in Bengal.

As he walks closer to the next compartment nearby, he can see the restless energy of the parents, who are with their respective sets of children outside B3 bogey. Just as he walks back toward the ice-cream vendor, Kiran bursts onto the platform, with the other two children in tow, dragging their own bags. He is about to rush to her and remembers, the official purpose of the visit, and thankfully turns toward the ice-cream vendor. "Two cups please, plain vanilla" he says.

"*Gooood maawwninng teacher!*" the children sing out nearly in chorus. The parents a bit furious till then, now appear more relaxed and facially constipated hiding their angst, not wanting to say anything upsetting the teacher who is going to be in-charge of their children for the week ahead.

Kiran looks at Ashu, gobbling the first ice-cream cup and about to dig into the next, "Hey, why don't you come here and help us with the bags!"

Ashu nearly drops the second ice-cream in reaction.

He is totally taken by surprise by her candor and yet no introduction to the children. His travel was supposed to be hidden on the train. At least that is what they had decided yesterday.

Megha turns around and asks Kiran, "Who is he?"

"Remember, I told you we will have a Rajasthani guide joining us, just so that we have no trouble on the train and in Jaipur."

All the parents turn around to give him approving looks, convinced for good that there is a man accompanying the two teachers onto the trip.

Luckily for Ashu, despite some drops of vanilla ice-cream on his shirt his clean-shaven look makes him look genuine and clean. "Moustache and stubble do not suit you" he remembers Kiran's feedback and Father D'Costa nodding, conveniently sipping into his glass, himself a clean-shaven priest.

He thanks himself for having shaved in the morning. He realizes that Kiran can continue to surprise him.

"Hey children, will you all like to have an ice-cream cup?" he says, before any of them respond in the negative. "Ok, get inside the train and I will get all your cups inside."

The children hurriedly say goodbye to their parents, who are off and about and begin to exit the platform.

Ashu takes Kiran's bags and asks her to stay with Megha and rest of the children bags and follows the students into the train. He makes two more trips to get all their bags inside the correct compartment, escorts Kiran and Megha to their seats and makes a final trip to pick up the ice-creams for the students.

"What about us Guide Babu?" asks Kiran, indicating herself and Megha.

"Here you go," espouses Ashu, as he pulls out two mango duets for them.

He had planned to sit with Kiran and enjoy the mango ice-cream, but makes the sacrifice for Megha instead. "Enjoy, I will see you both before *Sawai Madhopur,* as they change train engines there." Saying that, he departs into the passage way of the compartment.

Rupa is seated at the back of Sonny's car, with Hari seated ahead of her as Sonny takes the wheel. They only bag, is that of Sonny in the boot, as Hari has his cloth bag diagonally across his broad chest. Rupa has a tiny air bag in her feet and a food bag as she knows Sonny will eat all the way, the sandwiches prepared by her at six a.m.

Though she is the domestic help and cook in the house, she treats Sonny like a kid brother, and has the same equation with him, that Sanjeevni shared with Sonny over a period of time. They both had agreed, that one of the reasons it is worthwhile to work at the Malhotra Niwas, is Sonny, his easy-going behavior and kindness.

Infact till Hari came as a replacement, it was perhaps the only reason for Rupa to continue working. She looks at his strong forearms from the back seat and admires his large shoulders on both sides of the front seat. She believes that the sense of compassion of both the brothers is the same.

Sonny looks at her in the rear-view mirror, noticing her admiring Hari and she looks down at the bags. The second bag, has her two Bengali sarees with matching blouses and the morning prayer ensemble she carries everywhere, including her Durga Goddess mini-photo frame. She has visited the temple aside to Sanjeevni's Krishna temple, before the journey and made the two men wait impatiently for five minutes after they both were ready.

"It is always better to leave impatience behind" said Rupa, as she dropped a flower outside the main door of the house and one in the security cabin where Hari, and earlier Sanjeevni would be seated.

Hari watches amused. "Quite superstitious unlike *BhabhiMa*" he says to himself. Yet he admires her plain simple bare feet, as she puts on her '*chappals*' before entering the car.

Rupa has picked up some living '*Sanjeevni Booti*' herbs, from around the Durga idol at the next-door temple. Those herbs are in the side pocket of her air bag. The temple priest had offered her some flowers too, which she had accepted and later placed one in her oily hair, leaving the other two at Malhotra Niwas' entry points.

The road side temple she had visited is a makeshift one, with a large Goddess Durga idol, placed in-between an engraved cut out of the Banyan tree's strong bark. The idol is adorned with flowers and the *Sanjeevni Booti* herbs around it. The wife of the priest hands her one flower and the priest blesses her with another two.

Recognizing her Bengali sari, he asks her "*Bhalaubasa?*" as she blushes, she picks up three stalks of the herbs, with piqued interest, from around the idol. The priest's wife blesses her too, as she is the only early morning, bathed, clean, beautiful visitor and worshipper – making their early morning '*aradhana*' and puja relevant and complete.

Futile feels the priest, who has no other worshipper but only himself in company of the Goddess.

The earlier three nights Rupa has been sleeping above at the terrace of the Malhotra Niwas, alongside Hari, who neither seems to mind, nor does anything about it. They have formed their silent alliance in pure friendship and joint solitary adjustment to the present moment of their lives.

Hari's male presence, has aroused in Rupa an interest to relive her life all over again, afresh. Yet she hopes for Hari's first move, which is yet to happen. She understands Hari's test of patience as his youthful restraint and respect rather than scorn or neglect. He does enjoy the occasional embrace during sleep at night, yet perhaps in full fairness is not aware of her life's background at Malhotra Niwas, earlier houses in Delhi, and prior to that in Bengal.

As the car speeds out of Delhi city, it is Rupa who keeps thinking of it and finds a semblance of balance after weeks of her Nepali husband's death.

She is both thankful in a certain way and also happy, to be able to move on.

She had been married off to a man twenty years her senior, with not much sense for matrimonial life. Hers had been a life more of captivity and forceful matrimony without consummation of the marriage. A year after joining Malhotra Niwas, it was proposed as a package deal for Mony Malhotra's family benefit to allow them to live together.

He treated her more as a slave than a partner. There was never any love between them nor a physical relation between them,

Hari was around the same age, and she had fallen for him the first night she had slept at the terrace. She had been drawn to him perhaps not just due to hormonal reasons, but also to share her grief and life experiences. He was the first person, who had ever listened to her, without any judgement.

She could not understand her mixed emotions of sadness and a desire for freedom, and felt much lighter being around him.

Hari had not disturbed her, yet had allowed her to sleep alongside in embrace and had so naturally accepted her without any intention of stoking her interest, or compromising her with force. As a man he was also new to the man woman experience and

Rupa understood it. He had the raw physicality of *Sanjeevni* and it appeared to her that his elder sibling had actually gifted Hari to her knowing fully well what would happen.

Hence the brother's absence had helped to cement a relationship she hoped for and pined for years. She wondered and thought about all this and how she would face Sanjeevni with Hari together.

This was not at all on Hari's mind. He continued to enjoy the journey with Sonny, and the drive backwards to Nawalgarh. He was busy talking about how Nandu had aged and slowed down, and his missing the fields. He had promised Sonny he would teach him to plough the fields for fun, acting as the second Ox himself to Hariya. If BootiBhai and Maya would permit he could take Sonny on a trip to the nearby '*Gaushala*' and teach him to make cow dung pancakes to cool walls of smaller homes, nearby.

Listening to all this Sonny just nodded as he had already booked himself to stay for a week at the Indian Hospitality Resorts nearby.

It was the same hotel recommended by Ashu to Kiran and Megha and the same had been booked by them for their school trip.

"Jyoti Bhabhi's mother still works there", said Hari. "You will get a five-star experience sir. But you must have your day meals with us and go back only in the evenings."

"Who will take care of Rupa?" asks Sonny

"Oh, don't worry, BootiBhai and Jyoti Ma are there for that…" and places the radio into action.

The rains are trickling in, as the car nears the *Jauhri* bazar of Jaipur, where the trio make the traditional break for lunch at the *Laxmi Mishtan Bhandar* restaurant – discovered years back by Khazan Chand.

Maya's excitement knows no bounds. She has kneaded the wheat three times than what is usually needed, knowing that the next two days will create a few home meals.

She has Sudarshana over at nights to see Jyoti and is only aware about Ashu's trip. Maya has made extra chutneys, and '*gattey-ki-sabji*' for Ashu and brought all the pickles out in full force for Jyoti, though it is Sanjeevni who is gorging on them at this lunch time.

Nandu is chewing the cud, appearing half asleep and Hariya is grazing at the grass left over by Sanjeevni the previous evening.

"Is it you who is about to deliver?" she fools with Sanjeevni and pats his stomach, which has developed a bump two weeks after returning home.

Jyoti looks content, round, and herself about to burst anytime soon, appearing to carry twins.

"It is just one tall boy" says Maya, "That's why the stomach is so big and protruding." Hariya looks up at the reverse of the house and nods as if in agreement and goes back to eating his green meal.

"I just pray for a normal healthy baby." retorts Sanjeevni.

Tiger barks, from behind the house, tied as he is near the back door as if to acknowledge and agree with his master.

As the train pulls into Jaipur station, Kiran rolls her hair into a bun and pokes it with a long sharp plastic hair holder, that has its own mini-bun at the end of it. She quickly puts kajal in her eyes as she throws her used toothbrush quickly into her purse. Megha, on the other hand, is hungry, tired and looks like a mess, but is excited for her fortnight holiday ahead with the children. It is her first experience in Rajasthan and she wants to explore the city and surrounding areas properly.

The children are huddled into the passage of the train, with their small bags and knapsacks, and Kiran is expectedly awaiting support from Ashu at the railway station.

As the train strolls in leisurely into Jaipur station, Ashu jumps off his bogey and runs alongside the train, holding the rails of the compartment that Kiran is in.

Both Kiran and Megha feel comforted as they exchange knowing looks. Kiran is visibly looking diffident and bashful. Megha pinches Kiran, who squeals and tells her to stop hounding her for any answers, as she has none.

Heart of heart, Kiran is over joyed, as she is getting to go on a holiday together with her *beau*, yet not decisive of their relationship, but not dismissive either.

A *Maruti Gypsy* and a *Boxy kind of Mahindra Jeep-like vehicle* is waiting outside Jaipur junction station. They all troop out together and are amused as a tall '*Darbaan*' with very large and long moustache greets them with a '*Namaste*' as they step out of the station. The '*Darbaan*' does a namaskar to each and every child as well, with the same zeal and enthusiasm.

The children quickly huddle into the vehicles with Megha and Kiran taking their seat in two different vehicles. As they board from the back of the vehicle Ashu jumps on to the one which has Megha on it, leading the way to *Jauhri Bazaar* where they all intend to freshen up and have breakfast.

Ashu has managed to convince them to stay first at Nawalgarh's Indian Hospitality Resorts, so they intend to travel out of Jaipur the same day. He has made arrangements for a short break at the *Laxmi Mishthan Bhandar.*

As the jeep drivers are related to the same driver who has dropped Hari to Delhi two weeks back, Ashu makes enquiries at the reception of his youngest kid brother chatting up the drivers.

The driver hits the radio, and a song comes lilting out of the speakers of the stereo into the Rajasthani air, "*Har kisi ko nahin milta…yahan pyaar*". "Oh ho, to find love, one has to give love also!" says the driver very abruptly toward Ashu. Ashu lightly smiles on.

"You are making us travel for two days, non-stop. What was so urgent In Nawalgarh?" asks Megha.

"I rather you all see Nawalgarh first", he says, as he turns at the back putting on his glares. "Madam, Jaipur is about splendor and royalty, while Nawalgarh is about history and serenity" he continues. The jeep rolls on and so does the singer Manhar who while singing is putting his life into the *Jaanbaaz* song. The beats of the song have some sort of whip lashing effect and Ashu hits the off button on the radio.

Ashu has been thinking that Kiran is quite urbanized and is a bit concerned about his own simple roots. Though he has schooled in Calcutta and Jaipur city, he wants to show Kiran around with some aplomb, yet knows the setting in Nawalgarh is quite rustic and the song playing on radio has kind of sounded a warning to him.

"We all will get to see Nawalgarh or you just wish to show Kiran around?" says Megha bluntly.

"No, no, madam, it is not like this," replies Ashu, though he knows that's exactly how it is, he just looks back at her and smiles sheepishly.

His flat reply ends the conversation and he does not try any further to convince Megha otherwise, as she appears keen and sharp to him and there are four other children in the jeep as well.

As the passengers alight from the jeeps at *LMB* they are all led to the waiting rooms. Megha tells Kiran she would like to take a nap, while each of the children want to bathe and change their clothes.

Kiran takes her leave and bids time for a couple of hours. She tells the children to be ready by 2pm. As she steps down towards the reception she meets Ashu at the main road just outside the lobby.

"Some sweet lassi?" he says as he wipes off the milk from his lips and offers half the glass to Kiran. Kiran looks around, realizes she knows no one in Jaipur and takes the tall glass from Ashu. She holds on for a while, looking back at him.

"We have an hour to kill."

"Ok. Let's hurry then, take your glass with you and finish in the gypsy. He pulls Kiran by her hand and seats her hurriedly into the front of the vehicle. He beckons the driver, who throws the keys from across the road, landing in Ashu's cupped right hand. The vehicle lurches forward as Ashu slips it into the second gear quickly putting it into high speed.

Ashu gives Kiran a city tour, driving around Agra Road, the Rambaug Palace, Birla Mandir and the City Palace. They alight near the 'Jantar Mantar' where they get off.

He lets Kiran silently walk inside. She is amazed to find shops inside the city palace where she picks up some bedsheets and Jaipuri red salwar kameez.

As they sit, she asks him, "You went to college here, it's a beautiful city. What drew you to Bombay?"

"The desire to seek a life in a new city, get lucky and find someone like you" he replies flatly.

She swats him with a newspaper bag of her shopping, hardly any force in her blow, more affection rather than spite. He senses his chance.

"Actually, I was destined to meet you and see I have come back with your student trip. Bombay was just the means to my end. I sensed it was a big city and I always had big ambitions. Films we saw living here, the movies, they gave a sense of hope. I wanted to move away from the northern influences and this empty life of traditions. The city here is nice, but there is a leaning on Rajasthan's own rituals and customs which people here will never let go. I grew up in Calcutta and have travelled with my father in trains. If you really ask me, home for me is where I wake up. As long as there is someone to make home with in future, I can wake up anywhere. Currently it does appear to me that Bombay has a nice mix of people, from all religions and customs and everyone is able to mingle and practice what they want. Yet the neighbors don't know you and there is no patronizing of people. Everyone is free to experiment and go do their own thing, go about making their life. It's a city in strife, people in a perpetual struggle, all wanting to become someone."

"True, that's what led my father to Bombay also, he fell in love with the sunsets at the beach and his work place. He became so used to the sea, its salty air and the views, that he could never go back. He spent his entire life in a small five hundred square feet place." Kiran has spoken freely about her family without getting emotional

"Why? What was the reason? When you live in Bombay city, you stand by at the sea and stare at its expanse, you can see the open horizon, it gives you an open sense of space. The sea, the sun, the birds, walk in the sand, pray at a church or temple and you still catch a train on Monday morning and head to work. In my case I just walk from Father D'Costa's house to the school next door and the church, and the hospital. I love that. The college is coming up speedily too…I aspire to teach someday."

"History?" pops out of Kiran's mouth. "No, English." Says Ashu slowly but surely.

"Oh!" Kiran looks surprised. "I did not know you had aspirations for teaching."

"Why, do you think I cannot? I have been writing like my father, some small prose and poetry here and there. I do take interest in Wordsworth more than Shakespeare. The school library has so many books, I read during the recess and church hours in the morning, as I have to wait for Father D'Costa so many times, reading becomes the natural pastime."

Ashu walks up the steps of an enclosed sheltered structure, away from the sun, and seats himself on a natural marble slab. From his position he has a 180-degree view of the entrance hall of the city palace and behind him are rifles mounted on a wall like the rays of the sun, while before him is his own reflection in an imposing wall sized mirror. His head appears like a dot between the rifles for target practice.

Ashu continues, "I have just to decide if I teach in school or college, it requires me to complete my M.Ed.; English teaching is more to expose the children to what is out there, discover and understand the language, what the poets and writers have spoken before us. Analyze their stories." He looks at himself in the mirror, and thinks about staying intentionally focused on staying in Bombay.

"Did your parents have a story?"

The two remain seated for half an hour inside the '*Jantar Mantar*' as Ashu tells Kiran about how his parents met at Solan and migrated back from Calcutta to Nawalgarh.

"I knew less about my father; he was close to *SanjeevniBhai*. But what I know from mother, it was her decision to move back to her hinterland. They had spent years away from home somewhat detached in Calcutta. In the same way, I do not belong here,

I feel my heart beats more in Bombay. I feel constrained here. I do enjoy the weekly movies and churches and once you get used to walking by the sea you cannot walk in a place that is land-locked. The sea gives us the opportunity to feel you are on the periphery between land and sea and it liberates me from this land. Someday, when I am much older, we will see. My father could not go back where he belonged. That is why belongingness should be to people not to places."

"So, to whom do you belong?" asked Kiran naturally.

"Well currently to mother. But not to our place *Moh & Maya*" he tells her about their house, their land, how it was bought in the circumstances of travel and how Maya settled down there and became a widow after Hari was born.

"Bhai has a sense of loyalty to the mother, Hari has the loyalty to the land, as he was born on it. I have love for all of them, but I am not glued to the land. I'm more like a kite, willing to rise, fly and explore, but I need someone to reign me in."

"Hmm, so have you found someone then?" as Kiran asks the question her oxidized silver earrings, mirror the *jharokas* that adorn the city palace.

"Kiran, will you marry me? It will take me a few more years, but I will like to settle down in Bombay. There is a mesmerizing quality about you, not just in your eyes, but it's the way you look at me. I know you love me. Your eyes always reflect your feelings."

"Is this a proposal or an assumption about my likes and dislikes?" says Kiran, play acting angrily.

"Both." Replies Ashu.

"C'mon, let us go back, Megha and the children will be waiting for me!" Kiran ignores the question and desists giving an answer, walking away in her trademark style, stepping out of the tourist spot, toward the area where the Gypsy is parked.

Ashu follows silently behind wondering if he has let out the proposal too soon, or shared his feelings which he should not have.

As the vehicle turns back into *Jauhri Bazaar*, a sullen Ashu parks the jeep. They have not spoken in the vehicle at all and the silence has made Ashu feel dispirited and low, thinking he has mistimed his proposal.

The travel to Nawalgarh suddenly feels too heavy and he does not know how to now show Kiran his family. He has not received an answer from Kiran, so he is forced to wonder about the questions, Sanjeevni, Jyoti and mother may ask.

He has not told anyone about Kiran, Megha and the school children. The booking is in the resort but he has to take them around to show the havelis.

As Kiran disappears above, he decides to dial Father D'Costa in Bombay.

Kiran descends from upstairs with the children and Megha and their bags in tow. She can hear him, "Why? What happened Father?"

As he places the phone back on its cradle, he wipes off a tear and Kiran notices the visible change in mood. She thinks he has been affected as she is resisting an answer to his proposal

"Cheer up *Raja- Rajasthani* lets go see your home." Kiran is keen to meet Ashu's mother and full family before she can actually decide or answer. She knows she likes Ashu but she has no experience in matters of the heart. She is also concerned that they are not from the Sikh community and though she herself believes to have a multifaith demeanor toward religion and community, she thinks it is in their best interest that she makes an informed decision. She can't imagine the house he describes, but the name '*Moh and Maya*' intrigues her.

She is also perplexed on Ashu's choice of Bombay over Nawalgarh the way he himself makes it sound, a town with heritage and havelis.

This time Ashu sits in the gypsy holding Kiran and she has to transfer the one extra child from her vehicle into Megha's jeep.

"Father D'Costa was hospitalized due to diabetes. He passed out at home and no one found him till noon today morning. He is better now and recuperating at the Holy Family hospital" says Ashu, a bit tersely.

The mood in the gypsy is now sullen and all members are quiet, as the vehicles speeds on toward Nawalgarh.

The radio plays the Pankaj Udhas song "*Chitti aai Hai, watan se...*" and sets Ashu thinking about home away from home.

Where is his home?

Ashu wonders again about his belongingness as he is going toward home, it is Father D'Costa he worries about more, than feeling excited about meeting his mother after so long. He takes notice of his affections tilting and yet accepts them truly to himself.

Kiran is comfortable simply observing Ashu and his silence, in her own thoughts weighing her options.

She is not as spontaneous as him.

Sonny's car is just about an hour ahead of Ashu's jeep. Sonny has had an accidental encounter with Megha at LMB Jaipur. As she had hurriedly made all the children eat, Sonny from the table afar had watched Megha's movements.

Megha had gotten the waiter to visit their table a dozen times and repeated several mammoth orders for the children.

Sonny was amused to watch one woman manage her eight children and wondered who their father maybe. Since the children were of unequal heights and chubbiness levels, Sonny never imagined that Megha could be a school teacher on a field trip. He knew of no one who did such things from Delhi and his circle of influence never had teachers in it. He was usually a back-bencher himself all through college and school was a distant memory.

Since Megha used glasses, Sonny even dreamt which spectacle frame would suit her and make her look more beautiful.

"Hmm, more beautiful..." thought Sonny to himself.

Hari and Rupa had barely eaten and were shy to eat with 'Sahib' at the same table and silent with their backs toward Megha.

As Megha hurriedly left upstairs, she left her sling bag at the chair, which was noticed by Sonny. He pointed that out to the waiter and passed it at the cash counter, making sure they called the traveler upstairs and conveyed to her, that her purse was left downstairs. He made sure the zipper was sealed and tied up with a mini lock before he passed it on.

Sonny did not wait, as once the hotel owner assured Sonny they would pass the bag back to Megha, he stepped out of the hotel cum restaurant onto the road, where Rupa and Hari waited. Sonny looked backwards, but since he was himself the driver, he inserted the keys and unlocked the car to hurry onward to Nawalgarh.

Sonny had been to Jaipur several times, but he had not eaten such a tasty meal, nor seen such a beautiful yet industrious woman in Delhi before. He only found her carelessness and approach toward money a bit endearing, as she worried more for the children than her purse.

He wondered to himself as he commenced the last leg of the journey, '*Is it yesterday's pakoras or the meal giving him some acidity?*'

Perhaps it was good old heart burn.

16

THE REUNION

Maya is seated outside in anticipation. She expects Ashwini to reach anytime soon and her expectant eyes are pregnant with tears and a crazy sense of yearning.

Sanjeevni had stepped out into the verandah and observed Maya listening to the radio and carried on toward the well to fill pots of water and an extra drum so that there is enough water in the kitchen for drinking, cooking and washing.

Maya listens to Dev Anand's Prem Pujari, "...*badal, bijli, chandan, paani, jaisa apna pyar....Phoolon ke rang se....*" she is in a world of love. Her love for Khazan Chand, was like this song, pure like still water and sandalwood...a cooling influence on her life.

She remembered fondly this song had been heard by her just once then in the past and it comes down hitting her senses hard with many images flashing before her eyes. Her time in Calcutta with Khazan, and how Ashu was born, the way their youthful lives were spent in parks and at *Chowringhee.* The movies they would see and her argument that it was Dev Anand and not Raj Kapoor who was the more debonair actor.

She wished Khazan was there to listen to the 1970 film song playing today, but she knew she should not turn back the clock, at least not today. If only her spouse had taken care of his own health and not just the refugees from the partition and war.

She consciously deflects her mind toward her son. She knows she has to make the effort as she has a chance to meet him after so long. Her desire to see her son Ashu, more than a few years after he has left, causes a strange excitement and a pining heart. A sweet pain pounding inside, making the afternoon feel rather crisper than it really was on the outside. Luckily there was no rain today and she felt optimistic about her plans to host the bonfire at the back of the house.

Her eyes looked fleetingly toward the main gate of '*_oh_ Maya*', as the M from *Moh* and the '*ampersand-&*' had fallen off. It reflected a status as if Khazan was calling out to her, *'Oh Maya' make it happen you have your family together today!'*

She awaited Ashu's arrival to fix it as he would do so the same day usually in his D.I.Y. style. She realized she doubly missed Ashu because of his ability to get things done outside the house, as he was of not much use inside the house or the farm. The saw, the nails, the hammer and some of his metal equipment was just lying in Khazan's cupboard now for years, and their property had suffered as much as she in his absence.

The song on the transistor, changed to the 1973 number from Sanjeev Kumar's "*Oh Manchali, tu kahan chali…?*" Maya snapped out of her slumber day dream, as if Kumar was singing it for her. As she moves toward the veranda and is about to enter the house, she hears some tires screech that bring her to a halt. She spots the large vehicle of Sonny Malhotra stopping outside the gate.

It was the kind of size of a car not usually seen in Nawalgarh.

Maya walks a few steps to see who it was, and is surprised to see the tall and handsome youngest son Hari disembark from the car to open the metal gates of '*_oh _ Maya*'

Maya runs out, shouting for Sanjeevni, while running toward Hari. The transistor turns to the 1981 song in the background "*Aati Rehengi Baharen….*" The song speaks of watching the world from the heart's eyes.

A mother can't believe her own.

Maya's teary eyes are watching, shocked, that her youngest son is here and not Ashu. She is extremely pleased upon the possibility now of a full family reunion. The car moves up the gravel path toward Maya.

Hari walks behind the car hurriedly.

Sonny parks the car and gets off from behind the steering, bends forward and touches Maya's feet, and says, "*Pranam mataaji!*" making Maya feel immediately older and the most responsible.

Rupa descends from the car, with her sari over her head, saying very softly, "*Nomoshkar*". Maya recognises the Bengali tinge, as much as the border of her sari and smiles back, folding her hands.

Hari thuds into Maya, embraces her, almost lifts her from her hips and makes her go around in a circle, "Ma I am back for a feast for a week!"

"Put me down..." says Maya and Hari obliges, still holding onto his mother, his head over her head, she struggling to break free. The mother is a tad bit embarrassed while the son is more than just euphoric.

"*Arrey*, you are coming with guests, at least keep me informed, I would prepare the food and beds accordingly..." retaliates Maya as she moves toward Rupa, beckoning her to come forward.

Hari quickly makes the introductions and tells his mother of Sonny's plan to check into the Indian Hospitality Resort, for need of better bathing and toilet facilities and an air-conditioned room.

Maya raises her eyebrow at Hari hinting a question on Rupa's relation, but Hari ignores and walks toward the veranda of the house, where he can see Sanjeevni waiting with a bemused expression.

While Maya helps Rupa with the bags, Hari runs empty handed to embrace his father figure, touches his feet and whispers, "*BootiBhai*, what do you think of Rupa? You never told me about her, before we swapped places."

"How come Sonny drove you here?" replies Sanjeevni his mouth open, perplexed about how soon Hari is getting a vacation and a free ride back home, ignoring the question asked by his younger sibling.

Sanjeevni has always put Rupa in the background, as if she does not exist, but today seeing them all stand in their home compound he too blinks his eyes slowly. He is over awed by the situation and his younger brother's luck, to have the '*sahib*' drive him back home.

Sonny walks up to him, while holding Maya in an embrace, his arms around her shoulders, "Your son is very selfish, he wants all his attention from his mother and wife alone for himself. So, we decided to pay him a visit and welcome his new baby together. We have done the right thing *Na, Mataji*?"

"It is your own home beta, why will you stay at the hotel?" responds Maya.

Sanjeevni folds his hand to his '*Chottey Sahib*' and straightens out his kurta a bit wet at the tapering end from the water filling exercise.

Jyoti in full bloom, with her *sari 'pallu'* over her head, is standing at the '*dahleez*' of the house, with a large *thaali and diya*. The noise outside has reached her and she is ready to welcome her young brother-in-law. Expecting to see Ashu, she is also taken aback to watch Sonny comes up first followed by Hari.

Jyoti gives him the welcome placing a tikka on his forehead. Hari is up next, being welcomed, he takes the *thaali* from his *BhabhiMa* hands and does the Aarti on her.

"See I'm here to welcome my nephew. We have to go back in a week, please gift my elder brother his baby so that we can go back."

Jyoti knocks him a petite punch, clinging onto her *sari pallu* with one end in her mouth and the other hand taking back the *aarti thaali* from him. She raises her eyebrows toward Rupa and looks at Maya, before Hari speaks…

"Oh, she is here to help…she had no work since Sonny bhai sahib drove down with me. There is no one at home….at Malhotra Niwas", he looks around for Sanjeevni who is glaring at Rupa.

Jytoti calls Rupa forward and the rest of the members enter the house, leaving Jyoti behind alone to welcome Rupa. As Jyoti does the aarti, Rupa has her feet twitching with tension to enter the house, a tear coming out of her right eye.

"You are more beautiful than what I expected. May Goddess Durga keep you safe and healthy." Rupa places the bag down and bend to touch Jyoti's feet.

Jyoti stops her mid-way and seeks an embrace instead.

She whispers into her ear, "Hari is a foolish fellow, he has never stepped out of the house, leave aside look at a girl. I can see who he has brought to our doorstep!" Jyoti places her fingers on Rupa's chin making her break into a smile.

She can read Rupa's eyes well and understands from her blushing, that she is fond of Hari.

Rupa thinks to herself that Sanjeevni really deserves to be back with his wife.

However little does Jyoti know about her married past, or her attempts to flirt with her own husband. She is aware that Maya has just ignored Rupa and is concentrating on making Sonny comfortable. It is left to Jyoti who has taken her into the kitchen straightaway and shows her the way to the back of the house for the toilets. She urges Rupa to hurry and freshen up and then come and give her a hand in the kitchen.

Sanjeevni takes Hari out to collect some dry wood for the evening bonfire.

As Rupa returns to the kitchen with Jyoti they sit together to gossip, another vehicle at the gate is blowing its' horn asking to be let inside. Ashu has arrived with just the driver, having dropped the children, Megha and Kiran at the Indian Hospitality Resorts.

Maya peeps through the windows to see who it is and spots the jeep in which Sanjeevni had returned just couple of weeks back.

Maya is back inside the kitchen, with a flash she takes the *thaali* and stands at the entrance of the house, as Ashu jumps out of the jeep. His long legs come out like the oars out of a docked boat. He has brown leather shoes on, his acid jeans and a light brown kurta with a leather vest. He takes his glares off and runs towards Maya.

"My Maya darling..." confesses Ashwini to his mother, two arms outstretched.

The transistor beaks into "*God promise, hum sach kehta hai....humko tumse..*" from *Amar Akbar Anthony.*

It is surreal experience as Ashu mimes the song from his favorite movie, lip synching, going down on his knees to his mother, as if he is Anthony Gonsalves himself.

He shows her the cross in his neck, something he has picked up from outside Mt. Mary in Bandra. It is a stainless-steel contraption with a thick steel chain, that also has a key for his trunk under his Bombay bed.

"*Chal* do not do your drama with me. Stand up! I am your mother not your beloved" says Maya.

Ashu continues to kneel and embraces his mother's legs, and places his head at her waist. Water rolls down the cheeks of Maya, and she quickly wipes it.

"You are my first beloved ma, off course after *Bobby*!" This son, has left his muse at India Hospitality Resorts, little to his mother's knowledge unlike Hari who has brought Rupa along.

He plans in style, to get Kiran here later in the evening.

They both laugh, hug and continue to stand there for a few extra seconds till Hari and Sanjeevni see them at the threshold walking back with long dry sticks in their hands.

"Lo there are the farmers of Nawalgarh." says Ashu, raising both his hands.

"*Oh ho – Bombay ke Babu!*" says Sanjeevni.

He walks slowly but assuredly towards the threshold of the house and embraces his younger sibling.

Hari bends to touch Ashu's feet and Ashu stops him mid-way, much like Jyoti had stopped Rupa.

"*Oye Pehelwaan*, you are back? And with a *Bengalan* for mother?" winks Ashu at Hari.

"*Arre* brother, first day first show, and you have started" responds Hari.

They all three enter and introductions are made between Sonny and Ashu.

"Basically, they are Amar and Akbar, and I am Anthony" says Ashu.

"Hmm,...and she is then *Nirupa Roy*." pointing toward Maya.

"Sir have you eaten something, or has Jyoti just served you tea?" Just as Sanjeevni completes, Rupa comes walking out with some wheat biscuits and '*mathri*' in two plates. Ashu pounces on one of them, before Sonny, and Sanjeevni taps him with a loose wooden stick, "Wash up first!"

"Where will you be staying?" asks Ashu to Sonny, talking to him as a mere equal.

Sonny encourages the conversation and they both realize they have to head back in half an hour to the same location.

Ashu briefs his family on the Bombay school teacher trip and the school children and informs them that he will get Sonny back by seven that evening, so that they can all dine together, minus the school children.

He keeps mum on Megha and Kiran's names, and the unsuspecting Sonny offers to drive him back.

Ashu releases his jeep and driver, deciding to return with Sonny in his vehicle.

Maya and Hari go up to the terrace, where under the enclosed roof area, she has laid out mattresses under the sun. She makes Hari lift the mattress and lay it out to get the beds ready for the brothers atop the roof and transfers an extra mattress for Rupa with Jyoti to the room below.

Hari tries to argue a few minutes that he would like to sleep below in his old bed, and Maya brushes him off, urging him to sleep with the men, seeking privacy for Jyoti more than shielding Rupa from any of them.

Jyoti is wearing her orange *ghagra* and has made Rupa dress up in the similar outfit in yellow. Sanjeevni has seen Jyoti wear that before in her shapely avatar, and now has to deal with Rupa making the moves dressed that way.

He watches her eye Hari all the time and is deeply thankful that her attention has moved away from him.

He believes Hari is oblivious to all the attention he is getting.

Maya is in a crimson maroon sari, with her head covered, supervising Hari to straighten all the '*char-pois*' around the fireplace in a diamond shape.

In between each bed, she has made Hari erect a makeshift pile of large cushions for those who can sit without back support, and laid out the four single seater armchairs that they have.

Her own place is at the head of the diamond, like a tikka on the forehead of the back veranda and she has got her chair from the front of the house moved to the back.

Sanjeevni is planning to be seated around the well on two wooden cartons that are usually used to pack the mangoes he sells before the rains. He can see all the beds from there, and it becomes immaterial on which one Jyoti will be seated as he will have a clear view of all her potential seats, from his seat.

Presently, his cycle is leaning against the well, so he takes it out of the way and places it at the support of the main- door, so that Ashu understands that they are assembled at the back of the house and can walk around it.

He goes up to the terrace and overseas the arrangements for the night laid out by Hari, and checks on the pot of water and the glasses. He is at an angular position on the terrace from where he has a view of the main gate of '*Moh & Maya*'.

In a few minutes he watches the Malhotra vehicle that he has washed so often back in Delhi, drive up to their gate. It has passenger like two '*sahibs*' and Sonny and his own brother Ashu.

They enter the gate followed by two damsels dressed in green and red kurtas, wearing them over pant like narrow trousers. He observes them walk at the same pace as the men, sure of themselves compared to the Nawalgarh women that he has been watching over in the last two weeks.

Sanjeevni realizes he is more plainly dressed in his white kurta dhoti, as he whips out the Himachal 'topi' his father had presented to him during their Solan visits to their grand-parents residence.

He walks backwards on the terrace, so that he is not seen and peers over the side where Maya has finished the arrangements, the bonfire is lit.

Hari is seated very casually in full comfort on the stack of cushions, with Jyoti and Rupa atop one of the *charpoi* beds. Their outfits in orange and yellow in stark contrast to the dark red sheet on the bed – make them look brighter for the evening compared to the two urban women walking alongside Ashu.

Earlier at the hotel lobby of Indian Hospitality Resorts Sonny was waiting on Megha and Kiran. He was startled by the noise made by the two peacocks crying outside, as he saw Megha come downstairs from the staircase, her painted hands on the banister, with her handbag slung over her shoulder.

He observes the compliant position she took with Kiran, who had ordered the children to be in bed by nine and warned them that she would return and check on them by ten. She has given them grace one hour to fool around in their rooms.

Sonny is now outside in the courtyard of the hotel by his car, smoking a cigarette and can see Kiran requesting Ashu about the next morning travel while Megha is quiet.

As the women are led by Ashu toward Sonny's car, Sonny throws his cigarette and gets seated inside keeping the car engine running.

As all are seated in, Megha pronounces, "Driver, lets hurry to Ashwini's house, we are already late, its seven." In the front cabin, Ashu looks sheepishly at

Sonny, who winks at him and lets Megha assume that he is the driver hired from the resort.

When they alight, Megha has forgotten her bag in a hurry at the foot of the seat, and follows Kiran hurriedly into Moh & Maya.

"What a large house they have, compared to the matchboxes we live in Bombay. Look at the courtyard and the veranda…so grand." points out Megha.

Kiran takes in the surroundings quietly, as she and Ashu have had a formal understanding after his proposal. She is keen to meet his family and is anxious on how his mother and elder brother take to her. She knows the bonfire is followed by dinner, but she is also concerned for the school children back at the resort. Kiran is the sort of efficient task master, finding it hard to relax, yet the importance of this trip and visit is not lost on her. To top all this off, she has to fend off Megha's concerns and deal with an irritably quiet Ashu after the Jantar Mantar visit at Jaipur.

She assumes he is overly concerned for the priest back in Bombay, who is both his host and boss. She worries about Ashu's future and what he will make of his life in Bombay, and whether she should submit to him. As these thoughts pre-occupy her, she walks into the side garden pathway area adjoining the house, following in Ashu and Sonny's footsteps.

As the introductions go around for Megha and Kiran, the teachers in them notice that Sonny is not introduced. They believe him to be part of the Nawalgarh retinue of India Hospitality resorts or a representative of Ashu and family.

They next witness Sanjeevni come, with large brass glasses on a wooden tray, as the women remain seated and are impressed by the care and sensitivity of the men, as he starts serving his wife Jyoti and Rupa followed by them, and then at last to Maya and the other men.

As the fire warms up, pieces of charcoaled cottage cheese and pakoras are served around. Maya feels the sense of pride as a host, enjoying the glory of having guests, with all her three sons with her, and their loved ones.

She appreciates Sonny's humility and willingness to be with all of them, equating himself to them, understanding from her, how they moved from Calcutta's life to the one in Rajasthan. Maya decides to involve everyone together in a perceptive question and answer session.

"Can I ask all of you young souls a simple question, which each of you will answer honestly?" quizzes Maya.

"Sure!" reply both Megha and Sonny at the same time.

Both disconnected from the family, none having any shyness, are willing to open up. Megha twitches her nose looking at Sonny. "That will be fun!" she says.

Sonny's heartbeat goes up, but he appears the most relaxed from his outward appearance. Hari tries to go inside the house and is stopped by Sanjeevni, while Ashu sulks into the bed opposite the one on which Kiran and Megha are seated.

Jyoti shifts the bulk of her weight and places her hand on Rupa's shoulder and retorts, "Ma, you should ask the young souls and not us."

She is referring to herself and Sanjeevni.

"*Oye*, you are not so old yet, just about to become a mother, not a granny. Tell me all of you, what is your concept of love and romance in your generation. If you cannot express it, do take the liberty of singing out a song from any Hindi movie. It will help us to spend the next couple of hours before dinner at nine."

Sonny asks, "Mataji, you start, and tell us what is yours? And then each one of us will do the same"

Maya relents straightaway as she is prepared with her clear thoughts and years of listening to songs on the radio.

"Son, in our times things were very slow. Their father was even slower than slow. I had to net him myself. He had a weakness for sweets as he had grown up in a mithai shop. He never knew how to start a conversation. So, we took the help from Hindi movies. '*Mughl-e-azaam*' scared me, as I never wanted to lose my love. I recognized Khazan, his moods, his choices, more than he knew himself. His attention was on his family members who were not around him and those that were, were often ignored due to his day-to-day obsession on religion or farming pursuits."

Ashwini listens to all this and his heart aches.

He suddenly misses his father greatly and looks toward Sanjeevni, who is watching Hari very intently.

Ashwini can see the distance that has come between them and the years spent in Bombay has made him even more different from his brothers.

"Well, *Maataji*, my idea of romance, is to have some '*kadak*' chai following samosas and chat at South-Ex market outside my shop. If the right girl comes along, I will like to walk the Janpath market with her. Delhi is in my heart and my heart is in Delhi."

"So crazy and food oriented!" states Kiran flatly, rolling her eyes.

"And you madam?" asked Sonny, looking toward Kiran, but intending to make her companion speak.

He checks out Megha who is awaiting Kiran's response and hopes that Megha would take the indication and have something to say.

"Let the men go first, else they will never speak." says Rupa.

"Yes, that's a good thought. We should have the last turn and option to speak." Jyoti spoke affirmatively.

'My love is sitting inside you" says Sanjeevni dryly, pointing at Jyoti's stomach.

"Arre kya Bhai, be serious, Bhabhi Ma wants an intense answer" interjects Ashwini.

"And what about you, *betta*?" questions Maya, looking at Ashu as if asking for an explanation on why the two school teachers were added into the family tonight so hurriedly, and if he was hiding something.

Maya was hoping, heart of heart he had settled for Kiran, though her strong demeanor and poise, made her seem a bit arrogant and sure of herself. Megha was too short for Ashu.

The external appearances were important to Maya, and she knew instinctively it was Kiran who Ashu would be with, if at all between these girls.

"In our community, they look only for Sikhs." Said Kiran suddenly.

Ashu straightens up on the bed, getting up from his slanting position. Maya and Sanjeevni take note of his change of mood since he is back in the evening, as Ashu is quieter than normal, perhaps a tad bit tired from his journey. They all realize that Ashu is listening to Kiran with rapt attention.

Kiran has come to see Ashu's family, though she knows that Ashu is not expecting any family support or opinion, as he seemed to have made up his mind. Her response does not go well with Ashu as he looks upon it as a blunt reaction rather than a deft reply to ward off any suspicions.

Meeting Maya in few minutes Kiran has to decide to be more direct and open, and not appear backward, considering she is visiting from Bombay. Yet she must not come across as rude or too bold and forward.

"We have to look for turbans and a sense of humor" she laughs. She is hoping to hint to Ashu, to break the ice and lighten up himself a bit. The days leading up to the trip were so romantic and now he had completely switched off, after throwing her into the bonfire, she felt. She could see his brooding nature come to the fore in his own house and familiar setting rather than the free-spirited light manner he carried himself with in Bombay.

Maya laughed, and that lightened up the mood, between not just the two women, but all of them.

"Well Rajasthan is also filled up with turbaned men!" she retorted, proud of her own background and family.

Megha took over, "Men do not speak so easily, that's why I believe a man, who is expressive and can talk, will be fun to be with, as I hardly speak much myself. I am scared of pets and I hope he is not an animal lover. A visit to the movies is surely my idea of romance, chomping on the same popcorn."

"Ma, make your sons also talk…." Jyoti takes over, "…else we will never come to know."

Maya turns toward Sanjeevni, who is straightening a straight enough stick, with another stick. He throws them both into the bonfire, and realizes he is pinned down, being the eldest.

"Well, someone who can cook well, make pickles for me, wait for me to call her and someone who can be a good mother to my children. A very patriarchal way of thinking, but it boils down to that in day-to-day life. There should be respect between both, for only then there can be love. I also think there is no ideal partner, after a few years one has to adjust to each other's nature that does not stay stagnant."

"Whoo…hoo BhabhiMa. There is our BootiBhai's response" goes Hari.

He looks at Ashu who re-assures him, that he can speak out of turn. Ashu restrains himself from saying anything.

Hari opens up, "Well, someone who can play cards with me, sleep silently, alongside. Someone who is a bit naughty." He speaks innocently, making all the women laugh and giggle.

Rupa grows a bit bashful and this time Sonny takes note of it.

Hari intentionally looks at Maya and talks, as if he is addressing her, so there are no glances and looks, with Rupa, throwing Ashu off guard.

Sanjeevni already knows of Rupa's naughtiness and simply thinks that Hari is not aware of her background.

Everyone looks at Jyoti and Rupa now as Ashu retains his silence.

"Someone who calls his wife, more often every week, especially after a phone has been installed in the wife's house after so much of hassle." Ashu and Sanjeevni laugh aloud. Maya too is exasperated, with Jyoti's response.

Her mother, Sudarshana brings another round of food and snacks and settles down at Maya's side.

She urges Rupa to also talk.

"Well, someone who can just give love and knows how to take love. Someone who can be devoted to me and not abuse or get violent."

Everyone grows silent and goes completely quiet.

Sanjeevni can understand her pain.

Sonny is surprised, as he has no clue of Rupa's married life and the violence she has faced. Rupa has been as a girl child, whisked away from home, with no family life and has been working hard as a helper even before she was a woman.

Kiran relates to her plight of not having parents and quickly hides her sympathy, realizing the tough life that Rupa may have led.

No one there knows of her first marriage, despite the open talk, Sonny and Sanjeevni remain quiet and let it pass.

"It is your turn Ashu..." says Sanjeevni decisively. He knows only he can prod his brother for a reply.

"Well. I have seen so many movies. But 'Devta of Sanjeev Kumar comes to mind. It has a song... "*Chaand chura ke laya hu, Ke chal bethe, church ke peeche....*"

Kiran takes the hint, as he she understands Ashu is referring to their bandstand walks in Bandra, behind the slopes of the Mt. Mary church. They had their walk in the day, and perhaps he is referring to the moon above in the clear sky now.

He has done it silently and made a direct reference to his own affiliation to churches and still kept her picture in the reference. She understands from his frame of mind, that he appears to be anchored in Bombay.

"In our times, it was the houses the men built for us" comes in Sulakshna. She remembers her own life, the house in which Jyoti grew up. Each woman defines her need based on what she has not got in her life.

The men over simplifying it, from food to children like Sanjeevni.

Hari's response appears tender enough to Rupa, to continue to love him.

Jyoti's expectation is laid out threadbare that Sanjeevni just does not talk or call enough, making Sanjeevni rue his migrant life in Delhi. He is happier back home in Nawalgarh, Ashu is thinking of Father D'Costa and is upset with Kiran for no reply to his proposal, now that he has even shown her his family and home.

Ashu is neither proud, nor shy, as his own anchor is shifting base into Bombay. For now, he has lost the desire to buy the next-door plot to *'Moh & Maya'*, as he has obtained complete clarity that he cannot live the life his mother has been living. Nor does he want his wife, in his absence to live alone in these surroundings and have his children distant from him.

Besides, he misses his father more here.

It tugs at his heart, that he finds it difficult to bear.

Living in Nawalgarh, reminds him of Calcutta railway station and the double treat ice-cream.

Perhaps that's the main reason, but he does not want to think about that. He accepts, his '*father is not there.*' While Ashu himself lived in the future, chasing Jaipur dreams, he now does not want to *recollect his missed* past with his father.

He remembers Father D'Costa in Bombay.

He tries to cling to the present that he has created chasing his future.

In that respect, he is identical to his folks.

Sonny and Megha have spelt out their urban requests from romance. A day in the city, doing the common place thing. They both munch the snacks, polishing off the chutney before their last cubes of cottage cheese disappear. They enjoy the change of their surroundings, more so Megha, who feels a bit bewildered with the noise of crickets and the food in her hand.

Sonny just regales in the group setting and comes across as reasonably human and trustworthy to her.

She passes on the plate to him and is taken aback by the speed with which he gorges on his food.

Rupa's need, from love, is merely that of no violence.

It is the most basic expectation to have according to Maya and she is a bit taken aback at the revelation. It appears more retrograde than her own times, and Maya wonders what it is in Rupa's past life that has made her talk about it. She can see, that Rupa is barely as old as Hari and yet does not see the same maturity in Hari, though she sees Hari is easy to trust and love.

Rupa is encouraged with Hari's response, and loves the man for his decency, like his elder brother. She wonders how these men can show so much of physical restraint. She has offered herself physically to Hari for over a ten-day period and he has barely touched her other than embrace her in sleep.

Perhaps he does not know what he has to do with her, she wonders.

'Tee-hee' she giggles in her soul. Keeps it quiet on the outside with a deadpan expression.

She knows she will be judged by both Jyoti and Maya.

She can feel Hari's male presence now, and she knows she will miss it at night, as she will not be able to sleep together tonight. In a way she is thankful, as she is not sure of her own restraint.

She already feels the love, and stares at the flames in the bonfire to cool herself down in comparison.

Sanjeevni, without intending to ridicule, cannot understand the time and space that has come between him and Jyoti.

He is a loyal man and has unidirectional love toward each of his relation. He has noticed the change that has come over her, but decides to give her time, patiently till the delivery, as their plans ahead are a bit fuzzy. He has enjoyed the weather here and remotely misses the Delhi city and the temple there. He has lost his routine. But he is okay with that.

He prefers his work at the small family farm and it makes him realize a bit of age that has happened to him, as he has acquired Tiger, lived at another house like Malhotra Niwas. He has come to understood that they have over ten times the size of house and land, and there is nothing pulling him back toward Delhi; *he is concerned for his brother Hari*, but he knows that Sonny is smart enough to take care of him and yet Rupa can also tide over Hari, if need be.

He watches over her, as she makes the overtures now toward Hari, and Hari being Hari, is in his own oblivion. He decides to let Hari face the consequences and make his own decisions on Rupa and not call him back to Nawalgarh. He expects his kid brother to return on his own, sooner than later, expecting him to get fed up of Delhi city life. He thinks Hari is a man of this land and he knows that Hari will return. Sanjeevni chooses at that moment, to himself stay back at Nawalgarh, give Jyoti time and work on the family land, that can still feed all of them. Besides, he has been enjoying the mango pickles and the fruit and flower trees he looks at so much. He has spent a few quiet days sitting before the trees, and talking to them in an imaginary way the manner in which he used to speak to Khazanchand, as if his father was still alive. He has not yet entirely realized that it is he who is the son of this land as much as he thinks Hari is.

He is also the duty-bound son, of '*Moh & Maya*' as he feels protective toward his ageing mother who has alone steered the family ahead. He wants to be there for her. In those moments, Sanjeevni understands his three pronged 'dharma' toward his land, his wife and his mother, all converging in his heart. He keeps the secret treasure quietly to himself, that not one is more precious than the other. He needs them all in alignment.

Maya on her part, has an air of self-assurance tonight.

They have not spent this kind of time, since the earlier days when they had just moved to Nawalgarh.

Ashu has always been away due to education and then Sanjeevni had to be away due to work.

She has been so used to just having Hari and Jyoti with her, that a full house, so many guests and Sulakshna still by her side, makes her feel relaxed and enjoy these moments. There is the shining moon and the embers from the bonfire going up slowly with the smoke at the center. From where she is seated, she looks at each one of her guests through the fire.

A trial by fire of sorts.

They have all come true, and appear loving and genuine to her.

That is all that is important for her, at that age.

She does not have a worry in the world.

Her own trials by fire are now nearly over, and it is the time of the next generation.

The bon-fire allows her to let the focus fall on them, rather than herself and Khazan Chand, and she has made a concerted effort for that. She no longer enjoys herself being self- conscious all the time, stuck in her flash backs of sorts.

She just wants herself to be, *conscious of her conscience.*

As the guests decide to go back after dinner, it is Sonny who drives Megha and Kiran back. Sanjeevni assures Ashu that Sonny can be relied upon as he comes from the well to do Malhotra family. The girls get off the car in a hurry at the India Hospitality Resort and go to their respective rooms.

Sonny lingers back, putting his seat in relax sleeping mode and lights up a cigarette. He notices Megha's same sling bag, in the back of the car.

"What a careless girl" he says to himself.

Inquisitive he opens up the bag, to check its contents and peers over the car window and windshield as it has a clear view in the parking lot from all the room windows.

The noise of some frogs croaking occasionally at night, interspersed with the crickets, makes Sonny feel he is committing a bank vault robbery as he opens Megha's bag.

He gazes at the '*darbaan*' in a red turban at the door of the hotel who smiles back and fingers his twirled-up moustache.

He is amazed to see a packet of cigarettes inside. "Hmm, madam remains quiet, but has her husky voice coming from here" speaking to himself, he picks up her handkerchief and smells the perfume, that Megha had on that night, and that still lingers in his car.

It is nowhere close to the '*Poison*' used by his mother, but nevertheless still smells exquisite.

He flicks off the ash from his cigarette, has a long drag and throws it into the bushes on the periphery of the parking spot. He locks the car, as he steps toward the '*darbaan*', who gives him a smile, as he is carrying Megha's bag on his shoulder.

Once he enters the elevator, he takes out the hotel room key from Megha's purse. He holds it in his hand and thinks of keeping it, to enter her room later at night, and take her by surprise.

As the lift goes upwards to the fourth floor, very slowly, his thoughts get scattered. He realizes he is thinking incorrectly. He decimates and reconstructs a plan repeatedly in microseconds as the lift propels him upward.

He has not had anything to drink and is sober since Maya's family has served no alcohol. He thinks, a futile failed attempt, can backfire. 'What if I scare her?'

There is no indication from Megha that she wants him to pay a visit to her room. He is surprised that Megha has not come back, to fetch either her bag or her room keys.

As he gets off on the fourth floor, he steps out silently onto the foyer, making sure, that he shuts the grills of the lift very carefully. Though the hotel has all modern amenities, it has an old-world charm and the slow, quiet lift helps to make Sonny's heart beat relax.

Sonny remembers the green kurta that Megha has worn, the conservative neck, and her lime green dupatta across her shoulders.

He is intrigued by her choice of eating popcorn at the movies. Sonny has always wanted a partner, who does not consider his family wealth, while choosing to be with him. He finds the girls in Delhi, with their predominant accent and conservative yet providence attitude, to not gel with his own preferences.

He wants to invest his family wealth in a place like Singapore or Hong Kong, to build his franchise overseas. His mind has been set thinking, due to Maya's question and answer session at the Nawalgarh farm, getting him off-centered a bit, like a side-pass on a football field.

As he walks toward Megha and Kiran's room, looking at the hotel key, the metal frame looking up at him with the number 44, he stares at the walls in the passageway.

He realizes he is just directly below Megha's room on the third floor at room 34.

The uncanny camel and horse photo frames on his floor, are absent on the fourth floor. Here the walls are adorned with the tiger and cheetah stuffed heads and there are three artificially created wolves and bears as well. These are at a lower height than the wall paintings on his floor.

In a reflex gimmick, he picks up the wolf stuff head and stops by the large full-length mirror, looking at it like a helmet held between his arm and waist in the mirror. He uses his left hand to touch the teeth of the wolf, and thinks of Megha's neck…

"What has gotten into him? Is it the food he's eaten in the open farm?", he thinks to himself.

He remembers the number of large stray dogs he has avoided hitting on the highway from Jaipur and wonders, why he himself feels an animal like desire in himself. He stares at himself in the mirror, a menacing look having developed on his face, an expression he thought he was never capable of giving.

His inner voice asks him "Why has talk about romance and love, caused an uncovering of such instincts within me?" he wonders to himself. There is still an element of rationality within his mind and he notices he is very human.

"Is it the animal like spirit, coming from the wolf head into me? A mask of animal emotion?" he snarls at himself in the mirror.

He remembers Tiger, sitting at Sanjeevni's feet and visualizes Tiger, panting, without a growl and he can almost hear Tiger's breathing within himself.

His human emotion again gets back within him making him ascertain that he was okay, with Tiger going back with Sanjeevni.

Yet, he almost cringes on why he feels jealous of Sanjeevni's free spirited nature, his farm, his life, his mother, and his expecting wife. *The simpleton* Sanjeevni, fits well into this simple life.

Sonny burns with a sense of jealousy, despite having come all the way to see Sanjeevni's life and his to be born child. He burns from a sense of emptiness in the life his father and mother have given him and the lack of family cohesion that he has just witnessed at '*Moh & Maya*'.

Sonny feels the heat rise up from the back of his neck and come riding up the crest of his head, like a mane of burning displeasure.

He moves the stuffed head, from the helmet position and pats the two short ears, feeling the rubbery element inside the fur, as if they are Tiger's ears. He randomly chooses to place the stuffed wolf over his head, looking back at it from underneath with crossed eyes, into the mirror. He puts his head through the narrow opening below, as he is curious to feel the animal head, from within.

His own barren brains have tipped over.

Sonny stands there silently, not being able to see himself.

It is very dark, and he cannot see a thing, the fear of human emotion, comes back and his hearing sense kicks in. He wonders if it would startle Megha, if he opens her room door that way.

He walks a few paces, goes up a mezzanine level of two steps and reaches the room #44, as he had stopped a couple of paces before it on the last mirror in the passage. He leans over to her room door and tries to listen standing at the shut door, with his double ears. He tries to arch the rubber ears above his head on the wolf head- attempting to listen in to the happenings in that room. There is only silence.

From outside, the scene appears like a wolf, prying and spying over its unsuspecting prey.

He can hear the voices coming from the room behind him, with a light song on the television, so he turns around to stand before room 45.

"*Mehbooba, Mehbooba....*" Belts out R.D. Burman, its lilting tune comes out softly in the throaty crooning voice.

It makes Sonny sense he has become worse than *Gabbar Singh*, relenting to the evil side of his jealous wolf spirit thinking incorrectly about Sanjeevni's circumstances and family.

"No doubt he's cute, but intense." He can hear Megha,

He wonders whom she is talking about.

He moves the strap of Megha's handbag, as it slips over his arm, back on his shoulder.

He looks like part vampire, part portly Rajasthani man, with his state '*jootis*' adorning his small feet. His pink sleeveless jacket, over his light cream shirt, is filled up of his sweat. He luckily uses the strong Brut perfume he picked up from Singapore and he visualizes the *brute* he must appear like. He feels like one.

His head inside the stuff wolf head, now perspiring, makes his hair stick to his head like a wet coconut's coir. He wonders what he has got himself into and still patiently tries to listen on.

It appears that Megha is in Kiran's room, and Kiran is now telling Megha something, to the effect over the music, "Gulshan main gul khilte hain….~ …..*they are a nice family, but Ashu appears more like himself in Bombay. He is out of sorts here….*" Sonny notes that it is Kiran talking about Ashwini.

He feels hurt and forlorn.

Now there is a second brother to feel jealous about.

They are not even well off enough.

The voices get nearer to the door.

Sonny hurriedly walks away, down the two steps, the wolf head still atop his face and he goes and stops, approximately before the mirror where he was earlier and stands there.

It is barely a few paces away, yet nearby the same mirror where he had put the stuffed head on.

Kiran has deflected into the toilet door, inside the room and luckily not opened the room door.

As Sonny struggles to get his wolf head out, the room no. 45 opens up and he can hear Megha say her good-byes to Kiran inside.

Megha has taken a duplicate key to her room and has that swinging, rattling with the metal surface of the rectangular metal keychain in her hands. She had thought she had left her purse at Maya's place and would fetch it tomorrow. The lobby had passed her the duplicate key.

Sonny strains the rubber wolf ear again, listening to the key, wondering if it is Kiran locking her door, or Megha trying to open hers. As Megha steps out, so does Kiran till the edge of the door.

They are both taken aback, as they see Sonny standing a few inches away from the mirror, with the stuffed wolf head on his head, a couple of feet away from their rooms.

"Who is that?" shouts Kiran indignantly.

"Sonny???" interrogates Megha loudly, literally shouting. She can recognize his pink jacket.

A few seconds pass...Sonny turns around slowly to face them, his wolf head hanging down in shame. He is stuck inside, at an angle away from them, not able to estimate accurately whether he is facing them, or the other fellow wolves on the wall.

He does not know what to say. All his options of surprise, scare, and ambush are lost. He just takes a few steps forward, and drapes Megha's bag, from his shoulder onto the crevice of his right arm, offering it ahead to them.

Both the girls blink at each other, dumb founded.

"What are you up to?" says Megha, finding herself.

"Mmph, bhaaaghhhh.." he points out to the bag first using his left hand, and then points to his head... "Hhhhhhallp"

Both of them walk toward him and put a lot of force together, but fail to get the wolf head off while standing. Both the girls are nearly his height at five feet six inches.

He is eventually made to lie down on the floor, holding the side railing of the passage way on the side of the rooms wall as they pull upward and get the wolf head off. It takes them three to four minutes of a struggle to succeed, and Sonny is red faced, wet with perspiration and embarrassment, a slight bruise on his right cheek from the wiry end of the wolf stuffing.

"Yuck!" says Megha. "Why in the hell will someone put this on?" as the head goes rolling onto the side wall near a room door.

"I, I… don't know what came over me. I saw them on the wall and was intrigued to see how I would look and realized the eyes were blocked only once I had it over. My curiosity took the better off me and it blocked my vision. I have been struggling for the past five minutes to get it off."

He hides his reason and contrived plans and feels very sheepish to have to be rescued by both the girls.

Megha bursts into a loud laughter, almost cries as tears fall off her cheeks.

It increases Sonny's anguish.

Kiran interjects after a full minute, to make her realise that Sonny was actually feeling miserable and giving them both embarrassed expressions.

"Oh, thank you for getting the bag upstairs." says Kiran.

Sonny digs the key out of his pocket and tries to hand it over to Kiran, with Megha looking on puzzled, as to how the key came out of her purse. "Well actually I am in the room 34 below and my key is lost. I thought maybe you would also need your keys… and I thought, I thought…."

As Megha tries to conceal, she breaks into peals of laughter again making Sonny breathe easy, seeing that the girls are not upset, and he simply regrets his own stupidity.

Yet he is relieved to be able to breathe in the open. He invites them to a cold coffee at the 24hour café below.

Kiran declines and urges Megha to accept the invitation, taking her turn to be with the children early morning for breakfast.

"I hope you are not the wolf in sheep's clothing." shoots Megha, doubtfully.

"Well, I can't get you popcorn here, but some sandwiches with the cold coffee could be possible." Kiran walks away saying goodbye, as Megha helps Sonny to get up from the carpeted floor and joins him at the cafe.

Sonny reveals who he really is and his real intention to make the trip from Delhi just to be with Hari and Sanjeevni's family. His childlike story-telling and good nature surface to the fore.

Megha orders some jelly with vanilla ice-cream, while Sonny sips from his tall cold coffee mug, as the only turbaned waiter on shift, waits their table till past mid-night.

They spend two hours chatting and Megha looks happily onto Sonny, enjoying her vacation cum work trip.

She acknowledges that she has had a very *'unlike Bombay kind of day'* and mentions it to Sonny.

"Well, its' not like a Delhi kind of day for me either." he replies.

The café is an open one, at the lobby and reception level itself.

Sonny can see the '*darbaan*' security guard outside the glass façade, giving him a zealous smile as he watches Sonny talk to Megha, her back towards the hotel entrance. Sonny wonders about the assumptions the *darbaan* guard would be making.

They both sign off to head upstairs to their respective rooms. Megha chooses to forget how Sonny suddenly found his own 'lost' room key, when he steps out on the third floor.

She says goodnight, waving at him through the grilled collapsing doors of the lift.

Megha takes out her two sets of keys from the back pocket of her trousers and walks towards her room door, staring down the stuffed wolf-head on the side of the carpeted floor. Her Bombay etiquettes and defense mechanism with North Indian men, can now be at a complete relaxation. She pantomimes a 'growl' as she looks back at it sideways with her head tilted from her room entrance.

She enters her room door closes it silently, and then bolts the door from inside.

She places her desk chair before the door.

The Bombay beauty, has tamed the Delhi beast.

17

TIME & THOUGHTS

It is 6:30 in the morning.

Tiger wakes up his droopy eyes, resembling his closed ears falling over his sullen face. He moves gradually from near Sanjeevni's mattress away to the steps of the terrace. He stops and looks back for a minute as he watches Ashu and Hari, steer, their legs raised, yet their bodies asleep.

Unlike Tiger's master who sleeps face and chest down as if fallen into a swimming pool in a diving pose, his siblings sleep with their faces looking up. Ashu has his arms across his face and forehead while Hari has his arms locked between his legs in a fetal position with the sheet thrown away.

Sanjeevni steers and realizes that Tiger is moving about. He observes Tiger's movements and directs him with his left arm.

It has been two weeks and he has made sure Tiger urinates, near the *gulmohar* and mango trees.

Tiger listens to his master, without a bark and lumbers down to the end of their plot of land. He wets the grass behind the mango tree and on his way back, slurps some water from an open pail of paint. He topples the water over and wets his feet, feeling the cool moisture from the earth. He sniffs around the diamond arrangement of last night looking for crumbs of wheat and cottage cheese near Hari's sitting area.

Tiger decides he is the happiest here compared to the old Sikar railway station from where he migrated with Sanjeevni to Delhi. '*Moh & Maya*' presents him with ample running space, two large tree trunks, a circular stone walled well, and ample farm area. Though he has been distraught not being allowed to run through the farm land by his master, he hopes for a second chance to try that once the season changes along the side lines.

Tiger finds the land airy with ample water and trees and grass to run about and play on. He feels as free as a man could in the company of humans.

Entering the house from the veranda at the back, he decides to cosy up under Jyoti's laden bed, rather than go back up the steps to his master. As he enters from the back door, pushing the door inward, the breeze stirs up Maya, who looks at him disgustingly, but does not curse him.

Maya is habituated to the early morning leaks due to Khazan's habit of awakening twice in the middle of the night. Khazan would replenish the water discharged, by a large glass of water and repeat the virtuous circle of events. At least with Tiger, she is disturbed just once, that too just half an hour before her own wake up time since Tiger moved in.

Tiger in the meanwhile is resting for his second but short siesta, his chest heaving with breath like a running car engine due to his morning walk for the piddle. His eyes and mind relaxed finding sleep, with his ears alive in his dreams, cropping up for every chirp of the squeaky sparrows and his friend the squirrel from the adjoining land. He prefers them to the grunting pigeons he decides, and falls deep into his nap.

Maya awakens and goes about the virtuous water cycle, first to the toilet and bath area, then back to fill water from the well. She thinks about her family life and her choices and how that has impacted all the three sons lives. She has got what she wanted from her life. She hopes they can attain the same. Their freedom of choice to travel and return is something she does not wish to curb.

She estimates that Sanjeevni provides her with loyalty and security while it is Ashu who treats her like an equal and a woman, not really revering her, yet exuding love for her.

Due to Hari, she feels connected to the youth and her kitchen. She has to respond to his food needs and yet knows that Sanjeevni will eat whatever he is served. She must wait to enquire what Ashu wishes to eat and keep that in the night dinner menu. She ponders at the differences, yet the sameness of the brothers in their body frames and large foreheads with square chins. Their eyes sparkle differently and it is Ashu's eyes that drive her to think, something is amiss in his life.

On the terrace as drizzling drops of rain faintly fall, Hari realizes a sense of moisture on his sheet over his face. He opens his eyes and looks back at the clouds, as he throws off the sheet, as if beckoning the clouds to send him a pour. It takes him a few seconds to realize that he is not in Delhi.

He has forgotten his Delhi duties for the day and enjoys the sense of abandon and comfort that the home provides. He feels pleased with himself as Rupa's coming with him and staying back, gives him the feeling of impersonating marriage, a woman he can claim to be his contribution to the mother and the house. Yet he feels free from the impediments that marriage can bring upon his life. He feels no physical need, despite being attracted toward Rupa, he cannot understand what it is that keeps him far yet so tantalizingly near. He wants her in his company, yet he is not sure of his family's opinions. He seeks a sense of comfort in the fact that no one has expressed negatively the reason of Rupa's presence, yet Jyoti's acceptance does not exhilarate him. He wants a green signal from his eldest brother

Sanjeevni and wishes to have it before they return perhaps. These are his thoughts as the drizzle converts into a small shower at 7.30am in the morning.

Ashu and Sanjeevni awaken abruptly and help each other to collect their mattresses and carry them under the shelter area of the terrace tank. They crouch on their knees under the tank, looking on at Hari, gazing at his childlike behavior and enjoyment to get wet in the rain.

They can see their own younger selves play on the terrace under the tank from where they would have to collect the cricket ball for their '*pittu*' game downstairs. They know they are all grown up men in that moment and they cannot scold Hari, nor warn him of Maya's consequences letting him deal with the outcome of his choice.

"So, have you found your love?" asks Sanjeevni questioning Ashwini under the tank. He looks at him in the eye.

"He sure seems to have found his" replies Ashu, avoiding his sibling's gaze.

"You seem to deflect these days, questions that are directed at you" retorts Sanjeevni. "It has been sometime since we met together on this terrace."

"Well, the home coming tugs at the heart. It reminds me of everything that I do not wish to be. I do not wish to re-visit our past. I do miss father a lot though and that's why I have been keeping a bit silent" admits Ashu.

He goes on, "This place makes me feel small, not young anymore. And I can see we are grown-ups, we have to provide for ourselves, our existence and we ourselves are now faced with the choices we have to make with our lives, that Ma and Baba made with theirs." He has taken time to choose his words, as it takes a toll on him, to admit it to his eldest sibling that he is not overjoyed about returning home. Yet he does not want to argue or debate with his brother. He has spoken his mind, though not entirely. His thoughts are still etched with Father D'Costa's hospitalization and the fact that he is not there by his side in Bombay affects him.

He has also discovered that he now finds the roads and streets dusty and the largeness of the house and land, makes him feel lost. He likes Bombay, its compactness and the house he shared with the priest, its walls, his simple bed, in the small room he spent the better part of the past few years.

Ashu wonders about the sense of space Bombay city, the sea, gives outside the home and the sense of proximity and closeness it gives within the four walls of the house. He decides not to disclose any sentiments about Kiran to his sibling as he does not know where he himself stands with the woman. He feels it is premature to share anything with the family and awaits and hopes for a positive closure with the woman first. These events make him appear aloof and guarded which his close sibling can recognize from childhood experiences.

In those moments under the tank as water falls with now a larger force, Ashwini finally turns and looks back silently into Sanjeevni's eyes.

Ashu does not understand that Sanjeevni was holding so much back just like their father. To not burden the younger with the responsibilities and the load of the elders, was the way Khazan had taught Sanjeevni.

Sanjeevni was to become a father and could sense his own disconnect with Jyoti. But he too chose not to speak about it. In those minutes of physical togetherness, both the brothers were aware of their distant approach toward each other and yet felt the other sibling to be more afar than themselves to the other.

Ashu in the meanwhile has a momentary self-realization as it dawns on him, that he has completely changed living in Bombay and that was what he was intending for himself from the time of his higher studies. He was seeking a change, to bring that about on his own life, a sense of liberation which the migration had given him. He now had a complete sense of closure. Even if Kiran declined his proposal, he decided not to be sad, though he realized he felt sulky, since she had not responded. He told himself her presence in his city and to come till here, was enough, as she had liked him that much to make the adjustments and come down till Nawalgarh. Yet there was a bitter sweet tinge of sadness, as he had expected an immediate reply, which was akin to his own quick-silver like thinking as he knew they both liked each other and were just meant to be together. He also knew the metamorphosis he had himself been through in these preceding years and felt that Kiran too needed the same time to overcome her own changing hearts. He wanted Kiran to come entirely out of mourning and fall deeply enough in love to be able to spend their lives together.

"Well, it can be said, father is the one, who loved us all equally, yet he was compassionate about his choices. He always gave me time and sometimes I feel he was the only one who loved me, as he had no expectations back in return." says Sanjeevni slowly. "I too miss him very much and can see him mirrored in this land everywhere. I am myself anchored to the farms due to that. Look at our kid brother. He is drenched, and so must be the soaked cotton inside his mattress. Get up!" he yells toward Hari.

Hari looks at the two of them his two elder siblings, crouched like young boys under the water tank. Their knees now wet with the ends of their kurtas, as the water rolled all over the terrace and toward the pipe trap, tapering toward their end of the terrace to fall below in the side of the house.

The side of the entrance from where all the guests had entered yesterday had a small storage area made of cement and tiled walls, and the falling water from the pipe trap off the terrace created an artificial waterfall, with a small man-made pond below.

Maya used that water effectively to water the trees and plants she had on the periphery of the entrance during sunny days when water was scarce. The noise of the waterfall was loud enough and it rang into Hari's ears, who danced in his bed shaping his hands as if miming the shapely figure of a woman.

"That's a man in love for sure." Speaks Sanjeevni.

"Oh, with whom?" quizzes Ashu alarmingly, coming back to the moment. He chides himself, not to worry too much of the future, just like forgetting about his past.

"Did you not see the third woman sleeping in our house last night?" answers Sanjeevni.

"Rupa? The maid? How are you so sure?" 'I can tell. Look at him, not a bother in the world. His youth, carrying him forward. Love does not seek social position. He appears happy with her. She is a woman looking out for love, so she will absorb whatever he gives her. This is a man who did not want to leave this land. His zest for life unchanged, but his heart, now carries his pride and sense of madness with it. This is the way to be in love. When you have now found it yourself, why are you saddened by it?" puts across the elder brother bluntly to the younger.

Since Ashu had not responded with the first gentle query, Sanjeevni had decided to press on.

"Well, I am not saddened, but neither am I enriched by it. I feel it. When I am with that person. I do not carry it around. I worry about it as it may not forever be reciprocated. Lucky is Hari, for he never yearned to be in love like me. Being the youngest, he is always automatically loved by all. His happiness is a feeling he can carry, so his love is not just a fleeting experience."

"Is yours a fleeting one?" worries Sanjeevni as he looks into Ashu's eyes again searching for some honesty and confessions. The deep valley inside them gazes back silently at him.

"No. No one's real love is fleeting. I do not know why I said that. What I find is, perhaps when you find the person, the one who adequately warms your heart, the person does not deliver on the expectations you have from her" responds Ashu finally trying to give his candid thoughts back to his brother.

"Expectation is not love. Set her free, give her the freedom to express when she wishes to. Do not control the expression, as that will repress her love." Sanjeevni attempts to coach his brother, to give Kiran some time, reading his thoughts and last night behavior correctly.

"Wah brother, you seem to know a lot more, without watching movies, reading anglicized books and without stepping into Bombay" says Ashu.

"It comes naturally from my heart, perhaps from father. See how much he accepted of his Maya. He even built a home where he did not belong. He let her lead. I think that's love. He realized she had been following him in his work life. He let her lead during his retirement years. I saw them before Hari was born. They were still deeply in love. A sustainable sort of love is what one must build, with patience and care towards each other. Later once children go away, what is one left with? Today mother reminisces him and still listens to every song on the radio, with only him in mind. She values him more now when he is not there. Each one's love has a different nature. That's the marvel of the world. No two people can love the same way. Mother finds him in music, I find Jyoti in Tiger and in my food at times, for the companionship we used to have during the meals. With every morsel of food, I have remembered her and I have to yet tell her, as she feels otherwise. Her love is in her anger, for she has been separated from me."

Sanjeevni now, goes on, softening his pitch, "And if we merely want to love our own reflection, then why do we need another person. We have to accept our partner with what she brings to the marriage association. Her uniqueness her perspective must enrich your life. What you seek is difficult, as you are making two transitions, one from the land and place you come and one of your heart. In matters of love, please let your mind rest."

"Happiness is the fleeting feeling, that love seems to be compensating Hari with. Lucky Hari."

"Be careful Ashu, your passion and intensity may not get absorbed fully by a woman. Love maybe soft and independent in another person. Do not base all your love only in passionate and intimate love. Have the love of your life before your eyes, but also love all of us in the family back in return. Mother needs it the most."

"Thanks brother your wisdom is not with me, as I think from my heart. You have a deep mind and the inputs you have shared I will carry in my heart and I assure you, I will be patient and wait for the lady of my life to vouch her love for me." Ashu creeps out and shouts out loud, "Oye Hari, come here..."

It is 8.30 am in the morning. They three sit under the tank for a few minutes together as they watch the rain drop back to a drizzle.

The sun takes over and the clouds disappear. A new day has dawned and reunited the three brothers together. They revel in each other's company for a few minutes till they hear Maya move around the kitchen below.

They eventually step down as the rain returns, and the shower increases in force yet again. It lightens the day and the feeling the brothers have for each other, it is like a bond created as much by the weather that day as much by their roots at '*Moh & Maya.*'

Ashu pulls Hari away from his escapade of joy in the rain, but hugs him, hanging on to him for dear life, as if Hari was the elder brother. What Ashu was really trying to do was get some of Hari's luck and sentiments to rub off on himself. He was seeking the same kind of altruistic love that Hari had found, that had been illusive for him.

It is 9.30 am in the morning.

Kiran wakes up amidst the crumpled white sheets on the four-poster bed in her Indian Hospitality Resorts room. She puts aside the off-white net across the two column sides on her side of the bed and places her feet into the Bombay Hawaii slippers she had carried from Linking Road for the trip.

She hated walking inside hotel rooms on her bare feet, as despite using foot lotions at night, her feet were dry every morning. She has missed the nightly beauty regime last night, making her feet ache with dryness.

Her thoughts meander toward '*Moh & Maya*', the very name of their house, the setting last night around the bonfire and the arrangements made by Maya, despite her simple existence. While she looked up to her with respect, she realizes she can never live there in Nawalgarh. To that extent, she is happy that Ashu was not too happy to return home, but the fact that he was not proud of his own roots still bothered her.

She found his hunger and appetite to break-free from that life to be attractive, but his lack of interest in his own family a bit brazen and too independent. Here she was yearning for her own family and folks while Ashwini ran away from them all the time.

She stared at herself in the bathroom mirror, gazing at the mirror work around the frame of the mirror, rather than her reflection. She clumsily drops the toothpaste from her brush into the wash basin. It happens every morning. She would then push some paste again from the tube onto her left forefinger and apply it into her teeth, and then commence brushing.

She looked at herself eventually, smiling back with froth and foam coming out of her mouth, her child like moment of exhilarating experience that she would have with her own father. As a child, she now missed her parents and was alone by herself in this world. She was here, in this most unique place which she had never travelled to despite her school experiences.

She had her freedom, the question that she had in her mind, was '*Would she be fine in letting her liberated sense of life and freedom come to an end?*'

She knew she was alone, yet she felt a sense of independence and abandon, an existence which marriage would not give her. She sought no further security as she lived in her small family home in Juhu, with an uncle for a neighbor. Though she liked Ashu as a friend and his rural roots even engaged her in a rustic sort of way, she was not able to pin herself down to a commitment which she would be comfortable with. She also wondered if the divine love she had for her various Gods in the temples and shrines of Bombay, would simply disappear. She was fulfilled enough in his friendship which she liked a lot and she could be herself in his company. She recognized that she felt comfortable with him around.

Yet his angsty and irritable restless ways bothered her. She cleaned up her toothbrushing activity and decided to get ready quickly to step down for breakfast with the school children early in the morning, as promised by her to Megha.

She wanted to face Ashu on the trip to the havelis, with her '*Indian*' look as she had promised to him.

Megha wakes up in her room at 10.00 am and senses a headache.

She drinks a large gulp of water from her bedside glass, throwing aside the coaster. She has no thoughts of the previous night other than remembering the milkshake Sonny had ordered last night.

She convinces herself, dopey eyed that she is, that she would happily miss her breakfast and goes back into dreamland.

The breakfast in the resort lobby all laid out has the head Chef himself preparing hot '*puris*', with large stoneware bowls lined out in a row like a neat stack of trees.

The first section of bowls is filled to the brim with potato parathas, followed by hot piping samosas, ending with a large dome of kheer.

On the opposite side of one table is another filled up with an assortment of chutneys and two large domes of the same kind of hot diced potatoes with light turmeric, one of them being labelled '*Jain*' and the other being labelled 'just potatoes' perhaps cooked with some dash of garlic and onions.

Kiran dives into these with a large helping for herself and a small pile of '*puris*'. She avoids the samosas and sweets, as she can see the school children walking down alighting the steps, singing aloud jointly "Good Morning Ma'am!" in a chorus.

As the children are getting to travel outside today they are excited and in high spirits. Each of them winds up their dining in ten minutes and Kiran is just placing her coffee cup back in the small saucer, when she observes Ashwini drive into the hotel reception in the jeep outside, followed by another car.

The trip to the havelis he had promised is finally happening and they all troop out of the hotel lobby in few minutes.

The hotel guard opens the door, and gently smiles at Kiran, acknowledging her as looking ready for the morning saying, "*Shubh Diwas, Maam*", she retorts hurriedly with a quick '*Namashkar*' and hustles the children towards the two vehicles.

The children dutifully take their positions at the back of both the jeeps, allowing Kiran to be seated in the one with Ashu.

"Oh, Good morning, someone is seating herself in my jeep today?" sarcasm dripping from Ashu all over the floor of the jeep. The early morning crisp air, the freshness of dew on the leaves in the hotel parking lot, and the misty vapor on the few car windshields is still not off, but Ashu is off the blocks in a jiffy.

"Shall we not wait for your friend and leave ahead, as I have to fill fuel in this tank. My companion will bring her along and catch up on speed at the market temple. You can pay your obeisance to Lord Shiva and I can fill the two jerricans of diesel and stock up for the journey."

Though Nawalgarh had been developed with a proper narrow two lane road, and had Indian Hospitality Resorts as its only famous hotel, it still had not a full-fledged commissioned petrol pump. Cars and jeeps were seldom here only to connect them to the state government buses toward Jaipur. The small kind of village appeal was retained by the place and hardly much of vehicular movement meant people had better air quality and no one really complained while riding cycles.

Before Kiran could really react and respond, her foot dangling outside the jeep, Ashu actually puts the jeep into low gear, starts the engine and revs off the stone pathway of the hotel, shouting "Hold on!" toward the children, each of whom catch hold of the jeep's inner cage of iron rods under the canvas top.

Kiran is thrown inward, as he takes a sharp turn deliberately sharper than necessary, her back juxtaposition onto his shoulder, finding herself off balance. She quickly gets both her feet into the jeep.

As she straightens herself before her students, giving Ashu a silent glare, she shoots off, "Ah, the famous Rajasthani hospitality. The resort should have their own drivers and cars to keep the dust out."

"This is what I say madam, this is not Bombay. I appreciate you coming all the way here, our development is still fifty years behind, but you will get to witness and see the grand havelis which are over hundreds of years old, their murals and ceilings having the love and romance of Radha and *your* Lord Krishna."

A tinge of jealousy in Ashu's voice is apparent.

Kiran ignores him. They drive in silence. The children fooling around at the back. She observes the many rural folk, wearing their white kurtas, dhotis and colorfull turbans, pat comes her question, "How come you do not wear a turban, when you are back home?"

"I just never did." quips Ashu, quickly tossing his hair from the left of his forehead upwards to the right side.

He stops the jeep near a mid-size grocery store and whisks himself off the jeep holding the top, jumping out into the street. She observes his lithe body, moving in his sleeveless leather jacket, his pockets stuffed with something, his white kurta over the same jeans of last night. He puts his left hand into the back of his head, combing the tufts of hair at the back, and uses his right hand to point toward a small Shiva temple urging her to pay her respects.

She gets off, after checking with all the school children who do not wish to join. As he is filling the first jerrican with diesel and placing a '*beetel leaf paan*' into his mouth, he wipes his finger at the back of his head. She walks into the archaic heritage kind of structure of a temple, its walls barely ever painted lying in ruins.

An old head shaven frail monk, a Hindu '*Pandit*' comes out to welcome her with a steel plate of small pieces of coconut and a flower on it. He gives her a small amount of sweetened milk to drink, blesses her, and points toward the inner sanctum of the temple.

As she walks inside, she observes, she is the only devotee, a small bull shaped statue at the entrance. On the left is a well-oiled, bright saffron Hanuman idol before which she bends. There are strong sun-rays hitting the shrine through sections of leaves and branches of the only banyan tree in the complex of the temple, like gold dust, almost like bright sandal-wood talcum powder onto the Hanuman idol.

As she straightens herself, some of the sun rays hit her face and her own salwar kameez figure, like a kaleidoscope of changing patterns, illuminating the mirror work on her garment around her neck.

She stands before the '*Shivling*' observing in silence the milk drops coming from the pot strung above it, her back turned toward Ashu who enters the temple complex. She turns to step back and descend the small two steps of the temple's inner sanctum, the kaleidoscope of color illuminating her face, throwing off a myriad of psychedelic colors due to the sun rays. It hits Ashu's eye like a motley of many splendid paint explosions inside the complex.

He sees her like a Goddess herself, the divinity in her expression, the softness of her heart, the pureness of her soul reflects on her pretty face.

The *Pandit's* wife now, gets up to lift the same steel plate and welcomes Ashu, breaking the silence of the lovely moment he has experienced.

"So, you have come finally *Ashu Betta*, it feels like so many years have passed by." The lady, in her white saree pulls upright a part of it and welcomes Kiran too.

"He would always pray for a pretty wife. I hope this fellow has not promised you the skies. He lives in a make-believe world."

"You are right mother, he does" replies Kiran, before Ashu can speak.

Ashu remains calm and quiet, still observing the shine on and around Kiran, as if the darshan has blessed her so much that it has lit her up in his eyes. He is oblivious to the little talk and is lost in admiring her rather than the Gods in the temple.

"I do feel all of divinity around me, as if I have been here before, whereas it is my first visit." muses Kiran. "This temple is 350 years old, maybe in an earlier life?" asks the seated '*Pandit*'. "May Lord Shiva bless you both."

"May the Gods give her sense *Panditji* to stand by me all my life." jokes Ashu.

"Oh, I am sure she will. Look at me, this Pandit has not even earned twenty rupees a day, but we both manage to eat and live here for forty-five years. Time passes you by, the memories remain of the good young years. Where will a wife go?" expresses the Pandit's wife freely.

She is looking to chit chat with Kiran, who says nothing.

There is silence.

"It is not like this in the city mother, girls have a lot of options." comes in Ashu.

"She talks too much" says the Pandit, taking the plate from his wife's hands shutting her up for any further responses.

He gets up and takes the flower from the plate and passes it to Kiran.

"Betta, take your time, what is the hurry, you are young. You will get many suitors like him, buzzing around like butterflies. The one who walks the snail's pace and stays, standing the test of time will be the one for you".

The Pandit has realized from Kiran's silence, that they are both unmarried and she is merely a visitor. He frees Kiran from saying anything, and yet gives her some direction in her thoughts.

Kiran smiles back peacefully.

"The temple is very beautiful, despite being old. It is like you. Years of wisdom captured inside. I am sure you have seen many like us visit?" she asks the Pandit.

"Yes, and they always return," he replies with pragmatism. "With their full family." He smiles at her, with his two buck teeth.

Ashu folds his hand seeking Kiran to leave as the children are waiting in the jeep outside.

They both step out and Kiran realizes that Ashu has made her visit complete.

She does not need to visit the havelis.

She feels a sense of tranquil after the temple visit. Peace has more power than just independence.

Far away from Bombay, the grief inside her, the chance to meet this '*Panditji*', his feeble old hands and white stubble, watching another old couple, besides her late parents. It makes her believe in a sense of time. An old time that has slipped away, and a future time that is upon her, her time too will come.

She realizes that besides divinity, time waits for no one.

This is her time now and it was destined for her to visit this small temple in Nawalgarh, that gives her a sense of completeness, by herself, despite having lost her parents. It has absorbed all her sadness within and sent her out of the shrine a new cleansed person.

A beau, knocking on her doors, awaiting her confirmation to stich her up.

She gathers her thoughts quickly and decides to keep them to herself, and share it with no one, not even with Megha.

She steps out of the colorful bright red painted compound of the temple, and turns back once more to take in the view of the shrine, its complex, the old walls inside, the ruin like structure, the brown unpainted look on the outside.

It all merges into the water carried by her in her kohl filled eyes.

The drive must continue with Megha's vehicle having just joined their jeep, as it waits behind theirs.

The havelis of Nawalgarh await them ahead. Kiran has to complete the trip for her students.

Both the girls, lost in thought, with the dust that rises from the jeeps as they leave the village, think of the numerous differences the place exhibits with their Bombay life. They both sitting in the separate jeeps, having experienced a little bit of dry Rajasthan life, the change in weather, sparse brown trees wet from early morning showers, have again dried up like the sand in a dessert. Far from the Arabian sea, no beaches no wet sand, the same sense of space and brown openness, the sand and dust replacing the sea and the shoreline.

A sense of distance from their Bombay lives makes them feel a bit lost, yet they do not feel like returning to their urban lives in a hurry. They can see the advantaged lives they live and perhaps the perspective that Ashwini has to migrate, comes into a clearer focus, despite the simplicity of the place he belongs to.

Kiran now gradually appreciates the amount of hard work and travel Ashu must have had to do, back and forth to Jaipur, to get where he has in life and the fact that he has to do that all over again, in Bombay to rise.

She realizes the village does not even have a proper painted temple, leave aside a petrol pump. She can see many travellers ride pillion with three adults to a motorcycle, with bright smiles on their faces, colorful turbans on their heads. She counts the number of cows she passes, aside and on the streets, open in gay abandon completely untethered. They appeared less lost, than Megha and Kiran in their midst.

She looks at many children closely as they cross when Ashu stops the jeeps to let them walk at their pace. Each child, flashes their teeth, many with dark skin exposed through their brown uniforms and small pair of shorts. Young babies stare back as they sit tucked away between the hips and arms of their mothers and aunts. Yet, a majority of the children always flash a smile, oblivious to their living condition, the lack of city life, happy and divine, like the sentiment coming from the '*Pandits*' of the Shiv temple.

Ashu looks at her, through his imitation Ray Ban glasses. He lowers the frame, to watch her from above. He can see her gazing at the children as they cross sheep like, joined in by more and more of school children hurrying for their early morning class in a nearby make-shift school.

He looks at her questioningly almost appealing.

His proposal has not met with any reply yet.

"When will the children come?" He thinks to himself.

She just pouts her lips, and points ahead. "Drive, mister!"

It is 11.00 am in the morning.

Rupa has started her day, with Jyoti. There is a shared sense of joy between them. Jyoti is relieved to have a younger pair of hands in the house and Rupa is pleased to meet someone with solid experience with Maya and her sons.

Jyoti almost takes her in like her kid sister. She has been living so many months with just Maya, an elder, an old mother. She loves her, as Rupa is closer to her own age company and enjoys the nuanced looks and fearful approach of Rupa, as if Jyoti is already now in Maya's footsteps.

She allows Rupa the use of the restroom first. She has many questions for Rupa and her background. As they sit to plan the meal of the day, while Maya goes for her elongated bath routine, Jyoti asks Rupa about their customs in Bengal.

Rupa removes the herbs of "*Sanjeevni booti*' from her airbag and passes them to Jyoti, telling her about the name of the herb and how it is always in the company of Ma- Durga. She speaks about the auspiciousness of the festival and the sweets made in that period.

Jyoti takes the herbs in her hands, places it around her face, and indulges Rupa, taking heavy breaths of it.

Rupa offers it to her as her gift, for seeing and meeting Jyoti.

Rupa has made Jyoti feel revered.

For that alone, Jyoti accepts her for who she is. There is, no longer any pretense between them.

Jyoti takes her hands and places them over Rupa's face. "Oh, lost sister of mine, I know you like Hari – he is a '*bondhu*' like his elder brother. Be prepared for a long life of a lack of *admittance of love*, yet be prepared to pine for him. He is as fond of his bulls as your *Sanjeevni Brother*."

"You can plant it aside the Gulmohar tree" Rupa continues to refer to the plant.

Jyoti realizes her story and affiliation to the herb is not over and she has to reverse back from the reference to Hari.

"If the plant has just been uprooted for one or two days, it will grow again, if replanted. It grows only in the foothills of the Himalayas. I am not sure if it will grow in this weather..."

"Sanjeevni can plant the '*Sanjeevni Booti*' says Jyoti laughingly.

"You are lucky sister. Your husband is devoted to you, he would never eye a woman in the streets of Delhi, the temple priest there, would look forward to his morning visit. He was such a simpleton, always eat what we gave him. He has always been kind to all of us."

Jyoti understands the '*we*' to be the Malhotras.

She nods.

"He is kind wherever he goes, he should be kind to his wife also."

"He is!" points Rupa to Jyoti's belly.

Suddenly Sanjeevni enters the kitchen area, accustomed as he is to his morning tall glass of milk. He is still attired in his white kurta, buttons open, his chest showing, he straightens his hair, and looks at Jyoti asking, "Where's my morning glass of milk?" irritated by the presence of Rupa.

He had expected to snatch a few moments with Jyoti, having observed Maya heading for her bath, from atop the terrace.

Now he knew the next few moments he would get later in the evening.

"Get prepared to do it yourself, as sister is going to have her own little '*Jeevani*' " ...retorts Rupa.

Jyoti observes the prompt repartee puzzled with Rupa's sense of forwardness to cut in, and her comfort in speaking out aloud before Sanjeevni -as if a friend.

Rupa gets up, stirs the already boiled milk with a ladle, and pours out a large glass of hot milk from the vessel and hands it out to Sanjeevni thinking nothing of it.

Sanjeevni turns a bit embarrassed, as he recollects the old odd moments in the Delhi kitchen with Rupa and can see the expression on Jyoti's face.

"Oh sister, it was me who would pour out the milk for him every morning, as he and our co-worker would use the toilets in turns." Says Rupa, thinking nothing much of revealing her ex-husbands presence in the kitchen.

"I was married off as a child, and I am on my first holiday after the mad man died." Jyoti is left aghast staring at Sanjeevni. He looks back at her reassuring her, pointing above at the terrace.

"Hari is going to step down soon. The man is the '*Shri Bheem*' of our family. Please get the stove ready and get the parathas going. Now that you are here, make yourself useful. If mother is not impressed, I and Jyoti alone will not be able to fix things with Hari."

"Don't worry about that. I have already fixed Hari with me back in Delhi itself. It happened in the first few days of you having left. We used to sleep together on the terrace", she says innocently, not realizing how it sounds.

She is leaving Jyoti further aghast, with every sentence, her holding the '*booti*' in her hand, inhaling the herbs, and breathing heavily back at them.

"And why will mother not accept me? I too will bear Hari the children he wants. We can stay on in Delhi and you can see Jyoti sister through her stages of raising your child. You are needed here more than in Delhi."

Rupa seems to have already decided everything for herself and Hari, in her youthful exuberance having said it directly as she sees it. She has spent all her growing up life in Delhi and has waited for this moment, to seize it entirely.

She is very sure of herself and does not understand the hesitating nature of Sanjeevni or his wife.

She looks back at both of them staring at her... and asks, "What?"

Jyoti continues staring, in turns at both of them, having this very convenient and domestic conversation, in her own kitchen, inside '*Moh & Maya*'. No one seems to be asking her if she would like to visit Delhi. But she is happy in her mind, thinking deeply for a minute. It would be good to have Sanjeevni back and make him lift the heavy water, help with the new born child, do the farming and tend to Maya also himself.

The mother and son could sleep outside when necessary, in Hari's room and Sanjeevni could join her inside, when nursing or as she required him.

She points at the herbs and wants to show who is the boss. She has few minutes before Maya arrives back at the scene.

"Can you try to plant these at the back of your trees and water them from the well. The parathas will be ready my lord in ten minutes. I am more worried for my child number one, so don't worry about Hari's appetite. Now Rupa is there to take care. Let's worry about this second monster to come out."

Sanjeevni has wrapped up the milk in one long swig and moves swiftly as he takes the plants and looks at them. Inanimate as they appear he speaks aloud… looking toward Rupa at the annoyance of Jyoti, "You are right, *'Jeev'* could be a nice name." He is responding to Rupa's reference to their baby. He walks out, holding the herbs in his hands to go and plant them outside immediately.

He knows fully well that Jyoti seldom has a request, and if she has made one, he should fulfil it.

He places the herbs on the foot of the bark of the *Gulmohar* tree, where he has engraved a Lord Hanuman on the tree bark. He bends before the make-believe idol. He bends to plant the same.

He folds his hands in silence for a few minutes.

Maya steps out of the bathroom at the back, clean, and fresh, in her crimson maroon saree. Rupa suddenly bursts out of the back veranda, where Maya had remained seated yesterday. "Mother, mother, mother!"

Hari comes running to the corner of the terrace, realizing that it is Rupa who is shouting from below.

Ashu had left over an hour back, as they allowed him to get ready first and use the service of the toilet and bath area. Hari had just piled up the beds and mattress together when he had heard Rupa shout out frantically.

"What happened?" asks Maya, sensing the panic in Rupa's voice.

Her water bag broke, call the Doctor, we need to take Jyoti sister to the hospital."

Sanjeevni has just finished planting the herb, his hands muddy, he stands paralyzed at the base of the tree. From afar, he can view all the spots on the land, he looks up at Hari on the terrace, Rupa below, his mother paralyzed outside the bathroom.

He thinks of Jyoti and her perplexed expressions in the kitchen. His son seems to have arrived, listening to the stories and plans of his future aunt- Rupa!

Sanjeevni chuckles to himself, and begins to take big strides toward '*Moh & Maya*' and collects Maya, by her arm along the way.

Both the mother and son, look at each other, and instantly embrace each other.

"Now Jyoti will also have, like me, someone like you, for herself." Maya realizes she must say the same to Jyoti, after the birth of her grand-child.

Only a mother can understand, what it can mean to a mother.

Thoughts...each one to theirs.

Sonny has just started eating, when he gets a call at the India Hospitality resort, reception, with Sanjeevni on the other line, looking for Ashu.

He agrees, to come over to fetch Jyoti. Sonny had been clear he was not here to see the havelis. He had forgone the company of Megha. He had thought he would visit the family for lunch. He wanted to make a difference in the life of Sanjeevni.

Here he was.

He leaves his breakfast unfinished and rushes out to get into his car, and transport them to the annexed building of the resort, where the small nursing home has got things ready.

He informs Sudarshana on the way.

He is God sent for the family,

Just like Rupa is.

Maya has taken note of it.

Everything seems to fall in place.

It is 12.00 in Nawalgarh.

A wet day in the morning, a dry one at noon.

An eventful and bright one for Jyoti and Sanjeevni for sure.

18

DREAMS

Eight years have passed.

It is 1996.

Its nearly two decades since Khazanchand is no more.

Maya has been deeply reflecting while travelling on the train.

She dives deep into her dreamworld and can see her make believe world. She collects her thoughts, to decide what she must collect to pack into her bags. She is unable to decide on the number of sarees and she has only one slipper, that she wears around the house outside while being barefoot inside.

Maya tells Jyoti not to be upset and reassures her that she will certainly be back. Till then, her own mother Sulakshana will take care of her and her house. The song, "*Pardesi, Pardesi, Jaana nahin...*" from the Hindi movie *Raja Hindustani* is blaring in the background from the next compartment, but the noise of the train rattling on the tracks is interspersed with her grand-son's voice. Sanjeevni's son, Ekjot, is asking her why she is sad. He tells her she should be happy to meet her own sons in Bombay.

Maya is thoroughly confused with the conversation and can see a saddened Jyoti, telling her, "Ma, just because I did not name my son on a God's name, please do not take him with you."

The mother in Maya, is able to see Sanjeevni, struggle to walk till the gate of 'Moh & Maya' after a padayatra of sorts, with worn out clothes, his face darkened with soot. While he awaits at the gate of 'Moh & Maya' he is looking for Tiger who is no more.

Sanjeevni opens the gates and walks toward the '*gulmohar*' tree without entering the habitable area of the house. He is disoriented and is looking for Tiger. Maya knows that Tiger died a few years ago, and cannot seem to tell Sanjeevni this. He walks into the farm land, while she remains perched on the '*charpoi*' at the veranda watching him like a hawk.

Maya is sweating profusely, her neck drips oceans of water from behind her head, her scalp wet and her blouse and underarms feel stuffy with her own odor.

She is worried, '*Who will cook the bottle guard and dal tonight?*' The moistness and sweat make her extremely uncomfortable and she suddenly awakens to realize that she is in a train compartment. The rattling of the train tracks below her, is music to her ears, and she is relieved to find her berth is facing that of Sanjeevni who is deep in sleep himself on the opposite berth.

Maya is now completely out of her dream and absorbs her surroundings in the compartment. She assures herself the train is hurtling with speed toward Bombay, to unite her with Hari and Ashu. Off course, the real reason behind her first-time travel to Bombay, is something else. She is more excited to see her own sons, whom she has not met since last two years. As she nods to herself, she can see the passenger in the passage look at her with a bewildered expression. She smiles back at him to assure him too, that she is not some old lady who is sick of mind or talking to herself. As a thinking mother, she does know when she has to fast forward to reality and that she has been stuck in rewind mode in the past repeatedly. She promises herself not to make references of Khazanchand when she is in Bombay, though she misses him the most.

Maya rarely had the entire family together now. The outing at Nawalgarh, when all her sons were together at the reunion and birth occasion of Ekjot, was now eight years in the past. Jyoti had delivered a baby boy and while there were numerous suggestions to name her grand-son, it was Jyoti's clear mindedness and choice that was selected by Sanjeevni as a sign of domestic loyalty and submission. Jyoti had looked onto Maya for her approval and sought one in each other's glances and recommended the name of Ekjot.

Jyoti was also signaling to Sanjeevni, that he was going to be their one – '*ek*' and only child. Ekjot was now seated on the top berth across his grandmother and above his father's berth. He looked down at his grand-mother, wondering what mumbo-jumbo she spoke to herself even on trains.

Below Ekjot, in the same compartment, Sanjeevni's dream makes him grimace as if in pain and at intervals of musical interludes from the train wheels and tracks, the dream evokes a smile as well. Like his son Ekjot the father too was wearing a '*Pathani kurta pyjama*' and looked like the epitome of blissful patriarchy. Becoming a father had made Sanjeevni calmer and more relaxed and still act younger by the day. He would be playing with his only son for hours in the fields of '*Moh & Maya*', in the mud and never on the terrace. Sanjeevni had locked up the area of the terrace to avoid taking Ekjot upstairs. It was in superstition of missing his own father while Sanjeevni was playing upstairs when Khazan had been with Hari when they had lost him.

The more Maya looked at Sanjeevni and Ekjot, the more she missed Khazan. She felt a mixed sense of joy and sadness, for she realized Sanjeevni had shifted his focus onto the next generation, one that Khazan had been unable to see. Her own affections had now deflected toward Ekjot while staying together at Nawalgarh and the rest were always with Ashu who was alone in Bombay.

Sanjeevni seemed to be now enjoying his dream. "I will certainly get our son back and don't worry I will not lose him in Bombay."

He could see himself assure Jyoti. Sanjeevni realised in his dream, that he was seeing a dream and enjoyed the sweet sleep in the rocking cradle of the train so much, that he wanted the dream to continue. He steered it in a futuristic sense, cajoling Jyoti to join them to Bombay. He knew fully well that Jyoti had stayed back at Nawalgarh.

He became consciously aware, '*Why am I getting to see this dream?*' as he clearly remembered leaving Jyoti behind with her own mother, on the pretext that his wife wanted a break from her duties and wanted to live with her mother for a while.

Sulakshna had also aged and slowed down. It had been decided that she would move into '*Moh & Maya*' while they were all away. This was why Jyoti had sought a promise from Sanjeevni, that whether he came back or not, he was to send Maya and Ekjot back home. Maya had always been her companion from day one of her marriage.

Ekjot enjoyed his father's company so much, but Jyoti always restrained him, even reprimanding him to be with her more often. She was keen that he educated himself like his '*Ashwini Chacha*' whom Sanjeevni never despised.

Yet the father in Sanjeevni neither wanted his son to follow in his footsteps nor in Ashwini's. He wanted Ekjot to make his own choices. Both father and son would spend carefree time on the farm, in the fields, and in delivering the amazing bottled pickles that Jyoti had begun to specialize in to India Hospitality Resorts. As a father Sanjeevni knew, it was a matter of time when Ekjot too would move out of 'Moh & Maya' for his own future and he enjoyed the moments he had with his son.

Hari was asleep on the bench outside the room of Holy Family Hospital in Bandra and was about to have a '*dream*' day.

In the maternity ward inside, was Rupa, who was due to deliver her first baby. Rupa was going through her last-minute checks and had been '*cleaned up*' for the delivery. Having hospitalized her late before midnight, Hari had barely slept a few winks after nodding off at 4am.

Rupa and Hari had come visiting to Bombay to meet with Ashu just a week back. He had hoped to go back to New Delhi, where they were now settled at the back of Sonny Malhotra's shop. Rupa had been keen to visit Bombay and Hari had taken special leave granted by the ever-gracious Sonny, for them to take a holiday. The shop in Delhi was now lying shut, with orders from customers un-delivered. Hari and Rupa were both stuck in Bombay awaiting the pre-mature delivery of their child due to last night's complications.

In his dream, Hari could visualize his pregnant plump wife from behind the optician's curtain, as he spoke out to her aloud, *"Dear, get the glasses off, you will not need that in the delivery room."*

In the dream, Rupa is wearing her Delhi sunglasses, not willing to take them off and is standing behind the curtain at the shop. Hari is staring at her from the cashier counter, aghast, thinking to himself, "*This does not make sense, why is she wearing a patient's hospital robe in the shop?*"

However, deep in the dream he seems to know the precautions he needs to take, "Be careful" he says, "…it has a slit at the back, and you are not wearing anything inside. For the sake of Lord Govind, *pleeaaase…*, customers will start entering the shop anytime soon, return the sunglasses on the glass shelf." It is usually his habit to correct the annoying children who accompany his lady customers in the shop.

Rupa is just provocatively looking back at Hari, her pregnancy in full view, rubbing her right hand on her rotund belly. Her left hand on her hips, her red sun-glasses perched at the bridge of the nose, winking at him from her right eye.

"First you promise me, you will take me to Bombay, I want to wear these glasses there. Call '*Ashu Bhai*' now and let us take off for a few days. You keep just working and guarding the shop as if you own the business. Sonny bhai has gone back to Singapore and is not expected back for six months."

Sonny had moved to Singapore a few years back. The Nawalgarh trip had ended, with both he and Ashu going back to Delhi and Bombay respectively – empty handed, with none of their proposals accepted by Megha and Kiran.

Sonny had decided to open an import business, importing frames of high quality from Korea via Singapore and exporting the same to India, where his father would run the retail business. Even though his father died last year, Sonny had closed down Malhotra Niwas and had moved Hari into the shop. The two of them had developed a good rapport with each other, based on their travels, mutual trust and love. Hari had thus inherited Sanjeevni's goodwill with the Malhotra family, while Sanjeevni himself had moved back to Nawalgarh permanently. This was for the good of Jyoti and Maya, who were both mighty pleased with that situation.

Hari could now see his dream reaching a conclusion, with Rupa having got out of her maternity robe. She was now on the delivery bed. But no, it was actually the optician's chair on which you could do your eye tests. Rupa was hell bent to have her delivery in that space, with getting her eyes checked on the optotype - the Eye test chart. She was still bulgy and blown to new proportions in size, with no baby in sight but lying prostrate face-up on the chair with her glasses on.

Hari could not understand his dream, as he could see his wife, sprawled, bloated and without her robe, on the optician's chair. His scale of worry was on the increase, as he felt he was running against time, to get back to Delhi as he knew in his dream that he was now in Bombay. It was nearly time when customers would enter the shop and leave them exposed for the untimely delivery, making his heart race.

Ashu, in comparison was scared to sleep. He had turned from an optimist in love, to a spurned friend, who had lost interest in day-to-day life. He was barely earning enough from the School Canteen job and would see Father D'Costa in and out of hospitals. That greatly disturbed him.

Ashwini's life had become one of dependency, needing shelter to live with Father D'Costa – who provided his house, and work at the nearby school due to him as well. Thus, his care for him was Ashu's reciprocity for Father D'Costa. Due to that, Ashu was trapped in a vicious circle of School, home, hospital, and late evening simple cooking work, to keep the house chores of Father D'Costa going.

He was engaged in service due to his attachment to the '*father*', missing his own all through the years. He had never despised nor felt jealous at that time of Sanjeevni as he had enough attention from Maya, but now he missed his own father Khazanchand too. This in a way united him with Maya, in pining for the same person and also his love.

Ashwini was spending this night sleeplessly as he realized that Sanjeevni was not just lucky, but had dutifully served their own father, and had been rewarded with a life of love, domesticity and stability at '*Moh & Maya*'; Ashu in contrast had walked out on a similar life, seeking a better future for himself.

At that young age, the rebel in him was keen to explore, but till now with so many years of life in Bombay he was yet to really settle down into a better future. A school canteen's contractor's job was hardly a future. The part time tutorials he ran for the children, barely earned him some savings to invest in his government bank PF account, a habitual investment discipline he had overhead from his father.

Those were his only savings and were nominated to Maya.

All through this paternal vacuum his own yearning for love was not being fulfilled. He had religiously every Sunday, lit a candle at the Mt. Mary open shrine opposite the main church building, and always looked around if Kiran would by accident be visiting.

Despondent, he would walk away downhill from the steps, to hurriedly escort the *Father* back from hospital to his home. At times, Father D'Costa would accompany Ashwini in a wheelchair and a taxi, an old Fiat Safari car, and sit alongside the cross and witness Ashu go up the Mother Mary steps in front of the church.

While the Father's company was enjoyed by Ashu, once at that spot, Ashu would take a few minutes of personal solitude in praying and Father would sit silently, in his locked wheelchair and observe, in repentance of his own lack of discipline. The human D'Costa in him would yet express gratitude before the 'cross' for all that he had received in his life and asked for nothing for himself. Father would spend a few minutes praying for Ashwini, hoping he would find his love.

In the run up to the previous weeks, Ashwini had been in and out of the Holy Family hospital with Father. His dialysis and one foot amputation had left Ashu scarred and scared at the same time. Ashwini now realized that life will not go on forever, even for himself. He felt alone, despite living permanently with Father D'Costa and being preoccupied in care giving activities. Though lonely, his exterior façade of stoicism and resolute singlemindedness, seeking love from Kiran, had come to a dead-end much earlier after the Nawalgarh trip.

Having fallen into grief with so many years of abandonment, he at times felt angry and missed Kiran who had never visited him, or father D'Costa either. Yet he also accepted heart of heart, even if only to himself, as he realized how much more he now needed Kiran, than ever before, as he had failed to get her out of his mind. He was older, weary, and tired, to play the charades games with any other woman, as he only sought the same pleasure of her company, that he had lost eight years back. He had no clue, if she had settled down herself and he only knew, that she had stopped teaching at the school she would teach in Juhu. Repeated trips to the Krishna temple at *ISKCON Juhu,* led to no new discovery, other than attending aartis, imagining her standing by his side.

As he would pray and eventually open his eyes, he would find himself alone. In this way the picture in his mind sharpened and he yearned for Kiran even more. He would assure Maya back home, that he was fine, but he missed her, his own father and yet saw the steady deterioration in Father D'Costa plunging him into an abyss of melancholy.

Kiran had come back to Jaipur from the Nawalgarh trip, unconvinced on the *nature of love* that Ashu had sought from her. She herself had just discovered her own independence and having seen Ashu's family from the inside, she felt the misgivings of his desires and questioned her ability to deliver on them during that time. She recognized that he was in love with her and she had respect for his family. She was also keen to take up a pure spiritual path in her life and live the life of a devotee, but in her inability to see the clear vision and choose between the church and the temple institutions she visited, she was unable to leave her own affiliation to either and leaned back on the learnings of the '*Granth.*'

She did not want to adopt and adapt to matrimonial life as there was a sense of yearning in her to adopt the life of '*bhakti*' and pure devotion to the supreme force.

Hence at Jaipur she was still on the fence as she failed to understand her own self completely; and it was this same sense of confusion toward each faith, yet belongingness to all, that made her appear so endearing to Ashwini.

The internal confusion toward religious belief, yet the ethereal acceptance toward all forms of spirituality had dawned on Kiran, but she saw in Ashu, some strong pre-conceived notions about the way he wanted to live his life. She knew she may not find solace in it herself, but she was even more ill at ease, and doubted if she would be able to provide Ashu the same sense of love he expected from her.

She simply felt he was too passionate for her.

To an extent love also scared her, as she had lost her own loved ones she loved earlier. This sadness overwhelmed her. To give her heart completely away became difficult and was seen by her as an impersonal task. It had hardened her seeing premature deaths in her own family and her focus in life tilted away from life itself and more toward departure from it. Death had become a reality for her at a very young age.

It had been no different for Ashu, but he was carried by his '*desire*' while she was marred by her knowledge of her own '*fatality*'. Building affiliations and attachments frightened her. In that sense, her sense and grasp of spirituality took her far away from the sensual and physical forms of love, as she knew Ashu would expect that from her, which she was ill at ease to provide. Her attempts at love were for some invisible force she experienced in religious institutions, which she was waiting to encounter and ready to embrace. She also knew that death would eventually snatch her from Ashwini and land a double blow on him, after the loss he had had at a young age of his father.

These opposite ways of thinking and ideology, tore them apart from each other. This in a way relieved Kiran who had been overwhelmed with love and was heavy from her own sadness. She became a very different individual by way of her travels and realized she was a mere mortal. Her sadness instead transferred over to Ashwini who could not fructify his love for her, and this desolation permeated deep down into his heart.

Initially it had been a very short cultural school trip, so she had sought more time from Ashu to make up her mind. He had seen this as a rejection and mindlessly, tried to hurry her, seeking an embrace while boarding the train at the Jaipur railway station after the Nawalgarh trip. He had been angry and frustrated, that she had not warmed up to his proposal, even after he had entertained all her requests on the trip.

Kiran had pushed him away, near the toilet passage area at the back of all compartments. They were hidden from view of all other passengers but this had upset Ashu. Even though Kiran had made the trip, it had been muddled for her, as she still emotionally remembered her own folks and had also missed their opinions for her to concur before taking any decision. Her visits to the *Shiv* temple had calmed her, but had not helped her to make up her mind in Nawalgarh. She also knew that Ashu was not yet in a stable profession. This lack of reciprocity had led to Ashu getting hurt and both of them getting off at Bombay central station and going their separate ways.

That was eight years back.

This meant Ashwini still lived a bachelor life by himself and though Maya and Sanjeevni had played no role then, they now understood that Ashu was in a tough situation. With Hari having landed at Bombay and Rupa having gotten into a complication and admitted at Holy Family hospital they had decided to travel as an emergency.

Ashu had the same small house where he lived with Father D'Costa. They both occupied the two bedrooms and he had agreed to host Maya and Sanjeevni in the living room, based on which they had sought the emergency tickets and travelled via *Sikkar, Rajasthan.* Though they had been wait-listed, the T.C. on the train had confirmed their travel status. Once they crossed *Sawai Madhopur*, all three of them had gotten comfortable on their three berths.

For the brothers in Bombay, Ekjot was the surprise package of the trip, as he was anxious to see where '*Ashu Chaccha*' lived, and meet his new born brother or sister – which Rupa and Hari had been nervously expecting.

Maya knew it was the first time for them and Ashu would need her presence to rock the cradle and stabilize his boat. Hari and Rupa had been staying with Ashu, for the past three days and been using Father D'Costa's room. It was fully occupied with Rupa's bags, her hand beads and many other paraphernalia she had accumulated in the trip.

Hari, had carried the Tanjore painting from his Delhi shop as a souvenir for Ashu, as a gift from Sonny Malhotra. None recognized the value of Sonny's gift, but the painting had baby Krishna's image, which led to a rejection from Ashu as it had to be put aside on the nail next to the Jesus Christ crucified sculpture on Father's wall.

Ashu felt that Father D'Costa would feel bad upon his return from the hospital. Hari felt that if the '*Father*' was genuinely a religious man, he would appreciate the culture and the artistry represented by the painting. It had led to the first crack in their relations, as both brothers had evolved away from home and no longer shared any common bond, nor had visited '*Moh & Maya*' in the preceding two years.

Their migration to their two respective cities had made them inhabitants of those cities, imploring them to adapt.

Ashu had become like any '*Bombayite*' a bit cut and dry, lacking ethos. Hari on the other hand, was the proverbial garrulous '*Delhiite*' who had benefitted from the Malhotra family, was joyously in love with Rupa, who had reciprocated his love and was to even start his own family. This accentuated the gap between the two brothers wider than the age gap between Sanjeevni and Hari.

Ashu had also carried the burden of being a solo act, in a new direction and travels from Bombay to Rajasthan's small town Nawalgarh had been a challenge. Silently he despised his family as none had made any efforts to ever visit him, forgetting that it was he who managed the expenses and difficulty to host his own family. Fact of the matter was that even after nearly a decade in Bombay, he had not risen in work, and his personal life was yet to find a firm footing. Father D'Costa was his only savior, and now he was not able to act as a savior in return to the Father as he saw his second limb being lost to amputation that same week.

Ashu had broken into a fight with Hari the previous evening. Hari and Rupa had desired to visit the Juhu beach, which had been facilitated by Ashu, despite being harassed and torn in different directions. He had to care for the Father and also care for his younger sibling, who appeared more mature and set in his relations with his wife, than what Ashu could achieve in the next decade. This had set Ashu thinking, about his own future in a dejected sort of way.

On the return journey, Hari, Ashu and Rupa had taken a rickshaw from the beach area and the bumpy ride back had been inconvenient for Rupa. Her system was shaken and this led to a complication and discomfort for her, requiring the hospital visit next-door to Holy Family.

Both Hari and Rupa had thought this was an innocent visit, but the doctors had decided to hospitalize her instantly to save the baby and the mother. Ashu's long, solitary period of depressed state of mind, his tiresome travails of care for Father D'Costa, his searching eyes at Juhu Beach and the Sun & Sand Hotel, looking out for Kiran, and the stay at home with Hari, seeing him so much in love with Rupa had triggered anger and near despicable behavior toward Hari and Rupa.

It was Rupa's calmness and pleading, that she needed to see a hospital, that had broken the verbal duel between the two brothers. Hari had stayed quiet and calm while Ashu had broken into a diatribe of expletives and blamed Hari for having come to Bombay amidst the tensions that he was already facing.

It can be said in favor of Ashu, that he had to arrange the money with the help of Father D'Costa, who himself was hospitalized for treatment post his second leg amputation. The father had offered his personal security to the hospital and assured payment of money from his own savings. Ashu had broken down in tears in Father D'Costa's room, sobbing while holding his hands. Ashu had returned from the hospital leaving Hari on the bench outside Rupa's room, to fend for themselves. The deposit required for the room had been arranged with the contacts of Father D'Costa.

Ashu had slept around 5am in the morning, and knew, that his mother and Sanjeevni would be at his house – arrive as they would have to on their own. He had luckily not promised to receive them, but had sent his address to them in an earlier letter and photograph with Father D'Costa he had clicked at the school *Andrean Fair* four years back.

He knew his mother had his residence address.

Yet the dream Ashu saw, made his heart rate rise and his worries quadruple. He was astride on a horse at Juhu beach, in his wedding attire, and could see Rupa and Hari on the pavement away from the sandy beach. It appeared that Rupa was clutching her tummy – crying out loud to him to join them. On the other side of the beach, were Sanjeevni and Ekjot, egging him on to ride a horse they were astride on. The father son duo riding towards Ashu in the direction opposite to Sun & Sand Hotel.

Maya, stood in her trademark wine maroon Saree as did Kiran, on the beachfront facing the Arabian sea, both walking together towards the waves.

Kiran turns back to call Ashu toward them. Ashu suddenly finds everyone looking up to him to fulfil their need of his company and their responsibilities.

The horseman whipping the horse is Father D'Costa without both his legs. Ashu is struggling to find *Father's* feet and can see only the four horse-shoe clicking on and the tail swishing with Father D'Costa having suddenly disappeared.

The horse unable to move, in the confusion, decides to let go off himself and relieves himself urinating into a puddle on the beach. He can now see *the Father* in front of Hari and Rupa, suddenly embedded into the sand dunes, no feet all bandages asking him to go toward Rupa.

As Ashu looks up from the sand dunes, he notices Tiger, walking sullenly toward two sand sculptors of Jesus & Krishna, both made by Jyoti Bhabhi on the beach. Tiger goes and takes his position in the center, while Jyoti Bhabhi asks "*Which God will you choose Ashu? Kiran always wanted to know how religious you are?*"

"But I thought Tiger had died five years ago, what is he doing here?" asks a confused Ashwini.

Jyoti Bhabhi again asks him, "Do think about our Krishna too and give our love to Jesus. By the way, did Rupa get you the '*Sanjeevni Booti*' plant from Delhi?"

"Oh, I had to plant the *Sanjeevni Booti* at the back of Father D'Costa's building compound. There is a small garden patch there. Rupa had brought it four days back, and I left it immersed in a glass vase." Ashu replies and admits to his forgetfulness.

"Let the life in any green plant around you, not die Ashu. It is important for the future of our children. Complete that Ashu, it is important, Sanjeevni is important. The *booti* is important. It will bring a new life ahead for you. It has worked wonders for us at '*Moh & Maya*' Listen to Rupa. Listen and plant Sanjeevni. The booti. Not your brother. Please send him back with Ekjot soon after you give us the good news."

Ashu can see the sculpted sand images of Jesus and Krishna, and Tiger melt away into the beach while the image of Maya and Kiran glitter in the backdrop of the Juhu Beach sun. That remains his last image of Juhu in his mind.

His mother and wife together.

Jyoti Bhabhi, puts the phone back on the phone cradle and there is a loud click in Ashu's mind.

It wakes Ashu up from his dream.

At 8.00 am he feels very rested despite a short nap of few hours. He feels serene. In that peaceful mood, the old '*prophecy*' suddenly dawns on him from the rays of the sun coming into his bedroom window. He remembers his father's written words in '*Degrees of Separation*' and understands why his yearning love for Kiran, has not been fulfilled.

There will be just no, None.
No degree of separation from being one.
No degree of separation, between us.

Perhaps that is why he can see all his family characters in his dream. *'Does he have the same sixth sense that his father had?'* He thinks to himself, and tosses his hair from left to right, with his habitual head spinning action. He realizes his drift away from his own family, something that he was not supposed to in his own assessment he had failed. In his pursuit of a companion and love, he had lost his love for his own family. He gained back his excitement to look forward to meet Maya and Sanjeevni, and it infused him with a sense of hope and optimism that he lacked for so many years.

He decides to call Jytoi Bhabhi back in Nawalgarh from the PCO phone booth outside his apartment. He looks at the clock adjoining the table stand that has the Bible on it. It is quarter to nine in the morning and despite the short nap, in those few hours he feels refreshed and bathed as if under a waterfall at some mountain. He dresses quickly, sports on his jeans and kurta shirt and dashes out of the house, carrying the keys in his neck chain merged with the cross locket, that has Jesus on it.

"How are you Bhabhi? I have been remembering you. Why did you not come along?" asks Ashu

"I and Ma got to spend some time here itself. You all are '*Pardesis*', like your mother, '*travelers*' of the dessert.

We are stayers and someone had to stay back here at '*Moh & Maya*'... and who will water the Tulsi plant for your mother and the booti for your brother – planted at Tiger's feet behind the Gulmohar tree?" retorts Jyoti.

She continues with an afterthought "Get married soon, and I will come to see you."

Ashwini listens silently and the imagery of '*Moh & Maya*' the fragrance of the *Gulmohar* flowers and the mixed fragrance of the Ponds dream flower, the image of his mother Maya comes to his eyes. He thinks, if his mother is with him, he will perhaps never go back to Rajasthan.

Suddenly his despair, anger and sorrows wilt away, and his consciousness comes back to him. He can see his mother, coming toward him from the dust of the dessert. She has travelled for the first time with his eldest brother- making the visit to his abode in Bombay, and to see Hari and his child too.

Ashu realizes the date, at the PCO phone booth, shows 05/05 – it is the 5th of May – the two fives that Hari had in his hand, at their father's demise, suddenly flashes like a lightening image in Ashu's mind.

The blind man running the booth, has an "*Ace of spades*" stuck on the wall with the message – "*ONE RUPPEE*" for a three-minute local call.

"Ok Bhabhi, I have to go...." Ashu has only Fifty rupees in his top pocket and since he is not making a local call, the STD meter of the PCO gallops away toward thirty- nine, way ahead of the Rupee One.

He intends to also buy half a loaf of bread with the balance from the same blind guy operating the telephone booth.

"Please keep Ekjot safe, Ashu! He is all I have got."

"Arrey, why do you worry Bhabhi? *BootiBhai* and I are both there."

"Your mother has three of you, I only have one son, Ashu" replies Jyoti.

"Ok Bhabhi, I promise." Says Ashu as he rests the black phone receiver back on the cradle.

The blind man running his phone service shoots, "Miya, tell me what the counter says, and please give me exact change. You are my first lucky customer of the day, and the first customer is God."

"Allah you mean," replies Ashu.

He notices that the blind man, has a '*taweez*' on his right arm, and wears the Lucknow Kurta, which habitants of the state of U.P. wear. He smells of betel leaf so early in the day...he notices the same *Mashq* of water, his mother had presented to each of them, to carry and keep cool water.

"Same thing, my son, for your Bhabhijaan, you are God, as I could see you had to promise her something. For me, it is you today morning" cuts in the man with the Ace stuck near his head on the PCO booth wall, returns him the Rs.1 change, and hands over the Ten Rupees bread to Ashu.

Ashu looks at the ace....and with a wry grin, accepts the message.

God is Allah or Ishwar, it's the image you wish to carry in your own consciousness. He rushes back, crossing the road, goes to the back of his apartment complex.

He pulls out the glass vase from the window, adjoining the balcony of his ground floor apartment.

He takes the shoots of the "*Sanjeevni Booti*" that Rupa had carried from Delhi, and looks for the loose soil at the periphery of the compound, to implant it at the back side of Father D'Costa's building.

It has been four days, but the plant is still alive.

Ashu exhorts himself that he must bolster himself to look after his elder sibling and deliver on the expectations of his nephew who is arriving in Bombay, at a much younger age then himself. He thinks of the boy in his mind, as he plants the stalk of his father's namesake into the Bandra soil, behind his Catholic Priest's apartment.

He wonders, remembering the pious Muslim's message from the phone booth, 'All Gods are one' – or perhaps in the Indian pantheon of Gods, there is One God or another, for all.

As he dusts soil from his hands, his pain of missing Kiran, is washed away.

He falls back in love with her memories at the temple in Nawalgarh, where the priest had blessed them both. He can see the sunlight on his own face bouncing off the windows of their apartment and the kaleidoscope of images it creates on his face. With his reflection in the glass windows, he feels united with Kiran and a supernatural force rejuvenates him.

He believes in himself and his love, knowing fully well, that he will meet Kiran someday, soon.

At 1030am in the morning, Ekjot has been lulled into sleep as their Taxi wizzes by City Bakery at Worli. The song on the Radio is from the famous King Khan's "*Dil Wale Dulhaniya*" ....and Maya enjoys the melody. "Yashji's movies have managed to retain the romance and the melody of love in their songs."

Sanjeevni looks out and notices the posters of the other famous Khan of the city, the romantic hero- "Aamir' with the upcoming release of '*Raja Hindustani*.' Ekjot is oblivious to these landscapes and movies are not much of his interest.

"Well Ma the '*Kapoors*' are no more the heroes, as all the three Khans have now taken over." Sanjeevni's retort falls flat on the dashboard of the taxi as the vehicle jerks and pulls ahead toward Mahim Church.

As a son, Sanjeevni remembers the tussle between Maya and Khazan on *Raj versus Dev.*

"Every new decade brings new heroes and visitors into the city." speaks the taxi driver, talking to no one in particular. He looks around as if to detect the smells of Bombay that arise from the refuse and waste in Mahim creek.

"Welcome sir." he looks toward Sanjeevni, who feels proud of himself for being called sir ignoring the multitude of rotten whiffs that every light breeze carries into the speeding cab.

"Look *Baabba,* the Arabian sea on the left." The father tries to arouse the interest without hopefully arousing the sense of smell in his son. All at once the father notices that his son is asleep and is missing the scenery.

Ekjot in his dream, can see his *Chacha,* whom he looks forward to meeting, sitting with him at Juhu Beach, eating the ice-colored '*Golas.*' He remembers the photograph his 'Chacha' had sent to Maya a few years ago.

As the wet sand dries between their toes, they both play a contest, of moving their toes one by one, while Ashu loses as all his toes move together. Ekjot exults at the fact, that he can do it better than Ashu, moving them gently one at a time.

The taxi halts at the Bandra Masjid red light signal jolting Ekjot out of his dream. He gets up, rubbing his eyes seated in the back seat with his grand-mother.

The taxi driver watches the three of them silently, watch the pedestrians cross over from the Masjid side of the road to the Lucky restaurant side of the road. The driver places his Fiat car, into the first gear, moving the stick-shift upwards towards the steering wheel, dries his forehead sweat with the red handkerchief behind his collar and puts the car into the Hill Road side lane of Bandra, leaving Lucky Restaurant and the waft of meat smells behind.

Maya notices the big city smells, how they change, from one green light to another and is shocked at the density of people crammed into the city.

The taxi reaches its destination, ten minutes later, Ashu comes running out from the apartment block and opens the compound gate. He directs the taxi to enter the building compound to make it easier for him to unburden the cab of its luggage.

As the three members alight, and so does the driver, to untie the rope with which the luggage is affixed onto the external ceiling of the cab, Ashu rushes to touch Maya's feet.

He embraces Sanjeevni as Ekjot flies onto him and jumps to throw a tight monkey hug at him.

Ashu is pleasantly surprised at the affection he receives and reciprocates with a light bear hug. He hides his emotions in that hug, to wipe his tears, behind Ekjot's head. Maya takes notice of her son's emotions.

Sanjeevni taps Ashu's arm, after paying off the cab driver and they enter the apartment block with their two suitcases and two airbags, with Ekjot still hanging on like a chimpanzee on his uncle's shoulder.

The foursome enters next door at the hospital in time, and are made to wait at the Holy Family Canteen, for want of passes for all of them to enter. Ashu arranges for their breakfast, of '*Potato-Vadas*' *with* '*Pau*' a Bombay delicacy, and special Aloo Parathas for his nephew and *BootiBhai*. It all gets done for barely fifty rupees, including the 'cutting chai' in the mini-glass cups.

Sanjeevni is surprised at the taste and effectiveness of the food though it is not home-made. In fifteen minutes from there, they are all inside the hospital ward with Hari. After exchanges of pleasantries, they all start the usual guess work of boy versus girl, and the decision making of name keeping.

"Ma, here, you will have to play a role, as Rupa has completely blanked out. We did not expect to have the delivery here…and it has been heavy trouble for Bhai." Hari breaks out in tears, as he is under stress seeing his wife go into surgery and his family members arrive.

Ashu approaches him, "Hari, it is all my fault, I could not take good care of both of you. It is all taken care off by *Father D'Costa* as the Church trust will take care for the room expenses, we have to only pay for the Doctor's fees and any surgery expenses."

Sanjeevni compliments Ashu reassuring him with his usual elder sibling '*BootiBhai*' look. Maya gets all her sons into a huddle.

"I am proud of all three of you. This is what family is all about. We will miss Jyoti today. But her representative is there." She caresses Ekjot's hair, and asks him, "So betta, what name suggestion do you have? Entire journey in the train he has tried and confused me with so many names."

"We could keep Simran, if it's a girl." comes in Sanjeevni. *DDLJ*, the Yashraj Movie has popularized the name all over India.

"Let us wait for the suspense to end first." Says Ashu, as he rubs Hari's back.

After a precarious and tiring two-hour wait, the doctors come out and pronounce the birth of two girl twins.

A relieved and simultaneously shocked Hari sits down on the hospital bench in a collapsed heap of stress busted out from a punctured tyre. Maya and Ashu embrace each other with a loud jubilant celebration forgetting their presence in the hospital.

Ekjot looks on dumbly at his father while Sanjeevni bends on his knee, to reach the level of his seated kid brother Hari and embraces Ekjot, hugging them both together – "Congratulations Hari, you have attained what none of us, our earlier generation could. There is now Lakshmi in our house. Get up and go see Rupa inside and comfort her"

"Lakshmi and Durga" says Hari, looking back at Sanjeevni.

He gets up and goes into the patient's shared maternity room, to reunite with his wife, and carry his two darling daughters in his arms. He comes out of the surgery room, taking turns with Maya to let her go in and see her daughter in law and grand-daughters.

After an hour, the happy family decides to head to Juhu beach in the evening.

They all want to celebrate the arrival of two darling daughters for Hari, and yet selfishly leave Rupa to fend for herself alone in the hospital. Ekjot cannot conceal his excitement, as there has been too much for him to handle in one day.

He has set foot out of Nawalgarh for the first time, and that too, to Bombay, seeing different kind of roads and buildings and the huge hospital.

He proclaims to his uncle, "*Ashu Chaccha*, I will grow up and become a Doctor" The child in him has spoken aloud.

"And why is that?" Asks Ashu

"To deliver the children of all our family members." replies the child to guffaws from his father and Hari.

"That will be the choice of a new profession for our family" chipped in Maya.

"It is the safest one, you will surely become a big man. It is possible Ekjot." Says Ashu. "Anything is possible, in this city, if it is in your imagination. You must simply try and study very hard."

At five that evening, the family group of five of them leave Rupa and the two daughters asleep at the Holy Family hospital and head to Juhu Beach in the two rickshaws they hail from outside Father D'Costa's apartment.

Maya, Ekjot and his father are in raptures in their rickshaw, watching all the buildings they pass. Hari and Ashu, sit together in the leading rickshaw, asking the second to follow. They are all in an elated mood with even Ashu smiling after many hours of feeling the burden of responsibility. He does not want to think how Khazan or Sanjeevni would have handled it, as he knows he succumbed to a bit of the pressure. Ashu feels like making it up for Hari, and wants to in a way also see if his last night dream can come true at Juhu.

"I'm waiting to see your daughters, they will be brought out tomorrow to the children's area, after a day's time and rest with the mother."

"Yes, Rupa has her hand's full, I must help her and I will have my meals at the hospital itself. Don't worry for me." replies Hari. He remembers the words of Sanjeevni and the understanding he needs to demonstrate.

"I am sorry Hari, I was not able to…"

"I understand Brother, don't worry, all is well that ends well." replies Hari.

"Have faith in Lord Krishna, you will find your love." Hari catches hold of Ashu's folded hands and gives him the most devoted look he has ever got from his brother.

The hospitalization has brought the two together and closer, for till now Sanjeevni has always been the focal point for both of them, the bridge at which they would meet on two opposite ends.

Water flows, from one to another,
like love of the family.
It collects itself from well, to your home vessel.

Ashu remembers his Late Khazan's words and Sanjeevni's reciting of the poem on their Nawalgarh terrace. He can see for Hari, the true benefit of their family bond and feels the love he has missed for so long. Overwhelmed he becomes quiet. He realizes that there is no '*degree of separation*' currently, and shares the 05/05 story with his brother Hari, and the two matched playing cards that were found in his hands. Perhaps they represented the two girls born today on the 5th of May. The rickshaw is upon Juhu and the next one also stops behind them as they finish paying the fare. They both take their father's name silently and stare ahead at the turn of Juhu beach near Gandhiji's statue where they alight.

Ekjot runs and tears ahead at the expanse of the beach with Sanjeevni the worried father chasing him from behind.

"See how fatherhood pre-occupies him now, I hope you are also ready?" speaks Maya, looking at Hari.

"Ma, I'm just relieved for now, that Rupa and the girls are okay" he is the son, who always lives in the 'now' moment.

Don't seek the past, the present is the only continuous
We should live in the moment,
The future only then rapidly unfolds upon us.
How you lived and loved,
Will return to you.

Ashu, looking at the beach, the sunset, sending countless crimson like colors, in a spray all over the sky. It is deep orange in places, and light blue in some, with the soft cotton clouds turning peach pink like the soft candy floss being sold at some stalls.

Ekjot insists to his father, to try the bullet pellets on the small archer like balloon stalls and Sanjeevni relents. He has to help his son take aim.

As the rest of them take seats in the dry sand a bit away from the main center of the beach, Ashu gazes and looks toward the Sun & Sand Hotel far away and then at his mother.

He observes, as Hari suddenly gets up, and goes to admire the sand statues sculpted by some artists, using the wet and dry sand mix of the beach. Hari leaves the mother and son pair together and moves toward some stalls, where they ask Hari to try some rings, to lasso some wins of gifts placed on the beach pyramid built by the gamesman.

From far, Maya can see Sanjeevni and Ekjot negotiate with a horse man, to seat the boy and the father together. As they go into the opposite direction of the beach, galloping slowly away, Maya decides to ask Ashu to walk with her toward the Sun & Sand hotel, in the wet part of the sand.

Ashu joins and keeps pace with his mother, walking silently.

"So, how are you, my son?"

"I am fine mother."

"Has your heart mended?" Maya is keen to broach the topic of an arranged match for Ashu, as he remains the unsettled son.

We will reach our mend,
As only time will make us bend
As life and love flows within us.
It is in our children's lives, and before us.

Maya awaits Ashu's reply patiently.

"I'm still in love mother." replies Ashu.

He is the 'different' son, unique, entrenched in emotion, his love, permanent, yet suspended for a final expression.

As if a blessing from past life, my most pretty one.
Moh and Maya, makes me swell with happiness,
My heart soar with bliss.
There comes a separation,

Albeit a short one,
There is no real end.

"How many more years will you spend like this?" asks Maya.

"I'm not a settler mother, I'm a traveler." retorts Ashu very readily using Jyoti's argument. "Hari is settled well in Delhi and Bhai is with you in Nawalgarh. Two of your three sons are well *settled.*"

"You had originally planned to buy the plot of land alongside. Is there no *Moh for Maya*?" asks Maya trying to look deeply into the eyes of her son, she loves so much.

Ashu tosses his hair aside in the same fashion, as if he is standing outside the plot of land of '*Moh & Maya.*'

"Mother, you are always with me, wherever I go, I live every day, remembering you and Bhai. It is not as if I do not love my family. But I have to find my own feet and bearings in this city, here is where I have had all my struggles."

"Why do you wish to struggle against yourself? From a young age, you keep going away and stay away. Right from the Jaipur days, what has all this given you?"

"*Anubhav.* An experience" replies Ashu.

"Ultimately in life, everything is just an experience. You are attached to the place you chose with father for yourself, I am attached to this place, I have chosen for myself." Ashu is direct, without coming across as selfish, as he lays out the details simply.

"All your life will you keep walking alone?" worries the mother.

"No mother, I am walking with you now, let me live in the present."

Maya turns silent, she listens to the waves, and after the short ones break and terminate the larger waves recede into the sea with the current. So does her worries. She comprehends the firmness of her son's thinking and decides to leave it that way.

She is reminded of Khazan's talks with her, that they must allow their children the same kind of freedoms that they enjoyed. She remembers Khazan's parents, and tells herself, maybe like them, she will have to live away from her son. Her favorite son? The son that is left far away from the mother becomes the favorite. She is pleased with the devotion shown by Hari, toward her and Rupa.

Hari has been sending her money, which Ashu has failed to.

Sanjeevni has been dutybound, taken care of her and the small farm, from the day their father left her. She looks up at the landscape of colors on the canvas of the beach. She realizes she has to let go of her son, for his own progress.

I pray, they too find love.
They will need it more, than us folks

Preach nothing else, but 'pure love'
For there are no real degrees, that separate us,
Me from you, my love.

"Can I join the mother and son on their walk?" comes a feminine voice.

As Maya slows down her walk, she realizes that Ashu has stopped a few steps behind her, paralyzed, as if in fear, his feet sinking like quick sand into the wet beach area. A few small waves come and surrender into his feet. He does not turn back, his face turning from crimson to metallic orange. The voice is very familiar.

Maya turns back and cajoles him to look behind himself. He waits. From the side view of his right eye, he can see a girl with very long hair dressed in a *salwar* with a floral *dupatta* walk toward his mother before him.

Kiran goes and faces Maya and they chat for a few minutes. Ashwini remains standing in the sand, sinking deeper and deeper, observing from behind her nail-painted fingers held behind her.

She is moving her palms and fingers calling him toward her, while still holding her salwar above her similarly painted toes. The color of the salwar and kameez same as his mother.

"Sure, please join...." As Ashu replies walking up to her.

His tongue is heavy and cannot move inside his dry parched mouth. He looks back and can see Ekjot astride on the horse with Sanjeevni. He looks on the other side of the beach to find Hari with rings around his arm, inserted like the Rajasthani ladies bangles up to his shoulder. He is still attempting to win himself a gift in the sand pyramids game.

When he turns back, he can see Maya and Kiran have gone ahead of him around a hundred meters towards the receding waves, leaving a wet trail of four prints of footsteps for him to follow. He can see Kiran and his mother's silhouettes against the setting sun. They are the two most precious images he can see in reality, grinning happily alone, with no one to witness his bashful joy he scratches himself to see if he is genuinely awake.

It is his dream come true.

Both the women are lost in conversation, their crimson maroon outfits appearing like the dark brown sand they stand on. The outgoing low tide tries to sweep them back with it, but they stand firmly planted, as if moored yet unchained to Ashwini in loyalty.

As he walks up to them, he can hear Maya speak.

"No *beti*, you both go ahead for the walk, I was tiring in any case. This fellow has been patiently waiting for years and on tenterhooks these last few minutes." says Maya.

Ashu looks up in shock at his mother then with his mouth agape stares at Kiran.

As Maya walks away, Kiran takes his hand, makes him turn and starts to lead him to walk further away from the Sun & Sand Hotel and away from Maya. Maya is headed in the direction of Hari at the pyramid game stalls.

As Ashu turns back from looking for his elder sibling and Ekjot, Kiran leaves his hand and walks ahead. Ashu is looking around for his mother. Maya looks at Ashu, scowls at him, and hurriedly asks him to go behind Kiran, with both her hands gesticulating, as if pushing him away.

Ashu breaks into a smile, takes a new stride walking back-wards facing Maya and gesticulates back, as if to indicate that he will see her in half an hour, putting one arm at the elbow point of the other arm.

He can see Sanjeevni gallop back on his horse with Ekjot and Hari wave at both of them. Ashu turns and flips backwards and falls in the wet sand on his belly. Kiran watches Ashu break his fall, and walks back to pick him up while laughing aloud joyously.

Ashwini gets up with Kiran's help and takes her hand in his. She closes her hand around his and tightens her grip, squeezing some wet sand out.

He tries to pull her down slowly into the wet sand, but she firmly yanks him upwards. Ashu's jeans and Kurta are soiled and now appears as dark brown as Kiran's in the sunset.

"Where have you been?" asks Ashu, looking up at her. Her skin is glowing, she is looking ravishing, beautiful as always, unchanged with time.

"I have just returned from Dharamshala, after spending a few years with the Tibetan monks in Himachal. They protest peacefully for their land, while they live in ours, displaced permanently. I could imagine and see their peaceful anguish and follow the teachings of the Dalai Lama for many years. Upon my audience with their spiritual team of monks I saw the suffering faced by the people of Tibet, due to their displacement from their country, despite having a new one. I could not stop thinking of you. I understood while living in the monastery, that it cannot be my life permanently, a life of monkhood. They set me free as easily as they took me in and rehabilitated me. I returned three days back and today is the first day I could collect the courage to come here. Since afternoon I have been waiting here at Juhu, waiting…" replies Kiran. "Waiting for you."

She looks up at him, matches his gaze and smiles knowingly, that they will have a future together in this city.

"Sorry to keep you waiting for so long. It took me time to figure myself." Kiran looks sheepish, like Mary's little lamb.

Pat comes the reply from Ashu, "Sorry to keep you waiting in the sun since morning!" He is grinning from ear to ear and is too ecstatic to be grumpy.

He opens his arms for the embrace he sought at Jaipur station.

She responds in a cuddle into his chest.

Ashu cannot believe his change of luck and tosses his hair from the left side of his forehead back to the right where they belong.

Juhu beach. On a hot sunny day, becomes the ideal cool evening spot at sunset. It's a golden moment on a golden day on the 5th of May 1996.

As Sanjeevni gets off the horse and makes Ekjot alight, he tells him, "Son, I have a special thing to share with you, besides a story."

"What is it father? Is it a gift from Bombay?" queries Ekjot.

"No son, it is a gift from a father." He hands him the old, torn playing card of the joker. Ekjot looks down at the card, and the card simply smiles back its golden yellow smile back at him.

Sanjeevni smiles broadly and takes in the salty sea air in a deep breath, "I like to see everyone happy and smiling. Remember your father, as the Joker in Bombay."

Khazan's words ring true…

He is like salt, you cannot eat without him,
You cannot live with all life excesses, minus him.
From the joker, 'the booti' the infuser of life.
Save him. And you all will be one.

19

TWENTY TWENTY-ONE

2021

Two decades have passed.

The story telling session between Maya and Mohini has gone on for the better part of 2020 and has come to an end in April of 2021.

Maya is now permanently stationed with Ashwini and Kiran at Bandstand's Captain Villa apartments, and has witnessed the typical Mumbai household when it is devoid of *Sukku Bai and Kamla Tai.* With no maids and all the work load shared between Kiran and Ashwini, the only respite everyone gets from each other is when Mohini visits her Goan friend at the neighboring Mehboob Studio Café and Ashu and Kiran go in opposite directions from the Mount Mary steps for their walk.

Maya survives on the basis of her *Caravan device* and also the old transistor besides old and new seasons of Indian Idol on Television, devouring songs of all generations.

Maya's mind is now a jukebox of songs, which hums tunes and melodies based on real life situations. She has done her part by convincing Mohini, to reconsider her decision to shift to Goa for higher studies and has ensured that Ashwini's daughter stays put at Mumbai with her father and mother. Maya's influence on her is complete, without Mohini ever setting foot at '*Moh & Maya.*'

Ekjot has experienced in the government aided hospital the death of over three hundred patients since a year. Exhausted and emotionally completely empty, he goes about his mechanical yet compassionate service, by helping the families identify the support staff needed at the crematorium grounds in Shivaji Park. He does not participate in any strikes or call for action with other make-shift centers that staff the fight against the pandemic. He does what he can.

He has not met with Maya or his '*Ashu Chacha*' despite all being in Mumbai, due to precautions for them. He has as a health worker only received one out of the two necessary vaccinations.

Maya finds the current life very deplorable, and wonders, where they started from and where life has come to a standstill. Since March, the wait for the illusive vaccine is endless. So much for being stationed in India's financial capital!

Sonny has over the past decade expanded his south east Asian business and is living alone in his semi-detached house in Holland Village of Singapore. Hari is driving his master's car, a 2006 Lexus model at East Coast parkway in a loop exiting the Bayshore exit towards Upper East coast road. He has switched from the popular musical tracks of the movie soundtrack of '*Disco Dancer*' to an oft ignored song, "*Krishna, Dharti pe aaja tu...*" from the same film original soundtrack. He remembers fondly how he would dance on the veranda of their house in Nawalgarh and make his disco moves like the hero '*Mithun*', duplicating the artists pelvic thrusts after watching the songs on television.

Hari pines for his family, for Maya, and for India. He rues the fact that she did not fly overseas to be with him and the girls before the international flights stopped operating last year. He is cut up with his mother for their argument over phone calls and has stopped talking with her since late last year. Today, he wants to make a call to her, but is circling his car in a loop on the Singapore expressway, listening to the same '*Krishna song*' of a time that can never return. His images of the 'blue' Gods framed and placed on the walls of '*Moh & Maya*' remain with him. He wished Maya would be with him at his Tampines residence. He is himself stuck in Singapore and cannot fly to India due to restrictions and rules of both governments.

The second wave of the pandemic in India has been a stronger one.

Ashu is sad that it is nearly a year since his favorite actor *Rishi Kapoor* is no more. It was his acting in Bobby that started his movies obsession. Followed up with Saagar that sealed his choice of residing in Bombay, now Mumbai. For many common movie-going fans, watching a movie in a cinema hall is now not possible due to government restrictions as vaccines are being administered to the population at large. A big part of a simple human life is gone forever, when your favorite movie artist and work done by him, and the times you have spent watching those movies is gone forever.

Ashu has also realized with the movie star's departure, a sense of his own mortality and yet he has to be there for his own family, his mother and most importantly Mohini. After all, he too must be worried for himself and his life! He has been aware that Mohini has been acting differently for a few months and upon investigation with Kiran's intervention, they both know, that there is a boy Mohini is confused about.

This 'puppy' love is seen by the father as a stupid crush and not love, though it is a sense of confusion like the mother Kiran had for him years back. The same man looks at the same situation at a very different time very differently. He is protective and most concerned for Mohini.

Sanjeevni has made the mistake of setting out of Delhi without proper transport arrangements. He makes his spontaneous oft repeated travel back as a migrant and hopes it is his last move back to Nawalgarh.

He has been the replacement this time for Hari at the Malhotra's shop. Their business has completely deteriorated in Delhi after Hari's move to Singapore. Jyoti had been incessantly asking him to return back to their land. Maya is in Mumbai since a year and Jyoti awaits eagerly since the past week for him to reach Nawalgarh. She has been watering the '*Sanjeevni Booti*' behind the *Gulmohar* tree repeatedly as a superstition. The mango tree has no fruit this year.

In the past year of the lockdown across India, Sanjeevni had with great difficulty found a train out of Delhi and been back with Jyoti till Diwali. After the government had re-opened business in the country's capital he had gone back to Delhi in January when the pandemic re-surfaced. Oblivious to the simpleton Sanjeevni, many journalists had been writing about the similarity with the bubonic plague and the global crisis in 1929. The mood everywhere around has been sombre, dark and dull. Sanjeevni dejected with the fall in city incomes and his trade, decides to pack his bags forever. It has been kind on Ashu's part to take care of Maya and at the same time send money for Sanjeevni and Jyoti to supplement their meagre farm income.

It has taken Sanjeevni five days of travel by cycle, then train and lastly by foot, to reach the plot of India Hospitality Resorts near the outskirts of Nawalgarh. He has no energy left to walk any further and he takes a break, to seek drinking water from the security guards outside the resort. The set of guards from the new agency do not recognize him. The resort security mistakes him to be a passerby '*fakir*' and send him away aggressively. With masks atop everyone's faces, the sheer anger, rejection and aggression is too much for a travel weary Sanjeevni.

He knows he is so near and yet so far, from his love. Jyoti is his first and only love, and '*Moh & Maya*' his home is his second love. He has no strength to walk any further, peters out from the gate of the resort and goes across diagonally on the other side of the road. He trips on a big stone at the side of the wild grassy patch in to an empty sewage ditch.

In Mumbai the Covid-19 virus has created havoc and plundered the health of many as lives are lost in thousands and hospitals get flooded with more patients and lesser oxygen then desired.

The dull nights have merged into breaking news days, and very few people step out of their houses anymore, as Bandstand Bandra residents are in cluster zone of a lockdown imposed by the state government.

The local municipality in Mumbai, with the help of local police is patrolling roads to prevent residents to step out of homes. It's a soft version of a city curfew, with streets resembling eerie sets created at Mehboob studios in Bandra.

The film industry in Mumbai faces losses in crores of rupees as India is forced to bunker down like its army personnel in the previous year on the India China border. There is tension on both borders for India to handle and luckily it has able leadership in the country and the defense forces are at alert.

Maya wakes up, feeling fatigued, tired and still sleepy, but so conscious of her wakefulness, that she fails to fall back into slumberland.

The mind naturally worries and wanders. She knows that Sanjeevni has commenced his journey toward Nawalgarh, and left Malhotra Niwas in Delhi for good a few days back. However, her inability to talk to her eldest son, and no confirmed news from Jyoti makes her feel despondent.

The depression of not being able to speak to her youngest sulking son also makes her feel depressed, but she knows that conversations with Hari now are impossible with the permanent fallout he has had with his mother.

She is able to accept that as her current position, due to her own knowledge of Hari's behavior as a jealous son. It is he who has wanted Maya to be with him and her stay with Ashu has caused this rift. She has already prayed for his wellbeing and she knows that he with his daughters and Rupa will have the best medical care if needed due to Sonny's presence in Singapore.

However, with Sanjeevni she is more worried for Jyoti back home in Rajasthan, holding fort alone at the '*Moh & Maya*' ancestral property.

Though Ashu has not progressed as much, she knows he is never keen to return there, since she is with him. Hence it is just fair that Sanjeevni and Jyoti get to stay and enjoy the farm land life. She hopes the decision taken by her and Khazanchand come true for Sanjeevni and blesses him the most in her mind as she gets out of bed.

There have been times during the pandemic that Maya wonders, if she should have disbanded the property, when she was a bit younger and shared the proceeds between all the three brothers. "But would that have kept them together and the family united? Would that have robbed her off her own security of a roof over her head, in an ownership sense? Would she be able to live with Ashu and in '*Kiran's home*', for the rest of her life with no house of her own to return to? This way she can still threaten Ashu about her impending return, though she is no longer in a shape to travel back. Oh, so lucky was Khazan who went so early, and left her pondering about their children for so many years, and recite their life story to their grand-daughter."

She looks at herself coming in focus in the mirror and realizes she now talks a lot to herself. She must hide her thoughts before her son, lest he think she has become mentally unstable. Living in the past is the favorite pass time of a grand-mother and she is the happiest for Mohini, with whom she has managed to form a bond and share the story about *'Moh & Maya.' She has withheld some intimate details and edited out many years of strife and only shared what she felt would be relevant for the genZ.*

As she puts on her eye liner, she thinks to herself, "Every son, had his own destiny, and yet chose so differently."

The youngest, Hari, had settled down in Singapore, following his own boss Sonny to expand their optician business overseas and travel. He had even during the pandemic moved to and fro to New Delhi in 2020, but was not willing to meet his mother later in the year or now.

Little does she realize or understand the strong quarantine rules of the city state back in Singapore. Hari had been upset, that when Rupa had moved with the young children, the mother had not relocated to live with him permanently. He had offered his mother the comfortable life of an overseas Asian country, a country that had now managed the virus problem the best, like New Zealand.

She had not reciprocated his letters as she was always '*obsessed with Ashu*'. He also felt cut up that when the family needed him to stay back at Nawalgarh and take care of the mother and his Bhabhi Ma, it was he who had ploughed the farms and taken care of the interest of his parent's ancestral property. Now when he had found his career opportunity taking him overseas, he wanted his mother to be with him, to allow him to continue to take care of his mother. This was at the onset the cause of the rift between the mother and the youngest son, and Maya in her old age style, let things be the way they were, expecting to be asked as she was the mother.

Maya knew, she could never gel living outside her own country and that too so far away from her own house and home. She chose her country, and the two other sons, over one son, who had migrated for the betterment of his own selfish future. As a mother, she did not hold it against him, as she felt she had spent the initial time of Hari's years of life with him.

How does a mother balance her time with her multiple children? That too all boys. Thank God she never had a daughter, as she recognized her own patriarchal leanings as a mother. How would she ever cater to the needs of an obsessive daughter if it was not for Hari?

The girl child she never had, was fulfilled by Rupa and now with time in the pandemic spent at Bandstand with Mohini.

Her first daughter-in-law had learnt the most from her in kitchen duties and cooking styles. In a way she had always seen a daughter in Jyoti and for so many years it was she who had taken care of Maya, their family and interests. Maya had depended on Sanjeevni to run the family affairs for the years when Ashwini was chasing his dreams.

She also knew, that Sanjeevni and Jyoti could always be depended upon, to take her back in at '*Moh & Maya*' and still be held responsible to distribute the rights between the two brothers, who no longer needed the family property in the first place. It was now Sanjeevni's home and no longer hers or Khazan's place to rest, and she hoped, that her eldest son, could put her to rest back at their home, when her time would come.

It was Ashu on whom she entirely depended now. She had always depended on him emotionally and had the least time with him.

Her state of mind was always that way, something she had not shared with Mohini while reciting their family story and tracing the stories she had been sharing with her grand-daughter in the past year of the pandemic.

Time had thrown them together.

Like any doting grand-mother she saw comparatives and similarities between herself as a teenager and Mohini, with adequate tweaking from the lens of time.

It appeared that both Kiran and Ashu were happy to have her with them temporarily. Mohini had bonded so well, that Maya now did not feel like returning to Nawalgarh.

The Arabian Sea, its humid yet putrid smell at times, the summery weather and the heavy rain had captured Maya's imagination last year, and she thought she would return after the winter this year – perhaps for good.

Ashu never asked his mother to stay or till when she would continue to stay, nor whether she would prefer to return. He took her for granted as a son would his mother, and enjoyed her presence around him.

They always had this unspoken, open arrangement as part of their mother and son relationship, where he never felt responsible for her the way Sanjeevni did. He knew she could eventually go back to her '*Moh & Maya*' abode, and she also knew that he knew, that she would like her life to come to an end with Sanjeevni and Jyoti.

That was her 'ideal' scenario.

She was just living in the moment, and had merged her ideology to Ashu's comfort. She had not anticipated such a long stay, but her health, blood pressure issues and the pandemic situation meant no travel and a comfortable trap in Mumbai for her with '*her*' Ashu. She remembered a part of Khazan's words...

This trade has been on since Maya's time immemorial
Love often ends feelings mercurial.

In these circumstances, the inability to sell their ancestral property, settle and give Hari a leg up in his life, and spend time with Rupa, something she had never done, were the only regrets of Maya's life. But she also felt that the passage of time, now had shifted her interest from being the central fulcrum of the family and instead allow the three sons to find their own feet, on their own.

She was willing to be a mother on the move.

The true and original *migrant.*

She was happy drifting from one house to another.

She secretly even enjoyed the tussle in the minds of the sons to want her to spend time with each of them.

She harbored a minor grudge that except Jyoti, neither of her daughter-in-laws would speak to her telephonically or call her over to stay with them.

In the days of *whatsapp,* now the family would communicate with small chats on the messenger service, but the younger daughter-in-laws rarely spoke, or wrote.

She rarely expected reverence, but she also took for granted their deference.

Kiran was always amicable in presence of Ashu, but her vibe was never too warm, that could allow Maya a feeling to die in their house.

Somewhere, all these details had been concealed by the grand-mother from Mohini, who had spent the entire year during the pandemic, to record *'Maya's version* of the family story. This had made Maya re-live so many of those memories she cherished and had got Mohini to record that for her own future.

Her cousins Lakshmi and Durga in Singapore did not know this much.

These exchanges and small new memories were fresh for Maya and made her feel special enough. She had been able to see how much Ashu had changed and adjusted into becoming a fulltime Mumbaikar.

He had adapted well to having his Sikh wife alongside always, and Mohini had grown up into a nice modern, yet loving child.

It appeared that Ashu needed her the least, as a mother, as his own family unit was self-sufficient.

So many such matters of her children's lives still pre-occupied Maya's thoughts. They robbed her sleep and prevented her at times to want to live her life in a carefree manner.

'Oh, her three boys! Men now, raised by her, enjoying with their respective wives."

She had stopped being carefree once Khazan was gone.

She knew she was now an octogenarian and the lights could go off anytime, any day. She was satisfied to have shared with Mohini, her story, and having put so many minor details, insisting that Mohini records even the name of some film songs.

She hoped somewhere someone from the family would look back at her story, and realize how she had held the family together, got each one to love each other and yet see them through the toughest times of life, without their father.

She knew, it was only Ashu who was unhappy to have stayed back in Nawalgarh and he had managed his way out of the north and settled in his city of dreams. To that extent, he was still in the center like the position in the family, as Hari had progressed even further to have shifted overseas.

Each of her three sons, now lived in different locations and that was merely a logistical inconvenience she had to cope with. It was a similar irritant to Khazan's *permanent absence,* something she had gotten used to. She knew she would overcome this too and work on the logistics once the pandemic was over. She peered over the living room window and set up the dining table, putting up the plates and pickles ready for action.

She looks at the opposite building watchman, grease his palm with some sort of tobacco and white powder and shove it in his mouth under his tongue. "What a lousy fellow! At least they have a security guard, our building lacks one" she thinks to herself.

While these thoughts pre-occupy her, she has had her morning cup of tea, and put on the FM Channel that Ashu frequently turned on for her.

Kiran and Ashu had slipped out quickly for their morning walk and left Maya to make the parathas breakfast today as it had been decided the previous night.

Kiran was efficient and would communicate effectively and ensure she gave Maya some presence in the kitchen to still make herself feel useful. Her health condition had now stabilized and Maya herself did not want to live in a sense of fear all the time. As she turned the music on, she heard Mohini wake up and head towards the toilet, to spend the next day recording the concluding part of the story with Maya.

"*Roz roz ankhon tale, ek hi sapna ....*" A song from the '*junior Dutt*' movie played on the FM channel, setting the tone and ambience to grate some cauliflower and potato, and mix it with the branded *Aashirvaad* wheat. She hoped the wheat would taste the same when she churned out the parathas, as she uses a generous hand of lassi and ghee in the dough mix. She knew Ashu had another hour to return as they would come back with some grocery shopping, as Kiran had taken the red shopping bags from the kitchen. He would be hungry on his return and he usually liked to eat immediately and bathe later after his long walks.

Ashu walked out hurriedly from Captain Villa and began walking in a huff toward Mt. Mary's Church and school, as Kiran tried to give chase with haste.

The watchman from the opposite building, noticed the drift of the '*sahib and memsahib*' having a bit of a tussle, and dialed some numbers on his old Lumia cellphone. He speaks nonchalantly to his buddy over the phone. The tobacco and white paste had begun to foam in his mouth into a liquid mix that looked like pale blood. He spits it outside his security cabin.

"How can you hide, the existence of your aunt for so many years? God damn woman, do I even know you? A maternal aunt, like a *Masi*, is supposed to be, supposed to be...." he struggled for words. "An alternate mother"

"Precisely...," responded Kiran, "...and that's why I cannot say no to her. She has been living alone, for so many years in Amritsar and now feels, with her age, she could lose her life. She just wants to be close to someone who can perform her last rites. That's all there is to it."

"But why did you hide these facts for so many years?" Confused and angry Ashu feels spiteful. He has lost his cool, his temperament and feels he does not know his own wife. He used to feel the same way during their serenading and dating year and flashes of memories of that trip to Nawalgarh come back to him.

Like any other couple, the daggers are drawn in minutes after two decades of living together with each other. The home lockdown imposed due to the pandemic, has also created a hostage kind of feeling between many spouses and with permanent pressures of Mumbai life, *Ashu and Kiran were no different.*

The underlying tensions due to Mohini's choices and Maya's presence meant, they had little time for themselves. The unique age they were now themselves at meant the path to walk on, literally speaking, at Bandstand too, had two opposite directions from their building. Their individual personalities had crept back in and the couple had become two different people instead of one married soul partnership.

"Is this about your mother now?" shoots Kiran.

"Now how does everything have to involve my mother? She is here barely few months." hits back Ashwini. "It is actually the first time in my life that she is living with me. Us, I mean"

"Well, it is more than a year, if you take notice, Covid 19 lockdown happened last year and we are well into the break the chain lock-up with you, its past Maharashtra day sir." Kiran speaks with agitation and some aggression in her tone.

"So now you are in a lock up with me?"

Ashu stops in his tracks, looks at Kiran, glances away with hurt and dejection in his eyes, and out of reflex, tries to move the small lock of hair on his forehead backwards like his old childlike days. The hair moves back with resistance, like a stray dog's tail due to the wind from the slope coming upwards, carrying the whiff of corn, humid hot perspiration from countless couples strolling around the Arabian sea.

The air comes up Ashu's nostrils and he is equally piqued with the lack of fragrance and the presence of this putrid smell, as he is filled with dejection on knowing a sudden hidden truth. Strangers ambling along past all the entrance gates of hospice and old age homes on that street, look them up and down, as they both stand on two different sides of the street now.

They have been speaking at each other, rather than to each other.

Kiran shouts across, "So now your mother lives with you, and not us? We can go on and on Ashu, you know that. Let's go by to our favorite spot near the rocks opposite the juice center and we can speak there with peace and quiet. It is impossible to have a conversation with you here, or at home. I promise, I will buy you a cheese grill sandwich." retorts Kiran, keeping her cool, but not shedding her sarcasm.

Ashwini, suddenly walks in the opposite direction, back toward the church, away from the sloping downhill walk they were having few seconds back.

Though he breaks the argument, he also breaks his stride with quick paces away from Kiran, leaving her alone, gaping at his back. She smirks and admires his flabby backside. "He's put on weight", she wonders to herself like a typical wife.

Kiran collects her thoughts and her ear-pods, and just starts her own slow paced jog downhill, letting the matter be, and offering space with few '*degrees of separation*' to Ashwini.

She hopes he would climb down the Mt. Mary steps and meet her on the other side of Bandstand and join her at the Juice center, while she could have her run at the promenade, feeding her favorite pigeons the lose biscuit crumbs she has in her inner jacket pocket.

Her slate grey Puma jacket and black tracks, merges well with the crows as Ashu observes her from the top of the hill, where he has perched himself after stopping his walk.

He feels more infuriated with his wife and wonders, "Can you really know a woman?"

He thinks about Maya at home, after all, he does think about his mother, and expects the same of his wife.

"Does Mohini not do the same naturally? Why is it a big deal if a guy does the same?"

He shares Maya's worry about Sanjeevni having left Delhi, but not having reached Nawalgarh, and rues the day that Hari had flown out with Rupa to join Sonny in Singapore. Ashu had gone to the Mumbai International airport to see off the family.

Kiran was upset even on that day with him, for having delayed their late-night film at PVR Juhu. It felt like a different time, almost like partition days- the way Maya spoke about them to Mohini at home.

Their family was now split and all were in different places, like planets in space. Maya had always been like Mother Earth, with multiple moons around her and that importance had ebbed a bit, like the waning moon. She was now just another planet in the solar system.

This irked Ashu.

However, he knew Maya felt more like the diminishing sun herself, except that Kiran felt the same too. He saw them as planets, they saw themselves as the sun.

'These damn women of your life.

You can love them from the bottomless pit of your heart. But they just don't love you back hard enough, till they grumble and gripe about their own selves and before you know it, voila – they pull a bunny rabbit like aunt from their hat of hidden secrets.'

Comparatively, his daughter was his radiant star.

You could count on Mohini to give that balance to their lives. Ashu does not know, that Maya has talked Mohini out of going to Goa.

Maya and Kiran are aware, that Moh is just treating the Goan kid as a friend and there is no love interest in Mohini's life.

"*What would he do, once she relocated to Goa, for her university studies?*" she is now his center of love and the centrifugal force that binds his and Kiran's marriage.

He is scared that all wheels of their house will be off, if Mohini leaves from Mumbai. As the concerned father descends the Mt. Mary steps on the other side, he notices his daughter enter the *Good Luck Café.*

She is with someone who looked like Tony Fernandes, the son of his Allied Garage repair shop owner.

Ashu's heart races and sweat trickles down the temples of his forehead, going into his ears on one side and falling off on the side of his neck, on the other side.

He is now furious and upset at the same time, yet helpless and disappointed already with his own wife too.

He walks slowly toward the shuttered *Mehboob Studios,* as nondescript as he can be, and stands across the pavement facing *Noble Chemist.* He waits in queue with others and acts as a waiting customer outside.

He has time till 11 am to head back when the so-called curfew is imposed by the State Government and he knows his mother would be restless and waiting for breakfast at home. He feels like the constrained balls inside the triangle placed on a billiards table and feels for all three women of his life, who seem to be busy knocking him around the rectangular table.

Maya receives a call at 10:10am, on her cellphone with the number showing a +65 sign and picks the call, places it on the microwave oven. She puts it on speaker, as she pulls out the salt box from the second shelf of the open white cabinets before her.

"Hello, Ma..." is followed by silence.

Hari is on the other side of the line.

Maya is not able to speak.

Her mouth opens, forms a shape of a gaping bowler's hat, with no head inside it.

She is unable to find her speech. She has been slowing down and feeling the fatigue and tiredness for a few months, but she finds herself drained of energy all of a sudden.

Sanjeevni has managed to get up with the help of a cycle passerby, and directs him toward '*Moh & Maya*'.

In ten minutes seated at the back of the cycle as a passenger, Sanjeevni is dropped off at the house, whose name just reads incompletely as "*..h _ Maya*" Some lettering have come off permanently and the nature of human neglect combined with passage of the years and environmental damage has changed the sign for some time.

As Sanjeevni enters his home gate he wipes the dust of the words Maya, he does not enter the residential abode. He can see Jyoti seated at the *charpoi* where his mother used to be seated.

Sanjeevni opens the mask covering his face and he throws it at the path, as he walks toward the trees, with a gaping wife in tow. She is comforted when he walks ahead of the well and goes and bends on his knees below the *Gulmohar* tree, picks up the fresh leaves from the '*SanjeevniBooti*' herbs and smells them. He dunks his head into the pail of water outside the well, turns around to face his wife and gives her a reassuring look that he is fine.

He throws the rest of the water from the pail, into the soil for the tree and the booti plant around it. He has Tiger in his thoughts and misses him immensely.

Jyoti comes and first sits at his feet and observes his wounds and then gets up and sits with him. She has with her the passion flower, that she places in his palm as they both with their backs to the wall of the well, heave a sigh of relief to be reunited.

No amount of money and progress is worth this separation they understand silently. They both promise each other to be wedded to each other and their farm land for the rest of their life.

Hari at that instant is in tears on the cell phone wirelessly playing via the blue tooth in his car.

"Ma, I am sorry I did not call you for so many months, and was upset that you did not..." Hari's few words are lost on Maya.

He will never know, if she has heard and forgiven him.

Maya has collapsed and fallen in the kitchen.

As she falls, her head hits the edge of the marble and granite counter-top of the kitchen, on which is placed the microwave oven, on which is placed the cellphone.

She can see the strong battery and signal connection, as she breaks her fall with her left arm, she can also hear her elbow crack.

Her head now rests near the garbage can holding the dry paper and refuse of the clean floors and she can see vapor of hot air rising from the frying pan she has kept on a slow gas to shallow fry the parathas in ghee.

The aroma of dry wheat and the chopped yet uncooked cauliflower and boiled potato are in the air, but not on the pan.

She's thankful she has not put the milk to boil, for it would have spilled and that would have been a *bad omen.*

She prays, that Sanjeevni has made it home.

As a pool of blood spreads around her, she passes out for nearly a hundred and twenty seconds.

In those two minutes, she has lost a lot of blood from the deep gash around her eyebrow.

Hari has spoken many things but has not been heard. Maya can see, Sanjeevni cross the road in her dream, and enter the gate of '*Moh & Maya*.'

She is standing inside the gate to welcome her son and looks at Sanjeevni, her tallest and rustic looking son, sun burnt, thirsty and thankful at the same time, to be able to set his eyes on his mother, … or is it his wife behind her?

Maya looks over her shoulder behind to see Jyoti, right enough standing there, and instructs her, "*Do change the name of the place and put a new board, when I die.*"

As Kiran walks back up, disappointed with not having seen Ashu at the juice center, she huffs and puffs her way to the edge of the Mt. Mary hill, about half a kilometer away from their Captain's Villa.

As she is about to cross her hands before Mother Mary, a darkish man, walks up to her and suddenly pulls at her *gold mangal sutra,* ripping the edge of her skin on her neck.

Another man, comes from the edge of the steps and hits her left hand with a large metal rod causing her a piercing pain till her upper arm and shoulder.

Her phone falls from her left hand, as she falls on her right side when the chain snaps on her neck.

She falls and hits her head on a strong stone island of a large white and red cross. She feels her wet hair with her wincing left hand. She can smell and feel the red blood on her hands as she can see the inverted shrine of the church across the road as a crowd of candle sellers gathers around her.

From the pavement queue, Ashu can see Mohini weep and see the youngish boy, step out of Goodluck Café, hurry away on his bike. He observes his daughter from outside carefully and makes no move, allowing the next in line customer a chance to enter the chemist shop.

After about three minutes Mohini steps out of the café, and walks slowly back towards the Mt. Mary steps, attempting to walk back toward Captain's Villa.

Ashu briskly walks and catches up with her.

He takes her by surprise and is himself unexpectedly astonished, that she has managed to change her mood dramatically. As they both reach their apartment complex, he puts his arm around his daughter.

The Watchman across from his building gets off the motorbike and quickly takes the metal stick from his friend and places it inside a hollow bamboo stick inside the security cabin. The security guard removes his double mask and hangs it on the nail inside his cabin and ties the handkerchief from his forehead and ties the reverse ends of it around his neck. He removes his dark black sunglasses, removes his plain shirt used for washing cars in the morning. He wears the security uniform full-sleeves shirt over this vest and starts his duty at 10.15am, relieving his namesake Yadav Watchman who has been sitting on the stool since last midnight. It was both these *Yadavs* that Maya never liked, while observing them from her lighthouse position at the window of Captain's Villa.

"You ok my star?" asks Ashu

"Yes Dad, why?" responds Mohini, albeit a bit dryly

"No, just asking…anything you want to share?"

"Nothing worth it Dad, I am not going to Goa after all, that's all."

Ashu smiles.

He is happy with the outcome and does not want to dig any further.

"It is you after all, with whom I can spend the rest of my life my love." They both stand at the gate, and ponder at the crowd gathered ahead near Mt. Mary Church.

"What's happened there…." Asks a bystander to a passer-by.

"Someone got knocked down, daylight robbery these days", comes the reply from a woman jogging past. "And no one gives a damn, anymore in *Mumbai*."

As Kiran lies in her own pool of blood, she can see the Mt. Mary shrine fade in and fade out. She focuses on the cross atop it.

She wonders, whether the thieves were Christians or Hindus.

She remembers the kind face of Father D'Costa, his kind deeds and surprisingly has no worry in her mind about her husband, her daughter or her home.

"Krsna, take me to you in one clean sweep, and don't leave me here as a crippled vegetable. That's my only wish" says Kiran to herself.

"Dad, let us go back to *Good luck* café and have a chai and noodles meal there."

Ashu thinks for a second and in a split second says, "Why not, after all I love their *bun-maska*, and it is rare that wc father daughter get to have our meal out. Maya memsahib can wait."

Ashu believes it is his lucky day, to join his daughter '*Moh*', for the date, which she did not have early morning today. The father in him gives in and he thinks it is fair to forget for a while that he is also a son and a husband.

He can always recover those elder and mature women later.

After all love is such a strange feeling. You can only do justice to one relationship at a time.

Maya can hear the last words of Hari, still speaking in his monologue and she can barely think at the same time. The pain in her lower back, elbow and hip is excruciating.

She has thoughts of Sanjeevni in her mind.

Her conscience says a silent prayer for Ashwini, to find his true love.

Maya can smell the frying pan burn and the garbage bin that has not been washed since a week.

She can see her own blood reach the bottom of the washing sink on one side and the refrigerator on the other side of the kitchen. She seems to have her own sea of blood to float in, merge with her crimson red color saree.

Far away, in that pool of blood she can see the shadow of Khazan beckoning her.

"Here I come my love!" It has been a long time away from you. She remembers his writing while working as a teen in the Solan shop…

UNATTAINABLE

"Physical is ephemeral, Mental is mindful.
It is the spiritual that is unattainable.
Life is short and you still get to stretch it.
Take it in your hands - Wrench it.

She had stretched it for over 45 years after his departure.

It was again a date to reckon with 05/05 in the year 2021, the year which also added up to the number 5.

What was it with the role of fives in their lives?

She gave her sincere last blessings to Lakshmi and Durga whose birthday it was and a silent prayer for Moh.

Having blessed all her three grand-daughters, Maya struggles for her last breath, as the FM Channel radio in the background, dishes out the song "*Wahan Kaun hai tera...Musafir*" from Dev Anand's Guide.

Surprisingly it was the opening song of that film, but it turns out to be Maya's swan song.

The End.